THINGS HAD CHANGED IN BLANCO SPRINGS

And not in a good way.

But Bull had changed, too. At just short of twenty-one, he was a man—the last of his family. His father had left him a legacy of tragedy and ruin—along with a choice. He could sell the ranch and leave for good, with enough money to make a new start anywhere he chose. Or he could stay, pay off his father's debts, rebuild the ranch, and create a legacy of his own—a new dynasty of Tylers who could look any man in the eye and face any challenge together.

"Dailey vividly brings to life the mystique that embodies Texas . . . artfully weaving romance, intrigue, greed, jealousy and murder."—*Texas Tea & Travel*

L- HiWAY
44

TEXAS FIERCE

JANET DAILEY

ZEBRA BOOKS
KENSINGTON PUBLISHING CORP.
http://www.kensingtonbooks.com

ZEBRA BOOKS are published by

Kensington Publishing Corp.
119 West 40th Street
New York, NY 10018

All Kensington titles, imprints, and distributed lines are available at special quantity discounts for bulk purchases for sales promotion, premiums, fund-raising, educational, or institutional use.

Special book excerpts or customized printings can also be created to fit specific needs. For details, write or phone the office of the Kensington Sales Manager: Attn.: Sales Department. Kensington Publishing Corp., 119 West 40th Street, New York, NY 10018. Phone: 1-800-221-2647.

First Kensington Books Hardcover Printing: September 2017
First Zebra Books Mass-Market Paperback Printing: July 2018
ISBN-13: 978-1-4201-4368-3
ISBN-10: 1-4201-4368-9

eISBN-13: 978-1-4201-4371-3
eISBN-10: 1-4201-4371-9

10 9 8 7 6 5 4 3 2 1

Printed in the United States of America

Special thanks to Elizabeth Lane, without whom this book could not have been written.

CHAPTER 1

Pecos, Texas
June 1970

THE RODEO GROUNDS SIMMERED UNDER A TORRID Texas Sun. The dusty air was rank with tobacco smoke, diesel fumes, and the earthy smell of manure. Cattle shifted and lowed in the stock pens. Flies swarmed in the heat. Riding the updrafts, a lone buzzard circled in the sky.

Behind the chutes, cowboys waited their turn to ride for glory. Some lounged, chewing wads of tobacco and spitting in the dust. Others paced. A few of them prayed.

They were young, mostly, all of them hungry to win prize money and the coveted belt buckles that served as both honor badges and woman-bait. The cowboy who wore one could count on plenty of attention from the rodeo groupies known as "buckle bunnies."

From the arena beyond the chutes came the sounds of cheers, groans, and occasional laughter. The Pecos Rodeo claimed to be the oldest in the country—which meant that it was most likely the oldest rodeo in the world. Size-wise it might not be up to much. But the fans loved it, and they crammed the covered bleachers for every event.

Not that Virgil Tyler gave a damn about the rodeo's history or its crowd size. He was here to ride bulls for enough cash to get him to the next rodeo town and enough points to boost him in the rankings. If he won, he'd have his choice of the buckle bunnies, too. But right now his mind was on other things.

At twenty, he'd been on his own, and on the circuit, for three years. Big and rangy, with dark hair and arresting blue eyes, he'd started with broncs and last year moved up to the ultimate ride—the bulls.

He'd broken his wrist and his collarbone, cracked three ribs, and dislocated his shoulder so many times that he'd stopped counting. None of the injuries had kept him from missing a ride. He'd taped up, clenched his teeth, and climbed into the chute every time. Eight seconds to hang on to a bucking, twisting three-quarter-ton tornado of an animal. For eight seconds, he could stand any pain.

His dogged determination had earned him a new nickname—*Bull. Bull Tyler.* He liked the sound of it—helluva lot better handle for a cowboy than Virgil. Maybe he should use it in the arena. But he would think about that later. Right now the PA system was announcing the rider just ahead of him in the lineup.

Tex Holden was a good cowboy, and he'd drawn a decent bull. But the groans of the crowd told Virgil he'd barely made it out of the chute before being tossed off in the dust. The rodeo clowns were already rushing in to head off the bull while Tex scrambled to safety. Now, with the bull headed into the pens and the arena clear, it would be Virgil's turn for the last ride of the day.

His bull, a foul-tempered Brahma–Angus cross named Sidewinder, was already in the chute. Virgil had ridden him before. On a good day, Sidewinder's spirited performance, which counted for half the score, could rack up the points. On a bad day he could be peevish, surly, and downright murderous. When Virgil settled onto the wide, brindled back and noticed how the brute tried to crush his leg against the chute's metal side bars, he figured this was one of the bull's bad days.

Wrapping the rope around his gloved left hand and gripping the leather-bound handle, he raised his right hand high in the air and gave a jerk of his head. The gate opened, and Sidewinder barreled out of the chute in a cloud of dust and fury. The heavy bell that hung from the rope behind the bull's front legs clanged as he bucked across the arena.

Using his core strength to balance, Virgil dug his blunt-rowel spurs into Sidewinder's loose hide and hung on. The bull jumped like a rocket and landed like an earthquake. Pain from old injuries shot through Virgil's body as the huge beast tilted, spun, and changed direction with dizzying speed. Just a few more seconds . . .

The buzzer signaled a successful ride. Virgil tensed for the dismount and flung himself free of the raging animal. Only then did he realize that the rope had tangled around his hand, tying him to the bull. He landed upright. But when Sidewinder swung his upper body around, trying to hook him with a horn, the sudden strain pulled Virgil off his feet and almost yanked his arm out of its socket. He fought to get his legs under him. If the brute broke into a run, he could be dragged to death.

The two rodeo clowns, heroes in face paint and baggy clothes, charged in to save him. While one distracted the bull, the other managed to free Virgil's left hand from the tangled rope. He would've helped Virgil out of the arena, but Virgil motioned him away and walked to the gate, alone, head high and hurting like hell, to the cheers of the crowd.

Safe behind the gates, he sank onto a bale of hay. Nothing was broken or bleeding, but he felt like he'd been run over by a freight train. He swore as the announcer gave his score. Seventy-eight points out of 100—respectable but barely in the money. He loved the challenge and the danger of bull riding. But at times like this, it struck him as a crappy way to make a living.

From the tobacco plug that he'd buttoned into his shirt pocket, he twisted off a wad of chew and slipped it into his mouth. Filthy habit, but at least it helped calm his nerves.

"Virgil?" A familiar voice spoke his name. "Damn it, but you're a hard man to track down!"

"Jasper!" He stood to greet the cowboy who'd worked on his father's Rimrock Ranch since Virgil was twelve. Jasper Platt would be in his late twenties by now. Beanpole thin with a drooping mustache and a slow way of talking, he was the best all-around rider and cowhand Virgil had ever known. Maybe the best human being, too.

Virgil might have hugged him. But sore as he was, the best he could offer was a handshake. He hadn't seen anyone from the ranch since he'd run off at seventeen, after a gut-wrenching showdown with his father. The fight had been a long time coming. When it was over, Virgil had bundled up his gear, walked two miles to the highway, hitched a ride on a cattle truck, and never looked back.

"Bless my soul, boy, you've sprouted like a blasted weed! What are you now? Six foot two?" Jasper stepped back to look him up and down. "You're a grown man, all right. But what a sorry sight you are! You look like you got run down by a cattle stampede!"

"Did you see me ride?" Virgil asked.

Jasper nodded. "Not bad."

"Not bad?" Virgil had hoped for higher praise from his old friend.

"Let me tell you a hard truth," Jasper said. "A big *hombre* like you ain't got a chance in hell of makin' it to the top as a bull rider. It's those quick, little wiry guys that can stick on and bounce off like monkeys that rack up the points. You might be strong, but you're draggin' those long arms and legs and that extra weight. And I'll tell you somethin' else. The way you were gettin' slammed around by that bull, if you keep it up, you'll be crippled by the time you're twenty-five—if you even live that long."

"I'll keep that in mind." Virgil studied the man who'd been like an older brother to him during his early teenage years. Jasper wasn't here by chance. He'd clearly gone to a lot of trouble to find him. There had to be a reason.

"What are you doing here, Jasper?" he asked. "You didn't track me down just to see me ride bulls."

Jasper lowered his gaze to his dusty boots, as if summoning his resolve. In the beat of silence that passed before he spoke, Virgil sensed what might have brought him. But Jasper's words, when they came, still struck hard.

"Your dad's gone, Virgil. He passed away two weeks ago."

"Two weeks." A strange numbness was setting in. *Two weeks?* "What the hell happened? Was he sick?"

Jasper shook his head. "His horse came home late one mornin' with an empty saddle. Carlos and I went out lookin' for him, but it was almost sunset before we saw the buzzards and followed 'em. We found him in the escarpment at the bottom of a cliff. I'll spare you the details, but it looked like he fell off the top."

"That doesn't make sense. My dad knew every inch of those canyons. He would never have wandered up there and fallen off a cliff."

"It didn't make sense to us, neither. But since he wasn't shot or stabbed or anything like that, the sheriff called it an accident. We put him in the ground next to your ma."

Virgil's jaw tightened as the news sank in. Williston Tyler had been a miserable son of a bitch who took out his failures on his motherless son. Virgil's last words to him had been, "Go to hell!" Now Virgil didn't know what to feel. Grief, anger, and numb indifference warred inside him.

"The Rimrock is yours now," Jasper said. "It's in a

pretty sorry state, but your dad left the land free and clear—not a cent owed on it."

Virgil had given little thought to the ranch—two-thousand-some-odd acres of scrub below the caprock escarpment that separated the rolling hill country from the high, flat Texas plain. His memories of the place were mostly bad—drought, mesquite thickets, rattlesnakes, coyotes, and skinny cattle that were always getting lost. He'd spent his childhood riding herd, eating dust, and growing up with a father who'd never forgiven him for being born and causing the death of the wife he'd loved.

He'd have to be crazy to go back there.

"The Prescotts have been itchin' to add the land to their big spread," Jasper said. "I can't tell you how many offers they made your dad over the years, but even when he was as poor as Job's mule, he always turned 'em down. Now that you're in charge, you'll no doubt be hearin' from 'em."

"How much do you figure the ranch is worth, Jasper?" Virgil asked, thinking of all he could do with the money if he sold out to their wealthy neighbors.

Jasper scowled. "I reckon that's up to you. But remember what your dad always said. 'Trust a skunk before a rattler, and trust a rattler before a Prescott.' "

"I know what he said. But I sure as hell could use the cash."

"Money goes, boy. Land is forever, and there's only so much of it on this earth. That's another thing your dad used to say. That ranch is your legacy, boy. Think long and hard before you let it go for a stack of paper that'll be spent and gone afore you know it—especially if you're dealin' with the Prescotts. Those rich buzzards will take one look at you and see fresh meat. If you let 'em, they'll strip you to the bone and pick you clean."

Jasper glanced at his battered Timex wristwatch. "The day's gettin' on. I didn't come all this way to talk to you. I came to fetch you home." He fished a ring of keys out of his pocket, took a few steps, and glanced back over his shoulder. "Well, are you comin' or ain't you?"

Virgil sighed. He'd sworn he would never set foot on that ranch again. But now that the place was his, he had little choice. One way or another, he needed to settle his father's unfinished business. "I'm coming," he said, spitting his chew in the dirt. "Just let me pick up my prize money and get my gear."

There wouldn't be much money to collect, or much gear to haul away. The rusty, old pickup he'd driven here had blown a head gasket and wasn't worth fixing. Aside from that, and his modest savings account in the First Texas Bank, all he owned was a bedroll and a duffel with a shaving kit and a few changes of clothes.

Walking to the office to pick up the few hundred dollars he'd earned, he met Tex Holden, the cowboy who'd ridden just before him, coming the other way.

"Sorry about that last ride, Tex," he said. "Bum luck."

"It happens. At least I made it off the critter in one piece." Tex gave him a good-natured grin. "Will we be seein' you in Abilene?"

"Not this time." Virgil shook his head. "I'm headin' out. Got word my dad died, so I'll have business at home to take care of."

"Sorry about your dad," Tex said. "But I'll wish you good luck, all the same. See you around, Bull." He ambled off toward his truck.

"Bull?" Jasper had been close enough to hear.

"It's a nickname. That's what they call me these days," Virgil said.

"Bull Tyler . . ." Jasper rolled the name around on his tongue, trying it out. "Sounds like somebody you wouldn't want to mess with. I kinda like it."

"Yeah," Virgil said. "Me too."

They'd eaten dinner in Pecos and spelled each other driving for the rest of the night. By the time they pulled into the small town of Blanco Springs, the morning sun had cleared the caprock escarpment, which rose above the ranchland in a labyrinth of cliffs, turrets, and deep, shadowed canyons.

Above and to the east of the escarpment the land leveled off to a high plain so vast and flat that the early Spaniards who rode across it had driven stakes in the ground to mark their path and keep from getting lost. They had named it the *Llano Estacado*, the staked plain. Three centuries later, in the canyons below, the Comanche nation had made a last bloody stand against the invading whites, who slaughtered their horses by the hundreds to make sure the tribe would never ride to war again.

To the young man who called himself Bull Tyler, this was the country where he'd grown up—the country he'd never wanted to see again.

As Jasper drove the familiar road into Blanco Springs, Bull could see little that had changed. They passed the high school, which he'd left a year short of graduation. There were two churches—Protestant and Catholic, neither of which he'd ever attended. There was the movie theater he'd snuck into because he was too poor to buy a ticket, and the

Blue Coyote Bar, where he'd waited outside in the truck to drive his father home after a drunk.

The little mom-and-pop grocery store was the same, as was the garage and gas station. But there was a shiny new restaurant on Main Street called the Burger Shack. This was where Jasper pulled in, parked, and turned off the engine.

"They're open for breakfast," he said. "Might as well fill up and get coffee here. No tellin' what you'll find at the ranch."

"Isn't Carlos there?" Bull remembered Jasper mentioning the Mexican cook earlier.

"Carlos hasn't been paid since before your dad went missin'. He promised he'd stay and take care of the stock while I went to look for you, but don't expect a meal on the table. Come on. We'll both feel better with somethin' in our bellies."

Aching in every joint and muscle, Bull climbed out of the truck and followed Jasper into the restaurant. If Carlos hadn't been paid, then Jasper probably hadn't been, either. And what about the other ranch hands? If Carlos was tending to the stock, they'd probably left to find other work.

What was he going home to?

The Burger Shack was clean and cheerful with photos of classic cars on the walls and red Formica-topped tables in the booths. The menu was posted above the counter.

The waitress, a shapely brunette in a pink uniform, gave Bull a look that only a blind man could've missed. Bull didn't miss it—and he didn't miss seeing the gold band on her finger.

"Howdy, Jasper," she said. "I see you brought in a new friend. How about an introduction?"

"Sure," Jasper said. "Bonnie, this here's young

Bull Tyler. Bull, this is Bonnie Treadwell, the best damn waitress this side of the Rio Grande."

"Pleased to meet you, ma'am," Bull said, tipping an invisible hat.

"Tyler?" Her eyebrows rose slightly. "Then this must be Williston's boy. I'd know those blue eyes anywhere."

"That's right," Jasper said. "If you're ready to take our order, we'll have coffee and two breakfast specials."

"Comin' up," she said. "And I'm right sorry about your father, Bull."

Bull already had his wallet out to pay. He handed her a twenty. She brushed his hand as she took the bill. Up close she looked about thirty, but she was pretty enough to stir a tingle with her touch. His gaze caught the sway of her hips as she walked back toward the counter.

"Don't even think about it," Jasper said. "She's married and she's trouble."

"Not to worry. Don't get me wrong, I like the ladies. I've had my share of the kind that hang around rodeos waiting to give a bull bucker a different kind of ride. But I know better than to mess with other men's wives."

"Smart." Jasper glanced toward the counter where Bonnie was setting up their coffee mugs on a tray with cream and sugar. "Her husband's a trucker. Good man. Loves her like crazy. But when he's on the road she gets lonesome, and she's got a powerful itch for young cowboys. Not that I know firsthand, mind you, but I've heard the other guys talk. Trust me, you don't want to get involved with her."

"Got it. I'll keep that in mind."

Bonnie brought the coffee mugs and set them on

the table along with change from the twenty. Her breast brushed Bull's shoulder as she leaned over to pour the coffee. He willed himself to ignore the tug of arousal that tightened his jeans.

"You haven't said much about the ranch, Jasper," he said as Bonnie sashayed back to the counter to greet an older couple. "If the news is bad, I might as well hear it now."

Jasper added two packets of sugar to his coffee, stirred it, and took a sip.

"It *is* bad, isn't it?" Bull said.

Jasper nodded, pausing to take a breath. "You knew your dad was a drinker."

"Yeah. But he pretty much kept it under control, didn't he?"

"For the first few years I knew him, he did. But after you left home, it got worse. He stopped fixin' up the place, let the sheds and fences fall to ruin, stopped clearin' pasture, and quit workin' on the house. He cleaned out whatever was in the bank to feed the stock and pay the men. When that was gone, he started sellin' off the cattle and horses."

Bull felt a hollow burn below his ribs, as if the coffee in his stomach had turned to acid. The Rimrock had never been a showplace of good management, but at spring roundup, before he left, there'd been at least four hundred head of Hereford cattle on the range. It had never crossed his mind that conditions would go downhill—and so fast.

"How many cattle are there now?" he forced himself to ask.

"There's Jupiter—your dad was savin' him for last. And besides him there are about twenty cows and a dozen spring calves. The steers are all gone."

"What about horses?"

"Four. All of 'em old."

"Lord Almighty." Bull barely noticed when Bonnie set their plates on the table. At least his father had kept Jupiter, the aging Hereford bull. As long as the surly old boy could do his job, and the cows were healthy, there would be more calves. But the time and money it would take to get the ranch running at capacity was staggering. He had $7,000 in the bank, saved from his rodeo winnings toward a decent truck. That would barely make a dent in what he needed for the ranch.

Maybe selling out to the Prescotts would be his only option.

"Eat your breakfast. You're gonna need it." Jasper was already digging his fork into the heap of scrambled eggs, hash browns, and bacon, with a short stack of pancakes on the side. Bull gazed down at his plate. Jasper was right, but his appetite was gone. He forced himself to chew and swallow each bite.

What if he'd stayed—taken his father's abuse and worked to make the ranch a success? Would his father still be alive? Would the Rimrock be a profitable, working ranch?

All he'd ever wanted was to be free of this place. But what if he'd made a different choice back then? What would he be looking at today?

After they'd finished breakfast, they left a tip for Bonnie and went back outside to the truck. "I'll drive," Jasper said, climbing in. "That'll give you a chance to look around."

Bull buckled his seat belt and rolled down the window as Jasper started the engine. The sun blazed in the cloudless sky. The morning was already hot.

By afternoon, heat waves would be rippling off the molten asphalt streets.

"Doesn't look like much has changed," Bull observed as they drove out of town. "Same old houses. Same dried-up lawns and dried-up people."

"Not much changes around here," Jasper said. "Except that your dad's in the ground and the ranch is within a gnat's eyelash of goin' under."

"Why didn't you tell me about the ranch when you found me?"

"Would you have come back if you'd known? Or would you have already decided to sell out to the Prescotts?"

"Who's to say I won't do that, anyway? It might be the only choice."

Jasper pulled off the road and turned to give Bull a stern look. "So you'd let them dirty skunks win, without even puttin' up a fight?"

"Ask me again after I've had a look at the place."

Bull didn't say any more. It would be wasted breath to argue with Jasper before he'd had time to weigh his options. He was the boss now, he reminded himself. Jasper, for all his value as a friend and mentor, was his employee. For both of them, that would take some getting used to.

He waited until Jasper had pulled onto the road again and driven half a mile into the open country before he spoke.

"Speaking of dirty skunks, how are the Prescotts? Is Ferg still around?"

"Yup. I seen him last time I was in town. He was drivin' around in a fancy red convertible with a couple of girls who looked young enough to still be in high school."

"I thought maybe he'd have gone off to college or something. His folks could afford to send him, that's for sure."

"Can't argue with that. But Ferg's too lazy for college. Besides, why should he go when he's set to inherit the biggest ranch in these parts?" Jasper gave Bull a knowing glance. "I take it you haven't warmed any toward him."

"No way." Ferguson Prescott, the neighbors' only surviving son, had been Bull's boyhood playmate. But years before he'd left home, an incident so horrific that they'd vowed never to mention it again had torn them apart. Distrust had made them rivals, then enemies.

"Was my dad still feuding with the Prescotts?"

"Not so much after the heavy drinkin' started. But he always said they'd get their hands on the Rimrock over his dead body."

Jasper fell silent, as if realizing what his words had implied. Bull gazed out the window at the drought-yellowed pastureland and cedar-specked sagebrush flats. A loose cow grazed in the bar ditch where the grass, watered by spring runoff from the road, still bore sprouts of green. Jasper slowed down and swung across the painted line to avoid spooking the animal.

"The sheriff called my father's death an accident," Bull said. "That's what you told me. Do you believe it?"

Jasper hesitated, as if weighing his reply. "I might . . . if I could figure out what he was doin' on top of that cliff in the first place."

"Did anybody look around up there?"

"The sheriff did. So did I. The back slope of the

ledge ain't all that steep. It wouldn't have been a hard climb. But it's solid rock up there. No way to see tracks on it."

"So there'd be no way to tell if somebody pushed him off the top."

"No way to know if he was pushed, or if he stumbled over, or if . . ." Jasper let the words trail into silence.

A shudder passed through Bull's body. "You mean, he might've *jumped?* Good Lord, Jasper, was he that bad off?"

Jasper hesitated, his eyes on the road. "Coulda been. But I don't like to think so. He never gave any sign of it. Just like he never gave up hopin' you'd come back."

"My dad wanted me back? After all the hateful things he said to me?"

Jasper nodded. "You were Williston's only flesh and blood—and all he had left of your mother. That's why he wouldn't sell. He was savin' the ranch for you."

Bull gazed through the dusty windshield, eyes following the flight of a red-tailed hawk. He swallowed an unaccustomed tightness in his throat. "I'll take a look at the ranch," he said. "Then I want you to show me where my father died."

CHAPTER 2

*T*WENTY MILES OUT OF BLANCO SPRINGS THE PICKUP swung off the paved highway and onto a rutted dirt road. The tires raised clouds of dust that filtered through the vents and drifted in through the open side windows. Bull could feel the grit when he ran his tongue across his teeth. The beating sun was hotter than a forge, and the old truck had no air-conditioning.

Still at the wheel, Jasper gave him a cheerful grin. "That's Rimrock dust you're eatin'. Welcome home, Bull Tyler."

Bull spat his chew out the window. It was still sinking in that the place was his—every dusty, rocky, snake-infested, mesquite-clogged inch of it. Given the value of ranchland these days, he was a rich man. But nothing above ground looked to be worth fighting for.

As the truck neared the heart of the ranch, he spotted the old wooden windmill that pumped well water to supply the house and the tanks for the stock. Missing several vanes, with others hanging loose, it turned sluggishly in the hot summer breeze. Off to one side sat the house that had been grandly planned but never finished. Its plywood exterior had weathered to match the blowing dust. The corrals were empty, the barn roof sagging. Bull couldn't see into the machine shed beyond the house, but he'd already guessed that anything usable would've been sold.

Jasper cursed as they pulled into the yard and drove up to the house. "Carlos's car isn't here. The bastard must've given up on us and lit out. Come on, we've got to see to the stock. In this heat they could all be dead of thirst by now."

He flung himself out of the truck and raced for the hose connection next to the barn. Bull sprinted after him, falling into the old routine as if he'd never left. While Jasper cranked on the spigot, Bull followed the long hose line around the barn to where it ended at the horse paddock.

The four horses were on their feet, thank heaven, but their heads were drooping, and the outline of their ribs showed like the tines of a pitchfork through their hides. The grass in their paddock was eaten down to bare dirt, and the watering trough was bone dry.

Bull directed the thin stream of water into the trough. At the sound of it, the horses came shuffling toward him. They were old animals—he'd ridden them all, growing up. There was Bess, the gentle bay mare, Pete, the roan stallion, and the two dun geldings, Cap and Chuck. Bull had long since learned not to show his emotions, but they almost broke his heart.

As the water rose, the horses pushed their way

around the trough and lowered their heads to drink. He would need to find them some hay or turn them into fresh pasture. But first he needed to help Jasper see to the cattle.

The cows and spring calves had been herded into the winter pasture to keep them close for feeding. Bull could see Jasper standing over a downed calf. It wasn't moving, probably dead. And the others looked close to it. He broke into a run, dragging the long hose behind him to fill the three water troughs through the fence.

At the sound of water, the cows and calves moved in, the stronger ones drinking it up almost as soon as it poured out of the hose. Bull kept running water into the troughs until there was enough for all of them. So far they'd lost only one calf, but some of the others looked almost too far gone to survive.

Jupiter, the massive bull, waited at the fence. He was gaunt but still rock solid. Williston Tyler had won the calf in a poker game and raised him to be a giant. He'd long since proven his worth, siring a good crop of calves every season. But unlike most Hereford bulls, a breed that tended to be easygoing, Jupiter was mean to the bone.

Wasted as the huge animal was, the white-rimmed eyes that watched Bull fill his trough gleamed with malevolence. There was good reason for the stout metal fence that confined him to his pasture.

"Damn that Carlos to hell!" Jasper swore as he closed the gate of the cow pasture. "I can't believe he'd go and leave these animals to die of thirst. If I ever catch up with the bastard—"

He paused to pick up a rock and fling it at a buzzard that had settled on the dead calf. His aim was

true. The bird squawked and flapped away. "Nothin'
we can do now except bury the dead one and try to
keep the rest of these poor critters alive. Williston
sold the backhoe last year, but there should be a couple of shovels in the barn. While you're getting
them, see if there's any hay. If it's all gone, one of us
will have to make a run to the feed store and load a
few bales in the pickup. Hopefully they'll let us have
them on credit."

"I'll do it," Bull said, "after I see how much hay's
left in the barn."

Leaving Jasper to refill the troughs, Bull sprinted
back toward the barn. For now, he willed himself to
focus on the task at hand. If he took time to think
about what it would take to get the ranch up and
running again, the worry would paralyze him.

At times like this, selling out to the Prescotts didn't
strike him as a bad idea.

He remembered Carlos, the longtime ranch cook,
who'd promised to stay and take care of the stock. He
was a good-hearted old man, not the sort who'd drive
off and leave helpless animals to die of thirst. Something about his absence didn't feel right.

The barn door stood open, light falling in shafts
through the sagging roof. An owl, slumbering on a
rafter, screeched an alarm and flashed upward to
vanish into the shadows above the loft. Bull could
see the shovels propped against the side of an empty
stall. Toward the back of the barn, he could make
out a wheelbarrow, a pitchfork, one rectangular bale
of hay, and scattered pieces of another—barely
enough to keep the precious stock alive.

Leaving the shovels for a second trip, he strode to
the hay, hefted the bale into the wheelbarrow, and
gathered up the rest. He was pushing the wheelbarrow

through the barn door when a metallic glint in the dust caught his eye.

Bending, he picked up a silver crucifix dangling from a broken chain. His pulse slammed. Carlos, a devout Catholic, had worn that crucifix day and night, as his father had worn it before him. He would never willingly have taken it off.

A chill passed through Bull's body. Something had happened to the old man—maybe the same thing that had happened to his father.

After dropping the crucifix into his shirt pocket, he pushed the loaded wheelbarrow out to the paddock. Sharing his discovery would have to wait until the starving animals were fed.

The horses crowded in as he forked the precious hay over the fence. There was barely enough for a few bites, but for now it would have to do.

Jasper was still running water into the cow troughs. Leaving the hose, he helped Bull pitch hay over the fence for the cows and calves and for Jupiter.

"That'll have to do till we get more," Bull said. "But right now I've got something else to show you. I found this coming out of the barn."

He reached into his pocket and pulled out the crucifix on its broken silver chain. Jasper's breath sucked in as he recognized it.

"Damn!" He took the crucifix from Bull's hand and clenched his fist around it. "I should've known Carlos wouldn't go off on his own. Now I'm wishin' he had. Anything would be better than that poor old man lyin' dead somewhere."

And the old man would be dead for sure by now, Bull thought. If Carlos had been gone long enough for the animals to run out of hay and water, he wasn't coming back.

"Maybe he caught somebody tryin' to steal his car," Jasper said. "It's gone, same as Carlos. He loved that old Buick, restored it himself, paint and all. It was his baby."

"Or this could be the Prescotts' way of spooking us into selling," Bull said. "I wouldn't put anything past them."

Jasper's eyes narrowed. "Watch what you say and who you say it to, Bull. Placin' blame where there ain't no proof will only get you in trouble. Anybody could've stole that car—teenage thugs, wetbacks cuttin' through the property—*anybody*. Carlos would've tried to stop them, but he couldn't have put up much of a fight. Poor old man didn't even own a gun."

Bull nodded. Jasper was right. The Prescotts might be looking to take over the ranch, but that didn't mean they'd commit murder to get it. That sort of thing only happened in the movies. Unless he could find solid proof, he'd be smart to keep his mouth shut.

"We should at least call the sheriff and have him put out an alert on the car," he said. "That old Buick should be easy to spot."

"Good idea." Jasper dropped the crucifix into his pocket. "Trouble is, the phone company shut us down a couple of months ago on account of not gettin' paid. If you want to talk to the sheriff, you'll have to drive into town."

"Give me the keys. I'll pick up some hay and a few groceries while I'm there. Is Sam Handley still sheriff?"

"Sam keeled over from a heart attack last year. Vern Mossberg is sheriff now."

"Do I know him?"

"Not likely. He's new in town. That's just one of the things that've changed since you left. While you're still settlin' in, you might want to play your cards close to your vest."

"Thanks for the warning." Bull took the keys. "I'll try not to be gone too long. And I'll help you bury that calf when I get back."

Jasper watched the pickup disappear down the bumpy road. Maybe he should've gone along on the ride back to town. Williston's boy had grown up big and strong. But young Bull had a lot to learn. He was bound to make mistakes. Maybe that was the only way to get smart.

Keeping a sharp eye out, Jasper walked around the barn and past the sheds to a patch of cleared ground on a low rise of land. There, bordered by rocks and marked by crude wooden slabs, were two graves. The older, smaller one was covered with the dry remnants of spring wildflowers, now gone to seed. The newer grave was a narrow mound of raw earth, the dust lightly blowing off the top. Jasper stood at the foot of that grave and spoke out loud.

"Well, Williston, I kept my promise. I found your boy and brought him home. You'd be proud of how he's turned out. One day he'll be a man who can hold his head up anywhere. But Lord Almighty, thinkin' about the hard times he'll be facin' gives me the cold shivers."

As if in answer, a breath of wind blew over the grave, stirring dust into Jasper's eyes. Jasper blinked away a tear. Williston Tyler had been the saddest man he'd ever known, and one of the toughest. Even toward the end of his life, when he'd been in so much pain he could barely stand to mount a horse, Williston had insisted on working cattle with the hired hands.

"I know you was hard on the boy," Jasper continued. "And I know he hated you for it. Maybe one day he'll understand why you did what you did, and how much you really loved him. But since I promised not to tell him the truth right off, I reckon he'll just have to figure it out for his self."

Thrusting his hands into his pockets, Jasper turned and walked back toward the barn. He'd never promised Williston he'd stay on, he reminded himself. He had plenty of reason to leave, including a pretty girl back in the hill country, just waiting for him to come home, marry her, and settle down on her dad's farm. But he couldn't leave yet—not with the ranch teetering on the brink of ruin and Williston's boy so inexperienced and unaware of the dangers. Walking away now would be like leaving a half-grown pup in the path of a cattle stampede.

He would stay—not for long, but for now.

Lengthening his stride, Jasper entered the house by the back door, passed through the cluttered kitchen and down the hall. He'd moved his few possessions from the dilapidated bunkhouse into one of the spare bedrooms to keep an eye on Williston. After the old man was gone, it hadn't made sense to move out.

The Colt .45 Peacemaker hung from its belt on a nail in the back of the closet. He took the heavy pistol down, strapped it around his hips, and went back outside to look for Carlos.

*　　*　　*

The sheriff's office, along with the jail, the court-room, and the library, was still housed in the old county building on Main Street. Bull parked the truck and crossed the lawn to the front door. So far nothing seemed to have changed. Same dingy beige walls, needing paint. Same creaky floorboard out-side the sheriff's office. The receptionist at the desk, though a little older and grayer, was the woman he remembered from the library, which she opened on Tuesday and Thursday afternoons. Same wire-rimmed glasses, same mole on her chin. Even her flowered dress looked familiar. Mildred, that was her name. Mildred Patterson.

He cleared his throat, causing her to look up from the romance novel she was reading. The puz-zled expression on her face dissolved as she recog-nized him. But she looked more startled than pleased.

"Hello, Mrs. Patterson." Bull remembered to take off his hat.

"Virgil Tyler! Heavens to Betsy, you've grown up!" Her voice seemed unnaturally shrill. "When did you get back into town?"

"Today. We've got trouble at the ranch. I need to talk to the sheriff."

She glanced toward the sheriff's closed door, then seemed to check the spiral notebook on her desk. "I'm sorry, but he's out. Would you like to leave a message?"

Virgil hesitated. He could ask the woman to pass on a report about Carlos and his car. But then he'd miss his chance to question the sheriff about his fa-ther's death.

"If it's all the same to you, I'd like to talk to Sher-iff Mossberg. When's he due back?"

"He didn't say. You could try after lunch. Again, I'd be happy to pass on a message."

Bull's eyes caught a flicker of movement behind the frosted glass pane on the sheriff's door. Was someone in the office, or was it just a trick of the light—maybe a tree limb blowing outside the office window?

"Thanks, but I'll come back later," he said. "Tell the sheriff I stopped by."

Tugged by a vague uneasiness, Bull walked back to the truck. Nothing was wrong, he told himself. Mildred Patterson had been cordial enough, and it made sense that the sheriff might be busy doing his job. But Jasper had said that things had changed in town. Was this what he'd meant?

He drove to the feed store, where hay was sold by the bale from a shed out back. It was expensive here. Buying a big load from a farmer would have been a better bargain. But this was an emergency, and he'd only be taking enough hay to fill the back of the pickup.

He parked around back where he could load and went inside to order and pay. The pugnacious-looking red-headed man behind the counter was a stranger. He glanced out the back window at the rusty pickup.

"If you're wantin' hay for the Tyler place, I can't sell you no more," he said. "Your credit's all used up, and your account's past due."

"I can pay cash," Bull said.

"You got enough cash to pay off the account? There's more than eight hundred dollars owed on it."

Bull tried to ignore the knot in his stomach. "I can't pay it off now, but I can pay cash for a pickup load."

The man folded his arms across his burly chest.

"No deal. Clear off the debt and we can do business. Otherwise, good luck findin' hay anyplace else."

Bull fought the urge to punch the man's smug, freckled face. Hay was scarce right now with last fall's crop almost gone and the spring crop still in the field. He'd be lucky to find any for sale, and the bastard knew it.

He pictured the starving horses and cattle. His hand went to his wallet. "Can you take a credit card?"

"If it's any good. And if you can show me some ID."

Bull had used the Visa card to tide him over between rodeos. Clearing the account and paying for the new hay would damn near max out his limit. But he didn't have much choice. He watched as the clerk checked his driver's license, ran the card, and handed him the slip to sign.

"Virgil Tyler." The man checked the card against the signature. "I heard that old drunk had a boy who'd lit out for the rodeo. That you?"

Bull held his temper with effort. "Williston Tyler was my father. But I don't go by Virgil anymore. The name is Bull Tyler."

"Bull Tyler, huh?" The man grinned. "Well, good luck livin' up to that one."

Bull took the receipt, walked outside, and gave it to the yard man, also a stranger, who loaded the bed of the truck with bales of hay. Bull climbed into the cab and drove off. Jasper was right. Things had changed in Blanco Springs. And not in a good way.

But he had changed, too. At just short of twenty-one, he was a man—the last of his family. His father had left him a legacy of tragedy and ruin—along with a choice. He could sell the ranch and leave for good, with enough money to make a new start anywhere he chose. Or he could stay, pay off his father's debts, rebuild the ranch, and create a legacy of his own—a new dynasty of Tylers who could look any man in the eye and face any challenge together.

But what was he thinking? Hell, even with his savings in the bank, he didn't have enough money to run the ranch for more than a couple of months, let alone make the repairs and buy new stock. He'd have to be crazy to bust his gut and empty his bank account when he could just sell out and leave.

He drove past the county building. The sheriff's big tan Jeep, which he'd noticed earlier, was gone from its parking spot. He would have to check back later. Meanwhile, he had time to kill, and he was getting hungry. He didn't plan to buy groceries until he was ready to leave town. Otherwise the food might spoil in the hot truck. It wouldn't hurt to grab a two-dollar burger and a Coke while he waited for the sheriff.

By now it was lunchtime. There were half a dozen vehicles in the Burger Shack parking lot. One of them was a sleek, red Thunderbird convertible, with its top down. As he drove past it, Bull couldn't resist slowing down to admire its flashy beauty. Never in his life would he own such a machine—or even want to. But it was no sin to look. Jasper had mentioned that Ferguson Prescott was driving a car like that. No surprise there. Ferg had always been a show-off.

Bull parked the truck, tossed his hat on the seat, and pocketed the keys. Sooner or later he was bound to run into Ferg. Here was as good a place as any.

After pushing open the restaurant door, he looked around. He could see Bonnie, busy behind the counter, but Ferg was nowhere in sight. Only as Bull walked up to place his order did he spot his onetime friend in the round corner booth.

Ferg had been a linebacker on the high school football team. He was no more than average height but was built like a brick wall, all muscle. Like Bull, he'd put on a good thirty pounds in weight since then. With his wavy chestnut hair carefully combed, his square-chiseled face clean-shaven, he could've passed for the star of a TV Western.

And he wasn't alone.

Sitting across from him in the booth was a girl. More child than woman, she couldn't have been much older than sixteen. Her blond hair was pulled back from her face in a messy ponytail. The fabric of her olive green T showed the firm buds of her breasts. Her bell-bottom jeans were stylishly frayed. All in all, she was just a gangly kid. But she had beautiful eyes—deep dove gray, strangely haunting. And her full lips formed a pretty, childish pout. Given a couple of years to grow up, she could be worth a second look.

But what the hell was a kid like that doing with Ferg?

"Hey, Virgil!" Ferg gave him a wave. He'd always been a friendly sort, but Bull knew better than to turn his back on him. Jasper's opinion of the Prescotts was spot-on.

He shifted over, making space in the booth. "Bonnie told me you were back in town. Come have a seat and tell us what you've been up to."

Bull would have ignored the invitation, but something about the girl intrigued him—maybe even worried him. And it wouldn't hurt to know what was going on with Ferg and his family. He placed his order with Bonnie, who gave him a smile and a wink.

Then, taking his Coke, he ambled over to the booth and sat down.

Leaning back against the corner part of the seat, Ferg appeared to be taking his measure. "Sorry about your dad," he said.

"Thanks." Bull held his tongue in check. He wasn't here to bait Ferg. He was here to listen and learn.

A slow grin stole across Ferg's face. "Bonnie tells me you're going by another name. Bull, is it?"

"That's right."

"Short for Bullshit?"

The jab hit home, and the bastard knew it. Ferg's grin broadened.

"No." Bull steeled his resolve to stay cool. "It's a nickname the other bull riders gave me because I could take a pounding without giving up. You might say I earned it."

"Is that right? I'd have guessed they called you Bull because you smelled like one." Ferg kept his grin. The girl sipped her Coke, her gray eyes shifting from one man to the other as if she might be hoping to see a fight. She had long, restless hands, the fingernails bitten to the quick.

Bull took a long draw on his Coke. "Question for you, Ferg," he said. "How much do you get paid for babysitting?"

Ferg looked startled. Then he laughed. "Bull Tyler, allow me to introduce my cousin, Miss Susan Rutledge. Her dad and my dad were stepbrothers growing up. I guess, technically, that makes us stepcousins. Her dad is here visiting from Savannah, so I volunteered to show her the town."

"My apologies, Miss Susan Rutledge." Bull gave her a nod, savoring the classy sound of her name when he pronounced it.

The girl glared back at him. "Ferg told me the people around here were ill-mannered bumpkins," she said. "Now I know what he meant. For your information, Mister Bull Tyler, I'm not a baby. I even smoke."

"Not legally." Ferg gave her a playful nudge. Her giggle was like a little girl's. Watching them, Bull felt a low-simmering anger. If Ferg was messing around with this underage child, he deserved to be shot.

"Do you chew, Miss Susan?" Bull's question dripped sarcasm. "I've got a plug of tobacco in my pocket. I'd be happy to share it with you."

The girl pulled a face. "Ugh! That's gross. Last summer I kissed a boy who chewed. It tasted awful."

"Suit yourself. No skin off my nose." Bull sipped his Coke. What the girl did was none of his business. But somebody ought to warn her that she was in bad company.

"So, *Bull,* are you home to stay?" Ferg asked.

Bull shrugged. "I just got here. Ask me in a week or two." No use talking about the dire condition of the ranch. He wouldn't be telling Ferg anything he didn't already know. "How are your parents?" he asked, making polite conversation.

"My mother passed on two years ago. My dad's as ornery and stubborn as ever."

"I didn't know about your mother," Bull said. "I'm sorry."

"Dad's already grooming me to take over the ranch. He keeps pushing me to get hitched and give him a passel of grandsons to carry on the family name. Hell, I'm too young for that! I've got a lot of living to do before I settle down."

"Smart thinking," Bull said. "I can't picture you as a father. Not yet at least."

Had Ferg just flinched? Dismissing the thought, Bull glanced around to see Bonnie coming from behind the counter with his burger on a paper plate.

"Here you are, cowboy." She set Bull's order on the table, bending close to give him a view of her ample cleavage. "The fries are extra special from me. Eat hearty."

Bull hadn't ordered fries. "Thanks," he said as she strutted away, hips twitching with every step.

Bull reached for the ketchup and was pouring it on the fries when he realized he was the only one with food. "Aren't you two eating?" he asked.

"Naw. We've got lunch waiting at home. We were just having Cokes. Come on, Cousin Susan, I need to get you back to the ranch before your dad sends a posse after us. Enjoy your burger, *Bull.*"

Ferg slid around the booth, pushing the girl out ahead of him. When she stood, Bull saw that she was surprisingly tall and as slim as a boy. Ferg's hand rested on the small of her narrow back as he ushered her toward the door. Neither of them looked back at Bull to say good-bye.

From behind the counter, Bonnie watched them go. Her mouth was fixed in a smile, but even from where he sat, Bull could see the troubled look in her brown eyes.

Bull finished his burger and fries. By the time he left, she was busy with other customers.

Returning to the county building, Bull spotted the sheriff's Jeep in its usual place. He parked the truck and went back inside. In the outer office, Mildred Patterson glanced up from her romance novel.

"The sheriff is expecting you, Virgil," she said. "Go on in."

Sheriff Vern Mossberg rose from behind his massive oaken desk. He looked to be nearing fifty, square jaw, square shoulders and chest, ramrod spine, close-clipped hair, and an immaculately pressed uniform. Retired military, Bull guessed. Army, or marines. He had that look about him.

"Mr. Tyler." He acknowledged Bull with a curt nod. "Please have a seat."

Bull lowered himself onto a straight-backed metal chair that faced the desk. Mossberg took his seat, fixing him with a steely gaze. "Now, what can I do for you?" he demanded.

"Two things," Bull said. "First, I want to report a missing man and the theft of his car."

"The man's name?" Mossberg picked up a pen and slid a yellow pad to the front of the desk.

"His name is Carlos Ortega. He's our ranch cook, and he was gone when we—"

"Ortega, you say?" the sheriff interrupted. "He's Mexican?"

"Yes. He's worked for us about ten years. He—"

"Is he here legally? Does he have citizenship, or maybe a green card?"

"I never thought to ask." Bull's frustration seethed. "Look, the man's missing, along with his car. I found the crucifix he always wore. It was broken, like it had been ripped off him. All I'm asking is that you put an alert out for his car—it's a restored Buick, easy to spot. I can give you the plate number."

Mossberg shook his head. "Mr. Tyler, my policy is not to waste time chasing after illegal Mexicans or their vehicles. If you have proof that he's legal, bring it in. Otherwise, if you want to track him down, I suggest you contact the border patrol."

"Listen, Sheriff," Bull argued. "Carlos isn't a criminal. He's a harmless old man. He could be hurt somewhere, or dead."

The sheriff gave Bull a stony look. "I told you, it's not my job to track down illegals. Now, what was the second thing you wanted?"

Bull checked the urge to get up and leave. He already sensed that this errand was a waste of time. But whatever the sheriff had to say, even if it wasn't helpful, he needed to hear it.

He cleared his throat. "It's about my father. After he went missing, he was found at the bottom of a cliff. His death was ruled an accident. Why wasn't it investigated as a possible murder? How do you know he wasn't pushed, or killed before he fell?"

The sheriff scowled. "It wasn't a difficult call. There were no signs of a struggle, no injuries that wouldn't have been caused by the fall. He wasn't shot or stabbed or drugged—although there was plenty of alcohol in his system. As far as I'm concerned, the case is closed."

"Who did the autopsy?"

"The doctor who serves as county coroner looked him over. But given the condition of the body—" He shook his head. "Doctor Gaines isn't a trained pathologist, but he saw enough."

"Never mind. I get the idea. I hope you'll understand if I look into this myself. I owe my father that much." Bull stood and left.

After picking up a few groceries, Bull climbed into the truck and headed back to the ranch. Even with the windows down, the cab of the truck was an oven. Sweat glued his clothes to his body and trickled down his face. As he relived his visit to town, his hands gripped the steering wheel until the knuckles ached.

Through the haze of anger, frustration, and blame, one reality stood as solid as the rocky pinnacles above the ranch. He had no friends in Blanco Springs, no allies, no credibility, and no family honor. Except for Jasper, who couldn't be expected to stay and work for nothing, he stood alone against the avalanche of misfortune that had fallen on the Rimrock.

Selling to the Prescotts would be the easy way out. But one look at Ferg's smug face had been enough to convince him he couldn't just roll over and give up. The land was his legacy—to keep and pass on to his children and grandchildren. If he wasn't man enough to fight for it, he wasn't man enough to live.

He'd been proud of the name his fellow bull riders had given him. But staying on a bucking bull for eight seconds was child's play when compared to what he was facing now.

To save what was his, he would need the gut strength to do whatever it took. The rules of common decency would be out the window. He would have to be tough, hard, and ruthless.

Bull.

It was time he started living up to his name.

CHAPTER 3

JASPER WAS WAITING WHEN BULL PULLED INTO THE YARD. "How did it go in town?" he asked.

"Could've been better." Bull climbed down from the truck and spit his chew in the dust. "I got the hay. But with the cattle too weak to move to better pasture, it won't last long. And the sheriff was no help. According to him, hunting for a missing illegal isn't in his job description."

"That doesn't surprise me. The man hates Mexicans like a sheepherder hates coyotes."

"Was Carlos illegal? I never asked, and he never said."

"I reckon he was," Jasper said. "We talked a little. He's got family in Mexico—little town over the border. Rio Seco, it's called. Unless the old man was damned lucky, I don't suppose he'll ever set eyes on the place again."

"So you didn't find anything that might be a clue." Bull gathered the grocery bags to take in the house.

TEXAS FIERCE   37

Jasper shook his head. One hand rested on the heavy pistol strapped to his hip. "Not a trace. No blood. No tracks. No tire marks from the car or anything else. Between the dust and the wind, there ain't much left to find."

"Is the house all right? Whoever came by could've ransacked the place."

"Not much left to ransack." Jasper took the last grocery sack. "The house is fine."

"I should've asked if the icebox was working before I bought milk and butter," Bull said.

"The icebox makes more noise than a bulldozer, but it stays cold, most of the time. We got lights and well water. And the old TV works fine if you don't mind fiddlin' with the antenna."

"That's good enough for me." Bull followed Jasper into the house and helped him put the groceries away. The place didn't look like much, with its shabby wall, exposed plumbing and wiring, rough plank floors, and worn-out, secondhand furniture. But then, it never had. Maybe someday he could fix it up, make it something to be proud of. Right now that was a long way down the list.

"We'd better unload the hay and see to the stock," Bull said. "Then I'll have a look around and figure out what we can fix without having to buy anything. Something tells me the lumber and hardware store won't give us any more credit than the hay and feed place did."

Jasper looked hopeful. "You're talkin' like you mean to stay. Have you made up your mind?"

Had he? Driving home, he'd felt so sure of himself. But now, surrounded by memories of the place where he'd grown up, he could almost hear his father's voice.

Can't you do one damned thing right? You're worthless, boy! You'll never amount to a hill of beans!

What if his father had been right? What if he was taking on more than he could handle?

"I haven't made up my mind yet," he said. "But I might as well get a few things done while I'm thinking it over."

"I reckon that'll have to do for now," Jasper said. "Your old room's ready with clean sheets on the bed. You can put your gear in there. Your dad's old forty-four is in his desk. With all that's been goin' on 'round here, you'll want to keep it handy."

"Thanks, Jasper. I'll get my duffel after we've unloaded the hay and fed the stock. Fix yourself some lunch if you're hungry. I had a burger in town. Did I tell you I ran into Ferg?"

"How'd that go?"

"About the way you'd expect. He's the same spoiled shithead he always was."

"Not that hard to figure out, is he?" Jasper scratched his mustache. "You said you wanted to see where we found your dad. I can take you anytime, but we'll have to hike from the truck. Those horses ain't in any shape for ridin' yet."

"It can wait till morning, when it's cooler. Meanwhile, we need to get more feed to the stock and bury that dead calf. Then, if there's enough daylight left, I'll see what I can do about fixing those vanes on the windmill and oiling the pump. That should get us more water pressure, and—" He broke off, puzzled by the grin on Jasper's face. "What the hell have you got to be so happy about?" he growled.

Jasper shrugged. "Nuthin' much. Just thinkin' how good it is to have you home, Bull Tyler."

* * *

A waning half-moon rose above the escarpment, casting the gullies and canyons into a black shadow. Coyote calls echoed across the foothills, one joining another in a nighttime chorus of yips and howls. An owl swooped on silent wings to seize a ground squirrel in its talons and flap off to its nest.

In Blanco Springs, the houses were dark. The lamps along Main Street cast empty circles of light on the sidewalk. Even the Blue Coyote was closed, its parking lot empty, its neon sign sputtering on and off, unseen and unheard.

Three blocks away, in a small house on a quiet side street, Ferg Prescott rolled over in the bed where he'd just had wild sex with Bonnie. "Gotta go," he muttered, pleasantly sated.

"Why so soon?" she whispered against his ear. "Danny won't be home till tomorrow."

"You know why. You've got nosy neighbors, people driving by. If we get caught, it's all over."

"Don't go yet," she pleaded. "A woman needs a little snuggling after a good time. It *was* good, wasn't it?"

"It's always good. The best." Ferg sighed. Sure, it was good. It was sex, wasn't it?

She nestled against him, her flesh warm and yielding, like risen bread dough. Ferg liked her well enough, and she knew how to give him what he wanted. But at thirty, she was overripe and past her prime—especially for a man who liked his women young, firm, and tight where it counted.

"I saw what you were doing today," he said. "And I didn't like it, not one damn bit."

"What didn't you like, honey? I'm not a mind reader."

"The way you were rubbing up to that cowboy in the café—you know, showing off your boobs, giving him free fries."

"Heck, I was only having fun. It didn't mean anything. You know me, it's just my way. Besides, you had a girl with you."

"Her? She's a baby. Just a kid. And she's my cousin."

"Not your real cousin. I heard what you said about her."

"So you heard, did you?" Ferg rolled over and leaned on his elbows, scowling down at her. "Well, if you want to make me happy, you can put those ears of yours to good use. I need to know more about what Bull Tyler is up to. Anything you hear about his plans and how his ranch is doing, you let me know. And if you can find out more by getting cozy with him, I'll understand. Got it?"

She gave him a lazy smile. "What's in it for me, sugar?"

"What do you think?"

Her knowing laughter was interrupted by the roar of a huge diesel pulling up in front of the house.

"Oh, my stars!" Bonnie sat bolt upright. "It's Danny! He's home early! Out the back window! I'll toss you your clothes!"

Cursing, Ferg scrambled over the sill and dropped to the ground. The backyard was pitch dark, the unmowed grass flattened next to the house. No surprise. He wasn't the first man to crawl out of Bonnie's back window, and he wouldn't be the last. All the same, he felt like a character in a slapstick comedy—and he didn't like it. Respect was something he craved almost as much as he craved sex.

His boots and clothes landed next to him. While

Bonnie welcomed her husband in the front room, Ferg dressed in the dark, climbed the fence, and cut through the block to where he'd left the ranch pickup.

Still swearing, he started up the truck, turned onto Main Street, and headed out of town. Until yesterday he'd been feeling pretty good about himself. As sole heir to the Prescott Ranch, he had family prestige and all the money he wanted to spend. He had expensive clothes and boots, a flashy car, and lots of pretty girls to ride in it—even if most of them were jailbait. He'd felt like the uncrowned king of Blanco Springs—until Virgil Tyler showed up.

Bull Tyler. The name burned like acid in his veins. Ferg had hated him for years. Now that he was back, Ferg hated him even more.

Unlike Ferg, Bull had no family, no money, no good clothes or expensive car. But he had something that Ferg, as the son of privilege, would never have. Call it an *edge*—that air of determination, hunger, and raw courage that had driven him away from Blanco Springs to take up one of the most dangerous sports in the world. Comparing himself to his former childhood friend, Ferg conceded, would be like comparing a big, pampered hound to a wild wolf.

Now the wolf had returned to claim the land Ferg's father had wanted for years. Ferg knew about the condition of the Rimrock. He'd watched the place slide into ruin as Williston Tyler's health and fortunes declined. Williston could have sold the land anytime, but he'd refused to the very end of his life.

Now the Rimrock had passed to Williston's son. Any reasonable man would sell out for a fair price and be gone. But Bull was not a reasonable man. If he made up his mind to stay, it would be as if his feet were planted in stone.

But the Prescotts could be intractable, too. One way or another, they were determined to get the Rimrock. If Bull Tyler chose to stand against them, one thing was certain.

He would have a war on his hands.

Sunrise found Bull high on the platform of the windmill, replacing the broken and missing vanes, while Jasper fed and watered the stock. He'd hoped to do the job last night, but by the time they'd buried the dead calf, the light was fading. There'd been no time to start.

The windmill tower, which his father had built of scrap wood decades ago, was in dire need of replacement. Anchored to the ground with stakes, it quivered with every move Bull made. It was a wonder it hadn't blown over in a heavy wind. But for now, it would have to do. Money was too scarce for a new metal one.

Getting more water out of the ground was at the top of the list he'd made. Fixing the windmill was more urgent, even, than seeing the place where his father had died.

As the morning light stole across the yard, he could hear the hungry bawling of the cows and calves in the pasture. Meadowlarks called from the grasslands. A golden eagle rose from a cedar clump and circled into the dawn sky. Mornings like this were the best thing he remembered about being home, the coolness of dawn, the sounds of nature, the sense of peace that was all the more precious because he knew it wouldn't last.

From his perch on the high platform, Bull could see the land from horizon to horizon. The yellowed pastures were clogged with thickets of mesquite that would need to be chained down and cleared away. Prairie dog colonies, with burrows that could break the leg of a cow or horse, dotted the open spaces. Pasture fences sagged between rotted and broken posts. But the most urgent problem in this hot, rainless summer was water. Without it, the ranch would never support enough cattle to make a profit.

Digging more wells would be the ideal solution. But hiring the equipment to do the job would be expensive. Hell, everything was expensive. Restoring the ranch to working condition would take ten times what he had in the bank.

He wasn't ready to give up—not by a long shot. But at times like this, all that he'd taken on seemed impossible.

Bull worked as he pondered, tightening the loose vanes and replacing the missing ones with pieces he'd found in the shed. There would still be a few gaps, but the windmill should turn faster than before. After that, all he could do was clean and lubricate the pump, replace the gaskets if he could find any spares, and hope for the best.

By the time he got the pump running efficiently, the morning sun was already getting hot. Strapping on his father's old .44 Special single-action Colt and taking a canteen of water, he joined Jasper in the pickup. Dust plumed behind them as they drove across the scrubby flatland to the low hills at the base of the escarpment.

"We'll have to hike from here," Jasper said, pulling the truck to a stop. "The canyon where they found your dad is about a mile up. It's not too far, but it'll be steep going."

When Bull climbed out of the truck, he could see the faint tire tracks and trampled scrub where the sheriff's men must've parked and the barely visible trail they would have made through the foothills. A chilly premonition crept over him. "Is the place on Rimrock property?" he asked, already knowing the answer to his question.

Jasper nodded. "It butts right onto the line. The far side of it is Prescott land."

"Let's go." Bull slung the canteen strap over his shoulder and headed up the trail. He knew with sickening certainty where they were going. It was to a place he'd buried in his memory—a place he'd never wanted to see again.

His index finger traced the thin scar that crossed the pad of his left thumb. Ferg Prescott had a similar scar, dating back to the summer afternoon when, years ago, the two boys had taken a blood oath never to speak of the ungodly thing they'd done or the lie they would tell to keep it secret. After that day, they'd never been friends again.

The two men walked in silence. The shadows deepened as they passed into the escarpment, a labyrinth of lofty sandstone cliffs, towering hoodoos, and meandering steep-sided canyons. Here, sheltered from wind, the tracks of the sheriff's team were easy to follow. But Bull didn't need them to find his way. He knew where to go.

The sound of trickling water drew him to an opening in the canyon at the foot of a high ledge. It was a spot of stunning beauty, the canyon floor carpeted in coral-colored sand, the sheer wall of the cliff decorated with Native American petroglyphs of horses—scores of horses, in all sizes. A spring seeped down one side of the cliff, nourishing clusters of green before it vanished into the rocks. Beyond the spring, a steeply winding trail led to the clifftop where the land sloped off toward the Prescott Ranch.

Blocking the dark memories from his mind, Bull gazed at the broken boulders that formed a layer at the foot of the cliff. Nobody could have survived a fall onto those sharp rocks. "You found him here?"

"Right here. Carlos and I were searching on horseback. We saw the buzzards and followed them to this place." Jasper shook his head. "All we could do was lay a blanket over him to keep off the birds and flies while we went for the sheriff."

Bull forced the image to the back of his mind. "Did the sheriff find anything besides the body?" he asked. "Was my dad wearing a gun?"

"No gun, no watch, and his pockets were empty."

"So, he could've been killed and robbed."

"If he was robbed, it would've been up topside. There weren't any tracks down here where we found him."

"Any tracks at the top?"

"Nothin' but rock up there. Come on. You might as well have a look. Maybe it'll help settle things in your mind."

Jasper started up the steep, narrow trail. Bull followed him, knowing he had to see the place. Old memories crowded in. He steeled himself against them. If he could stay on a bucking bull for eight seconds, with his cracked ribs wrapped in duct tape, he could stand anything.

The trail stopped at a level clearing below the clifftop. The loose scree that had fallen from above almost concealed a low cave that served as an entrance to a winter rattlesnake den. The snakes would be scattered now, but the smell of the den lingered, foul and pungent in the air. Forcing his gaze straight ahead, Bull continued climbing behind Jasper, over the rocks and up the back of the cliff.

The cliff top, not much bigger than a large dining table, was solid sandstone. Scoured by wind and weather, it was as flat as a griddle. Footsteps would leave no trace here; and if there'd been anything else to find, the sheriff's team of deputies would have already picked it up.

"Nothing." Bull mouthed a curse.

"I told you. But you had to see it for yourself."

"Are they sure he was even up here? He could've been murdered and dumped at the bottom."

Jasper shook his head. "Like I say, when Carlos and I found him, there was no tracks anywhere. There's no way to tell if he was pushed or if he was just up there wanderin' around alone and stumbled over the edge."

"That doesn't sound like something he'd do."

Jasper took his time answering. "Maybe not to you. But your dad changed a lot after you left. When things got bad, he liked to go off and find a spot where he could just sit and think. Sometimes he'd take a bottle with him, sometimes not."

By now the sun was nearing the peak of the sky. Jasper raised his hat and wiped his forehead with his bandanna. "Put this mess behind you, Bull. What's done is done. You've got other things to worry about."

Resting a hand on the butt of the .44, Bull gazed out over the foothills and beyond them to the dry flatland, dotted with brush and scarred with trails and gullies. Jasper was right, he told himself. He couldn't afford to spend time investigating his father's death when he had a ranch to save. For now, at least, he would need to put the tragedy behind him and move on.

From where he stood, he could see all the way to the heart of the ranch. The house and outbuildings were as drab as the earth beneath them. Closer, at the base of the foothills, he could see the pickup where they'd left it to climb the trail.

A half mile beyond, in a dry wash, something caught his attention. Bull tensed, shading his eyes against the blinding sun.

"What is it?" Jasper moved to stand beside him.

"That wash, the one just past that big clump of mesquite. Can you see anything down there?"

"Hard to tell." Jasper squinted into the glare. "All I can see is a little bit of color. Might just be trash, but it wouldn't hurt to check it out. Let's go."

Bull had already started down the steep trail. Half an hour later they reached the spot where they'd left the pickup. Climbing inside, they headed across the rough, open land toward the wash.

As the truck pulled up and stopped, two ravens flapped off a gnarled, dead cedar on the edge of the wash. *Bad sign,* Bull thought as he swung to the ground. He could detect no odor yet, but odds were that something down there was either dead or dying.

The wash was about six feet deep and an easy stone toss from rim to rim. At first, when he looked down into it, Bull could see nothing but rocks, sand, and tumbleweeds. Then he saw it, sprawled facedown below the exposed tangle of cedar tree roots—the chunky figure of a man. Jeans-clad legs, faded, plaid flannel shirt, a thatch of silver hair—it was Carlos.

Half-leaping, half-sliding, with Jasper behind him,

Bull crashed down the side of the wash. Dropping next to the old man, Bull laid a hand on his shoulder.

Carlos stirred and moaned. Incredibly, he was alive.

But he wouldn't be alive for long, Bull realized as he and Jasper rolled the old man onto his back and saw the dirt-clogged wound below his ribs. Blood soaked the ground where he'd lain—more blood than a man could stand to lose. If blood loss didn't kill him, the infection would.

Cupping the back of Carlos's head in his hand, Bull tipped the canteen to the cook's lips. The old man could barely swallow. With that wound, he had to be in terrible pain.

"We've got to get you to the hospital," Bull said.

Carlos's lips moved. "No . . . no hospital, *por diós.* Don't let me die there. Take me home . . . to Rio Seco. Bury me with Rosita . . . *mi esposa . . .*"

His voice trailed off. His head sagged. But then he seemed to recover a little. With surprising strength, he seized Bull's arm, holding it like a vise. "Promise . . ." he rasped. "Promise to take me."

Bull's gaze met Jasper's. Jasper gave a slight nod of agreement. Carlos was too far gone to make it to the hospital, an hour away in Lubbock. If he died in the truck on the way to his village, at least he'd know that he was going home.

Bull lifted the crucifix out of his pocket and slipped the silver cross with its broken chain into the old man's hand. "All right, Carlos," he promised. "If that's what you want, we'll take you to Rio Seco."

Bull pulled off his shirt and singlet. After wadding the singlet into a ball, he pressed it over the wound and bound it tightly in place using the long-sleeved shirt. There was a moment's deliberation while they figured out how to move Carlos. Jasper used the tool kit to unbolt the pickup's tailgate and lift it off. They worked the old man onto it and found a sloping spot to carry him out of the wash. Bull helped slide the tailgate into the pickup bed and stayed back there with Carlos while Jasper drove.

The drive back to the house was hot, dusty, and bumpy. Bull used his hat to shield the old man's face, gave him a little more water, and used his bare arms to cushion Carlos's body against the jarring. The ride had to be agonizing, but no whimper escaped Carlos's tightly pressed lips.

"Carlos." Bull spoke close to his ear. "Who did this to you? Was it the Prescotts?"

"Didn't . . . know them. Two men. Mexican. One with a bad scar. They . . . take my car, drive me to that wash . . . I run . . . they shoot . . ."

Every word cost the old man. Bull gave him another sip of water. "It's all right, Carlos," he said. "Don't try to talk. Just rest."

At the house, they lowered Carlos to the ground while they lined the truck bed with a mattress from the bunkhouse and added a blanket and the shell that fit like a roof over it. Jasper came up with some nonprescription pain pills and helped Carlos swallow three of them before they eased him back into the truck bed and reattached the tailgate. Even if they'd had the skill for it, cleaning and dressing the bullet wound would only have wasted precious time, and there was no way to give him blood. All they could do was keep their promise and get the old man home.

"The trip to Rio Seco is about six hours each way," Jasper said. "One of us will need to stay here and keep an eye on the ranch. Shall we flip a coin?"

"I'll go," Bull said. "I had a tenth-grade Spanish class and picked up a little more on the rodeo circuit. It might come in handy."

"Fine. The map I marked is in the truck, along with the rest of those pills. You shouldn't have any trouble at the border. Now you better get goin'."

"Keep a sharp eye out," Bull said. "There could be more trouble headed our way."

Jasper patted the heavy Colt that hung at his hip. "Don't worry. If anybody shows up, I'll be ready for 'em."

Bull climbed into the truck, put it in gear, and drove slowly down the rutted lane toward the highway. He was careful going over the bumps and hollows. Any jarring would cause excruciating pain to Carlos.

A cold anger rose in him as he drove. Anybody who'd shoot a harmless old man and leave him to die in agony deserved the worst. Whatever it took, he would see that they paid the price.

Carlos's description hadn't told him much, except that there'd been two Mexicans, and at least one of them would've known about the wash. That didn't mean they had any connection to the Prescotts. But it did mean they were armed and ruthless. The sheriff had already washed his hands of the matter. That left Bull—and Jasper, if he felt the same—to see that justice was done.

By the time he turned onto the main highway, the sun was low in the sky. Bull checked the map, glanced back at Carlos, and kept driving south toward the Mexican border.

CHAPTER 4

SUSAN RUTLEDGE SAT ALONE ON THE FRONT STEPS OF the two-story frame house—the sort of house that passed for a mansion in rural Texas but would be nothing more than a rental in Savannah. At this late hour, almost midnight, no one else was stirring. At last she could be alone. At last she could breathe.

Striking a match on the heel of her boot, she lit the cigarette she'd pilfered from the gold-plated case on Hamilton Prescott's desk. Inhaling the bitter smoke, she coughed, then tried it again. Maybe if she smoked enough, she'd get to like it. Meanwhile, at least it gave her the rush of doing something forbidden.

She blew a puff of smoke into the darkness, trying to make a ring like she'd seen some people do. She and her father had been here for two weeks, with at least three more weeks to go. The days were long and hot and endlessly boring. She could have stayed in Savannah with her mother, but Vivian Rutledge's world of shopping, cocktails, and beauty treatments was even more depressing than being in Texas with her father and uncle—and with Ferg, who practically had to be bribed to entertain her.

At least the nights were pretty here, the stars big and bright, just like in the song. A crescent moon was rising in the east, above the rolling Texas hill country. Wind rustled the dry grass. Faint insect and animal sounds, few of which she could identify, drifted out of the night. If she closed her eyes, she could almost imagine being in some wild, exotic place, stalking like a lioness through the thorn bush.

In the distance, she could see headlights leaving the highway and turning up the long gravel lane toward the house. Even from here, she recognized the ranch's pickup truck. That would be Ferg, coming back from one of his late-night visits to town. The fact that he hadn't taken his convertible told her he didn't want to be noticed. He was probably seeing a woman—maybe that pretty, older waitress at the burger place who'd been paying him a lot of attention yesterday. At least she had been until that rough-looking cowboy had come in and joined them.

Bull Tyler. Susan had been intrigued by him—even though he'd called her a baby. There'd been something tough and raw about him. Something forbidden—like smoking, only more exciting and dangerous. Last night, lying in bed, she'd fantasized about kissing him. He would never kiss her for real, of course. But she could imagine anything she wanted to.

The pickup was getting closer. Not wanting Ferg to find her on the porch, she hurried down the steps, stubbed out the cigarette, and slipped around behind the house.

Shortly after her arrival in Texas, she'd discov-

ered the delicious pleasure of disguising her bed
with pillows, sneaking out at night, and wandering
the open land. Mostly she went on foot. But sometimes, if the moon was up, she'd saddle a docile
mare in the stable and go for a ride. Her father
would have a stroke if he were to find out. He would
ground her for the rest of their visit, or even put her
on a plane and send her home early. But so far she'd
been both careful and lucky.

She knew the night could be dangerous. There
were snakes, scorpions, coyotes, wild pigs, and cattle
roaming the dark. There were washes and deep gullies. And there were beasts in human form who
wouldn't think twice about harming a young girl.
But she was always alert and careful, even going so
far as to tuck her hair under a cap, making her look
more like a boy.

So, should she go tonight? After some thought,
Susan decided against it. With Ferg still awake, she
might be spotted. And she hadn't arranged the pillows in her bed before going out to sit on the porch.
She couldn't chance it. One mistake and she'd be a
prisoner in the house for the rest of the long visit.

Tomorrow, then. Or the next night. With a sigh,
Susan bade a silent farewell to the moon and stars
and slipped back into the house.

A few miles north of the border, Bull stopped for
gas. When he checked on Carlos, he saw that the old
man had passed away.

Gently he tugged the blanket over the lifeless face.
At least his suffering was over. He looked peaceful
now, almost happy, as if he'd known that he was
going home to his loved ones.

Bull bought some coffee to go in Del Rio and drove across the Del Rio International Bridge to Ciudad Acuña. By now it was after eleven. The Mexican border station was quiet. The guard blinked himself awake, checked Bull's driver's license, and let him pass.

An hour later, on a two-lane asphalt road crossed by wandering cows and goats, he reached the outskirts of Rio Seco. The village, its name meaning "dry river," was little more than a cluster of tile-roofed adobe houses around a public square with two iron benches, a well, and a single palm tree. On one side was a church that looked like something out of an old Western movie. The only place showing any sign of life was the local cantina across from the church. One side was open to the plaza. Bull parked the truck and climbed out.

Four men, of varying ages, were sitting at a table drinking beer and playing cards. Mariachi music blasted from a small portable radio. The bartender looked up as Bull approached the rough plank bar.

"En que puedo servirle, señor?" he asked. *"Quiere una cerveza?"*

Bull surmised that the man had asked if he wanted a beer. He struggled with his high school Spanish. *"No, gracias."* He pointed to his truck. *"Aquí tengo Carlos Ortega. El es . . . muerto."*

The men at the table were staring at him. One of them, who appeared to be the oldest, rose to his feet. "I speak English," he said. "Did you say that Carlos Ortega, my brother, is dead?"

Bull nodded, relieved that he wouldn't have to depend on his weak command of the language. "My friend and I found him dying. He asked me to bring him here. I'm sorry. He was a good man."

"You knew him?"

"He worked for our ranch as a cook."

The man extended his hand. He was a younger, leaner version of Carlos. His English, though spoken with an accent, was fluent, as if he might have worked for some years in the United States. "Ramón Ortega *a su servicio*. Did you say my brother's body is in your truck?"

Bull accepted the handshake. "Yes. He wanted me to bring him home. He died on the way here."

Ramón glanced toward a younger man at the table, who sprang to his feet and hurried off. "Tell me how he died. Was it an accident?"

"No." Bull explained what had happened.

Ramón nodded, a sadness in his intense brown eyes. "*Ay*, that beautiful car. He drove it here once, so proud. And now he has died for it. What about the law? Did they catch the men?"

Bull shook his head. "The sheriff won't do anything to help."

Ramón's expression hardened. "Please, I want to see my brother now."

Bull opened the tailgate and pulled the mattress out. Ramón lifted the blanket, gazed down at Carlos for a moment, and covered his face again. By then people were spilling into the plaza, a few still getting into their clothes. Some of the older women were wailing.

Two young men, about Bull's age, raced ahead of the others. Pulling Ramón aside, they exchanged bursts of rapid-fire Spanish. Ramón turned back to Bull.

"Joaquin and Raul—they are Carlos's sons," Ramón said. "After their mother died they grew up in my home. They are like my own children. They want to go back to Texas with you and find those evil men. They want justice for their father."

"But those men could have left the state by now. They could be anywhere," Bull argued.

"Joaquin and Raul know that. But there is no honor in staying here and doing nothing. If you take them, they will work to pay you back. They are hard workers."

Bull weighed what he'd just heard. Smuggling two Mexicans back to Texas would be illegal as hell. But Lord knows, he could use the free labor, and he owed it to Carlos to help.

"What about the border?" he asked. "How would I get them through?"

"Easy. Before the border, you let them out. They cut around and cross the river. You pick them up on the other side. The *coyotes* do it all the time." Ramón used the common term for people who dealt in smuggling Mexicans. "So what do you say?"

"Maybe. But I'd be taking a risk. I need time to think about it," Bull said.

"Fine. The burial will be tomorrow, after the grave is dug and the body prepared. You can decide then."

"I can't wait that long. I left one man alone at the ranch. There might be trouble. I need to get back."

Ramón turned and spoke to Carlos's sons. Again, they exchanged volleys of Spanish, speaking so rapidly that Bull could catch only a few words.

"They understand," Ramón said, turning back to Bull. "They will go when you are ready. But I ask you, please come to my house now. Have some food and coffee while they say good-bye to my wife and get their things. Give us a chance to thank you for bringing Carlos home."

It appeared the decision had been made.

Two men had come with a litter and taken Carlos's body away. The crowd was clearing, people going back to bed as Bull locked the truck and followed Ramón to an adobe house just off the square. Only now did he notice that the man walked with a painful limp. It was probably the reason he was here instead of working in the States and sending money home. With his brother injured, Carlos might have been the family's main source of income. Now even that would be gone.

The house was small but clean, with colorful blankets on the furniture and pictures of saints on the walls. Ramón's wife, a tired-looking woman who would have been pretty in her youth, was warming beans and tortillas on a makeshift wood stove. She gave Bull a weary smile as she dished up the food and poured the coffee, which they drank black, sitting at the table. The two young men ate hastily, eager to be off on their adventure.

"Do they speak any English?" Bull asked Ramón.

"Some. They are shy about using it, but they can speak if they need to. Don't worry. They are good boys. They will behave well. Yes?" He gave his two nephews a stern glance.

"Yes." They nodded, answering in English. Bull could only hope this was a good idea and that he wouldn't end up in jail.

He had just finished his coffee and risen from the table when there was a knock at the door. Ramón's wife hurried to open it. Three men, who appeared to be in their thirties, stood on the stoop. One of them, who looked a little older than the others, stepped inside.

"We hear you take these boys to Texas," he said in broken English. "You take us, too? We pay you. Four hundred dollars each."

Twelve hundred dollars! How much feed, fencing wire, and gasoline would that buy? He could even pay the phone bill. It was damned tempting. And damned risky.

"We lay down close in the back of your truck," the man persisted. "You cover us—nobody will see. I tell you what—five hundred each. Half now and half when you take us to Big Spring. We know a rancher there. He will give us work."

Fifteen hundred dollars. And Big Spring wasn't that far out of the way. Still, he'd be smart to think twice. There'd be hell to pay if he got caught.

"Escuche," the man said. "Listen—these two *muchachos*—it is their first time. They can get lost. They can get caught by the *migra*. We know the way to cross the river. We can keep them safe."

A glance at Ramón's worried expression was enough to tip the balance. True—the boys would be safer, and the whole plan had a better chance if the older, experienced men were along to guide the younger ones. And the idea of returning home with money for the cash-strapped ranch sweetened the temptation.

Bull nodded. "Fine. Get your things. We leave in a few minutes."

The man grinned. "We have everything, *señor.* Even the money. *Vámonos!*"

For Bull, the next hours crawled with gut-clenching tension. He drove to the border with four men riding in the truck bed and the older one sitting up front to give him directions. A quarter mile short of the border, he let them out in Ciudad Acuña, drove across the bridge to Del Rio, and passed through the border without a problem. From there he followed a hastily sketched map to a wooded park in the older, Hispanic section of the town and waited in a nervous sweat. What if he'd misunderstood the directions to the meeting place? What if the men had met with an accident or been picked up by the border patrol?

An eternity seemed to pass before his passengers showed up, damp and laughing. They piled into the pickup, fitting lengthwise, like cordwood, in the bed. Bull covered them with a tarp and piled the mattress from the bunkhouse on top of them. The ride would be hellishly uncomfortable until they put a safe distance between the truck and the border, but the men accepted the conditions cheerfully.

It was almost dawn when Bull let the three men off at the gate of a ranch outside of Big Spring. They gave him the balance of the money and shook his hand.

"Others want to come north," the oldest man told him. "Any time you want, they pay you. Some *coyotes* are bad. They take money, then rob my people and leave them, even kill them. But you are a good *coyote*. They can trust you."

The words, meant as a compliment, weighed on Bull as he drove the rest of the way to the ranch with Carlos's two sons. What he'd just done had been easy money, and it would be even easier the next time. One run every couple of weeks, with no free rides, would go a long way toward supporting the ranch until they could get the cattle operation paying again.

But what if he got caught and went to jail?

You are a good coyote.

Was he? That remained to be seen.

When he pulled up to the ranch house, Jasper was in the yard, hauling hay to the stock. He dropped the pitchfork and strode over to the truck as Bull climbed to the ground.

"You told me you'd be right back," he said. "What the hell took you so long? I was getting worried." He looked Bull up and down. "How'd it go?"

"Fine. Just more complicated than I'd figured." He pulled the crumpled wad of cash out of his hip pocket. Jasper's eyes widened as Raul and Joaquin spilled out of the pickup bed with their packs.

"What the devil have you been up to, Bull Tyler?" Jasper sputtered.

Bull gave him a quick rundown of what had happened. "These two men are Carlos's boys. They'll be working for us while they look for the men who killed their father."

"And what about the money?"

Bull told him about the other men. "There's more where that came from. If I can make a run over the border every week or two, it could make the difference between saving the ranch and having to sell."

Jasper swore. "It might sound like good, fast money, but you won't get rich runnin' Mexicans, you young fool. The border patrol's been playin' those games a lot longer than you have, and they know all the tricks. You were lucky this time. But keep doin' it and they'll nab you for sure. Then you'll be in for a long stretch behind bars—and believe me, this ranch won't be here when you get out. Think about that while you get these boys settled in the bunkhouse. I s'pose we owe it to Carlos to take 'em in. But if anybody comes around, you'd damn well better keep 'em out of sight."

Jasper stalked off and went back to work. Bull set Raul and Joaquin to cleaning out the bunkhouse while he made bacon, eggs, toast, and coffee for breakfast. He was starved. The boys would be hungry, too.

He'd been pretty much set on making more trips over the border. But Jasper's advice gave him pause. He had some serious thinking to do. Meanwhile, at least he had workers to mend the fences and maybe help shore up the barn roof. And he had a little cash for feed and supplies and to get the phone service back. For now, he would concentrate on getting some work done. The bigger decisions could wait until later—or at least until the money ran low.

Two weeks after Bull's return from Mexico, the weather was still bone dry. On the Prescott Ranch, the grass was turning brown. Cattle clustered in the shade or crowded around the watering tanks. Even the nights brought little relief from the dry wind. People grew tired and irritable. Tempers flared.

Susan had fled the house after a shouting match between Hamilton Prescott and Ferg, who'd crept in after one of his late-night visits to town. When Ferg had found his father waiting up for him in the living room, the confrontation had exploded, growing louder and louder until the two were practically screaming at each other.

"I'm not a baby, Dad! I'm a grown man, and a man's got his needs! What I do at night is none of your damn business!"

"Hell, boy, it was my business when you were fifteen and

got a preacher's daughter pregnant! It cost me a bundle to hush up her family! And you had to go and pick a girl who wouldn't get an abortion! I'm still sending them money to support the little bastard, and I'll be damned if you're going to saddle me with any more of them! If you've got needs, for Christ's sake get married and be done with it!"

Susan had buried her head in the pillow and done her best to ignore the raging quarrel, as her father was likely doing. But after fifteen minutes she'd given up. She'd rolled out of bed, pulled on her clothes and sneakers, and arranged the pillows in her bed. With her hair twisted under her cap, she'd pocketed her miniature flashlight and slipped out the back door.

Clouds drifted across the night sky, blown by the dry wind that never seemed to stop. Needing to stretch her limbs, Susan set out on foot. Maybe if she walked far enough and fast enough, she could forget what she'd heard. She didn't want to be privy to the Prescotts' dirty secrets. All she wanted was peace and quiet.

The neighboring ranch, the Rimrock, was a mile from the Prescott house by way of a dusty, rutted road. She knew whose land it was. Hamilton Prescott had told her one night over dinner about the penniless, alcoholic Williston Tyler, who'd owned the two-thousand-acre ranch and refused to sell so much as a pebble of it. Since the man's mysterious death, the Rimrock had passed to his son, Bull Tyler, the rugged, blue-eyed ex–rodeo rider whom Susan had met that day in the Burger Shack. Hamilton had expressed the hope that the young Tyler would have the good sense to sell out. But after meeting the Rimrock's new owner, Susan had the feeling that getting his ranch wouldn't be as easy as her uncle expected.

Before tonight, she'd limited her wanderings to Prescott land. But now she craved escape, and she was still highly curious about Bull Tyler. She felt a prickle of naughty excitement at the thought of seeing his house and imagining him sprawled in sleep behind its walls.

The heart of the Rimrock was no more than a fifteen- or twenty-minute walk. Stepping out with a long-legged stride, she left the Prescotts' yard, switched on her flashlight, and found the road across the scrubby sage flat. Soon she caught sight of a distant windmill, turning against the stars. Beyond that lay the low, sprawling house.

Switching off the flashlight, she crept closer. Seen by moonlight, the house, like the bunkhouse across the yard, had a ramshackle look to it. Its curtainless windows were dark. Except for the battered pickup parked next to the house and the subtle stirring of horses in the nearby paddock, the place might have been deserted.

Mildly disappointed, Susan had just stolen past the front of the house when she heard the creak of the screen door opening and closing. Bull Tyler came out onto the porch.

Had he heard her? Heart slamming, Susan flattened herself against the side of the house. Peeking around the corner, she could see him standing at the rail, clad in jeans, boots, and a singlet that displayed his sculpted torso in the moonlight. One hand held a heavy pistol.

Now what? She needed to get home soon. But if she cut back across the yard, the way she'd come, he was almost sure to see her. Even if he didn't shoot her, she'd feel like a fool to be caught sneaking around his house.

She glanced west, toward the fenced pasture and the moonlit escarpment beyond. Maybe she could cut behind the barn, make a wide circle through the pasture, and come back partway down the road, out of sight. It might involve climbing a fence or two, but she had long legs and it was nothing she hadn't done before. Besides, it would be an adventure.

When Bull Tyler showed no inclination to leave, she ducked into the shadows and headed for the far side of the barn.

A faint sound in the dark had awakened Bull and sent him bolting out of bed, grabbing for his clothes and his pistol. The sound had amounted to nothing, but now he was too restless to sleep. Pistol cocked, he stood on the front porch, gazing out over the yard. It was well past midnight, the sky showing only a few drifting clouds that would bring no rain to the parched land. Even the night wind was warm, sucking the moisture from everything that grew. From somewhere beyond the shadows, a lone coyote raised its yipping wail. There was no answer.

In the two weeks that had passed since Bull's return from Mexico, Raul and Joaquin had proven to be hard workers, cheerful and eager to learn whatever they didn't know how to do. The bunkhouse was now livable, including the bathroom and small kitchen, and much of the fence line had been mended using the old wire and the truckload of rough cedar posts that Bull had bought in town. The cattle and horses were strong enough to be moved to pastures where the grazing was better. But because of the drought they continued to get extra feed. The barn roof still needed repair, and the money for hay, food, and other supplies was flowing out like blood from a death wound.

Was it time for another trip to Rio Seco? Bull was already doing the math in his head. Five men at $500 each—that would fix the worst of the barn roof. And Jasper had yet to be paid. Nothing but loyalty was keeping him here. The money Bull had saved from his rodeo winnings was mostly gone. At this rate, he would soon be dead broke. But he understood the risks of transporting more illegal Mexicans. If he ended up getting caught and jailed, the ranch was as good as lost.

Something moved in the open yard and disappeared behind the barn. Though he'd barely glimpsed it, Bull was sure he'd seen a slender human figure. Was one of the Mexican boys up to some kind of mischief? Or was it an outsider, thinking to make off with some free beef? Whoever it was, they had no business being out here at this hour.

Keeping to the shadows, Bull slipped off the porch and followed on silent feet.

Susan rounded the back of the barn and reached the stout pasture fence. Gripping a solid metal post, and taking care not to snag her jeans, she eased herself over the barbed wire. The flashlight was in her pocket, but she didn't want to use it. She needed both hands, and a moving beam of light would attract too much attention.

Her cap blew off as she dropped to a crouch inside the fence. She fumbled for it in the dark, but it had already blown out of reach. Standing, she took a moment to get her bearings. The pasture was about the size of a football field. The only gate was some distance behind her, where she couldn't pass without being seen. To get where she wanted to go, she would have to cross the pasture and climb back over to the other side of the fence.

Maybe this wasn't such a good idea after all. But she'd already committed to her plan. Unless she wanted to risk being caught, she had little choice except to keep going.

Part of the pasture was still visible from the house. But clumps of invasive mesquite had sprouted here and there—not tall, but thick enough to hide her if she dropped low. Keeping her head down, she raced to the nearest one and paused to catch her breath. So far, so good.

She'd made it partway to the next clump when something stirred in the shadows at the far corner of the pasture. Something large and dark.

It must be cows, she thought—maybe a group of cows and calves, awake and curious. She spurred herself to move faster. By the time they wandered over here, she'd be gone.

But the dark shape was moving toward her now—moving faster, and not breaking up the way a cluster of cows would. Pausing an instant, she twisted the flashlight out of her pocket. Her hand shook as she switched on the beam.

The light revealed the ugly white face, blunted horns, and massive body of a huge Hereford bull. Head down, it was barreling straight toward her.

CHAPTER 5

*H*OLY HELL . . .

Bull reached the fence in time to see Jupiter pounding across the pasture. Fleeing from the monster, and losing ground fast, was a wisp of a girl, her long blond hair flying in the wind. For an instant she only looked familiar. Then, as something clicked, he realized she was the teenage cousin he'd seen in town with Ferg.

No time to remember her name or wonder what she was doing here. If he didn't act fast, Jupiter would kill her.

Keeping a grip on his cocked pistol, he vaulted over the fence. The barbed wire ripped his jeans and tore a long gash in his thigh. He ignored the pain. He would have to divert the huge beast long enough for the girl to scramble to safety, then get away himself. That would take speed, timing, and plain dumb luck. He didn't even want to think about the alternative.

Yelling and waving his arms, the way he'd seen rodeo clowns work, he fired into the air and rushed to intercept Jupiter's path. Startled, the fool girl looked around. "Run, damn you!" he shouted. "Get to the fence!"

Spinning away, she plunged ahead. Jupiter's near-sighted gaze had spotted Bull. The animal paused, swinging his massive head and horns as if uncertain which target to chase. Bull waved and darted away to one side, yelling a challenge as he cocked the gun again, inviting Jupiter to chase him.

For an instant the tactic seemed to be working. Then, a dozen yards from the fence, the girl stumbled to her knees. In a panic, she struggled to get up, her pale hair fluttering like a matador's cape in the wind. The bull's head swung from side to side. Then, choosing the more vulnerable target, Jupiter bellowed and charged her.

With the giant barely a stone's toss away from the girl, Bull leaped into Jupiter's path, aimed the Colt, and fired a bullet between the white-rimmed eyes.

With a moan and a sickening lurch, Jupiter collapsed onto his knees. A shudder passed through him as he rolled to one side, his massive body twitching in death.

Bull cocked the pistol and fired another shot into the huge head. His shoulders sagged as reality sank in. He had just destroyed the most valuable animal on the ranch—the key to the recovery of his herd.

Fury rising, he turned toward the girl. She was huddled where she'd fallen, sobbing. *Susan*—he remembered her name now. *Susan Rutledge.* Not that it made any difference. Neither did the fact that she was probably scared out of her wits. He was mad enough to slap her silly.

"Get the hell up, Miss Susan Rutledge." He nudged her leg with his boot toe. When she raised her tear-streaked face, he held out his hand. She took it. He jerked her to her feet. Her palms were skinned, and her jeans were ripped at the knee where she'd fallen on something sharp. Her hair was tangled, her face streaked with dirt and tears.

"I'm . . . sorry," she stammered.

"Sorry won't bring back my prize bull." He reined in the urge to grab the little brat by the shoulders and shake her. "What in hell's name were you doing in that pasture?"

Her lip quivered. Then, seeming to pull herself together, she thrust out her stubborn chin and met his eyes. "Taking a shortcut."

"A shortcut? To where?"

"Back to the road. I was just exploring. Then you came out onto the porch. I was afraid you'd catch me."

"*Exploring!*" Seething, Bull shook his head. "For hell's sake, girl, this isn't Savannah. You damn near died tonight! And that bull was prime registered stock! I'll never have the money for another one like him!"

Jasper appeared outside the fence, out of breath and still buckling his belt. "I heard a couple of shots," he said. "What the—" His words ended in a groan as he saw Jupiter lying dead on the ground. "Oh, Lordy, what happened?"

Bull unclenched his teeth. "Jasper, this is Miss Susan Rutledge, who's visiting the Prescotts. She went on a little adventure in the pasture. I had to shoot Jupiter to save her."

Jasper cursed under his breath, looking as if he was about to cry. Short of losing a man, the death of the stud bull was the worst thing that could've happened on the ranch. At last he sighed and spoke. "Well, I don't reckon we can afford to waste the meat, even though the old cuss is bound to be tougher than boot leather. I'll wake the boys to help dress and hang the carcass. Then we can haul it to the meat packer in the mornin'."

The boys would undoubtedly be awake. But they knew better than to come rushing outside at the sound of gunshots.

"Give me a few minutes to run Miss Rutledge home, and I'll come back and help you." Bull glanced at the girl. "Come on. We might as well go out through the gate. No reason to keep it closed anymore."

Jasper glanced down at Bull's ripped jeans. "Your leg's bleedin'. You might want me to take a look at it before you go."

"Later. I'll be fine." He opened the gate and steered the girl across the yard to the truck.

Susan glanced at Bull Tyler's grim profile as he drove the pickup over the bumpy road. Her adventure had caused unbelievable harm. She couldn't blame him for being furious.

"Are you going to tell my father?" she asked.

"I don't know your father. And I'm not exactly on good terms with the rest of the family. So, no. I'm just going to let you out by the gate. You can tell them whatever the hell you want to."

"I'm sorry," she said. "I really am."

"Being sorry won't bring Jupiter back. He had a vile temper, but he sired fine calves, and a lot of them."

"Would it make any difference if I thanked you for saving my life?"

He gave her a stony glance, his blue eyes glinting anger in the darkness of the cab. "If you want to thank me," he said, "you can do it by never coming on my property again."

She saw that he'd stopped outside the gate to the Prescott Ranch. Any closer and somebody might hear the sound of the truck. She glanced back at him. He sat looking straight ahead as if she wasn't there.

Without another word, she opened the door of the truck, dropped to the ground, and, willing herself not to look back, took off at a run toward the big, dark house. Behind her, she could hear the engine of the old pickup already fading down the road.

Three days later the written invitation came, hand-carried by a cowboy on a smart-looking bay that bore the Prescott brand. The cowboy remained in the saddle, waiting while Bull opened the envelope and read the handwritten note inside.

> *Mr. Tyler:*
> *My family and I would be pleased to have you as a dinner guest tomorrow evening at 6:00. If you'd care to join us, I have a business proposition you'll be interested in hearing.*
> *RSVP.*
> *Yours truly,*
> *Hamilton Prescott*

The cowboy on the horse cleared his throat. "They said to tell you that RSVP means—"

"I know what it means," Bull said. "Tell your boss I'll be there."

As the man rode away, Bull showed the note to Jasper, who read it and chuckled. "Just look at that fancy little note, and that pretty handwritin', with them little curlicues. Bet your boots ol' Ham didn't write that his self."

Bull had a pretty good idea who'd written the note for Ham Prescott, but he wasn't about to say so. "Well, whoever wrote it, I can guess what Ham wants. He'll be pushing me to sell him the Rimrock."

Jasper's eyes narrowed. "You don't have to show up, you know. That'd send the old bastard a message for sure."

"Maybe." Bull spat his chew in the dust. "But it won't hurt to know what he's thinking." *And if the talk gets around to it, maybe I can learn more about the way my father died.* Bull didn't voice that last thought. He knew Jasper had discouraged him from trying to blame Williston's death on the Prescotts. What he didn't understand was why.

"Any luck finding a replacement for Jupiter?" Jasper asked, changing the subject.

"Not yet." Bull shook his head. After Jupiter's death he'd weighed his alternatives—none of them good. This summer, with the troubles on the ranch and the cows in such poor condition, Jupiter had yet to be turned out for breeding. His male calves, the few that remained, were set to be castrated in the fall. If allowed to grow into bulls, they wouldn't be old enough to breed for another year, or ideally for two years. That would mean, if the ranch had to depend on them, there'd be no calves born on the ranch for at least two years. The fee for the loan of a breeding bull, along with transport and upkeep, was prohibitive. And buying a new registered bull, like Jupiter, was out of the question.

He'd even called a couple of breeders he knew from the rodeo to check on the chance of getting an animal that was unfit for the arena due to age or injury. They'd taken his number and said they'd call him if one became available. So far, he'd heard nothing.

He'd read about artificial insemination and knew it was commonly done, especially by the big breeders. But so far he lacked the equipment and the know-how to set it up here. Susan Rutledge's little escapade had turned into a calamity. The cows were doing better now, with a number of them showing signs of estrus, but if he didn't find a solution soon, there would be no new calves next spring.

"I guess we could always buy a bunch of calves on the cheap and raise them here."

"Maybe. If we had the money, even for cheap." At times like this, Bull was sorely tempted to throw up his hands, sell out, and walk away with the cash in his pocket. Jasper, he knew, would be dead set against the idea. But with Hamilton Prescott's invitation in hand, he couldn't pass up the chance to learn what the man had in mind.

At a time like this, he'd be a fool not to keep all his options on the table.

Showered, freshly shaved, and dressed in clean jeans and a plaid shirt, Bull drove the pickup over the bumpy road to the Prescott Ranch. He hadn't been inside the house since his boyhood, when he and Ferg were still friends. Things had changed a lot since then. But whatever he was facing tonight, Bull was determined not to let it rattle him. He was a man, he owned his own land and livestock, and he could hold his own with anybody, even the high-and-mighty Prescotts.

He parked the car out front, walked up the path to the front porch, and knocked on the door. He heard a rush of light, quick footsteps. The knob turned. The door swung open. He found himself face-to-face with Miss Susan Rutledge.

She was wearing a periwinkle blue sundress with thin straps and a nipped-in waist that made the most of her slender figure. The color brought out silvery glints in her gray eyes and heightened the pink in her cheeks. Her long blond hair was brushed to a sheen and caught back from her face with a blue ribbon, giving her the look of Alice in Wonderland. Innocent—except for those satiny, sensual lips that stirred forbidden questions in his mind. He had to remind himself that she was young enough to get a man arrested.

"Hello, Susan." He didn't smile.

Her lower lip quivered slightly. "How's your leg? I was worried that you might not have had a tetanus shot."

"It's fine, and I had the shot last year." Bull was still angry enough to turn the little brat over his knee, but since he was a guest here, it behooved him to be civil.

She stepped back, away from the door, giving him room to come in. "Dinner will be ready in a few minutes." Her voice was breathy, with a little nervous catch. "I'm under orders to keep you entertained until Dad and Uncle Hamilton come down."

"What about Ferg? Won't he be here?" He followed her into the parlor that adjoined the dining room. The long table was set with matching china and silver. The smell of roast beef drifted from the kitchen.

"Ferg just came in. He's washing up, I think." Her silvery eyes studied Bull's face. "You and Ferg don't like each other much, do you?"

He managed a wry chuckle. "What gave you that idea?"

"I've got eyes and ears. That day in the Burger Shack, I could tell something was going on."

"Ferg and I go back a long way. As the old saying goes, it's water under the bridge." Bull studied the array of framed family photographs on the wall. His eyes came to rest on a professional portrait, taken perhaps a dozen years ago, of a younger Ham Prescott with his family. Bull recognized Ham's wife, who'd recently passed away. Next to her was a robust, confident Ferg who, even then, had looked like—and had been—a schoolyard bully. Seated on his father's knee was a younger boy with a shock of white-blond hair and vacant blue eyes that looked too large for his delicate face.

Bull tore his gaze away from the picture. But Susan had noticed him looking at it.

"The boy in that photo is Ferg's little brother, Cooper," she said. "He was kidnapped and never found. Can you imagine that?"

Bull didn't answer.

"I was told that some Mexicans took him. He was out playing cowboys with Ferg and his friend when—" She broke off, staring in dismay at Bull's rigid expression. "Oh, no! Was that friend you? It was, wasn't it?"

"We don't talk about that anymore, Susan." Bull's reply was curt. In the awkward silence that followed, he turned back toward the dining room. "That's the fanciest table setting I've ever seen," he said.

"Thank you." Her smile lit her face. "I did it all myself—even though Uncle Hamilton said it wasn't worth the bother for having a Tyler to dinner."

Susan had spoken innocently, but Bull could imagine Ham Prescott's contemptuous voice saying exactly that. This was no social occasion. Ham would nail him to the wall if he could.

"Is that how you eat in Savannah?" he asked Susan.

"Only at dinnertime."

He shook his head. "Real cloth napkins and all those extra forks and spoons—is it some kind of test to see if I can get through the meal without making myself look like a west Texas bumpkin?"

"Silly!" She giggled. "It's easy to figure out. You start with the ones on the outside and work your way toward the middle. If you're not sure what to do, just watch me." The little minx knew how to charm, but Bull wasn't ready to forgive her. He couldn't help wondering whether she'd told anybody about her foray into the neighbors' pasture and the death of his registered bull. Probably not. The truth would have gotten her into a lot of trouble.

"Glad you could make it, Virgil." Hamilton Prescott walked in from the hallway. A big-bellied, ruddy-faced man, he was dressed in a plaid Western shirt with a buffalo-horn bolo. The big silver buckle that fastened his belt gleamed in the light from the deer-antler chandelier that hung above the table.

The man who followed him into the room was tall and elegantly slim, with a pencil-fine mustache and a haughty gaze. Ferg had mentioned that Ham and Susan's father were stepbrothers, so it wasn't surprising that there was no family resemblance between them. Both men shook Bull's hand. Ham's hearty grip was almost painful in its power. Cliff Rutledge's handshake was a gentleman's, restrained, even cautious, as if he might be afraid of soiling his palm.

There were five places set at one end of the long table. Ham took his seat at the head, with Rutledge on his right and Ferg, who'd just walked in, on his left. Susan sat next to her father, leaving a place for Bull next to Ferg.

The Prescotts' cook, a retired cowboy with a limp, had filled the glasses with ice and sweet tea. Now he carried a bowl of vegetable salad to the table. Susan raised her hands to signal what must've been a family ritual. Everyone joined hands around the table while she murmured a brief grace. The moment was awkward—Bull holding hands with Ferg on his right and reaching across the table to clasp Susan's soft, slim fingers in his callus-roughened palm. At least the contact was short, ending in a sigh of relief around the table.

They made polite small talk through the salad and the main course of overcooked roast beef, carrots and potatoes—the weather, the price of beef, and the bird hunting Ham and Rutledge had done on the ranch. Bull followed Susan's example and managed to get through the meal without any breaches in etiquette. Her eyes twinkled with secret amusement when he reached for the wrong utensil, then glanced at her and corrected himself. Why did the little scamp have to be so young, and so damned sure of her effect on him?

After a dessert of leathery apple pie, the cook cleared away the dishes and brought in a half-filled crystal decanter and some glasses. Susan was excused, although Bull had the feeling she'd have liked to stay. Ferg, too, wandered off as if he had better things to do. Bull was left alone at the table with the two older men.

He braced himself for whatever was to come next.

Ham poured three fingers of liquor into each glass. "Drink up," he said. "Fine peach brandy all the way from Georgia. Nothing better."

Bull took a sip from his glass, feeling the sweet burn all the way down his throat. He'd drunk his share of beer and whiskey, but this was his first taste of brandy. He liked it.

"I was sorry to hear about your father," Ham said. "I stopped by to pay my respects, but your man didn't have much to say to me."

"No, he wouldn't. I've been hoping to find out more about the way my father died. I don't suppose you can give me any satisfaction."

"I wish I could. All I know is what the sheriff concluded—that it was an accidental fall. I'm guessing Williston was drunk and just wandered off that ledge." Ham swirled the brandy in his glass and took a swallow. "Sorry, I know that must pain you."

"It does," Bull said. "But I know you didn't invite me here to talk about my father."

Ham's smile was cold. "No, I didn't. I know Williston left the Rimrock in a pretty sorry state—the buildings and fences broken down, the equipment and cattle sold off . . ." He took another sip of his brandy. "You can't be having an easy time of it."

"I'm doing all right," Bull lied.

"So what are your plans for the place?"

Bull shrugged. "Do what I can, when I can. It's all going to take time. But I'm not afraid of hard work."

"Hard work isn't enough if you don't have money. You know I made your father several offers to buy the Rimrock."

"And he turned them all down. So will I. The Rimrock isn't for sale."

Ham exchanged glances with Rutledge, who'd been listening in silence. "I understand that, Virgil. That's why Cliff and I are prepared to make you an offer that would resolve everything, for all of us."

"I'm listening." Bull willed his expression to remain uninterested. But he could feel the tightening, like a coiled spring in his gut.

Ham leaned closer. "What we're proposing is a three-way partnership. You contribute the land. Cliff and I contribute the money to transform the Rimrock into a first-rate working ranch—everything new, even the house. You'd manage the ranch for a good salary. At the end of the season we'd split the profits."

Stunned, Bull stared at the two men. What Ham was proposing sounded almost too good to be true— all the money he needed to rebuild the ranch, and enough to do well on after that. And he'd still be a one-third owner.

"Think about it, Virgil." Rutledge spoke for the first time. "It would be a win for all three of us."

"What about Ferg?" Bull asked.

"Ferg's the heir to this ranch. But he wouldn't be involved in the partnership," Ham said. "Neither would Susan, for that matter. It would just be the three of us. We'd set up a trust with the partners as heirs. So what do you say?"

"If it's a yes, I can have my lawyers start the paperwork tomorrow," Rutledge said. "We could have the cash flowing and the work started within a couple of weeks."

Bull emptied his glass. "It's a lot to think about. I'll need some time."

A flicker of disappointment crossed Ham's face. "Take all the time you need," he said. "For now, at least, the offer stands. Come to me if you have any questions."

"I'll do that." Bull pushed away from the table and rose from his chair. "Thanks for dinner. Give me a few days to mull this over. I'll get back to you."

The other two men had risen also. Ham Prescott gave Bull another crushing handshake. Cliff Rutledge's handshake was as coldly reticent as when they'd met earlier that evening. It meant nothing, Bull told himself. It was just part of Rutledge's manner.

All the same, Bull felt a prickle of unease as he walked out the front door and closed it behind him.

Night had fallen, the risen moon casting the covered porch into deep shadow. Something stirred in the wicker swing. Bull's reflexes jumped, then relaxed as he realized it was Susan.

She rose, smoothing out her skirt. "How did it go?" she asked in a whisper.

"Fine. They made me an offer. I'm thinking it over." He started down the steps, headed for his truck. She moved to his side, matching her steps to his.

"Did you tell them about the other night, and having to shoot your bull?"

"Nope. Your secret is safe." He reached the truck and fished his keys out of his hip pocket. Susan made no move to go back to the porch.

"My dad and I are leaving tomorrow," she said. "We're driving back to Georgia."

"Well, have a good trip. Texas will be a far less interesting place without you." Bull opened the door of the truck.

She touched his arm. "Look at me!"

He turned toward her. She caught the back of his neck with one hand, stretched on tiptoes, and kissed him firmly on the mouth. Her lips were petal soft and tasted lightly of apple pie. They molded to his in a way that sent a jolt of arousal through his body.

Before Bull could gather his wits, she released him. The pupils of her silver eyes were dark wells in the moonlight. Her lips were moist from their kiss.

"I'll be back, Bull Tyler!" she said. "And the next time I kiss you, I want that awful tobacco taste gone so I can do it right!"

Leaving him drop-jawed, she spun away, dashed up the steps, and disappeared into the house.

CHAPTER 6

*B*ULL DROVE THE TRUCK HOME AT A CRAWL, TAKING his time to sort out what he'd heard tonight. His lips burned with the memory of Susan's impulsive kiss. But this wasn't the time to dwell on that. He needed a clear head to think about Ham Prescott's business proposal.

He'd been braced against any offer to buy the Rimrock. But the idea of a partnership had come out of nowhere, catching him off-guard. On first impression, it sounded like a good idea—all the money he needed to build up the ranch, a new house, a regular salary, and a share of the profits. And he'd still be part owner, with two wealthy partners to back him.

So why was his gut warning him that something wasn't right?

Jasper was waiting on the porch when Bull drove up to the house. When he heard about Ham Prescott's offer, he shook his head. "I can't help rememberin' what your dad thought of the Prescotts. You know what he always said."

"I know. Trust a skunk before a rattlesnake, and a rattlesnake before a Prescott."

"That wasn't just idle talk," Jasper said. "Ham Prescott would swindle his own mother if it got him something he wanted. Whatever he's offerin', no matter how good it sounds, there's got to be a catch. And I'd caution you not to make a move before you figure out what it is."

"Good advice." Bull yawned. It had been a long, hard day, and the urge to drift into sleep, with Susan's kiss still smoldering on his lips, was impossible to resist. "I'll give it more thought in the morning, when my head is clear."

He'd started toward the door when Jasper called him back.

"Hang on. I'm not finished talkin'."

Something in Jasper's voice stopped Bull in his tracks. He paused, turning around.

"Before you think too hard, there's somethin' you need to hear," Jasper said. "I promised your dad I wouldn't tell you this, but wherever he is now, I think he'd forgive me." He nodded toward one of the two battered lawn chairs on the porch. "Sit down."

Wide awake now, Bull sat. Since his return to the ranch, he'd sensed that Jasper was keeping secrets. Whatever he was about to learn, something told him it would change his life.

Jasper took the other chair and turned it toward Bull. "I know you've had a hard time believin' your dad loved you. Maybe you'll believe it after you hear this." He cleared his throat. "Williston Tyler might not've been the best man who ever lived, but he sure as hell was one of the toughest. You been wantin' to know how he died and what killed him. Fine. Here's the real story."

Jasper paused for a moment, gazing out across the yard. In the stillness, the vanes of the windmill creaked in the wind. A horse nickered in the paddock. Bull waited, knowing better than to rush the story he was about to hear.

"Last year, Williston was having some pain in his gut," Jasper began. "At first I thought maybe it was his liver, from the drinkin'. When it didn't go away I finally talked him into seeing a doctor. They did an X-ray. It was cancer."

Cancer. The word sent a chill through Bull's body. He'd known a few people with cancer, and he'd seen what it did to them. All of them were dead now. "What kind of cancer?" he asked.

"I don't remember the details. It was a kind that spreads and kills if it isn't stopped. But the doctors told Williston he was one of the lucky ones. They'd caught it early. With surgery and chemotherapy, they said, there was a good chance they could save his life."

"What happened?"

"About what you'd guess. Williston found out what the treatment would cost. The only way to pay for it would be to sell the Rimrock. He refused to do that. He said he wanted to save it for his boy."

"Oh, Lord . . ." Bull hunched over his knees as if he'd been gut kicked. The awareness of what his father had chosen and why was like an auger boring between his ribs, drilling into his heart. He'd seen cancer—the wasting away, the ungodly pain. His father—the man he'd cursed and vowed never to see again—had gone through that hell, with no treatment, to preserve this land for his son—and his future descendants.

Jasper leaned closer. "Through it all, right up to the week he went missing, Williston dragged his body into the saddle every morning and went out to work the stock. Except for me, and maybe a couple of the hands who'd known him a long time, nobody knew he had cancer. They just thought he was drunk, which he pretty much was toward the end. It was the only way he had to dull the pain."

"So the Prescotts didn't know?"

"Not unless they guessed. Williston kept away from them as much as he could."

"So when he went over that cliff . . ." Bull swallowed hard. "He could've stepped off on purpose."

"Lord knows he was in enough pain. But it wasn't like him to quit that way. And I know for a fact he wanted to see you again before he died."

Bull gazed down at his hands, letting the words sink in. What if he'd forgiven his father and come home to make peace? But why wonder? It was too late to change things.

"Wouldn't the autopsy have shown he had cancer?" he asked.

"It couldn't have been much of an autopsy. The body was in bad shape from the fall, and old Gaines is just a general practitioner, not even a surgeon. He probably didn't do any more poking around than he had to."

Jasper rose from his chair. "The last thing Williston told me was to go and find you. That's what I did. So take that thought to bed with you, Bull Tyler. And ask yourself what your dad would want you to do about that partnership."

Jasper walked down the steps, then paused and looked back. "Your dad loved you all along. If he was hard on you, it was only because he knew you'd need to grow up tough." With that he headed across the yard, toward the horse paddock.

Bull watched Jasper's lanky figure vanish into the dark. Rising from the chair, he turned toward the screen door to go inside, then changed his mind and moved off the porch. Earlier, he'd been ready for bed. Now he was too strung out to sleep.

His wandering footsteps took him around the back of the house and up the slope of the small hill where his parents were buried. It wasn't his first visit to the spot. The day after his return to the ranch, he'd paused for a moment there, out of familial duty. But tonight was different. As he stood by the sad, bare mound of earth, he imagined his father, in the throes of excruciating pain, mounting up to work cattle on the land he loved—the land he was determined to save for his son, for his grandchildren, and for generations to come.

At that moment, something flashed in Bull's mind. He remembered asking Ham Prescott whether Ferg would be involved in the partnership. And he remembered the essence of Ham's reply.

Ferg wouldn't be a partner. Neither would Susan. It would just be the three of us. We'd set up a trust with the partners as heirs.

With the partners as heirs . . .

Bull swore out loud as the truth hit home. If Ferg and Susan wouldn't be heirs to the trust, neither would his own future family. At his death, which could come a lot sooner than expected, the Rimrock would revert to the partners. His offspring would get nothing.

Trust a skunk before a rattlesnake, and a rattlesnake before a Prescott.

His father and Jasper had been right. Once the partnership was drawn up and signed, Ham would pay some thug to see that Bull met with an "accident." After that, Ham would likely buy out Rutledge's share at half the ranch's value. Just like that, the Rimrock would be Prescott land.

Bull's curses purpled the night air. Why hadn't he seen through the scheme right off? Maybe the brandy had gone to his head—or maybe it had been the girl. For all he knew, she'd been told to flirt with him.

Never again, he vowed. If the Prescotts wanted a war, he would give them one. If they came at him, he would fight back double. If they were smart, he would be smarter, tougher, and meaner.

He looked down at the grave of the man he'd never understood until now. "I'm back, Dad," he said aloud. "And I'm back to stay."

At first light the next morning, Bull saddled Pete, the stallion that had been his father's favorite horse. By now, all four animals were sound enough to be ridden. It had become a pleasure to mount up in the fresh dawn air and ride the fence lines, looking for spots to be mended.

But pleasure wasn't what Bull had in mind this morning. He'd spent most of the night lying awake, thinking about the ranch and how he could keep it running. But he did his best thinking in the morning, in the saddle. And he didn't plan to come back to the paddock until he'd made up his mind about a few things.

This morning he chose to ride the higher pasture in the part of the escarpment that bordered the Prescott Ranch. It was a peaceful section of land, cooler than the flatland below. He could check on the grass, with the idea of moving his small herd of cows and calves up there.

As he rode, taking the old stallion at a walk, he pondered the decisions that had to be made. Williston had left the ranch clear of debt. That meant as long as no money was owed on it, the land would be safe. If worse came to worst, he could sell off all the cattle, get a job somewhere, hunker down, and let the grass grow, or even lease pasture to a friendly neighbor, until he could afford to start ranching again. He didn't like that idea, but he needed to keep it as an option.

He could also sell off part of the land for enough cash to keep the ranch going. He liked that idea even less. The Rimrock wasn't a large ranch. Every acre was precious and needed. And Williston had given up too much to keep it.

He weighed the idea of making more *coyote* runs to Rio Seco. If enough men wanted to come north, and if he didn't get caught, he could clear enough to cover food and supplies for the rest of the season. But no, Jasper was right. Smuggling illegals across the border was a federal crime. If he tried it again, and got caught, his father's suffering and death would be for nothing.

Somehow, he had to survive until the calves were ready to sell to a feed lot operation in the fall. With the profits, he could then buy enough harvest-time hay to tide the cows over the winter.

But that would be worth doing only if the cows

were pregnant. Otherwise, he'd be better off selling the lot of them.

Damn that fool girl and her nighttime adventure! Bull felt the loss, and the anger, every time he saw Jupiter's empty pasture. Without a decent stud bull, the small herd had no future.

By now he'd reached the upper pasture. Here the grass, though sparse, was still green, the older wood fence posts undamaged, at least on the surface, but it wouldn't take much to push them over. He was weighing the wisdom of moving the herd up here when a new sight riveted his attention.

The land here bordered a large pasture that belonged to the Prescott Ranch. In the near distance, he could see cattle grazing—white-faced, red-coated Herefords, all registered stock, he was sure. Among them was a bull—huge, healthy, and as horny as all get-out. The way he was going after those cows, licking, smelling, and mounting, was a beautiful sight to behold.

A hulk like that bull could easily push down a weak wire fence to get to more cows—especially if he had some help. And if a few stray cows wandered over the downed fence to the richer grass on the other side, who would be to blame except the bull?

Wasting no time, Bull dismounted, wrapped his rope around a fence post, and used the horse to yank the post off its partially rotted base. It broke easily, bringing the wire down as it fell. After toppling a second post the same way, Bull laid the wire flat and checked it to make sure no cattle crossing through the gap would become tangled and cut. That done, he coiled his rope, mounted up, and rode back down to the lower pasture to get help moving his herd.

Ham would be apoplectic if he learned what had happened. If he discovered the truth, he'd be capable of killing any Rimrock cattle on his property. But desperate times called for desperate measures, and that was a chance Bull would have to take. He could only trust nature to take its course.

As long as the partnership offer was on the table, he would probably be safe from retaliation. Since healthy cows came into estrus every two or three weeks, it would pay him to stall, to delay his decision as long as possible while the Prescott bull made babies with his cows and heifers. Once he turned Ham down and told the old bastard to go to hell, all bets would be off.

Three weeks with the bull should be enough time to cover most of his cows. He might be pushing his luck, but if the gamble paid off, at the end of the third week he would sort out his own branded stock from the Prescott herd, mend the fence, and wait for a nice crop of spring calves.

In his search for funds to tide the ranch over, Bull came across a newspaper ad for temporary work as a roustabout, helping dismantle a giant oil rig. The work would be hot, dangerous, and miserable, and he would need to drive to the Gulf Coast for the job. But the two-week window was perfect, and the money would be good, especially if he was willing to work double shifts, seven days a week. A phone call got him the job.

After renting a junk loaner from a garage, for Jasper to drive while he was gone, he loaded up his gear and left. He hated being away from the ranch for that long, but Jasper was capable, and the Mexican boys would be a lot of help. He could check in by pay phone to make sure everything was all right.

After two weeks of backbreaking work in the torrid sun, eating junk food, and sleeping in the truck to save money, Bull pulled into the ranch yard at dawn to find Jasper waiting for him.

"Damn it, it's about time you showed up," Jasper said. "I was beginnin' to worry that you'd got yourself crushed or drowned . . . Lord have mercy, you look like you've been broiled alive. You smell like it, too."

"Well, you won't have to worry anymore," Bull said. "As of now, I'm done with the oil business. Anything new around here? Are the cows all right?"

"The cows are fine. I checked on 'em yesterday. The fence is still down, and that big, old bull is goin' to town on both sides of it. But you won't want to leave your herd there much longer. Ham came by yesterday. He said to tell you he's waitin' on your answer to his business proposition. When you turn him down he'll be on the warpath. If he finds your cows on his side of the line, he's liable to shoot the lot of 'em."

"Let's chance it for a few more days," Bull said. "We can always claim the bull pushed the fence down, and we didn't know about it." He reached in his hip pocket, took out the wad of bills from his two-week paycheck, counted off $1,000, and thrust the money toward Jasper. "Before I forget, here's some of your back pay."

"No need for that." Jasper put up a hand in protest. "I know you need every cent to run the ranch."

"Take it," Bull insisted. "I'll manage."

Jasper knew better than to argue. He thanked Bull and pocketed the money. "One more thing," he said. "Raul and Joaquin came and talked to me last night. One of their friends spotted Carlos's Buick, with two men in it. They're camped down by that old gravel pit, about five miles from here."

"I know the place," Bull said. "But how in the devil did those boys get the word? They've hardly been off the ranch since they got here. They don't even have access to a phone."

"That's a thing about Mexicans," Jasper said. "They've got their ways of keeping in touch between the farms and ranches where they work. A few of 'em will have a car, or even a bicycle. They'll visit back and forth at night and out on the range. They'll send messages, have places where they get together and have a few beers. Somethin' tells me our boys have been busier than you think."

"All right." Bull stretched his cramped limbs and yawned. He'd been behind the wheel for more hours than he wanted to think about. He needed a good shower and a few hours of sleep. "So when do they want to go after those men?"

"They wanted to go last night, but I said they had to wait for you. They can't go alone and unarmed. One of us will need to go with them, that is, if the murdering buzzards haven't moved on already."

"I'll go," Bull said. "You stay here and keep an eye on things."

"You're sure? This is damned serious business."

"I promised myself I'd even the score for what they did to Carlos," Bull said. "I'm grateful for the chance."

"Fine," Jasper said. "For now, you might as well get some rest. The boys and I can take care of the chores. I'll tell them it's on for tonight."

* * *

Bull doused the pickup's headlights as he turned off the narrow asphalt and found the washboard road that led to the old gravel pit. Abandoned years ago, it had become a hangout for teenage alcohol parties, lovers, and homeless tramps. He could only hope the men who'd killed Carlos and stolen his car hadn't moved on.

Carlos's sons sat next to him on the truck's bench seat. They'd made a plan before leaving the Rimrock, but between Bull's high school Spanish and their limited English, he couldn't be sure how well they'd understood each other. Bull had strapped on his .44. Raul and Joaquin were unarmed except for their switchblades, some lengths of rope, and a six-pack of Dos Equis beer.

A quarter mile from the gravel pit, Bull pulled the truck onto a wide spot in the road. The three of them got out quietly, barely closing the doors. In the distance they could see the faint glow of a fire and hear the unmistakable blare of a radio tuned to a Mexican station. The two young men glanced at each other and nodded.

Bull carried the ropes looped over his shoulder, the pistol cocked and ready in his right hand. Joaquin carried the six-pack of beer. As they neared the gravel pit, Bull hung back, keeping out of sight among the clumps of sage and mesquite. The plan involved putting the two criminals at ease before overpowering them and tying them with the ropes. It would have been simpler for Bull to shoot them from cover, but Carlos's sons had wanted to take their revenge with their own hands. Bull understood and respected their sense of honor. If he ever learned who'd murdered his own father, he would do the same.

The stars were bright overhead, the moon just rising. A small animal—a mouse or lizard—skittered across the path and vanished into the long, dry grass. The pistol was cold in Bull's hand. He'd never killed a man. Neither, he suspected, had the two boys. One way or another, tonight would change them all.

Bull stayed in the shadows outside the shallow ring of the gravel pit as Raul and Joaquin walked into the firelight with the six-pack of beer. He could catch only a few words of Spanish, but he could make out laughter and sounds of greeting.

Carlos's Buick was parked a few yards from the fire. When the stockier of the two men turned into the light, Bull could see the ugly slash of a scar across his face. There was no doubt these were the murderers who'd killed the old man.

Bull kept the pistol cocked and aimed, ready to fire if either man made an aggressive move. He was a decent shot—his father had taught him, railing at him, even cuffing him, every time he missed a target. After a while he'd learned not to miss.

Now the four Mexicans were sprawled around the fire drinking beer. The two thugs didn't appear to be armed, and Bull couldn't see any guns within reach. They were downing their second bottles, laughing and singing along with the music on the radio, when Bull stepped into the firelight.

"*Manos arriba!*" he barked, ordering the men to put their hands up. Playing along, Joaquin and Raul raised their hands. The two thugs hesitated, but the sight of the heavy pistol in the *gringo*'s hand was enough to convince them not to try anything.

"*Bájense—en la tierra!*" He gave up on Spanish.

"Down on the ground, damn you! Now!" As the men prostrated themselves in the gravel, Bull tossed the ropes to Carlos's sons. "Tie their hands and feet," he ordered. "Do it!"

Still pretending to be frightened, the young men obeyed. Only when the two men were securely trussed hand and foot did their demeanor change. Standing over them, Raul spoke in rapid-fire Spanish. Bull caught the gist of what he was saying—that he and his brother were the sons of the old man they'd killed. Now the two *cabrones* were going to pay.

Bull's part was done. He kept his gun trained on the two bound men, but their fate was in the hands of Carlos's sons. Bull had resolved not to interfere. Even so, he had to stifle a gasp when the young Mexicans took the remaining rope, passed it around and between the bound ankles of the two men, then lashed it securely to the trailer hitch on the back of the Buick.

Still facedown on the ground, the men were blubbering and pleading now, tears streaking their dusty faces as they begged for their lives. Ignoring them except for a pause to check the ropes, the two young men climbed into the front seat. Raul, the driver, started the big car, switched on the headlights, and gunned the powerful V8 engine. The car roared out of the gravel pit and shot across the rocky, brush-strewn flatland.

Bull could hear the men screaming as he turned and started back to his pickup. By the time he reached it, the screams had stopped. As he stood by the truck and watched the red taillights grow faint with distance, the truth struck him.

Carlos's sons weren't coming back. They had all they'd come for—their revenge and their father's beloved car. Joaquin and Raul were headed straight for Mexico.

Bull couldn't help wondering if they had money for gas and food, or even if they knew the way. Never mind, he could only wish them well and hope they would reach Rio Seco, covered with honor and driving the most beautiful car in town. He would never know for sure. His business in Rio Seco was done.

The Buick had reached the road. Bull saw the taillights stop briefly, long enough, most likely, for somebody to untie the rope from the trailer hitch. Then the old Buick moved on and vanished into the night.

Much as he wanted to be out of that place, Bull knew he couldn't leave until he'd checked on the two men. Hopefully they were dead. If they weren't, they damned well ought to be.

He started the truck and drove back to the spot where he'd seen the Buick stop. In the play of the headlights, he could see a pair of bulky shapes in the runoff ditch next to the road. Taking his pistol, he climbed out of the truck.

The two murderers were unconscious but still breathing. Cocking the pistol, Bull stood over them, legs straddling the ditch. "For Carlos," he muttered, and pulled the trigger twice.

Afterward he took a moment to find the brass casings, then he got back in his truck, turned around, and drove back toward the ranch. Eventually the bodies would be found and reported. But the sheriff would do nothing. Mexicans weren't in his job description.

In the past, Bull had wondered how it would feel to kill a man. Now he knew. It was just business—

nasty, dirty business. He could do it again if he had to. But he wasn't looking forward to the next time.

The ranch was getting close. Jasper would be waiting to hear the whole story of what had happened. But Bull wasn't ready to tell it. He needed time to settle his nerves. It was barely ten o'clock. On a Saturday night, the Burger Shack stayed open until eleven. He could use the pay phone outside to call Jasper and let him know he was all right.

He wasn't hungry, but he could use a cold Bud Light. If Bonnie was working, she'd get him one without asking for ID.

As he turned onto the highway, the realization struck him like a lightbulb going on. Bull shook his head in disbelief. In the turmoil of the day he'd forgotten that this was his birthday. He had just turned twenty-one.

Reeling between exhaustion and euphoria, he drove into town, parked at the Burger Shack, and gave Jasper a quick call from the pay phone before going inside. Bonnie was working. She gave him a smile and a wink as he walked in and took a booth.

She brought him the beer and a glass without being asked. He wondered if he should tell her he'd just come of age, then decided against it. Birthdays were a kid thing, and he wasn't a kid anymore.

He sipped the beer and thought about his future plans. It would be reckless to leave his cows with the Prescott herd much longer. In the next few days he would take Jasper and separate his stock from the others. If Prescott's men showed up, the broken fence would give him a good excuse for being there. When the fence was fixed and his cattle safely moved, he would face Ham Prescott and tell the old bastard to take his partnership offer to hell.

Within a few weeks, he should know which cows weren't pregnant. With luck, they could be sold off for enough money to feed the others through the winter. If he could keep the ranch solvent till next spring's grass sprouted, hopefully the worst times would be over.

"Hey, sugar." Bonnie's sexy voice broke into his thoughts. "You look like you've had a rough day. Want to talk about it?"

Bull glanced around the restaurant and realized that everyone else had gone. He and Bonnie were alone.

She slid into the booth next to him, smelling of jasmine and bacon grease. Her finger brushed a stray lock of hair back from his face. It would be tempting to unload his concerns into her sympathetic ear. But he remembered what Jasper had said about playing his cards close to his vest. "Nothin' much to talk about," he said. "I'm just tuckered out, that's all."

"I know a cure for that." She ran a fingertip down his cheek. "Danny's in Albuquerque, and I get off in fifteen minutes. You can wait around if you want."

He hesitated, knowing it wasn't a good idea. But what the hell, he'd just killed two men, and it was his birthday.

"I'll wait," he said.

CHAPTER 7

Summer 1972, two years later . . .

*T*HE BARKING DOGS WOKE BULL IN THE MIDDLE OF
the night. He flung himself out of bed, yanked on
his pants, and reached for the loaded .44 he kept next
to his pillow. From the yard outside, drunken whoops
and laughter mingled with the roar of a heavy-duty
truck engine. Bull cursed. He could guess what was
happening, and he knew he'd be too late to stop it.

Barefoot, he charged out onto the porch to see
the wooden windmill tower come crashing down,
pulled by a rope tied to the rear of a black pickup.
Through the clouds of dust that rose around the
wreckage, he could make out a half dozen cowhands
in the back. The driver gunned the engine. The
truck roared away, amid hoots and catcalls, leaving
the rope behind.

Bull fired a couple of shots at the rear tires. But

between the dust and darkness, his aim was no more than a guess. Even if he hit his target, the truck wouldn't stop. And shooting at the men would only escalate the guerrilla war that the Prescotts had been waging against him for the past two years. It might even put his own hired hands in danger.

No question, the bastards were acting on Ham Prescott's orders. If pressed, Ham would deny any knowledge of the vandalism or dismiss it as a boyish prank. But Bull knew the score—and he knew that Ham would do anything to drive him out and get his hands on the Rimrock.

The windmill would need fixing at once. The well beneath it was the only reliable source of water on the ranch. In this hot, dry summer, even a day without water would be hard on both animals and men. Two days could be fatal for the smaller spring calves.

The commotion had awakened the two young cowboys who lived in the bunkhouse. They stumbled out the door, yawning and cussing. Bull hollered at them to get dressed and come help. They were good kids, but they were just out of high school, and they had a lot to learn. Bull did his best to teach them, though his patience sometimes had a short fuse.

What he wouldn't give for Jasper's calm wisdom at a time like this. But Jasper had gone home to the hill country two weeks ago, with plans to marry Sally, his pretty, patient sweetheart. Bull had wished him well and given him the old pickup, with new tires and an overhaul, in lieu of the back pay he was owed. These days Bull was driving a newer-model red Ford Ranger he'd bought from a man in town.

The dogs—big, shaggy mutts—trotted up onto the porch, panting and wagging their tails. Bull had bought them for five dollars each from a farmer whose bitch had had a litter of pups. They were too friendly to make serious watchdogs, but they barked when strangers came around, and they were learning to be good cattle herders.

Bull spat over the porch rail, cursed, and went back inside to put on his boots and make some coffee for the boys. At least there was plenty of moonlight. If the pump rod had only come loose and wasn't broken, and everything else was either intact or fixable, they could have the windmill up and working in time for morning chores. But if it needed parts, he might have to drive into Lubbock to get them. Just one more damned emergency in a season that was already draining his resources.

First chance he got, he would drive into town and buy enough concrete mix to anchor the legs of the tower into the ground, something his father had never done. Bull could only wish he'd thought of doing it sooner. For that matter, it would make sense to replace the old wooden tower with a sturdy metal one. The cost would be more than he could spare, but it would be better than pouring more money into something that was close to falling apart.

In this country, especially in the third year of a searing drought, everything was about water. And the Rimrock never seemed to have enough. By breeding the heifer offspring of the Prescott bull with his own yearling bulls, he had doubled the size of his herd in the past two years. But without adequate water, the land wouldn't support any more animals. His dream of a prosperous ranch, running upward of a thousand head, was just that—a dream.

He'd done his best with what he had. In the petroglyph canyon where his father had died, he'd dug out a tank at the bottom of the trickling spring and lined it to make a pool. But there wasn't enough water for more than a few cattle at a time, and it was too far from good pasture to be of much use.

The only way to afford a second well on the property would be to borrow the money from the bank to pay a drilling contractor. Bull didn't trust banks any more than his father had—and in these dry times, there was no guarantee that a new well would strike ground water. Somehow, there had to be another way to get what he needed.

The Prescotts had no such problem. They had three deep wells on their ranch, as well as a fair-sized stream, fed by a gushing spring in the depths of the escarpment.

But right now, Bull had more urgent concerns than his neighbors. If he didn't get the windmill up and running, there'd be no water tomorrow.

By the time the coffee was ready, the boys had wandered up to join Bull on the porch. Still yawning and swearing, they drank the coffee and ate the stale doughnuts left over from last week's run to town. Then they went to work.

By the next morning the tower was up, the blades turning sluggishly and the pump barely working. Given the makeshift repairs, mostly made with baling wire and duct tape, Bull knew that time was running out to replace it.

At the hardware store, he ordered a complete set of parts to be delivered to the ranch by truck in two days. Putting it together with the help of the young cowboys would be a lot of work, and the transition from the old windmill to the new one would have to be done fast. But the savings would amount to hundreds of dollars over having it installed.

He signed the order, grateful that in the past two

years he'd managed to pay off Williston's debts and establish decent credit. When the next bill came due, he'd probably have to sell off a couple of steers to pay it, but that couldn't be helped.

With that errand done, he picked up a few groceries and was about to head back to the ranch when he realized it was almost noon. He'd missed breakfast, and so had the boys. A couple of extra-large pizzas, which they'd doubtless wolf down in one sitting, would be a good idea.

He drove to the Burger Shack. Bonnie's old Studebaker was parked out back, which meant she was working. That would be all right. He and Bonnie had enjoyed a few romps, but when he'd discovered he was sharing her with Ferg, he'd backed off. True to her nature, she was still friendly and probably open to a rematch, but Bull had gone down that road for the last time. He'd never met her husband, but he didn't envy the man.

Ferg's red Thunderbird convertible was parked in the handicapped space. Bull resisted the temptation to gouge the shiny red paint with his key. He had no doubt Ferg was involved in wrecking his windmill, but keying his car, or slashing his tires, would be too much like a teenage prank. As Jasper might have said, revenge was best served cold. When the time was right, he would find a way. For now, he would at least have the satisfaction of looking Ferg in the eye, as if nothing had happened, and seeing him squirm.

Whistling under his breath, he walked through the door and up to the counter. Bonnie gave him her usual smile and wink, but as she took his order, her eyes flickered toward the corner booth. Without turning around, Bull knew that Ferg was there. He ordered a fountain Coke for himself, paid for everything, and took his soda from Bonnie. At last, taking his time, he turned around . . . and almost dropped his drink.

Ferg was leaning back in the booth, a self-satisfied smirk on his face. Seated next to him, his arm around her shoulders, was the most stunning young woman Bull had ever seen.

His eyes took her in—a mane of silky blond hair that framed her face in soft waves; cushiony pink lips; silvery eyes, their expression mysterious and unreadable.

As the shock wore off, Bull realized he was staring at Susan Rutledge.

Her mouth widened in a smile that left her beautiful eyes unchanged. "Why it's Bull Tyler!" she exclaimed. "Come sit down with us. How have you been?"

"About the same," Bull answered. "Ranching takes up most of my time."

Ferg's arm tightened possessively around her. He glared at Bull, as if daring him to say anything about last night.

Susan gave Ferg a playful glance. She was wearing a black tank top that bared her creamy throat and shoulders and showed off her womanly figure. The two of them were drinking chocolate shakes. She cradled her tall glass between her manicured hands. Bull was remembering those hands from before, the nails bitten to the quick, when he noticed something else—something that made him feel as if his heart had dropped into the pit of his stomach.

On the third finger of her left hand, Susan was wearing a ring with an impressive-looking diamond.

"How do you like it?" Noticing his interest, she held out her hand, tilting it to let the diamond catch the light. "It belonged to Ferg's mother. We just got engaged yesterday."

"Congratulations." Bull had to force the word. "I guess, since you're just stepcousins, that makes it all right."

"Hell, this is Texas. It'd be all right even if we weren't," Ferg muttered, then laughed at his own joke.

"When's the big day?" Bull's Coke tasted like acid in his mouth.

"Not anytime soon," Susan said. "I want to go to college for at least a year. After that, we'll see."

"I just wanted to get my brand on this filly before I turn 'er loose to run with the herd," Ferg said.

Bull stifled a groan. He couldn't help wondering what Bonnie thought about Ferg's engagement. But then, knowing Bonnie, it probably wouldn't make much difference.

"Bull, honey, your pizzas are done," Bonnie called from behind the counter.

Bull slid out of the booth, glad to be away from the two lovebirds—although they didn't seem all that lovey. Ferg was acting like he'd just bought a prize heifer. And Bull hadn't missed Susan's strained smile or the resigned look in her gray eyes. He congratulated the pair again, picked up the two pizza boxes, and headed out the door. As he carried them to the truck, Susan's words, spoken two summers ago, echoed in his memory.

I'll be back, Bull Tyler! And the next time I kiss you, I want that awful tobacco taste gone so I can do it right!

Bull had thrown away his chewing tobacco last year, after reading that it could lead to mouth cancer. This wasn't the first time he'd remembered Susan's promise. The words had triggered more than a few nighttime fantasies over the past two years.

By damn, he still wanted that kiss. One way or another, he was going to get it.

He left the pizza boxes on the passenger seat, closed the truck, and walked back to the red Thunderbird. After checking to make sure nobody could see him, he crouched behind the car, unscrewed the valve stems from the two rear tires, and used the tip of a screwdriver to let the air out. When they were both flat to the rim, he replaced the caps and pocketed the screwdriver. For good measure, he found a loose nail in the parking lot and jammed the point into one of the tires. That done, he strolled back into the Burger Shack.

Ferg glanced up at him. "Forget something, Bull?"

"Nope. Just bringing you some bad news," Bull said. "Your car's got two flat rear tires."

"What the hell—" Ferg's face reddened. "Who'd do a thing like that?"

"I saw some kids running down the block," Bull lied. "You know how it is with a fancy car like that. It gets a lot of attention. Some folks might even get jealous."

"Oh, no!" Susan gave her fiancé a stricken look. "I promised my dad I'd be home by one! I'll never make it if I have to wait for your tires to get fixed." Her gaze swiveled to Bull. "Could I trouble you for a ride home, Bull? If it's an imposition—"

Bull's pulse skipped. He faked an indifferent shrug. "It's fine, as long as you don't mind holding two warm pizza boxes on your lap. If that's all right, come on."

Holding the door for her, he glanced back at Ferg. "Sorry about the tires. If I see those kids again, I'll put the fear of God in them for you."

"Do that." Ferg's hateful expression hinted that

he might have guessed the truth, but there was little he could do now except watch Bull walk out the door with his girl.

As they crossed the parking lot to the truck, Susan gave Bull a knowing look. "That was a dirty trick if I ever saw one, Bull Tyler."

"It was, wasn't it." Bull opened the door and moved the pizza boxes out of the way. "And did you really promise your father you'd be home by one, Miss Susan Rutledge?"

She raised a delicate eyebrow. "Ask me no questions, and I'll tell you no lies."

Bull reined in a chuckle as he helped her into the truck and gave her the pizza boxes to hold. "I did promise to drive you home," he said. "But that doesn't mean we have to go the short way."

He closed the door and walked around the truck to the driver's side. As he climbed in he saw Ferg by the Thunderbird, scowling down at his flat tires. Bull gave him a wave as he roared out of the parking lot.

He had no expectations of the ride back to the Prescott Ranch with Susan. But he sensed that the two of them had formed a bond two summers ago. He had no reason to trust her, let alone like her. All the same, he couldn't deny that the bond was there, or that it was powerful.

Ferg mouthed a string of curses as Bull Tyler drove off with his fiancée. It was bad enough that Bull had flattened his tires—Ferg had no doubt about that. But the fact that Susan had asked Bull to drive her home was like rubbing salt on a burn. He didn't believe that excuse about her father for a minute. She'd wanted to go with Bull. It was like a conspiracy between the two of them—which didn't make sense. As far as he was aware, they barely knew each other. Maybe she was just trying to make him jealous. If so, damn her, it was working.

Not that he fancied himself in love with her. Susan had been like a kid sister for so long that it was hard to think of her any other way. But as long as he was being pushed to marry, he could do worse than a beauty with a father who was about to die and leave her a fortune. And he wouldn't have to spend time trolling for sex. Unless he was in the mood for variety, which was bound to happen, what he needed would be right there in his bed.

He glared down the street where Bull's truck had disappeared around the corner. What really ticked him off was that Susan was *his*. As long as she had his ring on her finger, no other man had the right to touch her—especially a lowlife like Bull Tyler.

If Susan didn't know that, maybe it was time she understood. Maybe it was time to teach her a lesson she wouldn't forget.

Bull felt Susan's eyes on him as he drove down Main Street. He wanted to say something clever, but he'd never been one for small talk, especially with pretty girls. He'd taken a gamble, flattening Ferg's tires in the hope that she'd need a ride home. That it had paid off exactly the way he'd hoped was almost too much to take in.

"You haven't changed much, Bull." She broke the silence as he turned onto the highway out of town.

"I can't say the same for you," he said. "I was surprised to see that ring on your finger."

"Oh, this." She twisted the ring, fidgeting with the

diamond, which must've been at least a full carat. "I know I don't owe you an explanation. But if you want to hear it, I'll give you one."

"Go on."

She took a ragged breath. "Ever since Ferg and I were children, our fathers have made it clear that they wanted us to marry someday—keeping my father's cotton and lumber businesses and Uncle Hamilton's Texas ranch in the family. Now that I'm almost nineteen . . ." Her words trailed off. She shrugged.

"That sounds like something out of the Dark Ages."

"I suppose it might sound that way." She shifted the pizza boxes on her knees. "Bull, my father has a weak heart. The doctors have said that, with treatment, he could live years. But if his condition takes a bad turn, he could go anytime."

"I'm sorry, Susan." Bull meant it. Cliff Rutledge had struck him as a snob, but it was clear that Susan cared about him. "Where's your mother in all this?"

"My mother and father are still married. But they pretty much live separate lives. She has her society friends and her cocktail parties, where she usually drinks so much that she can't get out of bed the next day. She likes showing off, and I'm sure she'll enjoy planning a fancy wedding for me. But we aren't close."

"I'm sorry." Bull steeled himself against showing too much sympathy. Susan hadn't had an easy life. But this was the girl who'd forced him to kill his prize bull, flirted with him at Ham Prescott's dinner, and was now engaged to his rival.

"I remember hearing about your father," she said. "Did you learn any more about what happened to him?"

Bull had, but he wasn't ready to share the story.

"Can't say I've had much time for that," he said. "But it still eats on me. I won't be at ease until I know how it happened."

"My father knows he's ill." Susan picked up the thread of her story. "That's one of the reasons he came back here to Texas. He wanted to see my future settled, with someone to help manage my affairs. Yesterday he took Ferg aside in the library. They talked a while, and then Ferg came out and proposed."

"And you said yes, just like that?"

"I said yes to being engaged, but I insisted on a year to go to college at Savannah State University. That way I'll be close to home if Dad needs me. The understanding is that Ferg and I will be married next summer. My father's promised he'll be there to walk me down the aisle."

"So you've got it all worked out." Bull couldn't disguise the sarcasm in his voice. What was it to him if Susan wanted to marry a jackass like Ferg, who'd likely burn through her fortune faster than fire through dry prairie grass?

"If that's how you want to put it, yes," she said. "My father needs to know that I'll be all right. And he needs something to look forward to. That's what I'm trying to give him."

Bull thought about Ferg and his reputation as a womanizer. Susan wouldn't be getting much of a bargain. But maybe she knew that. Maybe she'd figured that being mistress of a big ranch would be worth putting up with a lazy, skirt-chasing husband. As for Ferg, he'd be getting the beautiful, spirited heiress to a fortune. Now that was what most men would call a trophy!

But what did it matter? Didn't most marriages involve some kind of bargain—for sex, for security and social standing, for children, even for love, whatever that was? As long as both parties knew what they were getting—and what they were giving in return— maybe that was all right. But would it be enough for a woman like Susan?

Bull had taken a back road that wound among fields and small farms. Now he pulled off the road beneath some overhanging willows. Shutting off the engine, he sat in silence for a moment. The willow leaves made dappled shade over the truck. A light summer breeze rippled across the alfalfa fields and stirred a lock of Susan's hair.

"I haven't forgotten what I promised you," she said.

Bull's pulse slammed. "Well, for what it's worth, I haven't chewed tobacco in the past year."

"Good, because I've given up cigarettes." The pupils of her eyes were like silver-rimmed pools. Her satiny lips parted as she leaned toward him. The pizza boxes on her lap, along with the gear box between the seats, formed a barrier between their bodies. But when he pushed toward her, and felt the first brush of her lips, he forgot about everything except kissing her.

Her soft, moist mouth clung deliciously to his, lingering for breathless seconds. She tasted of sweetness and chocolate and pure, female sensuality. The flicker of her tongue against his sent a hot jolt of arousal down through his body. Bull savored the aching hunger, wanting his hands on her, and more, but knowing this was the best he was going to get.

They drew apart, both of them slightly out of breath. Bull leaned back in the seat and started the truck. In the awkward silence, he forced himself to chuckle. "Well, Miss Susan, all I can say is, when you gave your word to do it right, you weren't kidding."

She reached across the gear box and touched his arm. "Take me home, Bull," she said.

Bull drove back up the lane toward the highway. He'd told himself there was nothing more to say. But there was one question he couldn't stop himself from asking.

"Do you love him, Susan?"

She gazed ahead, through the dusty windshield. "I understand him. He's like a little lost boy who doesn't know his way. I suppose that's good enough for starters. The rest will come in time."

"And does Ferg love you?"

She glanced at him with a bitter smile. "You'll have to ask him that question, won't you?"

Bull had no answer. Minutes later he pulled up to the ranch gate and went around the truck to open her door. He held the pizza boxes while she climbed out to the ground. "Thanks for the lift," she said.

"Anytime." He watched her walk toward the house, her woman's stride all grace and power.

He would enjoy winning her away from Ferg, he thought. But what would he be winning her to? He had nothing to offer a woman like Susan. The sooner he forgot her, the better for them both.

Cursing the memory of that blistering kiss—the kiss that had made him want her—Bull climbed into the truck and drove back to the Rimrock.

As the truck pulled away, Susan turned back to watch it vanish in a cloud of summer dust. She wouldn't be seeing Bull Tyler again. Not alone at least. With Ferg hating him, and her Uncle Ham wanting his land, she'd be wise to keep her distance from the proud rancher. Any attention on her part would only give the Prescotts an excuse to harass him.

She had wanted to kiss Bull, and she wasn't sorry. It had been one small, selfish act of rebellion in her regimented life. For the few seconds their lips had clung, she had felt truly alive. But she couldn't allow it to happen again. Too many people could be hurt by the consequences.

So she would behave herself. She would be a dutiful daughter, a considerate niece, and a faithful fiancée. She would do her best to forget that soul-stirring kiss in Bull's truck. And she would accept the reality that her own wishes didn't matter—at least not to her family. She was only a woman, surrounded by strong-willed men who wanted to use her.

Could she really marry Ferg, knowing he might not be faithful and knowing that he'd already sired an illegitimate son? She'd told Bull the truth. She didn't love Ferg, but she understood him. She could only hope that underneath that brash, selfish exterior was a good man.

Brushing her hair back from her face, she continued on to the house. Sunflowers grew in patches along the path. She paused to pick some. She would trim the stems and put them in a vase to cheer the house's gloomy, masculine interior.

Only as she picked the last flower and turned toward the porch did she see him. Ferg was standing on the top step, waiting with his arms folded—waiting for her.

CHAPTER 8

*F*ERG LOOMED OVER SUSAN FROM THE TOP STEP, HIS
expression a stormy pout. "What took you so long?"
he demanded.

She lifted her chin, refusing to be cowed. "We
drove the back way. It was pleasant out, and we had
time."

"Time before one o'clock, when you promised to
meet your father? It's one-fifteen, Susan. And your
father's gone with my dad to look at a new front
loader for the hay barn. They were going to have
lunch in Lubbock. So, what do you have to say to
that?"

She sighed, knowing she was cornered. "All right, I
made up an excuse. Bull is a friend. I hadn't seen him
in two years, and I wanted a chance to catch up."

"A *friend?*" He came down a step, anger redden-
ing his face. "What the hell kind of a friend is he? By
my reckoning the only time you'd spent with him
was when you were with me."

"That's why I didn't think you'd mind." She took a breath. Her pulse was racing. "How did you get home so soon? I thought it would take a while to get the tires fixed."

"The garage sent somebody right over. It didn't take fifteen minutes to pump up one tire and put the spare on the other wheel. You should've waited, Susan. And you shouldn't have lied to me."

She met his gaze, speaking in a calm voice. "If you're expecting an apology, you're not going to get one. I may be wearing your ring, Ferg, but you don't own me."

He was down the steps in two strides, his hands gripping her shoulders hard enough to cause pain. "Listen to me! Bull Tyler is trash, just like his father. You're not to have anything to do with him. And you're never to lie to me again. Understand?"

Susan had never seen him like this. Momentarily stunned, she stared at him.

"Say you understand! Say you're mine and no-body else's!" His grip tightened. The sunflowers fell from her arms and scattered on the walk.

"*Let . . . me . . . go!*" The words exploded out of her as she twisted away from him and stepped out of reach. "People break engagements all the time. I don't have to marry you, Ferg!"

"Maybe not." His demeanor had changed. He was smiling now, as if he'd won some kind of victory. "But before you give that ring back, you might ask yourself what our breaking up might do to your father's health."

Susan exhaled her anger, knowing he was right. She couldn't give up on this engagement. Not if it would make a difference to her father. And despite the things she knew Ferg had done, he did have good in him. He could be kind and gentle—she'd seen it herself. Maybe with patience and affection, she could help bring out those finer qualities.

Needing a diversion, she bent to gather up the sunflowers she'd dropped. They looked bruised and had lost a few petals, but maybe some water could still revive them.

"I'm sorry, Susan." Ferg crouched beside her, handing her a few of the flowers he'd picked up. "I didn't mean to lose my temper. But I have to know we can trust each other. To have you lie and then go off like that with another man, especially *him*—it made me crazy."

"I'm sorry, too. In the future I'll remember that I need to be honest with you. And I'll do my best to make you happy." Susan had spoken carefully, keeping to what she knew was true. But she couldn't help wondering how Ferg would handle her being in Savannah for the coming school year, mingling with male students. Possessive as he appeared to be, would he pressure her to have the wedding sooner—even this summer?

If so, he was going to have a fight on his hands. She wasn't ready to get married yet, not before she'd had a taste of independence.

But what would she do if her father took Ferg's side—especially if his health was failing?

Ferg's big hand cupped the back of her head, his fingers weaving into her hair, holding her in place. "You and I were meant to be together, Susan," he muttered. "Never forget that."

His mouth captured hers in a forceful kiss. Susan responded, closing her eyes, softening her lips, and meeting the insistent thrust of his tongue. But it was all an act. What she felt was . . . nothing.

* * *

Wiping the sweat from his eyes, Bull used a wrench to tighten the bolts on a steel cross brace. The sun was blistering hot, the task seemingly endless. If he'd known how much time the new windmill tower was going to take, or how much work it was going to involve, he would have gladly forked over the extra money for a crew to erect the structure in a day or two. As it was, he'd been at it for more than a week. Working day and night, grabbing sleep and food as he could. The boys, Chester and Patrick, helped when he needed them, but much of their time was spent taking care of the stock.

Because the old windmill was still needed, the new structure had to be assembled next to it. When it was ready, the old tower would be taken down, the new one raised and moved over the well, anchored in the ground, and rigged with the pump. If everything went as it should, the new windmill would supply good water to the house and stock tanks through the next generation.

If everything went as it should.

The worry gnawed at Bull's gut. Every day the flow of water from the pump seemed weaker. Was it because of the ramshackle windmill or, as the water table shrank in the long drought, was the well that had sustained the ranch for as long as he could remember finally going dry?

He wouldn't know for sure until the new windmill was in place and working. But he'd already decided to anchor the legs in the ground with gravel instead of concrete—less stable, but essential if the costly structure had to be moved.

He reached for another cross brace, fitted it into place, and took another bolt out of the tool pouch at his belt. After weighing the options, he'd decided to assemble the tower on the ground, then raise it into place with ropes—safer and faster for a man working alone. He could only hope it would be strong enough to hold up to the pulling and shifting it would take to get it into place.

Sweat soaked his shirt and trickled from under his hat to form salty rivulets down his face. Hell, he barely had an idea of what he was doing. He was winging it from one day to the next, the work, the money, the stock . . .

When he could manage to sleep, he had nightmares about everything going wrong at once. He would wake from those black dreams in a cold sweat, pull himself together, and get back to work.

What he wouldn't give to have Jasper here. But Jasper, by now, would be settling down to a peaceful life in the hill country, with Sally, his lifelong sweetheart. Bull could only wish them the happiness they deserved.

He was bending down to tighten one more bolt when the snort of a horse startled him. Reflexively, he reached for the loaded .44 at his hip, but then he saw that it was Susan, riding across the ranch yard on a fine bay mare.

"Hellfire, I could've shot you." He wiped the hair out of his eyes. "What are you doing here?"

"I had some time on my hands, so I thought I'd pay you a visit." She was dressed in a light denim shirt, with faded jeans and pricey-looking boots. A battered hat, likely borrowed, shaded her face. The diamond on her finger flashed in the glaring sun.

"Where's your boyfriend?" he asked, knowing he shouldn't be glad to see her, and angry at himself that he was.

"He's at a horse auction in Wichita Falls, with my father and Uncle Ham." She swung off the horse, dropped the reins, and came to his side. "I see you're busy. Can I help you?"

"This isn't what you'd call woman's work. It's dirty and hot and miserable."

"I know. But I can hand you things. Just ask me." She moved an empty wooden crate closer and sat on it.

"Fine. Hand me that small socket wrench, the one by your foot."

She handed him the tool. "I can't believe you're doing all this by yourself," she said.

"Neither can I." He used the wrench to tighten a nut. "What are you doing here, Susan?"

"Nothing much. I was alone, and I got to thinking that I'd never seen your ranch by daylight."

"Well, you're seeing it." Bull gave the nut an extra twist. "Not much to look at, is there?"

"I wouldn't say that. It's got lots of . . . potential."

"You see potential. I see money I don't have and years of gut-busting work to turn this ranch into something a man can be proud of."

"And I see a man—a very dirty, sweaty man—who'll do what he sets out to do, no matter how hard it is. That's a compliment, in case you're wondering."

"I'll take dirty and sweaty. Not so sure about the rest." Bull glanced around for the boys, then remembered he'd sent them into town with a grocery list and told them to take their time. "Hand me that brace—the longest one."

She passed the brace to him and watched while he bolted both ends to the frame. He could smell her perfume, a scent that was light but, on her, strangely seductive. Her denim shirt was open past the second button, showing the barest hint of cleavage. Bull tried not to remember how it had felt to kiss her.

"You don't think much of me, do you?" Her question startled him. He looked up, catching the flash of vulnerability in her silvery eyes.

"What I think of you doesn't matter," he said. "But for what it's worth, I think you're selling yourself short. You deserve somebody better than Ferg."

"Like you?" She raised one eyebrow. Bull could only surmise that she was teasing him.

"Look around you," he said. "If you want to spend your life mucking stables and herding cows and sharing your bed with a dirty, sweaty, cash-poor rancher, I'm your man!"

She laughed. "Don't tempt me. It doesn't sound all that bad, especially the dirty, sweaty part."

Their eyes met in a breathless pause, as if they'd both revealed too much. Susan dropped her gaze, the color creeping into her face. "I don't suppose you have any cold beer in the house, do you?"

Bull took off his hat and raked his damp hair back from his face. "There might be a bottle or two of the Mexican stuff in the icebox. The back door's open. Don't look at the kitchen. It's a mess. The icebox is probably sprouting mold."

"Don't worry, I'll just grab the beer." Standing, she took off at a run toward the house. Bull watched her go, admiring her easy grace and the way her hips curved inward to her narrow waist. Too bad the house hadn't been cleaned since Jasper left. Even clean, the place was a dump. But it was what it was. He had nothing to hide, and no reason to hide it.

Moments later she came striding back across the yard, a single, open brown bottle in her hand.

"There was only one," she said, thrusting it toward him. "Here, at least it's cold."

"That's all right. You can have it," he said.

"Don't be silly. We can share." She swigged from the mouth of the bottle and passed it to him. He felt the fleeting warmth of her mouth on the ring of glass as he tipped it to drink. The chilled liquid flowed down his parched throat.

"Thanks." He lowered the bottle and passed it to her to finish. "That felt good. It's hotter than hell out here."

She took a sip, then handed the bottle back to him. "Here, take the rest. And you could use some shade." She tugged his arm. Bull had no cause to resist as she pulled him toward the nearby barn and through the open doorway.

After hours in the searing sun, the barn's interior was like a cool, dark cave. Susan looked up at him. Her eyes were soft in the shadows. A golden droplet hovered on her lower lip.

"You know why I came," she whispered.

"I know." The bottle dropped from his hand as he caught her close. She melted into him, their kisses wild, hungry, and desperate, burning with need. They devoured each other, a fierce heat rising between their bodies. His hand found the honey of bare skin beneath her shirt—the small, firm breasts, nipples that hardened at his touch. The press of her hips against his rock-hard arousal fired rocket bursts through his body. He thought of the darkness, the soft hay . . . She was wearing Ferg's ring, but he didn't give a damn about that. He wanted her. And he knew she wanted him.

She was tugging at his shirt buttons when they heard the dogs outside in the yard. He recognized their happy, eager bark. The boys were back from town, and the two mutts were hoping for a treat.

Susan had pulled away at the first sound. Bull caught the flash of fear in her eyes. Was she thinking that Ferg had set a trap and caught her?

"It's all right," he said. "My hired hands just pulled in. They're only boys."

"I need to go," she said.

"Yes, you do." He picked up the hat she'd dropped and walked her out of the barn. The boys were carrying the grocery bags into the house, fending off the excited dogs. No male with eyes in his head could fail to notice Susan, but they gave her little more than a quick look as she mounted her horse and rode back toward the Prescott Ranch.

Aching, Bull cursed as he watched her go. Damn the woman. Wanting her was driving him crazy. All he could think of was having her.

But there was more involved here than Susan. Stealing Ferg's girl would be the ultimate satisfaction—and the ultimate revenge. But what if he managed to make it happen? What then?

He sure as hell couldn't ask her to join him on this run-down ranch. And her father, who could barely bring himself to shake hands, would never welcome him into the family.

The only sensible action would be to walk away. Susan was a beautiful woman. If she didn't marry Ferg, there would be other men in her life. With luck she'd have the wisdom to choose the right one.

Taking Susan away from a brute like Ferg would be doing her a favor, Bull told himself. But he was rationalizing now—making excuses for the only thing that really counted.

He wanted her. He wanted her in his arms. He

wanted her in bed, her long legs wrapping around his hips, his kisses muffling her little cries as he pushed deep inside her.

He wanted her. And having her was all that mattered.

Ferg had disappeared outside after supper and driven off in his Thunderbird. When he hadn't returned by ten, Susan decided to wait up for him. It was time they had an honest discussion about his behavior, and what she expected of him as her fiancé. If he didn't come clean and promise to take their engagement seriously, it would be time for a talk with her father. Sick as he was, Cliff Rutledge would never force her to wed a man who didn't respect her.

She settled onto the couch with a paperback mystery novel she'd found in her bedroom nightstand—probably left behind by a houseguest. The Prescotts didn't seem to be much for reading.

By midnight, she was halfway through the book and had already figured out the ending. She'd even peeked at the last page to make sure she was right. With a weary sigh, she laid the book down on the coffee table. Her mind was beginning to wander forbidden paths, back to her ride that afternoon and the moments she'd spent in Bull's arms.

Shameless—that's what her mother would have called her. She'd thrown herself at him in a manner that wasn't the least bit ladylike. The worst of it was, she didn't care. Bull touched a place inside her—a place that was deep and wild and true. His kiss had taken her to that part of herself where she'd needed to go.

She remembered how he'd looked today—sweat

plastering his shirt to his body, his dark hair falling over eyes that were like the hot, blue jets of a gas flame. A man with nothing but land and pride. A man who would fight to keep what was his. Even the thought of him stirred her pulse.

But it was wrong to be thinking about him, especially now, when she was waiting to confront Ferg about his behavior. Not that she'd been perfect herself. She'd willfully kissed a man and enjoyed every second of it. Ferg, she knew, had done far worse. But she was just as guilty. Hers had been a betrayal of the heart.

One thing was clear. If she and Ferg were to marry, have a family, and build a life together, they needed to commit to being faithful—both of them.

By the time the Thunderbird pulled up to the house, she'd drifted into a light doze. Startled awake, she sat up as his key turned in the lock, smoothing back her hair and pulling down her shirt.

He walked through the door, blinking in the unexpected lamplight. His hair was rumpled, his shirt buttoned wrong. His lips looked slack and swollen.

Susan rose from the couch. He stared at her. "What the hell are you doing up?" he muttered, slurring the words.

"Waiting for you. We need to talk." Something told her this might be bad timing, but she'd made up her mind not to back down.

"We can talk in the morning. I'm goin' to bed."

"Now, Ferg." She stood her ground, blocking the way to the stairs. "I'm not as naïve as you think I am. I know you're seeing a woman in town. I even know you have an illegitimate son your father is helping support. What I need you to tell me is this. How can

I expect to stay engaged to, let alone marry, a man who behaves like you do?"

He leaned over her, seeming to swell in size. For a fleeting instant, Susan feared he was going to strike her. Then he turned away and slumped onto the couch. "Fine," he muttered. "You want to talk? We'll talk. Ask me any damn thing you want to know."

"The woman." Susan sat down at the far end of the couch. "Just one, or do you have a variety out there?"

"Just one. She's married. Her husband's on the road a lot, and it's all just for fun. No strings attached."

"I could ask you who she is, but I think I already know."

"Then you should know she's no threat to you. It's just sex, for both of us. That's all."

"I see." Susan gazed down at the diamond on her finger, scarcely able to believe she was having this conversation. "And the boy?"

"Hell, I was just a fifteen-year-old kid fooling around with the preacher's daughter. I couldn't believe it when she told me she was pregnant. My dad had to buy off her family. Otherwise, they'd have made a fuss and forced me to marry her."

"So where are they now?"

"Right here in Blanco Springs. Her folks sent her off somewhere to have the baby. When she came back, they made up some story about having adopted an orphan. The kid passes as her brother, but I don't suppose many people are fooled by that."

"What's his name? Do you ever see him?"

"Not if I can help it. His name's Garn—not my choice, believe me. The little wimp takes after his mother's family. If I didn't know better, I would never believe he was mine."

"But he's your son. Don't you feel anything for him?"

"Not a blasted thing."

"And his mother? What about her?"

Ferg raked a hand through his rumpled hair. "Hell, she was a cute little thing in ninth grade. But she grew up to be a prissy Bible-thumper like her mother. Believe me, she's nothing for you to worry about."

"I'm not worried about her," Susan said. "You ruined her life. I feel sorry for her."

"Well, don't. She was plenty willing at the time. And then her family tried to trap me. She's lucky my dad helps out with the kid. Even that's a helluva lot better than she deserves."

Ferg had been gazing down at his hands as he spoke. Now he shifted on the couch and fixed his bloodshot eyes on Susan. "Now it's my turn to ask a question. One of the stable boys told me you took the bay mare out today."

Susan had resolved not to lie. "Yes. I was bored, so I rode over to the Rimrock. Bull was busy working. His two hired boys showed up while I was there."

"I told you to stay away from him!"

"And I told you that you didn't own me." She shook her head. "I don't want to fight with you, Ferg. Maybe we aren't ready to be engaged. Maybe we should call it off and give ourselves more time."

"Is that what you want? What about your father?"

"He'll be disappointed. But he'll understand. He wants me to be happy. And I can hardly be happy with a fiancé who's sneaking out at night to sleep with another woman."

His jaw tightened, hardening his expression. "This is Bull Tyler's doing, isn't it? You were fine until you started getting cozy with that bastard!"

"This isn't about Bull." She rose to her feet. "It's about us and what you're doing."

"What I'm doing?" He pushed to his feet and stood glaring down at her. "Fine. Let me tell you what I told my father. I'm a man with a man's needs. Once we're married, you can take care of those needs at home, in our bed. Until then, you can't expect me to live like a monk!"

"And what about me?" Susan demanded. "Why am I expected to be totally faithful when you won't do the same?"

"Because you're a woman—my woman. And if you want to keep me at home nights, you know what you can do. Should I spell it out for you, sweetheart?"

Susan felt the blood drain from her face. Trembling, she slipped the diamond ring off her finger and laid it on the coffee table. "Good night, Ferg," she said, and turned to walk away.

He seized her arm, whipping her around to face him. "Fine!" he snarled. "Go if you want to. You'll change your mind once you've come to your senses. But remember one thing—if I ever catch you with Bull Tyler, or find out he's so much as laid a hand on you, so help me, I'll kill him!"

The next morning, Susan wandered downstairs to find her father alone on the front porch, enjoying a cup of coffee. It was early yet, the sun just edging above the eastern hills. Beyond the barn, the cowhands were busy with early chores. But here, with birds singing in the tall cottonwoods and roses blooming below the porch, the morning was as peaceful as the first day in Eden.

But as she leaned over to kiss her father's cheek, Susan had a feeling it wouldn't remain that way.

"Good morning, sunshine." He reached up to pat her hand. "What are you doing up so early?"

"I might ask you the same question." She sat down in the swing beside him, taking care not to tip his coffee.

"I just like the peace and quiet," he said. "That tends to go away once everybody's up and stirring."

"I know what you mean. Did you sleep all right?"

"Like a log. Better than in Savannah." He sipped his coffee. "I was just watching the light creep over the ranchland and thinking how happy I am that one day all this will belong to you."

Susan's heart was a leaden weight in her chest. She had to tell him. "Dad," she began, taking his hand. "Last night I gave Ferg's ring back. We aren't engaged anymore."

His hand jerked, spilling coffee on his immaculate khaki trousers. "What are you saying?" he demanded. "It was all arranged. Your future—"

"Listen to me. Ferg's got a woman in town. He goes to see her at night, when her husband's away."

"Yes, I know. But I wouldn't worry. Ferg will straighten up once he's married to you."

"You know?" She stared at him, dumbfounded.

"Ham told me. Naturally I wasn't pleased. But boys will be boys, and they do grow up. Heaven knows, I was no saint before I married your mother. But her daddy owned a cotton plantation, and I did my duty. Can't say I've ever regretted it, especially since I got you in the bargain." His eyes narrowed.

"I've a pretty good idea where this is coming from, Susan. You were seen riding back from the Rimrock yesterday."

"So now I'm being spied on?"

"A young woman like you has a reputation to protect. And Virgil Tyler isn't the sort of a man you'd want anything to do with. His father was a drunk, and young Tyler made his living as a rodeo cowboy before he came back to that run-down ranch. He's nothing but white trash. You're not to see him again."

Susan rose, fighting tears as she turned to face him. "I thought that you, of all people, would understand. I thought you'd be on my side."

"I am on your side," he said. "I know what's best for you, and as long as you're under twenty-one, you'll do what I say. Years from now, when you're well-off and surrounded by your family, you'll look back and thank me."

His expression froze. The china cup dropped from his hand to shatter on the porch. He clutched at his chest. "My pills!" he gasped. "Get them! And get some help!"

CHAPTER 9

*B*ULL LAY AWAKE IN THE DARK, TOO RESTLESS TO sleep. Nearly a week had passed without word from Susan. He could understand that she might not want to see him again. But what if something had gone wrong—an accident, or a clash with Ferg's explosive temper? He knew he had no right to be concerned about her. All the same, he was worried.

But Susan was the least of his troubles now. Three days ago he and the boys had erected the windmill tower and reconnected the pump. The new setup had worked perfectly. But the water flow was still dwindling. It was time to face reality. The water table beneath the land was shrinking. The well was going dry.

How much time did he have before the water ran out? Days? Weeks? Would the hire of a drilling contractor be a waste of time and money? What if he paid and the new well proved to be as dry as the old one?

If he could find another source of water for the stock, saving the well water for the house, maybe the ranch would be all right until winter storms replenished the ground. But what if those storms never came? And where was he going to find enough water for more than a hundred head of cattle? He might be better off selling the lot of them.

The spring in the petroglyph canyon was no solution. There wasn't enough water there to support more than a few cows. The neighbors to the south owned a patch of swampland that flooded with water when the rains were good. But this summer the place was nothing but a quagmire that trapped wandering cattle and stank from a mile away. Even if they'd sell the land cheap, it would be useless now.

Cursing, he swung his feet to the floor, sat on the edge of the bed, and cradled his aching head between his hands. The answer was out there, he told himself. All he had to do was find it.

The creek that ran through the Prescott Ranch flowed from artesian water high in the escarpment. Not only did that steady stream provide water for the cattle, it also irrigated hayfields for winter feed and made the difference between success and failure for that big ranch. Even in long droughts, the Prescotts had all the water they needed. There had to be a way for the Rimrock to get a share of it.

Barking dogs and the sound of a truck driving into the yard galvanized him to action. Without taking time to dress, he cocked the .44, charged out the front, and stopped as if he'd hit a wall.

Pulling up to the porch was the old ranch truck, the one he'd given to Jasper. The dogs danced and wagged as the truck door opened and Jasper climbed out with his pack.

Bull's first thought was that he'd brought his bride for a visit. But Jasper had come alone. He climbed to the porch with weary steps, ignoring the dogs that frisked around his legs. His eyes were sunk in tired shadows. He looked as if he hadn't slept in days.

"Jasper." Bull came forward, unsure of how to greet him. "Come on in. I'll get you something to eat."

"That can wait," Jasper said. "I'm pretty tired. Just point me to a bed."

"Your old room's the way you left it," Bull said.

"That'll be fine."

Bull went ahead of him and turned on the light. "What are you doing here, Jasper?" he asked. "I thought you were getting married."

"Didn't happen." Jasper turned toward him. In the glare of the lightbulb, he looked like a man in torment. "A couple of days before the wedding, there was a freak storm—a real gully washer. Sally was driving on a back road. Her car got stuck crossing a wash when the water came down. She couldn't get out in time. She drowned, Bull. She's dead."

By the next morning, after a few hours of sleep, some coffee, and a good breakfast, Jasper was alert and ready to start the day. He wore his heartbreak like a scar that had aged his features and left hollows of sorrow beneath his eyes, but he was outwardly cheerful and seemed anxious to get to work.

Despite the tragic loss, Bull was grateful to have him back. He'd missed, and needed, his old friend's experience and wisdom.

Over a breakfast of bacon and eggs, he filled Jasper

in on the water problem. "We can't depend on the well anymore," he said. "As I see it, the only way to keep our cattle watered is to get them to the creek. And that creek's pretty much on Prescott land."

"But not all of it," Jasper said. "The source, in the escarpment, is on government land."

"And there's no way to get cattle up those rocks to where it comes out."

"Let me finish," Jasper insisted. "You might or might not know this, but accordin' to law, surface water on the land—includin' the creek—belongs to the good old state of Texas. Anybody can use it. But the *access* to the water belongs to whoever owns the land. So if you can't get to it, you can't use it."

"Never thought about that," Bull said. "But I guess it makes sense. So how do we get to the water?"

Jasper put down his toast and began drawing an imaginary map with his finger on the table's Formica surface. "Right up near the mouth of that canyon there's a thirty-acre parcel of land where an old hermit lives. Cletus McAdoo showed up about the time you lit out, so you wouldn't know him."

"So, is it his land? Would he sell?"

"Hell, I don't know if he even owns the land. He just showed up and built a shack on it. Anyway he's as crazy as a bedbug, hates the Prescotts. He wasn't much for your dad, neither—wouldn't give him access even when he offered to pay."

"So where's the water on his land?"

"The creek is the boundary between his land and the Prescott Ranch. Like I said, the Prescotts don't own the water, just the access on their side. I reckon they'd do just about anything to get that old man's property. That would give the bastards control on both sides of the creek, so nobody else could use the water—especially the Rimrock. But the old man keeps a shotgun for anybody that comes on the property. He's been known to use it. That's probably what's kept the Prescotts from movin' in and takin' over."

"What about the land in between McAdoo's parcel and the Rimrock?"

"Open range for nigh onto a mile. Mostly sagebrush and mesquite. The graze is poor, and not a drop of water. But if we had access to the creek, there'd be no problem drivin' our herd across that stretch."

"Then I guess it's time to go and talk to McAdoo."

"You're sure you want to do that? He's liable to blow you full of buckshot, or worse."

"Do you know any other way to get to that water?" Bull finished his coffee. "Tell you what, I'll pay a call on the old man. Later today you can drive into town, check the records, and find out for sure who owns that parcel."

"Fine, you're the boss," Jasper said. "But be careful."

Half an hour later, with the sun just coming up and the two boys busy at chores, Bull buckled on his pistol, mounted up, and headed for the old man's property. Strange, he hadn't noticed the place in the two years he'd been home. But it was beyond the borders of the Rimrock, with federal land in between. If Jasper hadn't told him how to get there, he might have ridden right past it.

As he approached, the sound of the creek rushing over rocks reached his ears. Where the land leveled out on the Prescott Ranch, he knew that the creek slowed and widened, to make easy drinking for cattle in the Prescott pastures. But here the current was swift and musical. Water in this part of Texas was more precious than gold. He was hearing a treasure.

Now he glimpsed the shack, screened by a stand of willows. He could also see the barbed wire fence and the KEEP OUT, TRESPASSERS WILL BE SHOT signs boldly displayed in front. Jasper had told him that the property covered thirty acres. If so, its shape would have to be irregular. Here the distance was no more than fifty yards from the fence to the creek.

As an afterthought, Bull had tucked a white dish towel in his saddlebag. Now, after dismounting, he took it out and tied the end to a stick. It might not help, but it wouldn't hurt to let the old hermit know he'd come in peace. With his horse tethered in the willows, one hand holding the makeshift flag and the other resting on his holstered pistol, he walked slowly forward.

The shack was fashioned out of scrap lumber with a corrugated tin roof and a metal chimney. A ramshackle chicken coop stood at one end, with a well-tended vegetable garden in what would have been the front yard. A dozen yards away, screened by a few willows, stood an outhouse. The creek ran on the far side of the shack, reflecting glints of sunlight through the overhanging willows. There was no visible gate in the wire fence and no sign of human activity about the place.

"Mr. McAdoo!" Bull walked toward the fence, keeping the white flag in plain sight. "I don't mean any harm. I just need to talk to you."

He caught the movement of a wooden shutter. In the next instant, a shotgun blast roared past his head. The shot missed, but it was close enough to make him jump and leave his ears ringing. Recovering his equilibrium, he raised the white flag higher. "It's all right," he called. "I'm not here to hurt you."

"Lay down that pistol, Mister!" The voice sounded more like a child's than an old man's. "Nice and slow-like. No tricks, or I'll blast you to kingdom come!"

Moving slowly, Bull drew the gun from his holster and laid it on the ground.

"See that white rock? That's where the gate is. There's a wire loop. Lift it off and come in slow and easy with your hands where I can see 'em."

Bull did as he was told. A bead of nervous sweat trickled down the back of his neck as he reached the plywood door. The speaker didn't sound like a killer, but the first blast had come close. Now he was even more exposed.

"The door's unlatched, Mister. Open it a little, just enough to step inside. You can close it behind you. That's it."

Bull stepped into a dark, closed space. At first his sun-dazzled eyes could see nothing but shadows. He was aware of a sickly smell and the rasp of labored breathing.

Only as his vision cleared did he see the undersized figure standing in front of him—a pigtailed girl, maybe thirteen or fourteen, her arms barely strong enough to steady the heavy double-barreled shotgun she aimed at his chest.

"It's all right," Bull said. "I'm not here to hurt anybody. You can put the gun down."

Still tense, she lowered the weapon. Bull's gaze took her measure. Dressed in jeans and an oversized flannel shirt, she was lean and wiry, with plain brown hair and a face that was too thin for her large hazel eyes. As she turned toward a beam of light that fell through the shutter, he saw the port-wine stain that spattered the left border of her tear-streaked face.

Without a word she stepped aside. In the shadows behind her, Bull saw a narrow cot. On the cot, covered by a thin quilt, lay an old man with a scruffy, iron-gray beard. From the look of him, and the sound of his shallow, wheezing breath, he had to be in excruciating pain.

"My grandpa got shot last night," the girl said. "He's hurt bad. Can you help him?"

"I'm no doctor," Bull said. "I'll do what I can, but it might not be much." Bending closer, he eased the quilt off the old man, opened his stained canvas vest, and peeled away the folded sheet that served as a makeshift dressing. He stifled a gasp at the sight of the wound below his ribs. The old man appeared to have been hit by a high-powered rifle firing a soft-point bullet that had expanded on impact, tearing through vital organs. The amazing thing was, he was still alive.

His eyelids fluttered open. Bloodshot eyes glared up at Bull. "Who the hell are you?" he muttered.

"Bull Tyler. I'm a friend, Mr. McAdoo. What happened here?"

"Prescotts . . . bastards . . ." His face was grayish in the faint light, every word an effort. "Ol' Ham's been after me all summer t' sell. Came last night . . . said it was my last chance . . . I told him go t' hell . . ."

The girl hovered close. "Can't you do anything for him?" Her face was streaked with silent tears.

Bull shook his head. The old man was dying. All he could do was find out as much as he could before the end. "Who shot you?"

"Ham . . . hurt me bad." Cletus McAdoo closed his eyes, as if gathering what was left of his strength.

"Managed to crawl back inside . . . After Ham rode off, three of his bastards showed up. They would've come in, or torched the place, but Rose scared 'em off, shootin' through the window." His hand came up and seized Bull's wrist, his bony fingers like an iron vise. "Get her out . . . they'll be back. Mustn't find her here . . ."

Bull glanced at the girl. Rose. The name didn't suit her. She was more like a tough little weed than a flower. "Do those men know you're here?"

She shook her head. "I don't think so. Grandpa always made me hide when they came."

"Did you see the man who shot him?"

She nodded. "He was older, with a mustache and a big belly."

That had been Ham Prescott, all right. Lord, Ham had murdered this old man in cold blood, shot him with his own hands. Then he'd sent his thugs back to clean up the mess.

"Listen . . ." McAdoo pulled Bull down close to him. His whisper was so faint that Bull could barely hear. "When I go, this place is hers . . . Deed's in a wooden box . . . already signed . . ." He was slipping away. "Keep her safe . . . She's all I . . . got."

His eyelids fluttered and closed. His breath eased into silence. The girl's tears had become quiet sobs.

Knowing what he had to do, Bull covered the old man's face and drew a deep breath. Whatever happened next had to happen right. He couldn't be moved by pity or kindness. Everything he did now had to be done for the Rimrock.

"Listen, Rose." He gripped her shoulders, forcing himself to be gentle. "You've got to get out of here. Do you know where the Rimrock Ranch is?"

She nodded, wiping her eyes.

"Here's what I want you to do. Run out front and get my pistol. Bring it back to me. Then take my horse and ride like hell for the Rimrock. Find Jasper, my foreman—he'll be tall and thin, maybe driving an old pickup. Tell him everything that happened. Only him. Nobody else. Understand?"

"What about you?"

"When those men come back, I'll hold them off. With luck, they'll think your grandfather's still alive. When it's safe, I'll see that he's buried. Now get going. They could come back anytime."

"But . . . what about my chickens? I can't just leave them here."

"I'll save your damned chickens."

"Promise?"

"Hell, yes. Now go."

She was out the door like a shot, taking only a moment to find Bull's pistol before she brought it back to him.

"My horse is tied in the willows. He won't give you any trouble. Now, blast it, girl, get out of here!"

By the time she was out the door, Bull was already taking stock of the place. There were two windows, one on the door side and one on the creek side. Both were protected by drop-down shutters hinged at the top, opening inward. The window in front had a cracked glass pane. The one that faced the creek had none.

No doubt Prescott's men would be back. Ham would have told them that the old man was wounded. Once they felt confident that he was dead or helpless, they would either cross the creek and ransack the shack for whatever they could find or burn the place to hide all evidence of a crime.

Bull had to hold them off, at least long enough to find the deed and get away.

His .44 was loaded with six bullets, but he'd brought no extra ammo. Six shots wouldn't last long in a stand-off.

However, the old man's shotgun was a formidable beast of a weapon—a ten-gauge, breech-loaded, double-barrel model capable of blasting a man in two at close range.

The girl had fired one barrel when he'd arrived. Maybe the other one would still be loaded. But no such luck. When Bull thumbed the lever to break open the gun and check the breech, he found both barrels empty. He uttered a foul curse. He should've asked young Rose about extra shells. Now, if there were any left, he would have to find them himself.

But first things first. McAdoo's signed deed could make all the difference for the Rimrock. With that deed in hand—if it proved legal—he would have what he needed to gain access to the water. Find it before Prescott's thugs showed up, and he could simply take it and leave, without their knowing he'd been there at all. Let them rip the place apart if they chose to. They'd find nothing but the body of the man their boss had killed.

Which made Rose the witness to a murder.

But he'd think about that later. Driven by urgency, he tore into the clutter of the small shack, emptying drawers and cupboards, prying up floor-boards, dumping out bins of flour and sugar, even lifting up the mattress where the old man's body lay. No shotgun shells and no wooden box that might hold the deed.

And now, from the direction of the Prescott Ranch, he could hear the sound of approaching horses.

Swearing, he redoubled his frantic search for the shotgun shells. He'd looked every place he could think of. What was he missing? If there were any shells left, they'd be kept somewhere close, where they could be reached in a hurry, like . . .

Bull cursed his own oversight. Lunging for the bed, he lowered the quilt and groped in the pockets of Cletus McAdoo's vest. One pocket held two shotgun shells. He'd hoped to find more, but they would have to do. One thing was for sure, he couldn't afford to waste them.

The shotgun lay on the table, still open to expose the breech. Willing himself to stay calm and think clearly, he dropped the shells into place, snapped the weapon closed, and released the safety catch.

The riders were getting close now. Crouching below the window, he raised the shutter just far enough to see out. There were three men. This time Ham wasn't with them. Bull watched as they reined their horses on the far side of the creek and dismounted. Pistols drawn, they walked toward the flowing water that marked the property line. The current was swift but shallow. They'd have no trouble wading across.

The air inside the cabin was stifling. Sweat trickled down Bull's face as the men approached the creek, weapons drawn. His hands were sweating, too. After raising the heavy shotgun to his shoulder, he rested the barrels on the window frame. There were two triggers, one for each barrel, placed side by side and slightly offset. His finger rested on the nearest one. He would shoot one barrel, then wait to fire again when he knew where the blast would do the most damage.

He could only hope for a swift resolution to the

fight. After the second shot, he'd have nothing left but six bullets in his pistol. Once they were gone, he'd be lucky to get out of this mess alive.

The man in the middle was closest, a stocky fellow Bull recognized as one of the hired thugs who'd pulled down his windmill. Bull gave him time for a few more steps. He had one chance to stop the bastard. He couldn't afford to miss.

Bull aimed the shotgun at the man's chest. As his finger tightened on the trigger, he felt an unexpected resistance. He increased the pressure, squeezing harder. Sweat blurred his vision as he forced the gun to fire.

The shotgun blast roared in his head like dynamite going off in a cave. The recoil slammed his shoulder hard enough to knock him onto his back. Only as he struggled upright again did he realize what had happened. Somehow he had pulled both triggers. The two barrels had fired at the same time.

Still dazed, he cocked the pistol and raised the shutter far enough to see out. The two men who'd brought up the rear were backing off, dragging their comrade's body by the legs. The massive force of the shotgun blast had destroyed the man's torso. The rocks along the creek bank were spattered with his blood.

Gripping the pistol, Bull waited. Would the two remaining men take a chance and try to rush him, or had they seen enough? One of them carried a Colt .45 and wore a belt full of cartridges. The other held a high-powered hunting rifle. If they came for the shack, he would be hopelessly outgunned. His only advantage was the fact that they didn't know what they were facing. With luck they'd believe that the old man was alive and had an arsenal of shells for the massive gun.

He held his breath, clenching the pistol so tightly that his hand began to cramp. His shoulder throbbed from the pain of the recoil.

From back in the trees on the far side of the creek, the men stood watching and talking, maybe arguing. Then, decision made, they kicked some dirt and leaves over the dead man's body, mounted up, and rode off, trailing the empty horse.

They'd be back—most likely after Ham had torn a strip off their hides. That gave Bull maybe half an hour to find the deed and clear out. He'd be on foot, but he knew how to keep out of sight. With luck, Jasper might even get word from Rose and show up in the truck.

If he could find the deed and clear out fast, Prescott's thugs would never know anyone else, including the girl, had been in the shack. To make sure, he pulled the body off the bunk, onto the floor so that, if they came back, they'd think McAdoo had fallen after firing the shotgun and died alone.

Now where was the damned deed?

He'd torn the place apart, with no sign of the paper or the wooden box that held it. There was no place else to look.

Unless the deed wasn't in the house.

Gun in hand, he opened the front door, glanced around, then stepped cautiously outside. On the far end of the shack was an overhang with a tie post and a feeder that appeared to have sheltered a horse. But the droppings were old and dry, the hay gone. Bull checked for the box, kicking at the loose earth, finding nothing.

The coop was little more than chicken wire strung between posts and covered on top with loose boards. Inside were three friendly, speckled hens and a small rooster. They looked well cared for, likely by Rose. There were three nest boxes. Bull ducked inside the coop and checked each one. He found straw and a couple of eggs but nothing else.

That left the outhouse, the last place anybody would think to look. Was he wasting time? Opening the door wide to let in air and light, he stepped inside—and found the box. Wrapped in an old newspaper it was tucked into a dark corner, guarded by spider webs. Unwrapped, the box proved to be the kind that might have held note cards or a set of colored pencils. A rubber band held it closed. Bull's pulse raced as he opened it and unfolded the paper inside. It was the deed to the property, signed for transfer as the old man had said. He'd even had it notarized. No doubt he'd meant for the land to go to Rose. But Rose didn't need it. Bull did. This creased, yellowed piece of paper could be the key to survival for the Rimrock. He had killed a man for it, and he would use it as he saw fit. If it was authentic, all he'd have to do was add his name and have the deed recorded in the county office.

Closing the box, he secured it with the rubber band and slid it inside his shirt. He had no way to catch the chickens he'd promised to rescue, and no way to carry them. Maybe he could come back later in the truck, get the damn fool birds, and, if time and safety allowed, bury the old man. But right now he just needed to get the hell out of here.

He set off at a sprint. The impact of each pounding step on the rough ground sent a jolt of pain to his bruised shoulder, but he couldn't slow down. He had to get out of sight before Ham's hired goons came back.

By the time he reached a stand of thick mesquite, his sides were heaving. He paused to catch his breath, then continued at a quick stride. After another quarter mile, he saw the pickup coming over the horizon from the direction of the Rimrock. He groaned with relief. It was Jasper.

Minutes later the old truck pulled up beside him. Jasper was alone.

"It's about time you showed up," Bull joked feebly as he settled into the passenger seat. "Where's Rose?"

"I turned her loose in the kitchen to fix what she could find to eat. The little mite was half starved. Did you find anything that would help us?"

Wincing from the strain on his shoulder, Bull pulled the box out of his shirt and showed Jasper the deed. "Do you think this is any good?"

"Looks authentic to me. We'll know more after I check in at the recorder's office." Jasper drove in silence for a moment before Bull realized what was happening. Jasper was driving back toward the shack.

"Hey—" He gave Jasper a nudge. "You can turn around and go back now. We've got everything we need."

"Not quite." Jasper kept driving. "I made a promise to a worried little gal that I'd get her chickens."

"And get yourself killed while you're at it? Prescott's goons could be back there by now."

"Or not." Jasper kept driving, the truck bumping over the rough ground. Moments later they sighted the shack. Everything looked quiet. But Bull had Jasper stop the truck at a safe distance, behind the willows, while he circled the shack to make sure the coast was clear. There was no sign of the gunmen but his danger senses were tingling as he walked back to the truck. He didn't have a good feeling about this.

"Pull up to the fence," he told Jasper. "We need to do this fast."

"I've got a crate in the back."

"Fine," Bull said. "You catch the damned chickens. I'll keep watch."

They drove up to the shack. Jasper got the wooden crate, which had held parts for the new windmill, and stepped into the coop. Catching the chickens took him longer than Bull had hoped. The four birds were spooked. They pecked, flapped, and squawked, filling the air with loose feathers. It took Jasper several minutes to get them all in the crate and load it in the pickup bed. By then, Bull could hear riders approaching. They were getting close, too close. He needed a diversion to keep them from seeing the truck.

"Give me the spare gas can and get going," he told Jasper. "When you're at a safe distance, stop and wait for me. If I'm not there in ten minutes, go."

"Be careful." Jasper handed Bull the gas can, sprang into the cab, and gave the truck full throttle. The old pickup roared away, chickens bouncing and squawking in the open back.

With the riders getting close, Bull stepped inside the shack and doused the floor and surfaces with gasoline. Even the body of poor old Cletus McAdoo was soaked. It wouldn't be the proper burial the man deserved, but it might be better than he'd get from Prescott's men.

The shotgun was propped against the wall. A weapon like that one could come in handy if things got nasty with the neighbors. Bull grabbed it. He could hear the gunmen's voices from the other side of the creek. Time to get out and run like hell.

Taking the box of matches he'd found on top of the potbellied stove, he raced out of the shack and through the gate. There was just enough gasoline in the can to pour a trail, just enough time to light a flame that raced back to the house.

With a startling *whoosh*, the shack exploded in a ball of fire.

Later that morning, with the chicken crate safe in a shed and Rose sleeping off her long night in the spare bedroom, Bull sent Jasper to town with the deed. Two hours later Jasper was back, his face wearing a grin.

"So, is that deed worth anything?" Bull asked.

Jasper's grin broadened. "You're damn right, it is. The old man had legal title to the land—bought it cheap back in the fifties at some kind of bank repo sale. After he lost his wife and retired from teaching, he moved here. I'm guessing something might've gone wrong with his retirement savings, and this place was all he had."

"Wait, he was a teacher?"

"Yup, an honest-to-God Ph.D. in history. The clerk, that old lady at the county office, remembered him and knew his story. She even remembered that he rode in on a horse last year to get that deed witnessed and notarized. She said the old boy was lookin' pretty bad by then."

"And Rose? She must have quite a story to tell."

"I reckon so. But you'll have to ask her." Jasper's gaze narrowed. "That land is rightfully hers, you know."

"I know. But she's just a kid. We can make things right in time. Meanwhile, we've got legal access to water for our cattle."

Bull knew better than to voice his next thought.

And we've got a live witness who can nail Ham Prescott's murdering hide to the side of the barn!

CHAPTER 10

*C*LIFF RUTLEDGE'S HEART ATTACK HAD ROCKED SUSAN'S world. Although the episode hadn't been as serious as she'd feared, it had brought home the reality of his illness and the fact that he could die at any time.

The hospital in Lubbock had kept him for four days, giving him nitroglycerin tablets and blood thinners and monitoring his condition. Susan had stayed with him day and night, sleeping on an uncomfortable fold-out chair bed and cleaning up in the bath attached to his private room. As she sat by his bed, watching him sleep, she'd remembered, over and over, how she'd told him about her broken engagement and what had followed.

Had her father's heart attack been her fault?

Her uncle Ham had come by twice, once with Ferg. The two of them had been polite but distant to Susan, almost as if they blamed her, too. It was as if they were quietly piling on the guilt, waiting for her to break and change her mind.

On leaving the hospital for the ranch—a return trip to Georgia being out of the question—Cliff was ordered to rest and ease slowly into his usual routine. As his daughter and the only woman in the house, it was a given that Susan would be his nurse. He was a demanding patient, but at least caring for him helped ease her conscience.

Her mother had called and made excuses for not flying out right away—the heat, her busy schedule, the scarcity of airline tickets, and so on. Only after learning about Susan's broken engagement did she put the household on notice that she'd scheduled the flight and would be there in a few days.

Susan was dreading her visit. Where Vivian Rutledge went, drama followed.

On her father's fourth day home, Susan was tidying the neglected parlor. She was wiping dusty boot prints off the coffee table when the front doorbell rang. She suppressed a groan of dismay. Her mother wasn't due until after four o'clock. It wasn't even noon yet. Had she flown in early?

With the dust cloth still in one hand, Susan hurried to the door and opened it.

Bull Tyler stood on the threshold.

The cloth fell to the floor. A muffled whimper escaped her lips. He looked tall and strong and clean, his eyes even bluer than she remembered. The urge to fling herself into his protecting arms was like a cry inside her.

"What are you doing here?" she whispered.

"I've got business with your uncle." He took in her tired eyes, her gaunt face bare of makeup, and the hair she'd barely had time to finger-comb into a sloppy ponytail.

"Are you all right, Susan?" he asked.

Touching a finger to her lips, she motioned him out onto the porch and closed the door behind them. His gaze flickered to her bare left hand. She saw the question in his eyes.

"I broke my engagement," she said, the words coming in a rush. "When I told my father what I'd done, he had a heart attack—a real one. He's out of the hospital—I'm taking care of him here. And now my mother's coming today. Sorry, everything's been crazy." She glanced past the porch, remembering what Ferg had threatened to do if he saw them together. "We can't talk now. I've got to go in. But you said you came to see Uncle Ham, didn't you?"

"Yes. I phoned. He's expecting me."

"Come on inside. I'll tell him you're here."

He followed her into the parlor, his stride powerful and confident. The young man who'd once copied her table etiquette at dinner had come a long way.

Ham's office was open. When Susan told her uncle that Bull was here to see him, he frowned and nodded. "Send him in."

Susan stepped aside for Bull to enter. The door would be shut behind him. She wouldn't be able to see what was happening between the two enemies.

But no power on earth could keep her from listening.

Ham sat behind his heavy desk. He didn't bother to stand when Bull walked into his office—most certainly a deliberate slight. The head of the Prescott family was aging, Bull thought as he closed the door. Skin hung in pouches below his eyes. Jowls sagged over his jawline.

"You said you had business, Tyler," he growled. "Let's hear it."

"I just have something to show you." Still standing, Bull drew a narrow manila envelope from a pocket inside his leather vest. Unfolding the paper inside, he thrust it close enough for Ham to see. "This is a legally recorded deed to the former McAdoo property on the creek. The old man sold it to me before he died."

Ham's jaw clenched. His eyes bulged as Bull folded the deed again, slid it into the envelope, and replaced it in his vest.

"The property belongs to the Rimrock now," Bull said. "I have the right to water my cattle on that side of the creek, and you have no right to interfere."

Ham found his voice. "Don't think you can get away with this, Tyler. Run your cattle on that land and I'll shoot every last one of 'em."

"Like you shot Cletus McAdoo? I stopped by the place and found him dying. He told me you did it."

Ham's jaw quivered. "If he's dead, you can't prove a damned thing."

"That's what you think. McAdoo wasn't alone when he was shot. There was somebody else in the cabin, a witness who can testify in court that you pulled the trigger."

"Bullcrap! What witness? Who is it?"

"I'm keeping that to myself for now. I'm sure you can understand why."

Ham's face had paled to a sickly shade of gray. "You're lying," he said.

"Am I? You showed up on horseback. When the old man wouldn't let you take over his property, you shot him with a rifle. He made it back inside the shack, and when you sent your men in to finish him, he managed to put up enough of a fight to run them off. Does that sound about right?"

Bull waited while Ham struggled with his answer. He'd thought long and hard before coming to confront his powerful neighbor. He'd decided against reporting the murder to the sheriff. Ham would be more useful as a free man. And given the circumstances, he'd be easier to manage than Ferg, who would take over as the new boss if his father went to prison.

Ham's shoulders sagged. "What do you want?"

"Only what's fair. Just your guarantee that my stock and my men will be left alone to use the water on my side of the creek. And that your people will stay off the Rimrock and quit harassing us. As long as you keep the peace, I'll keep my mouth shut. Deal?"

"That's blackmail!" Ham growled.

"You're damn right it is."

"If you go to the sheriff, you'll be on trial for extortion and obstruction of justice."

"And you'll be on trial for murder. Your choice."

Ham swore, rose to his feet, and extended his hand to seal the bargain. Their handshake wasn't a friendly one. Bull knew what Ham was thinking. He'd been beaten. He was owned body and soul by this upstart son of a family he hated, and he was mad enough to spit bullets.

As for Bull, he might've won this round. But he knew better than to trust the wily, dangerous old man. From now on he'd be watching his back. He was still learning the game, and he was up against a master.

"One more thing." He paused with his hand on the doorknob. "I'm still looking into my father's death. If I find out there's anything you're holding back—"

"There's not a damned thing," Ham said. "I swear it on a stack of Bibles. If I hear any talk, I'll let you know. But your father's been gone more than two years now. It was an accident. Let it go."

"I'll let it go when I know the whole truth." Bull opened the door and stepped out into the hall, almost running into Susan, who'd sprung to one side. Guilt was written all over her pretty face.

Bull closed the door behind him so Ham wouldn't see her. "Eavesdropping, were you?" He raised an eyebrow. "How much did you hear?"

"More than I wanted to. But nothing that I'd care to repeat."

"Good girl. Your uncle wouldn't like it. Neither would I." He headed for the front door. She kept pace with him.

"Bull." Her voice was low but insistent. "You can't go off and leave me without explaining what's behind all this."

"I can, and I will. The less you know, the better." He opened the door and, without breaking stride, walked out onto the porch. "Stay out of this mess, Susan. It's none of your concern."

She followed him outside, closing the door behind them. "It's my concern if it involves people I care about. And I care about you!"

He swung back to face her. "Blast it, Susan, can't you see that I'm trying to protect you? What you heard—it's dangerous."

Tears welled in her eyes as she looked up at him, so determined and yet so fragile. It was all Bull could do to keep from catching her close and kissing her until they both burned with need. "I've got to go," he said. "Promise me you won't mention what you heard, not a word to anybody. We'll talk later."

"When?"

"We'll figure it out." His fingertip traced an imaginary line down her cheek. "Promise."

"I promise, but—" Before she could say any more, a high-powered car, its tires spitting gravel, roared up to the foot of the porch. There was no need for Bull to turn and look. Susan's stricken expression was enough to tell him it was Ferg.

She drew away from Bull as Ferg bolted out of the red Thunderbird, slammed the car door, and charged up the steps. His face was flushed with the heat of anger. "Get in the house, Susan! I told you what would happen if you went near that bastard!"

Susan stood her ground as he loomed over her, but Bull could see that she was trembling. He stepped between them. "Susan isn't wearing your ring anymore, Ferg," he said in a calm voice. "You can't tell her where to go. And she can see anybody she wants to, including me."

Rage glittered in Ferg's eyes. He looked ready to throw a punch. Bull shifted his feet, bracing for a fight. Ferg outweighed him by a good twenty or thirty pounds. But Bull was quicker and toughened by years of hard physical work. If his boyhood friend struck out, he'd have a fair chance of taking him.

"Stop it!" Susan cried. "You're acting like a pair of schoolyard rowdies! I won't have it!" She turned to Bull. "You'd better go. We'll talk later."

"I'm not leaving till I know you'll be all right," Bull said. "And as for you, Ferg, if I hear you've so much as laid a finger on her, you'll answer to me."

Ferg had taken a step back, but his face was still a mask of fury. He laughed, the sound dripping sarcasm. "Listen to the big-man talk, Susan. You probably think he's your knight in shining armor. But I'll tell you a dirty little secret—and I want you looking at him when you hear it." He paused. "Go on. *Look at him!*"

Susan turned toward Bull, eyes wide, lips parted. Bull had no idea what Ferg was going to say. But he should have guessed. It was the thing that would hurt her most.

"Listen, and listen good, sweetheart." Bull's grin was pure malice. "You know that woman you were so upset about, the one I was going out at night to see? Well, Bull's had her, too. He's humped her plenty of times. Go on, ask him to deny it."

Susan stared at Bull as if he'd slapped her face. He watched her expression change from shocked disbelief to hurt, and then to fury. What could he say? That he and Bonnie had meant nothing to each other? That he hadn't been with her in nearly a year?

But the damage had been done. Nothing he could say would make a difference. Helpless to stop her, Bull watched as Susan spun away and fled into the house.

Ferg paused to give Bull a last, triumphant sneer. Then he sauntered in after her and closed the door.

Bull drove back to the ranch in a black mood. He'd expected to be celebrating his victory over Ham Prescott. That part of his visit couldn't have gone better. But after that, Ferg had cut him down without a blow.

Susan was through with him for good; and he'd just begun to realize what she meant to him. She was a flash of golden sweetness in his drab life of worry, stress, and backbreaking work. She was like a sip of fine brandy, a fleeting taste of the quality he could never possess. She had never been his. All the same, her loss left an aching hollow that no ordinary woman could fill.

In those tough, early days on the ranch when everything seemed to be going wrong, Bonnie had been a diversion. They'd had a few laughs and parted friends. End of story. But Susan wouldn't understand that. She was a good woman with traditional values, maybe even a virgin. A man might view a roll in the sack with a willing female as harmless fun. But to a woman like Susan, it would be the ultimate betrayal of her trust—even if it had happened in the past.

At least he wouldn't have to tell her about the buckle bunnies who'd trolled the rodeo grounds and neighboring bars, eager for a hookup with a champion cowboy—and the times when he'd taken advantage.

He pulled the truck into the ranch yard and parked alongside the house. Jasper and Rose were out back, building a coop out of scrap wood and a roll of chicken wire they'd found in the shed. The two dogs lolled nearby in the shade of the house.

Rose waved as he got out of the truck. Bull hadn't made a conscious decision to keep the girl around. But something told him she was here to stay. Over the past few days, she'd proven to be a willing worker, a fair cook, and a good hand with animals. She was earning her keep, Bull told himself. And as an eyewitness to her grandfather's murder, she was his little insurance policy against any interference from Ham Prescott.

A cover had been needed to protect her identity

and explain her presence on the ranch. She'd gladly agreed to pass as Jasper's orphaned niece who'd come from the hill country to stay with him.

Rose had taken the subterfuge to heart. She tagged after her make-believe uncle like a puppy. As for Jasper, he'd begun to smile again. The grieving man and the lonely young girl were forming a genuine bond.

Bull climbed out of the truck and wandered over to join them. "So where are the chickens now?" he asked.

"In the barn," Rose said. "We put them in the tack room. It was the only place with a door. They've stopped laying, but they should start again once they're settled in the coop, with nesting boxes. You'll like the fresh eggs."

Bull studied the unfinished coop. "Are you sure that thing will be strong enough to keep out coyotes? One cackle will be like a dinner bell to those varmints."

"By the time we're done, it'll keep out an army of coyotes," Jasper said. "We're even digging a trench to bury the edge of the wire a foot down, so they can't dig under it."

"And snakes?"

"We're working on that. Aren't we, Rose?"

"Snakes shouldn't be a problem unless the hens have babies," Rose said. "The big chickens can kill any snake small enough to get through the wire. I saw them do it a couple of times back at my grandpa's place. They're tough birds, and smart, not like the ones on those big farms."

Jasper gave Bull a narrow-eyed glance. Bull knew what he was thinking. It was time to get a few things straight between them.

"Rose," Bull said, "it's getting close to lunchtime. Would you mind taking a break to whip us up a batch of sandwiches? I'll help Jasper while you're busy."

"Sure. No problem." She put down the hammer she was holding and hurried through the back door, into the kitchen.

Bull picked up the hammer and used it to pound down a loose nail. "I can tell you've got questions," he said to Jasper. "Go ahead and ask."

"I'm just wondering about that little girl's property. Her granddad didn't leave that parcel to you. He'd have wanted her to have it. So what have you done about that deed?"

Bull sighed. Only Jasper could pin him down like that and get away with it. "I think you know," he said. "Rose can't protect that land. We can. For now, it's part of the Rimrock. We've got access to the creek, and thanks to what Rose saw, we've got Ham over a barrel. He won't dare touch us."

"You owe that girl," Jasper said. "You owe her a lot."

"I know. But I can't pay her for the land. Not yet, at least. But hell, Jasper, what would she do with that parcel? Sell it to the Prescotts? God knows she can't live there alone, especially since the shack's gone. She's what—fourteen? I can give her a home and keep her safe. For now, that's the best I can do."

"Meanwhile, you're using her to control Ham. He could have her killed, Bull. We both know the old bastard's capable of that."

"He doesn't know who she is."

"He could guess. He's not stupid." Jasper shook his head. "I just want the girl to get a fair shake. Lord knows, she's had enough rotten luck in her life, starting out with that mark on her face." He was using iron staples to secure the wire to a post. Taking the hammer from Bull, he pounded one in and reached for another.

"How much has she told you?" Bull asked.

"Enough. Her single mother died of a drug overdose. Rose went into the system. After bouncing from home to home for a couple of years, she lit out and found her grandpa. You pretty much know the rest."

"Good God!" Bull muttered.

"She's as tough as they come," Jasper said. "But the last thing she needs is another raw deal. Her grandpa meant for her to have that land."

"And this ranch can't survive without access to the creek. I'll try to do right by the girl, Jasper, but until I can afford to pay her, I can't risk her getting that land and selling it to somebody else. Right now, the less she knows the better. If she has questions, you tell her to come and talk to me."

"Whatever you say." Jasper's tone made it clear that he didn't agree with Bull's thinking. But Jasper had a soft heart—and soft hearts never kept a ranch running in hard times.

"Something else," Jasper said. "She's expecting justice for the old man's murder. She keeps asking me when the man who killed her grandpa is going to be arrested."

"Does she know Ham's name or who he really is? I sure as hell haven't told her. Have you?"

"I know better than that. If Rose knew Ham was our next-door neighbor, she'd be on her way over there with a shotgun. But I don't know how long we can keep it from her. She's bound to find out."

Bull swore a string of oaths. "We can't turn Ham

over to the law. We need him to keep the peace. If Ferg takes over, there'll be blood. And if the girl comes forward as a witness against his father, her life won't be worth a nickel."

For once Jasper didn't argue. "So what do I tell Rose?"

"Stall her. Tell her the sheriff is looking into it."

"All right." Jasper sighed. "One more thing."

"Lord, what now?"

"I need to go into town and get her some decent clothes. Those rags she's wearin' ain't fit for muckin' out a stable."

"Fine." Bull fished his wallet out of his jeans and handed Jasper a few bills. "You can't take her along, looking like she does. Find out her size and get her a few basics. Once she's cleaned up she can go back— or better yet take her to Lubbock, where she's less apt to be noticed, and let her pick out more clothes there."

"Thanks. I'll go after lunch." Jasper tucked the bills in his pocket. "As long as she's family, she might as well dress the part."

As long as she's family. As he watched Jasper walk away, Bull had the feeling he'd gotten in over his head. Taking in a young girl, especially one who came with so many complications, was something he'd never imagined doing.

Having a warm, caring woman close by would make things easier. But the one woman he had in mind, the only woman he wanted, was far beyond his reach.

The tires of the red Thunderbird spat gravel as Ferg pulled out of the ranch gate and headed for

town. As he drove, he popped the tab on a can of
Budweiser and took a long, cold swig. He needed a
break. One more minute of the craziness in that
house would have pushed him over the edge.

Susan's mother, Vivian, had arrived three days
ago, blowing in like a hurricane and settling in like a
miasma of anxiety and tension. For starters, she'd
declared she wouldn't be leaving until her daughter's engagement was back on. In response, Susan
had made herself scarce. With her mother there and
her father mostly able to do for himself, she'd spent
her time riding or reading behind closed doors.

Ferg's father hadn't been himself, either. Sullen
and withdrawn, Ham had spent most of his time
closeted in his office or roaming alone on the
ranch's three-wheeled ATV. Maybe it was just because Vivian was here. Or maybe it had something to
do with Bull's visit a few days ago. The old man
might even be ill—which wouldn't be all that bad.
Ferg had never been crazy about herding cows and
mending fences. But the idea of taking over as boss
had some appeal.

As he turned onto the highway, Ferg downed the
rest of the beer and tossed the empty can out of the
car. To hell with the family drama he'd left behind.
He was ready for some fun tonight, and he knew exactly the kind of fun he wanted.

It was early yet, the sunset painting blood-red
streaks above the escarpment. Bonnie wouldn't be
off work until after ten. But he could hang out at the
Blue Coyote, have a few drinks, and play some pool
while he waited for her.

Sooner or later, he supposed, Susan would give in
to pressure and agree to be engaged again. Now that
Bull Tyler was out of the picture, she was bound to

come around. This time, when it happened, he would be expected to behave himself. But for now, he was a free man.

The Burger Shack was busy tonight. The high school baseball team had played a rival school that afternoon. The long game had gone extra innings. Most of the fans had left the ballpark hungry.

Bonnie and the high school boy who worked evenings were hustling. Unable to find an empty seat, Ferg stood by the door. A few minutes passed before he caught her eye. She gave him a tired smile as she hurried to a booth with a tray full of food and drinks.

At last she found a free moment to talk to him. He followed her down the hall toward the restrooms. For a moment they were alone.

"So when are you off tonight?" he asked her.

"Ten. But tonight won't work, Ferg. Danny's home."

So much for fun. But Ferg wasn't ready to give up. As far as he knew, Bonnie was the only game in town. "My car's outside," he said. "We could do a quickie when you get a break."

"Does *that* look like a break to you?" She glanced back down the hall to the swarm of customers who crowded the counter.

"I can wait till closing." Ferg didn't like taking no for an answer, especially when he was feeling the itch for a woman.

She shook her head. "Forget it, Ferg. I'll be dead on my feet by closing time. And my husband's waiting at home. You'll have to find your fun someplace else."

Rejection roused his mean streak. "You know, I've always wondered, Bonnie. Does your husband have any idea how you carry on when he's on the road?"

Her gaze hardened. "Let's just say he understands me. And as long as I'm there waiting when he gets home, he doesn't want to know." She stepped closer. "I might as well tell you now. I'm pregnant—it's Danny's baby, and I want it. I'm ready to be a mother. That's why I'm done fooling around with the likes of you. Now, if you'll excuse me, I've got customers to wait on."

She turned and strode away, her shapely haunches ripe and tempting beneath the thin, pink skirt of her uniform.

"*Bitch!*" Ferg muttered as reality sank in. Bonnie was pregnant! *Pregnant!* He knew better than to suspect the baby was his. She'd insisted that he use protection every time. But her husband, easygoing Danny Treadwell, had enjoyed special privileges.

So, no more fun and games with Bonnie. *Damn!*

Now what was he going to do?

He drove down Main Street to the Blue Coyote, where he had a couple of beers and played some pool. But it wasn't how he'd planned to have the evening turn out. He left forty-five minutes later, still in a sour mood. With no place else to go, he took a back road that circled the outskirts of town and eventually joined up with the highway that led to the ranch.

He should've known better. Reverend Samuel Timmons lived on that road, in a sprawling clapboard house with his fruitful wife and eight children, counting the one his firstborn daughter had contributed to the family. That daughter was sitting alone on the front steps, under the porch light, when he drove past. Recognizing his car, she stood and gave him a timid wave.

Ordinarily Ferg would've ignored her and driven

on past. This time he slowed the car and then pulled to a stop on the opposite side of the street. She hesitated. Then, glancing back at the house, she crossed the street and came down the walk.

Ferg lit a cigarette and waited. Edith Timmons wasn't a bad-looking woman, he reflected. With some makeup and the right hairstyle and clothes, she could be passably attractive. As it was, she was too pale and thin for his taste, with dowdy clothes and a shy manner.

Ferg knew she still liked him, and even nourished hopes that he'd come back one day to claim her and their son. Fat chance of that. But tonight he was desperate.

As she came closer, he reached across the seat, unlatched the passenger door, and shoved it open. That would be all the invitation she needed.

"Hi, Ferg." She slid onto the seat and closed the door. She was wearing a shapeless dress, its pale color indistinguishable in the dark.

"Hi." He tossed his cigarette out of the car and started to drive. "How're you doing, Edith?"

"Fine. So is Garn. He's getting big—maybe he'll be a football star like you."

Garn. Lord, how he hated that name.

"I wish he could meet you," she said. "You know, just as a friend."

"Better not to." Ferg pulled into a vacant lot, a half block past the reverend's house. "I've missed you, babe. Come here." He reached across the console between the bucket seats, pulled her against him, and kissed her, long and hard, shoving his tongue into her mouth. He hadn't made it all the way with her since the boy was born. But she'd always been up for their occasional necking sessions.

Maybe this time he'd be able to get her into the backseat. It never took much to get him hard, even with Edith. He was already there.

She moaned as his hand cupped her breast through the thin cotton dress. At least she had decent boobs. And squeezing them always got him going. He plucked at her buttons. "C'mon, babe, give me a feel. . . ."

She squirmed away. "No, Ferg. We mustn't . . ."

He took her hand and placed it over the bulge beneath his jeans. "Just feel that. . . ." he said. "That's what you do to me, babe. If you'd just—"

"I can't, Ferg." She pulled her hand away and reached for the door handle. "I can't do this with you, then go to church and sit there like nothing happened. I've never stopped loving you. But if you want me that way, you can marry me!"

With that, she shoved open the car door, climbed out, and stalked back up the road toward home.

Ferg's fist punched the steering wheel as he watched her go. "I'll marry you when hell freezes over, bitch!" he muttered, starting the car.

Swearing, he pulled out of the lot and roared up the road. In his rearview mirror, he saw the good reverend come out on the porch and shake an angry fist at him.

CHAPTER 11

Susan's mother stirred a teaspoon of sugar into her Jasmine tea and took a cautious sip. "You've been avoiding me, Susan," she said. "I've been here for days and I've hardly seen you."

Susan sighed. She'd come downstairs before the breakfast hour, hoping to grab a quick cup of coffee and disappear for a morning ride. But no such luck. Vivian had never been an early riser, but she'd made an exception this morning.

"We've barely had a chance to talk." Even at this hour, Vivian was put together for the day. Her still-pretty face was made up like a movie star's, her short blond hair freshly dyed and fluffed to perfection. Costumed in a turquoise silk blouse, tan skirt, and a coordinating neck scarf, she was the picture of a gracefully aging Southern belle.

"Sit down, dear." She tapped a manicured finger on the tablecloth. "You're looking peaked. Are you taking care of yourself?"

"I'm fine. Just need some coffee." Susan turned toward the swinging door that connected the dining room to the kitchen.

"You need more than coffee. Sit down." She rang a small brass handbell that stood next to her plate— a bell that Susan hadn't seen in her entire time here. The aging cook stepped through the door and stood at attention as if she'd trained him, which she probably had.

"Ma'am?"

"Get this girl some coffee with cream and some bacon and eggs with wheat toast. Pronto!"

"Yes, ma'am."

He vanished and returned a moment later with a cup of steaming coffee and a small pitcher of cream for Susan, who'd given up on leaving and taken a seat. "Thank you, Joe," she said.

Vivian shook her head as the old man returned to the kitchen. "What have I taught you about thanking servants?" she scolded Susan. "You're supposed to ignore them. They're just doing their jobs."

"Mother, this is Texas," Susan said. "It's good manners to be nice to everybody, even the hired help."

"Well, I taught you better." Vivian spooned more sugar into her tea, tasted it again, and nodded her silent approval. "Your father told me why you broke your engagement."

"Good. Then I won't have to explain it all over again. I can't believe Dad tried to talk me into changing my mind."

Vivian sighed. "You're very young, my dear. When you've experienced more of life, you'll realize that happiness doesn't always come in a perfect package.

Sometimes we have to accept the bad to get the good."

Susan had just finished stirring cream into her coffee. The spoon clattered to the table. "You're agreeing with him? I can't believe this!"

"Think about it, dear. Ferguson is a handsome young man, and he seems bright enough to be a good manager. One day he'll own this ranch. Combine that with what you'll inherit, and the two of you could be extremely wealthy. Think of it—anything you want. You could replace this hovel with a beautiful new home. You could travel, have the best of everything for you and your children—"

"Mother, don't you know what he *did*? Not just in the past, but after we got engaged. I caught him coming in after midnight. He didn't even try to deny that he'd been with a woman."

"He's young, dear. And young men have needs."

"That's what *he* said! And he told me that if I wanted him to stay home, I could take care of those needs myself. That was when I gave his ring back."

Vivian nibbled a slice of the dry toast that the cook had set on the table, frowned, and put it back on the plate. "As I said, Ferguson is young and running on male hormones. Once you're married, and he has you to keep him happy, he'll settle down."

"Did Dad?"

Vivian's expression froze. She took a slow sip of her tea. "Let's just say that I've never been sorry I chose him. He's given me a good life. And he gave me you."

"I see." Susan poked at the overcooked bacon and undercooked eggs on her plate. The last thing she felt like was eating. She understood the life her mother had created—the friends, the parties, the shopping.

But it wasn't the kind of life, or the kind of marriage, she wanted for herself.

"I need to get away from here, Mother," she said. "Take me back to Savannah with you. Take me home."

Vivian looked alarmed, then shook her head. "I don't think that would be a good idea. I have some pressing engagements, and somebody has to stay here to look after your father."

"He could fly with us. Surely he's well enough by now. We could all go home together. And I could spend some time getting ready for school in the fall."

"About school," Vivian said, and Susan's heart sank. "With things so uncertain between you and Ferguson, maybe you should stay here and try to work things out. You could even get married this summer, here in Texas. After all, why should you need to go to college? You'll have plenty of money as it is. And it's not good for a woman to have more education than her husband. It makes him feel inferior, less like a man."

"Mother, you aren't listening." Susan rose from her chair to face her mother. "I don't want to marry Ferg. I don't love him. And I'm pretty sure he doesn't love me. All I want is to go home and go to college."

"Well." Vivian's teacup clattered into its saucer. "You're not doing either unless we give you the money."

"I've got my credit card."

"Which your father pays—or his accountant does. That won't get you very far. As long as we're holding the purse strings, we'll be the ones calling the shots, honey."

"Then I'll leave on my own. I'll get a job. People do things like that all the time."

"Get a job?" Vivian laughed. "What kind of job? Scrubbing floors? Slinging hamburgers? We raised you to be a lady and to marry well. If you're smart and keep your looks, that's all you'll ever need."

"Mother, I don't know what time warp you're living in, but this is the twentieth century. I'm almost nineteen years old, and I don't have to do what you say."

Susan walked out of the dining room, grabbed her hat off the rack, and left through the front door. By the time she'd crossed the yard to the stable, she was fighting tears. She loved her parents. She'd always tried to please them, but marrying Ferg would turn her into her mother—an unhappy woman whose entire life was built on appearances. She wanted something more—something real and meaningful, even if it meant not getting married at all.

The young stable hand had learned to anticipate her morning rides. Her bay mare was saddled and waiting. She mounted up and took the road that wound among the pastures. The morning was still cool. A meadowlark trilled from a fence post. A flock of blackbirds lifted from a willow tree that overhung the creek. A few wispy clouds drifted in a clear sky that would become brutal as the sun rose higher. She wasn't sure where she was going this morning. She only knew that she didn't want to go back and face her parents, or Ferg, for a very long time.

Two days ago, Bull had spent a half day readying the old McAdoo parcel for cattle watering. While Jasper took Rose to Lubbock for more clothes shopping, Bull had taken the two young cowhands in the truck. They'd spent several hot, dirty hours taking down parts of the fence, knocking over what was left of the burned shack and outbuildings, and burying the charred remains of the old man's corpse under a fallen cottonwood, where the cattle wouldn't trample it. One of the boys had improvised a wooden cross and planted it in the loose earth. It wasn't much of a grave, but at least if Rose wanted to visit it, there'd be something to see.

They'd dug a shallow pit to bury whatever wouldn't burn, raked it over, and cleared the creek bank to make room for drinking cattle. Bull had half-expected to see Ham Prescott's hired guns come riding through the trees. He'd strapped on his .44 and stowed the big shotgun behind the seat in the truck, loaded with shells he'd found in the ranch house. But no one had shown up to bother them. So far, Ham was keeping his word.

The next day, when they'd run the cattle to water in batches of two dozen at a time, Bull had been extra wary. Leaving Rose to watch the ranch house, he'd armed Jasper and the boys and brought them along to make sure no Rimrock animals crossed the creek. Again, there'd been no trouble. But Bull couldn't help being nervous. Things were going too well. It wasn't like Ham to give up without a fight.

He'd already started thinking of a safer and more efficient way to use the water. If he could dig and line a catch basin to make a watering tank, or even install a metal one, a safe distance from the creek, he could then dig a ditch to fill it from the creek—or better yet, bury a length of PVC pipe with a hidden head gate next to the creek. For the time it would take to fill the tank, the creek could be diverted, say, at night, when the reduced flow to the Prescott Ranch wouldn't likely be noticed.

Jasper had reacted to the idea with caution. "Ham's

not gonna be too happy if he finds out you're blockin' the creek."

"Ham can't touch us as long as we've got Rose. We've got him over a barrel."

"That's what worries me. Don't underestimate the old buzzard. He didn't live this long by bein' stupid."

Bull had let the matter rest with Jasper. But he was already drawing plans and making estimates on renting a backhoe to dig the tank versus buying a prefabricated metal one.

This morning he would make some phone calls and get some bids. At least it was a start. But the creek water was only a stop-gap solution to a long-term problem. If he was to grow his herd in the seasons ahead, he was going to need an ample source of water and more land—enough water and land to start growing hay for a winter supply.

After a breakfast of ham and scrambled eggs from Rose's hens, he wandered outside. The ranch yard was quiet this morning. Jasper had left early and taken the boys to water the cattle. Rose was cleaning up in the kitchen. There was no sign of the dogs. Maybe they'd gone with Jasper.

"Right pretty day, isn't it?" Rose had come out to stand beside him. She had dressed in her old clothes, after insisting that the jeans and shirts she'd picked out in town were too nice for work. She'd changed into her new clothes only long enough to launder the old ones.

"Gonna get hot," Bull said.

"It's pretty anyway," she replied. "Where's Jasper?"

"He's herding the cows to the creek for a drink."

"My grandpa's creek?"

"Uh-huh." Bull could sense where this was heading. He'd avoided this conversation as long as he could. But there was no getting out of it now.

"Jasper told me my grandpa got buried."

"That's right. We buried him partway under that big fallen tree. One of the boys made a cross for the grave."

"Can I go see it sometime? I'd like to take some flowers."

"Sure." But he'd have to make certain she wasn't seen by the Prescotts, Bull reminded himself. "The house got burned down. But we cleaned the place up nice. The grave looks right peaceful."

The windmill turned slowly in the silence. "That land where the creek is belonged to my grandpa," Rose said. "Who does it belong to now?"

Bull had a ready answer. "It'll be yours when you grow up. But until then we're taking care of it for you, making sure that nobody else comes and takes it over."

"Oh." She sounded a little skeptical, Bull thought. The girl was sharp. Sooner or later there was bound to be a reckoning over that land. But for now, it was legally his, and nothing she could say or do was going to change that.

She might have said more, but just then two large, furry forms came bounding across the yard. The dogs had clearly been on an adventure. They romped closer, ears perked, tongues lolling, coats matted with mud.

"Oh no!" Rose groaned. "They're filthy! And just smell them!"

Even at the distance of a stone's throw, the rank odor was unmistakable. No mystery about where the two rascals had been. They smelled like the mucky swamp at the edge of their neighbors' property a

mile to the south. Judging from the foul aroma, the
happy pair had rolled and played in the fetid mud
and dug up heaven knows what, reveling in the
scents they loved.

"They can't stay like this," Rose said. "Keep them
here while I go for a tub and some soap."

"Maybe we should just shoot them and dig a hole."
Bull was only half joking. Rose shot him a glare over
her shoulder. He sighed and rolled up his sleeves.
He'd probably have to burn his clothes afterward,
but even he couldn't let the girl take on this dirty job
alone.

After calling the dogs over to the outside tap, he
began hosing them down. The well was still flowing,
but every drop was precious. He hated wasting water
on the blasted animals, but something had to be
done.

By the time Rose got back with a bar of soap, a
scrubbing brush, and the old tin washtub, Bull had
rinsed off the worst of the mud. But the dogs still
reeked. They would need a good sudsing and some
time in the sun before the stink was gone.

Tethering one dog to the water pipe, they coaxed
the other into the tub and began working the soap
into its fur. They were just rinsing off the suds,
laughing a little and struggling not to inhale too
deeply, when a rider appeared, coming from the direction of the Prescott Ranch. Bull's heart dropped
as he recognized the bay mare and the slim, erect
figure in the saddle.

It was Susan.

When she'd mounted up that morning, Susan
hadn't planned a visit to the Rimrock. But as she

rode among the pastures and hayfields, emotions churning from the clash with her mother, she'd realized she needed an ally—someone who seemed to see her as she saw herself. She needed Bull Tyler.

But why? What was Bull to her? A friend? But no. Even now, the memory of their torrid kisses stirred dark pools of heat inside her. Bull was not a friend—and not a lover. But he made her feel something she needed to feel again.

Ferg's stinging revelation that Bull had slept with the sexy brunette waitress—which Bull hadn't even bothered to deny—had left her stunned and hurt. Now she found herself wondering why. She had no claim on Bull. If her parents were to be believed, he was only guilty of doing what men do. So why should she care so much? Why did she find herself wanting to march up to the woman and slap her face hard enough to leave an ugly bruise?

Was she in love with him?

She was still wrestling with her emotions when she rode into the yard and saw Bull with a young girl and two large, shaggy dogs, one dog in a washtub. Whatever she'd expected to find, this wasn't it. Maybe she'd come at an awkward time.

She was about to turn the mare and go when Bull looked up and gave her a wave. It was too late to leave. Returning the wave, she rode closer. Now she could see that Bull and the girl were bathing the dogs.

"Do you need any help?" Deciding to be friendly, Susan dismounted, dropped the reins, and walked closer. That was when a nauseating odor stopped her like a wall. "Oh, my heavens!" she murmured.

Bull gave her a grin. He was wet to the skin. His clothes were plastered to his body. His dark hair sparkled with water drops. "You might want to keep your distance," he said. "These blasted dogs had a little too much fun last night. Rolled in some swamp muck. Sorry about the smell."

Susan led her horse into the shade of the barn, looped the reins over a hitching rail, and walked back far enough to keep from being splashed. Was Bull glad to see her? She couldn't be sure. And what was the girl doing here? She looked too young to be anybody's wife or sweetheart. "Are you going to introduce me to your friend?" she asked.

"Sorry," Bull said. "This is Rose. Jasper, my foreman, is her uncle. She's come from the hill country to stay with him and help out. Rose, this is Susan. She's visiting with the neighbors."

"Hi, Rose," Susan said. "Sorry we can't shake hands."

"Hi. I'm pleased to meet you." The girl sounded shy. Even soaking wet and dressed in ragged clothes that looked far too big, she was a pretty little thing. Her long-lashed, hazel eyes were set below striking black brows, her dark-blond hair caught back in a ponytail. Only when she turned away did Susan see the birthmark that spilled like a wine stain down the left border of her face. Even with that, Rose could be a beauty someday, she thought.

Bull and Rose worked together to wash the dog in the tub, Bull holding the big mutt still while Rose soaped and scrubbed its fur. Despite the horrific smell, which Susan was slowly getting used to, they almost seemed to be having fun. Crazy as it was, she found herself wanting to get involved.

"If you need an extra pair of hands, I could man the hose for you," she offered. "That way you wouldn't have to get up to turn it on and off."

"You're sure?" Bull's gaze took in her spotless white linen shirt, freshly washed jeans, and designer boots. "There's no way you won't get wet and smelly."

"It's only clothes. Besides, you two look like you're having way too much fun." Susan picked up the hose and took her place at the faucet. Close up, the mucky odor was even more powerful, but she resolved to ignore it. Somehow, helping Bull wash his dogs felt like exactly what she needed.

The dog in the tub was covered in soap suds. By now the big mutt was getting restless. It began to struggle, trying to climb out of the tub. Bull grabbed it around the neck. "Hose him off!" he shouted at Susan.

Susan turned the hose on full blast, stepped in close, and aimed the spray at the dog. Bull was getting soaked, as well. He was swearing and laughing. Rose was laughing, too.

Wriggling loose from Bull's arms, the dog clambered out of the tub. Susan managed to give the mutt one last blast with the hose before it shook its coat. Smelly water flew in all directions. Dripping wet, Susan collapsed in helpless laughter as the dog raced across the yard.

Rose turned off the tap. "Uh-oh. Now he's going to roll in the dirt," she said.

Bull pulled Susan to her feet. "Let him. With luck the dirt will soak up the rest of the smell and fall off as it dries. Right now we've got one more dog to wash."

The second dog was even more rambunctious than its brother. By the time it was rinsed off and set free, Bull, Rose, and Susan were all soaked and filthy.

Bull turned Rose toward the house. "You get the

first shower, young lady. And throw those clothes in
the trash, shoes and all. They're done for. And you can
add tying the dogs up to your nighttime chores. We
can't have those rascals running off again. Now go!"

"All right. I'm going." Rose scampered toward the
house. Susan stood next to Bull, watching her go.
"There's something about that girl," she said, thinking aloud. "She's not from the hill country, is she?
And I'm betting she's not really Jasper's niece."

Alarm flickered across Bull's face. "What makes
you think that?"

"I met Jasper the night you shot your bull to save
me. As I remember, that drawl of his was thick
enough to butter bread. Rose doesn't talk like that
at all. She sounds as if she's lived somewhere else,
maybe had some education. Why did you lie to me,
Bull?"

He sighed and shook his head. "The truth is we're
protecting the girl. She saw something she shouldn't,
and if the wrong people get wind of it, they'll come
after her. We can't let them find out she's here." His
blue eyes seemed to darken. "That's why I lied. But
now you know the truth. Can I trust you to keep our
secret?"

"Of course." Susan remembered eavesdropping on
Bull's earlier confrontation with Ham. He'd mentioned a witness. Now Rose's presence made sense.
But she wasn't about to bring it up. Bull had been
right. The less she knew, or pretended to know, the
better. "I'd never do anything that might cause harm
to a child," she said.

"Then you're not to say anything about her. Not
even to your family." He paused, as if leaving something unsaid. "If word gets out, Rose could die. I'm
trusting you with her life. Understand?"

"Yes. Your secret is safe with me. Cross my heart." She traced the imaginary X over her chest. Following his glance down, she realized that her wet shirt had molded to her skin. Her nipples jutted like dark nubs beneath the thin, almost transparent, fabric. Heat flooded her face. She *wanted* Bull to look at her, she realized. She wanted him to touch her . . . everywhere.

But wouldn't that just open up a whole new Pandora's box of troubles?

Needing a diversion, she reached for the hose and turned on the water again. "You need a good hosing down," she said, directing a stream at his hair, then moving it down to his clothes.

He laughed as the cold water flowed off him, washing away most of the mud and stench from the dog bath. "Now it's your turn!" he said, grabbing the nozzle and turning the water on her. "You can't go back home smelling like a swamp!"

Go back home. Yes, Susan reminded herself, she would have to show up at the Prescott Ranch like this. She was going to need a good story.

The water was cold, but it felt good to be clean— or at least cleaner. Bull turned off the faucet and dropped the hose. They stood face-to-face, the sun reflecting rainbows in the drops that clung to their hair and skin. Susan looked up into his eyes and saw the hunger—a hunger she felt to the warm, shimmering depths of her body. She was trembling. Her lips moved, releasing a whisper of need.

Without a word, he took her hand and led her into the shadows of the barn. With a little moan of surrender, she flung herself into his arms. He caught her close, molding her body to his as his mouth devoured her with kisses. They clung together, curves and hollows seeking and fitting as if their bodies had been fashioned just for each other.

Desire was a throbbing pulse in Susan's body. She felt him against her, hard through his wet jeans. She wanted what he could give her—and what she sensed she could give him. But no, they both knew it wasn't going to happen. Rose was nearby in the house, and the Rimrock's hired hands could show up at any time.

Cradling her head against the hollow of his throat, Bull held her. He swallowed, finding his voice. "Don't marry Ferg, Susan. Go home. Go to college. Wait for me to make this ranch a place you'll be proud of. It'll happen, I promise. And when it's ready, I'll come for you. I can't ask you to wait, but—"

"But I will wait," she said. "I'll wait as long as I have to."

He kissed her once more, then released her. "You'd better go," he said.

Her mare was tethered nearby. Susan swung into the saddle and rode out into the sunlight. Looking back, she paused. Bull stood framed in the doorway of the barn, his shirt open, his hair damp and rumpled. She filled her sun-dazzled eyes with the image.

"Go," he said.

Susan nudged the mare to a trot. "I love you, Bull," she whispered as she rode away. But she knew he hadn't heard.

The Prescott house showed no sign of life as Susan rode through the ranch gate. Her uncle's big Cadillac was gone from its spot next to the porch.

Ferg's T-bird was in its usual place, but she could see no sign of Ferg, who often slept until midday. With luck, she'd be able to slip into the house unseen, shower, and change before anyone noticed her appearance and started asking questions—questions she could only answer with a lie.

How much longer could she stay in this house with these toxic people? It was as if she was being crushed by the pressure from all sides. She needed to get out. She needed to go home to Georgia, move out of her parents' house, and find an apartment with some roommates.

But leaving here would mean leaving Bull.

The dimly lit stable was quiet except for the familiar sounds of horses drowsing in their stalls. Ordinarily, Susan would have turned her mare over to the stable hand to be rubbed down and put away. But the young man who'd readied her mount that morning was nowhere to be seen.

Never mind, she could take care of the mare herself. After unbuckling the cinch and straps, she lifted off the saddle, removed the pad and the bridle, checked the refilled feeder and water bucket, and let the mare into the stall.

She had stepped outside the stall to find a clean towel when she heard the bolt slide shut on the door and sensed a presence behind her. Turning around, she almost collided with Ferg.

She gasped as his strong hands seized her shoulders. His eyes glittered beneath heavy lids. She could hear him breathing in the stillness, the sound strangely terrifying.

"Let me go, Ferg," she said. "If I scream, somebody's going to hear me."

"Nobody who'd care. Your folks went to Lubbock with my dad. And I gave the stable boy the rest of the day off."

"I said, *let me go!*"

His grip tightened, fingers digging into her flesh. "Not until you tell me where you've been. Or maybe I know. You go out alone and come back smelling like a hog wallow—or maybe a Tyler. What've you got to say for yourself, girl?"

Susan willed herself not to show fear. "You and I aren't engaged anymore. Where I go and what I do is none of your business. You don't own me."

One hand released her shoulder. The palm came up in a resounding slap that blackened her vision for an instant. Stars flashed like midsummer fireworks before her head cleared.

"You're mine, you little bitch!" he snarled. "Your father promised me. We shook hands on it. So you might as well get used to the idea."

Susan knew he could hurt her again, but she had to make a stand. She glared up at him. "My father had no right to make that promise. And I wouldn't marry you if you were the last man on earth!"

The color darkened in his florid face—always a danger sign. "It's Bull Tyler, isn't it? The bastard's put his filthy hands on you, and God knows what else! So help me, I'm going to kill him! But first—"

His arms yanked her against him. His mouth came down on hers in a bruising kiss. "No—" Susan began to struggle. "Stop it! Let me go!"

She fought him, kicking, biting, and twisting, but she was no match for his strength. His hand ripped open her blouse and yanked her jeans off her hips. His weight pushed her down on her back, into the straw. One hand pinned her in place. The other fumbled with his belt. She screamed as he pushed into her, but she knew there would be no rescue. She could only lie sprawled beneath him, struggling as her world exploded in pain, humiliation, and a dark, helpless rage.

CHAPTER 12

SUSAN SCRUBBED HERSELF RAW IN THE SHOWER, SOAP-ing her body again and again. But it was no use. She still felt dirty. She might be able to wash the last trace of Ferg's rape off her skin. But it was embedded like a cancer in her memory. It would haunt her for the rest of her life.

Like a replaying loop, she recalled the moment he'd pulled back and sat up, leaving her bruised, bleeding, and utterly humiliated. "Served you right," he'd said with a contemptuous laugh. "Just so you'll know, I didn't use a rubber. If I got you pregnant, tough luck."

"I'll tell my parents . . ." she'd muttered, her throat hoarse from crying.

"No, you won't, sweetheart." He ran a fingertip down her cheek in a mockery of tenderness. "If you do, I'll tell them it was your fault. You came on to me. You wanted it. And they'll believe me because they want to—because believing you would be . . . *inconvenient* for them."

He was right, Susan conceded as she rubbed herself dry with a towel and put on clean clothes. When such things happened, it was almost always the woman who got blamed. She was asking for it, people would say. If she'd dressed or behaved differently, it would never have happened. Decent women didn't get raped.

So she would say nothing. But she couldn't stay here in Texas, not even if it meant leaving Bull.

Bull. Her heart contracted. She'd wanted him to be her first when the time was right. Now . . . no, she could never tell him what had happened. If he knew, he'd go after Ferg; and Ferg wouldn't fight fair. He would find a way to backstab Bull and hurt him, or even destroy him. Whatever happened, she couldn't involve Bull in this shameful nightmare. She would have to deal with it alone.

She had enough credit on her Master Charge to pay for the flight from Lubbock to Savannah. Getting to the airport would be a challenge. If she asked her parents to take her, they might try to stop her from leaving or, worse, invite Ferg to drive her. Any ranch employee she offered to pay would insist on getting permission from Ham. And involving Bull in any way was out of the question.

There was another option—riskier, but possible to do alone. She would buy her ticket over the phone, then make her escape plan. She had to believe it would work, that she would get home safely and somehow, later, find her way back to Bull.

* * *

Susan waited in her room until she heard Ferg's car heading down the lane, most likely for town. Alone in the house, she called an airline ticket agent from the phone in Ham's office. The earliest flight left at 6:15 that evening. She bought a single, one-way fare and packed her suitcase. The dirty clothes she'd worn that morning were bagged separately. She would toss them in a trash can along the way to the airport, where no one who knew her would ever find them.

Now came the risky part. If her parents, or Ferg, showed up before she left, she'd have a fight on her hands. She might not get away at all.

In Ham's office, she wrote a note and left it open on his desk. The keys to the ranch vehicles hung on hooks inside one of the cabinet doors. By now Susan was familiar with them. She pocketed the spare key to one of the newer pickup trucks and walked outside. Leaving her suitcase next to the porch, she went back to the vehicle shed. The ranch employees knew her. No one questioned her when she took the truck, pulled it around to the front of the house, and loaded her suitcase inside. Minutes later she was headed up the highway.

The note she'd left told her family that she was going home and instructed Ham that his truck could be picked up in long-term parking. The spare key and the parking ticket would be inside.

She didn't have Bull's phone number, or any way to get word to him now. But tonight, at home, she would get his number from information and try to call him. If she couldn't reach him any other way, she would write him a letter.

She was on her way. She could go back to Savannah

and take time to rest and heal while she made plans to move out of her parents' house. She was stronger than what had happened today, Susan told herself— strong enough to put the nightmare behind her and move on with her life.

An unexpected tear trickled down her face. A hidden voice whispered that she was still in denial—that the sick horror of what Ferg had done to her was still sinking in. Well, let it sink. Whatever it took, she would push her way through this and come back to Bull a whole woman, ready to love him.

Everything would be all right, she told herself.

But what would she do if she was pregnant with Ferg's baby?

Bull lay awake, gazing through the open window at the midnight sky. He was tired after a long day's work, but he was wide awake, the night too warm, the bedsheet wrapped around his body from hours of tossing and turning.

Today he had held Susan in his arms and made her a promise—that if she'd wait for him, he would make this ranch a place she could be proud of. It was a promise he meant to keep at any cost. But he was just beginning to realize what he'd taken on.

For the past two years he'd put his money and effort into the barn and other outbuildings, the fences, the watering tanks, and the new windmill. But a quality woman like Susan would need a quality home, and the ranch house was as ugly and dilapidated as it had been on the day he'd first come home from the rodeo.

Williston Tyler had designed and constructed the house for his beloved wife. When she'd died in childbirth, the grieving man had lost all interest in finishing the place. To this day, it remained as he'd left it—the outside covered with cheap "temporary" siding, the windows unframed, the walls bare, the floors little more than rough planks, the kitchen barely functional.

The house was solidly built, with a gray tile roof, a broad front porch, four bedrooms, a dining room, and two baths. But making it as fine as Susan deserved, even if he did all the work himself, would cost more than he dared think about.

He'd be selling off more than half his herd this fall, keeping only the pregnant cows, the immature calves and yearlings, and the two young stud bulls to winter over. There'd be money coming in, but much of it would have to go for wages, feed, equipment, and maintenance on the ranch. There wouldn't be much cash left for the house. To have it ready for Susan by next summer would take a miracle—and Bull refused to believe in miracles unless he could somehow make one of his own.

Nothing was sure in this life. Susan could easily change her mind about him. She could meet a more promising man at college or, God forbid, decide to go ahead and marry Ferg. But he had to believe she would come back to him. Only that belief would give him the resolve to finish the house.

But he couldn't even start without a way to earn more money. He turned over in bed, racking his brain for a plan.

That plan had just dawned on him when the telephone rang.

The phone was in the ranch office. Trailing the tangled sheet, Bull stumbled down the dark hallway.

He hoped to hell it was a wrong number. News that came in the middle of the night tended to be bad.

He grabbed the receiver in midring. "Tyler," he muttered.

"Bull, this is Susan." There was a faint crackle on the line. Her voice was faint, but something in her tone alarmed him.

"Are you all right, Susan? Where are you?"

"I'm . . . fine." He heard the hesitation and sensed that she was anything but fine. "I'm in Savannah, at the house," she said. "I flew home alone. Sorry, I couldn't tell you I was going. I just couldn't stand it there anymore."

"What happened—something Ferg did?" Bull's grip tightened on the receiver.

"It wasn't just Ferg. It was everybody—and everything. So much pressure all around. I had to leave without telling anybody."

"Then I'm glad you got away. But I hope you're planning to come back."

"Of course I am. Isn't that what I promised?"

He faked a laugh. "Just reminding you. The ranch will be waiting, and so will I." Should he tell her about his plan to finance the completion of the house? He hesitated. She was already under enough stress. He could sense it in the pitch of her voice. Something was wrong—something she wasn't ready to share with him.

"My parents will be here in a couple of days," she said. "Don't try to call or write. That could cause trouble for both of us."

"That's fine. This isn't a good time to push anything," he said, realizing he had to tell her regardless. "Just so you know, I'll be going back on the rodeo circuit for the next few weekends."

The catch of her breath told him she was worried. "Do you have to? I'll have nightmares thinking about you up on those bulls."

"The ranch needs the cash. I'll be all right."

"Promise you'll be careful."

"I'm always careful. I just wanted to let you know where I'll be in case you can't get in touch."

"I'd better go," she said.

Bull knew he had to let her. "Stay safe," he said.

"You too."

I love you, Susan. He might have said it, but the phone had gone silent. She had ended the call.

Was she having second thoughts about a man with so little to offer? Susan was young—maybe too young to know her own mind. But he couldn't let himself give in to doubt. She was the only woman he'd ever wanted. Whatever it took, he would make her his.

"You're going to do *what?* Are you out of your dad-blamed mind, Bull Tyler?"

Jasper's reaction, after hearing about Bull's plan to raise money and fix up the house for Susan, was exactly what Bull had expected. He was ready with his reply.

"You heard me, Jasper. I'm going back on the rodeo circuit for the rest of the season. It'll last for about six weeks, but I'll be gone only on weekends. The rest of the time I'll be right here running the ranch."

"Hell, it's not that I'm worried about." Jasper spat a stream of tobacco into the dust. "I can run this place fine. But you were no hot-dog bull rider in the first place—I know because I saw you. Now you're two years older and out of shape. You're going to break every bone in your damn fool body! All for a woman—and not just any woman. She's rich, spoiled, barely grown up, and kin to the Prescotts!"

"Not blood kin. And she's pretty much had it with the Prescott family."

"Have you forgotten how she made you kill Jupiter?"

"She was a kid then. She made a mistake. I can't fault her for that." Bull looked back toward the house. "My dad had big plans for this house. Finished, it could still be a fine place. I figure I can make some rodeo money while the season's on, then work on the house over the winter. When Susan comes back here next summer, I mean to have it ready for her."

"And if she doesn't come back?"

"Well, at least we'll have a house for the next woman who happens along." Bull made light of his answer. But the truth was, if he let himself doubt that Susan would come back to him, he wouldn't be able to sleep nights—let alone have the courage to go back to the rodeo.

"You're a crazy fool, Bull Tyler," Jasper said.

"I know." Bull shrugged. "Come on, let's get breakfast. Then, after I make some phone calls, we can ride out to the creek and you can help me figure out where to lay the pipe and set up that water tank."

The following weekend, Bull drove all night to Shawnee, Oklahoma, and parked behind the stands at the rodeo grounds. After a couple hours of sleep under the camper shell in the bed of his truck, he got up, swigged some coffee out of a Thermos, wolfed down a stale chocolate doughnut, and went back to the area behind the chutes.

He'd registered over the phone, so they already had him in the lineup. All he needed to do was show up at the table, draw his times, and draw his bulls. After that he'd have a few hours to rest, eat, and warm up the muscles that cramped from the long drive. Then it would be showtime.

Not much had changed since what he'd come to think of as the old days. Same sounds and cow shit smells; same flies, smoke, and dust. And at least some of the same people. A few even remembered him.

Most of the bull riders he saw were so young that they barely looked old enough to shave. At twenty-two, Bull felt like a senior citizen among them. He'd bought himself a plug of chewing tobacco. Filthy habit, but it helped steady his nerves. He wasn't out to win glory for himself. Just stay on the damned bull for eight seconds and avoid getting hurt on the way to the ground. That was all he needed to keep the money coming in.

"Hey! Bull Tyler! Is that you?" Bull turned at the sound of his name. Tex Holden, a friend from the old days, was striding toward him, a grin on his freckled face. "Hot damn! Don't tell me you're back. I thought you'd quit bull ridin' for good."

Bull shrugged. "I thought so, too. But I needed some quick cash, and so here I am. How about you?"

"Same here. I got married last year. Bought me a nice little spread outside Abilene and quit the rodeo— for good, I thought. Then we had ourselves a sweet baby girl. Those hospital bills—man, they just don't quit. It's ride the bulls or declare bankruptcy."

"Well, congrats on the baby. And here's wishing us both luck."

"Thanks," Tex said. "I've been on the circuit all

summer. Done okay so far, sendin' money home. But there's always that one bad ride just waitin' to happen. I think about it every time I climb into that damned chute."

"Well, you'd best not think about it too hard. See you around, Tex."

"Yeah. Good to see you, Bull. Maybe we can have a beer tonight, after the rides."

"Sounds good." Bull headed out to check his truck and put his paperwork in the glove box. He was too keyed up to eat lunch, but there was a bar down the block, and he liked the idea of a cold beer. After that he could walk off the stiffness in his joints or maybe find a shady place to park the truck and get a couple more hours of sleep.

The bar was dark and cool, the chilled beer like heaven going down his throat. He sat alone in a booth, nursing his drink. This was his least favorite thing about bull riding—the wait, trying not to think about what could happen in the arena.

"Buy me a beer, cowboy?" The girl who slid across from him looked too young to be legal, but that wasn't his problem.

"Sure." He caught the attention of the waiter, who brought her a Bud Light and a glass. The girl was pretty enough, with dyed black hair and an American flag tattooed on her bare shoulder. Two years ago, before Susan, he might have been interested. Now, not even a spark . . . and hell, she was just a kid.

"So, are you riding this afternoon?" she asked.

"Uh-huh." Bull sipped his beer.

"Bulls?"

"That's right."

She smiled, showing a gap between her front teeth.

"Meet me here after the rodeo, honey. I'll give you a different kind of ride."

Bull sighed. "How old are you?"

"Old enough." Her mouth assumed a childish pout.

"That's what I figured." Bull drained his beer, laid a couple of bills on the table, and left the bar.

He showed up early at the arena and checked his times. He had two rides scheduled in the afternoon. If he placed high enough, he'd be riding again that night for first place. The bulls he'd drawn were new to him. Too bad. Knowing what to expect from an animal could make a big difference. This time he would have to trust his instincts.

To finish in the money, he would have to qualify for the finals. Otherwise, his time and effort here would be wasted.

He checked the rest of the list. He would be riding third. Tex would be riding second, his bull an old acquaintance—the irascible Sidewinder.

The rodeo had already started, but the bull-riding event would be last. Bull buckled on his chaps and spurs and waited with the others, stretching and bending to keep loose, walking off nervous energy. The bulls were in their chutes. He studied the one he'd drawn, remembering what he'd learned from other riders. Nitro, a young animal, was big and full of spunk, but short on experience. Probably not a high scorer. *Just stay on him this first time,* Bull cautioned himself. *Go for the high points later.*

Sidewinder was in the neighboring chute. Bull recognized the brindled hide and the way the huge animal snorted, tossed his blunted horns, and body-slammed the sides of the chute in an effort to get out early. Tex had lucked out, drawing him. Sidewinder was getting old, but he'd been a champion in his day, and his performance in the arena could still rack up points for his rider.

"Hello, you old bastard." Bull spoke softly. "Nice to see you're still around. We'll get together one of these times, and when we do I'll show you who's boss. That's a promise."

Loud cheers from the stands signaled the start of the bull-riding competition. Bull took his old leather glove out of his pocket, slipped it on his left hand, and secured it at the wrist with tape. Then there was nothing to do but wait.

The first rider, a rookie, fell off at five seconds, landing unhurt in the dust of the arena. By the time the safety riders had driven the bull out through the gate, Tex was in the chute, ready to drop onto Sidewinder's back. The big bull was in a foul mood. He exploded out of the gate, bucking and spinning like a tornado. But Tex stayed on him like a champion, riding with style and control. The crowd cheered as the eight-second bell rang. Tex vaulted off his bull after a great ride.

Then something went wrong. As Tex landed, his leg gave way, and he went down. Before the clowns could move in, Sidewinder wheeled and was on him. A gasp went up from the crowd as the huge animal butted the cowboy with the weight of his massive head and hooked him with his blunted horns.

Already in the chute, with no way to get to his friend, Bull could only watch in horror as the clowns drove Sidewinder away and, with the aid of the two mounted safety riders, forced him out of the gate. As Tex lay sprawled in the dust, a team of paramedics rushed out with a stretcher and lifted his inert and battered body onto it. From outside the arena came the wail of an ambulance siren.

On with the show. That was the rule of the rodeo. The loudspeaker was already announcing Tex's score—an outstanding 86 points. And now Bull, still numb with the shock of what he'd seen, heard his own name. Settling his weight on Nitro's back, he gripped the rope handle, raised his right arm, and nodded.

Afterward, he remembered little of the eight-second ride except that he'd stayed on the bull and made it out of the arena on his feet. When he asked, repeatedly, how badly Tex was hurt, the only replies were shrugs and head shakes. Nobody knew.

He made it through the second round, with marks high enough to qualify for the finals that evening, which meant he'd be going home with cash in his pocket. He thought about the house and what the money would mean for his future plans. But when he closed his eyes, he could see only Tex's limp and beaten body lying on the ground.

With time to spare before the final event, he drove to the nearby hospital and found his way to the emergency room. The place was busy, but he finally found a nurse who was willing to talk to him.

"I'm sorry." She shook her head. "We did everything we could, but your friend never regained consciousness. He died on the operating table. We get quite a few cowboys here when the rodeo's on, but we've never lost one before. Were you aware that he was competing with a broken fibula?"

Shaken by the news, Bull managed to recall that the fibula was the thin bone in the lower leg. "God, no," he said. "He looked fine. Had a great ride. Then he jumped off and just went down."

"I can't say for sure, but I'm guessing the leg gave out on him. It should've been in a cast. He had it wrapped with duct tape."

Bull thanked her and made his way back to his truck. How many times had he taped his own broken bones and gone back into the chutes? How many other riders he knew had done the same thing? It was against the rules to ride injured, but desperate men were capable of desperate acts.

He couldn't stand the thought of carrying the tragic news back to the arena. He would keep his mouth shut and let word get around some other way. It would be all he could do to ride in the finals, collect his prize money, then drive back to the ranch. There was no way in hell he'd be able to sleep tonight.

When he got back to the arena, the times and bulls had been drawn. Bull would be riding last—and he'd be riding Sidewinder.

"We can get you a different bull if you want," the official said. "We'd have taken him out of the drawing, but somebody upstairs thinks it would give the crowd a thrill to see him out there again. It's up to you, Tyler."

"I'll take the bastard," Bull said. "And I'll ride him."

Six cowboys had made the finals. Tex would have been one of them. But Bull couldn't let himself think about that now. Nor could he put too much blame on Sidewinder. He was just an animal, following his nature. Tex was more at fault, doing a dismount on his broken leg. But how many times had Bull taken equally foolish chances? Life was nothing but a crapshoot. Some won, some lost. And usually there was no rhyme or reason why.

By the time he climbed into the chute, Bull had cleared his mind. Nothing existed except him, the animal under him, and eight vital seconds. Left hand on the rope; right hand high; knees gripping; spurs digging into Sidewinder's thick, loose hide. A nod, the gate swinging open, the clang of the heavy bell between the bull's thick front legs. Shift and balance. No fear. No emotion. Sidewinder bucked and twisted, putting on a good show. When the bell rang and the crowd erupted in a roar, Bull knew he'd won. What surprised him was, he didn't care.

He rolled to one side and hit the ground on two feet. By the time the clowns rushed in, he was safe.

His score was decent—not as high as Tex's but enough to win. As the crowd poured out of the bleachers, he went back behind the chutes to collect his prize—$5,000, most of it in hundred-dollar bills. The wad of money felt leaden in his hand.

Seeing the grim faces around him, he knew that the riders had gotten word of Tex's death. The man behind the table held out an open shoe box with a few bills in it. "Some of the boys are taking up a collection for Tex's wife and baby," he said. "Anything you'd care to contribute—"

"Oh, what the hell!" Bull tossed the bundle of cash into the box and walked outside into the summer night.

CHAPTER 13

*F*OR THE NEXT THREE WEEKS BULL WORKED HIS RANCH Monday through Friday and spent weekends on the rodeo circuit. He was doing all right, winning cash every time, but never again finishing in first place. It was as if seeing a good man get pounded to death by a bull had taken something out of him. He rode with a cold detachment that kept him in the money, but the passion to make it as a champion rider was gone.

The weekend rides were taking a toll on his body. He was nursing cracked ribs, a wrenched shoulder, and strained muscles that screamed with every move. Ignoring the pain, he would tape whatever could be taped, gulp down a handful of over-the-counter pain pills, and go back to the chutes.

His next event would be in Atlanta—a long drive, but it was a big rodeo, and the prize money was excellent. Unfortunately, so was the competition. Some of the top bull riders in the country would be there. He would be lucky to make the finals.

It hadn't escaped him that he would be within driving distance of Susan. The hunger to hear her voice and hold her in his arms had kept him from sleeping nights. He'd imagined storming her parents' house, kicking down the front door, and carrying her off in his truck. But he knew better than to act on his fantasies. She'd warned him not to contact her. And she hadn't called him since the night she flew home.

Was she all right? Had she abandoned her promise to wait for him? The questions chewed on him day and night. But pride and caution kept him from seeking answers. Whatever happened next would have to be up to her.

Meanwhile, he had a ranch to run.

Jasper tossed a shovel full of dirt out of the wide pit they were digging to hold water for the cattle. "Hell's bells, you didn't tell me this was going to be so much work!" he grumbled.

"We agreed that this was the best option." Bull straightened and massaged his aching shoulder. They'd talked it over and made the decision together. Hiring the backhoe would've been expensive, and the noise would have attracted too much attention from the far side of the creek. The same with having a prefab tank delivered. The safest and cheapest choice had been to dig the tank and the trench for the pipe by hand—at night, when the air was cooler and the work less likely to attract attention.

They'd chosen a low spot near the edge of the old McAdoo property, upstream from the open crossing where they'd been watering the cattle. Willows would screen the spot where the three-inch PVC pipe, now in place, emerged from the bank.

After digging the shallow trench and laying the pipe at an angle to carry water downhill, they'd started on the tank, which they'd planned to line with plastic sheeting. Digging out the mesquite, hauling rocks, and breaking the drought-hardened ground had been exhausting work, even without the beating sun. Bull and Jasper had taken turns with the two young hired hands, digging by night, tending the ranch by day, and, when their strength was spent, sleeping. But now the tank was almost finished. It needed only some leveling and the plastic liner. Then it would be ready to fill with water.

"You know they're gonna find out over there, if they haven't already." Jasper nodded toward the Prescott side of the creek. "Old Ham isn't gonna like it one bit. He'll raise hell any way he can."

"Let him," Bull said. "What we're doing isn't illegal. We've got as much right to the water as the Prescotts have. As long as we have a witness who can pin him to the wall, Ham's agreed not to interfere."

"Maybe." Jasper spat in the loose dirt. "But I wouldn't sell the old son of a bitch short if I was you. And Rose is gettin' anxious. She keeps askin' me when the sheriff is gonna arrest the man who shot her grandpa. If somethin' don't happen soon, she's liable to light out and go lookin' for him herself."

"She still doesn't know who Ham is?"

"Nope. But she's a sharp little cookie, and as tough as a rawhide ribbon. You can't keep her in the dark much longer, Bull."

They were talking in low voices. Only as they paused did Bull hear the rustle of willows from the far side of the creek. As he turned, something large crashed away in the dark, headed back toward the Prescott Ranch. Had it been a cow, a horse . . . or a man?

They waited in the silence that was broken only by the rush of the creek and the chirr of nighttime insects. Nothing. But by now they were both nervous. Bull's pistol was in the truck. He retrieved it and tucked it under his belt. But nothing happened. They finished their night's work and left.

The next morning, after a late breakfast, Ferg climbed into his red Thunderbird and headed for the Rimrock Ranch. He was in a good mood. Over the past weeks, he'd become impatient with his father's refusal to turn him loose on Bull Tyler. Now, while the old man was at the Cattlemen's Association conference in Fort Worth, and planning a three-day hunting trip at a friend's ranch on the way home, Ferg was boss. He planned to make the most of it, starting with a visit to stir things up at the Rimrock.

As he drove he hummed a tune. Last night he'd picked up Edith a block from her father's house, parked on the side of a quiet country lane, and had himself some rip-roaring fun in the backseat. It hadn't taken much time for Edith to come around. The hint that he just might decide to marry her had done the trick. They'd been a regular thing for more than a month. And it didn't hurt that she really liked sex. She'd liked it at fifteen when he'd knocked her up, and she liked it now. She even let him do it without a rubber, some nonsense about birth control being against God's will. Ferg wasn't worried. His father was already paying for Garn. No big deal if it happened again.

Not that he had any intention of marrying Edith. Especially not while there was a chance of getting Susan and her daddy's cotton fields. He'd been disappointed when she'd run home to Georgia. But the woman would come around—especially if he'd managed to get her pregnant. Meanwhile, there was no reason he couldn't have a little fun with the preacher's daughter.

His thoughts shifted as he neared the Tyler place. One of the men had reported some nighttime digging on the property. That could mean only one thing. Someone was planning to steal the water. It was time to make Bull Tyler squirm, and Ferg planned to enjoy every minute of it.

Bull wasn't surprised to see Ferg's red convertible pulling into the yard. He'd expected something like this after last night's suspicious sounds from the far side of the creek. Ham had probably sent him to find out what was going on, which was reasonable. But how much did Ferg know about his father's crime and the agreement not to interfere with the Rimrock? That remained to be seen.

Braced for anything, he came down the porch steps to greet his boyhood friend. Jasper and the boys were off with the cattle. Rose was in the kitchen. Bull was alone and unarmed, but he wasn't worried.

"Morning, Ferg." He crossed the yard toward the Thunderbird.

"Bull." Ferg touched the brim of his hat and climbed out of the car. He wasn't packing. "Nice new windmill you've got there."

"Thanks. Put it up myself."

Ferg glanced at the windmill. "Any water left down there?"

"Not much. A little for the house is about all. Hoping for rain and trying to make it last, like everybody else. What can I do for you?"

Ferg's stance widened, as if bracing for a fight. "You can start with an explanation. We've seen that hole on your side of the creek. We're guessing you want to run water into it."

"That's right. It'll water more cattle at one time, and we won't have to worry so much about them crossing the creek to your side. Better for everybody."

"But you're taking water out of the creek. That's stealing."

"No more stealing than what goes into the cows. We've got as much right to that water as you do. And we'll only be diverting enough to fill the tank. Your ranch won't even miss it."

"But you're upstream from us. What's to stop you from blocking the stream and diverting all the water for yourselves?"

Bull shook his head. "For one thing, we'd have no place for all that water to go, especially since the land beyond our property is open range. For another thing, it would only cause trouble between us and your ranch. We don't want a water war. We just want what we can use."

"Then why do all that digging at night?"

Bull shrugged. "Why not? We don't have to put up with the hot sun or take time away from the cattle. And the moon and stars give us enough light to work. As for diverting the creek, look at your ranch. You divert the water all over the place—to your hay-

fields, to your watering tanks, anywhere you need it.
By the time the stream gets to the end of your property there's no water left. We won't be using a hun-
dredth of that. So go on home, tell your father
exactly what we mean to do, and tell him he's welcome to come see it for himself."

"I'll do just that when he gets back from Fort
Worth next Wednesday. But he's not gonna like it."

Bull had wondered how much Ferg knew about
the murder and the deal Ham had made. Not much,
he concluded—otherwise Ferg would've let something slip by now. And it did make sense that Ham
would protect his son against any involvement in the
crime and its cover-up.

"If Ham doesn't like it, that's his problem. So run
along home now. When he gets back, tell him what I
said." Bull turned toward the porch, hoping Ferg
would leave. But the other man stepped back and
planted himself against the side of his car as if he
meant to stay all morning.

"I got a letter from Susan." The words stung like a
razor slash across Bull's face. "She told me she'd left
because she needed a break. But now that she's had
time to think, she wants to be engaged again. I knew
she'd come around, especially after that hot farewell
in the stable. You can't fake something that real."

Bull could only stare, his emotions too raw to
hide.

"She was unbelievable," Ferg said. "I'd meant to
wait till our wedding night, but she wanted it right
then and there, flat on her back in the straw. She
didn't even want me to wear a rubber—wanted to feel
it skin to skin. I'm tellin' you, man, when a woman
gives you her virginity, it's something to re—"

Bull's fist slammed into Ferg's jaw. Driven by pain

and fury, the punch crunched bone and knocked Ferg back over the hood of the car.

Ferg, a seasoned brawler, recovered fast. In an instant he was up and swinging. His knuckles cracked against Bull's cheekbone. Bull, in his murderous rage, barely felt it. He waded in close, hate driving every blow he landed, bruising and bloodying the man who'd claimed the woman he loved.

They traded punch for fury-driven punch, lunging, hammering. Kicking and head-butting. Bull slugged Ferg's mouth and felt a tooth give way. Ferg caught Bull's eye with a sharp left hook that shot arrows of pain through his head. Bull reeled, caught himself, and charged his enemy again, wanting nothing more than to tear Ferg apart and leave him bleeding in the dust.

A gunshot shattered the air, the sound freezing both men in midmotion. Startled, they turned and stared. Rose stood on the porch, Bull's .44 gripped between her hands.

"Stop it! Both of you!" she shouted. "Break it up, before I'm tempted to shoot lower!"

Ferg staggered back against the car, a smirk on his battered face. "Well, how about that," he said. "Bull's got himself a feisty little live-in honey. Kinda young, but not bad lookin', even with that ugly mark on her face. Wait till I tell Susan!"

Bull checked the impulse to leap for his throat. The fight was over—for now, at least. "She's not my little honey, Ferg," he said. "She's Jasper's niece, who's here to stay with him. So take your dirty mind and get out of here."

Grinning, Ferg picked up his dusty hat, climbed into the red convertible, and drove away. Bull stood looking after him, his gut churning. Was it true?

Could Susan have promised to wait for him, then gone right back to the barn and had sex with Ferg? He didn't want to believe it. But the doubt was there, eating at him and growing—fed by the fact that he hadn't heard from her in weeks.

He loved Susan, but how well did he really know her? Not as well as Ferg did, that was for sure. She and Ferg had shared family. They'd grown up knowing each other. Why wouldn't she decide to marry him instead of some dirt-poor rancher she barely knew?

The question was tearing him apart. But as he turned around and saw Rose on the porch, Bull realized he had even more urgent concerns than Susan.

Ferg had seen Rose. And once Ham got home and heard about the girl at the Tyler place, the wily old man would have little trouble seeing through the fake story and guessing that she was the unknown witness to his crime.

When that happened, not only would Rose's life be in danger but Bull's truce with Ham would be over. Once the girl was out of the way, the Prescotts could—and would—wipe him out.

That afternoon, Jasper showed up, hot and dusty after hours on the range. "You look like hell," he said.

Bull told him what had happened. Jasper shook his head.

"I told you that Rutledge girl was bad news. Sorry you had to learn the hard way."

"It's Rose I'm worried about now," Bull said. "We need to decide what to do."

"You're sure Ferg's been kept in the dark?"

"Pretty sure. If he'd known about his father and the witness, he would've shown some sign of it. Ferg isn't that cool."

"From the looks of things, I'd say neither are

you." Jasper's gaze took in Bull's swollen black eye and bruised face. "You say Ham's out of town till next week?"

"That's what Ferg said. There's always a chance he'll forget to tell his father about Rose, or that Ham won't make the connection. But we can't count on that."

Susan had seen Rose, too, Bull remembered. She'd promised not to tell anybody, but then she'd promised other things, too. He couldn't count her out as a danger.

"We can't count on anything," Jasper said. "We've got to plan for the worst."

"Will you be okay with my going to Atlanta this weekend?"

"And risking your damn neck again? I'll be okay, but will you?"

"The money's good. I could win a pile of cash."

Jasper sighed. "You're the boss. You don't need my permission to make a fool of yourself—especially if you try to see that girl."

"I don't plan to see her. She's in Savannah, and Georgia's a big state. Anyway, I'll be back before Ham gets home. Rose should be all right until then."

"You'd better be sure of that. If I see any sign of danger, I'll take her in the truck and drive her back to Sally's old farm in the hill country. You know, it might not be a bad idea to do it sooner. She'd be safe there. And Sally's folks would be glad to have her."

"We can talk about it when I get back from the rodeo," Bull said.

"We should ask her, at least. All she does around here is work. It can't be much of a life for a young girl."

"Fine," Bull said. "I'll leave it to you. You can ask her anytime. Meanwhile, we need to finish that tank and get the water in it before I leave. Tell the boys to be ready. We'll start after supper, when the sun goes down."

Rose had cooked a big pot of chili with beans and taken part of it out to the bunkhouse for the boys. As an extra treat, she'd made fresh baking soda biscuits that were still warm. She'd turned out to be a pretty fair cook, Bull mused as he filled his bowl. He would miss that if she left. But Jasper was right. She had to be protected, and the Rimrock wouldn't be safe much longer.

"This is a right tasty meal, Rose." Jasper gave her a smile. "We don't thank you often enough for all your hard work—do we, Bull?"

Bull looked up from buttering a biscuit. "We don't. Thanks, Rose. You do a lot around here."

Rose flushed and looked down at the table. Clearly she wasn't used to much attention.

"We were talkin' before supper," Jasper said. "Much as we like having you, this is no life for a young girl—cookin', cleanin', and washin' clothes for a bunch of men, with no woman around to mother you and no friends your own age. I know a farm couple back in the hill country—nicest folks you'll ever meet. Earlier this summer they lost their daughter. I know how lonesome they must be."

"How did they lose their daughter?" Rose asked.

"She drowned. We were plannin' to be married." Emotion roughened Jasper's voice. "That's how I know these folks. They have a little farm, with a nice house. I know they'd be happy to have you stay with them. You could even take your chickens."

"You're sending me away?" Rose's eyes widened. A spoon clattered to the floor as she rose out of her chair. "No! I can't go! I won't!"

Jasper looked pained. "But it would be so much nicer for you, Rose. You could have friends, go to school—"

"No more school! When I went to school, the kids made fun of my face. They said I had a witch mark. So I learned by myself. And my grandpa taught me. He taught me a lot.

"But that isn't why I want to stay here. I promised myself that I wouldn't leave until the man who killed my grandpa was in jail or dead. And nothing's happening! Why can't I talk to the sheriff? I could tell him exactly what I saw and what that man looked like!"

Bull hadn't meant to interfere. But with the girl so frustrated and Jasper slumped in defeat, it was time to step in. Rose was brave and intelligent beyond her years. She deserved some honest answers.

"Sit down, Rose," he said. "Sit down and I'll tell you as much of the truth as I can."

Rose lowered herself to her chair. "Go on," she said.

"I know who shot your grandfather," he said. "I won't give you his name, but I can tell you that he's very rich, very powerful, and very dangerous. If he knew you'd seen him, and that you could testify against him in court, he would likely have you killed. That's why Jasper wants to send you someplace safe—and so do I. Do you understand?"

Rose nodded, but her chin kept its determined thrust. "I understand, and I'll be careful," she said.

"But I'm not going anywhere. Not until that man is locked up or dead. Why won't you tell me his name?"

"Because knowing his name would put you in even more danger."

"Does the sheriff know?" Her sharp gaze narrowed as Bull scrambled for an answer that would satisfy her. *"Does he know?"* She was on her feet again, her hazel eyes blazing fury. "He doesn't, does he? Because you haven't told him! You haven't even told him my grandpa was murdered! You just stuck that old man in the ground and walked away, didn't you? And then the two of you lied to me! Why, Bull? What is all this buying you?"

Bull cleared his throat. "What it's buying me is more than I care to explain," he said. "But don't blame Jasper. He told you what I ordered him to tell you. He's been on your side all along."

"Let me take you away from here, Rose," Jasper said. "We both want you safe. When the man who shot your grandpa is arrested, we'll bring you back to testify."

"But he won't be arrested, will he? Not if I leave. You'll just go right on protecting him. Isn't that what you're doing?"

The girl was prodding too deep and cutting too close.

"That's enough," Bull snapped. "It's already been decided. You're going."

"No," she said. "If you make me, I'll run away on my own. You know I can because I've done it before. If I have to, I'll find the sheriff and tell him everything I know. Believe me, it won't be pretty."

With that, Rose spun away from the table and stalked down the hall to her room. For a long, silent moment the two men stared after her. Then Jasper shook his head and chuckled.

"This isn't funny," Bull said.

"That depends on your point of view," Jasper said. "From here, you look like you just tangled with a wildcat. That little gal has you over a barrel."

"We can't let her go to the sheriff."

"And we sure as hell can't risk getting her killed. What're you thinkin'?"

"As long as she's made up her mind to stay, all we can do is keep an eye on her," Bull said. "She should be safe as long as Ham's out of town. But we mustn't leave her alone. You'd better stay here tonight and make sure she's all right. The boys and I can finish the water tank."

"Suits me," Jasper said. "Somebody needs to keep an eye on the place here. Besides, if I went with you, I'd be worryin' about the girl the whole time."

As the sun sank behind the escarpment, Bull loaded the truck bed with a big roll of plastic sheeting, several packs of tape and some cutting tools. Taking the two young cowboys, Chester and Patrick, with him, he drove out to the tank. Tonight they planned to put down the plastic liner, then fill the tank with water from the creek.

Bull had left the shotgun in the house with Jasper. But he was wearing his holstered .44. Ham had given his word not to interfere, but his son didn't seem to be aware of that. After the fight today, Ferg would be spoiling for mischief. Bull hoped nothing would happen. But if trouble did show up, his first concern had to be the safety of the two unarmed boys.

They parked next to the tank, unloaded the

rolled sheeting, and began the work of putting down a waterproof layer. It wasn't an easy job. The slippery plastic had to be held in place while tape was applied to join the edges. Rocks, which they'd dug out of the hole earlier, were carried back to anchor the sheets at the bottom and around the top. Only after it was done, and the tank filled with water, would they know whether they'd succeeded in making it leakproof.

By the time the tank was finished, the moon had climbed to the peak of the sky. Sweaty and exhausted, they leaned against the truck to rest. "Good job," Bull said. "Now let's run some water down that pipe and see what happens. Chester, grab the flashlight out of the truck. We'll need to see up close. Patrick, you stay down here. Holler when the water starts coming out of the pipe."

With Chester holding the flashlight, Bull crouched next to the creek, raised the makeshift gate, and thrust it sideways against the current to force water into the pipe. Was it working? He bent closer, motioning for more light.

That was when he felt a slight vibration through his thin boot soles and heard, from the far side of the creek, the unmistakable rumbling of a cattle stampede.

"Run, damn it!" he shouted. "Get in the truck!"

Chester dropped the flashlight and bent to pick it up. "Leave it!" Bull grabbed his skinny arm and dragged him along, racing back toward the pickup. They had seconds to make it. If the stampede caught them, they'd be trampled to death by the thundering cattle.

Patrick had already clambered into the cab of the truck. Bull opened the door, shoved Chester inside, and, slamming the door, vaulted into the bed of the pickup. He could hear gunshots as the riders drove the panicked herd toward the creek. It was too late to get away in the truck. By the time they got moving, the cattle would be around them like a flood. They'd have nowhere to go.

Damn, Ferg Prescott! Damn him to hell!

Bracing his legs, Bull stood erect and drew his .44. He had six bullets in the heavy pistol. There was more ammo in the glove box but no way to get to it. He would have to make every shot count.

He cocked the gun and saw the herd burst out of the darkness on the far side of the creek. Pounding through the shallow current, they came on like a wave—two hundred head, at least, moonlight gleaming on their horns and chalk-white faces.

Flowing through the empty tank, they ripped the sheeting with their sharp hooves and poured toward the truck.

Bull took careful aim and fired at the leading steer, the bullet striking squarely between the eyes. The animal dropped just short of the truck. The cattle coming from behind stumbled over its body, jamming together before they separated and veered to the sides. Bull downed two more steers, creating a low barrier that would slow the animals and force them to go around the truck. Three shots. He had three more left.

By now the truck was surrounded by a sea of moving horns and bodies. Protected only by the metal sides of the truck bed, Bull braced for balance while they surged around him, rocking the pickup as they rammed and shoved in mindless terror.

Two more shots downed a huge steer before it could crash into the truck. One bullet left.

Beyond the truck, the herd crashed through the fence that marked the property line and fanned out over the scrubby open rangeland, where they would tire, stop, and be rounded up the next morning.

Now, finally, the stampede was thinning. As the last trailing steers raced past, Bull saw three riders emerge from the darkness. The man in the lead, mounted on a tall buckskin, rode toward the truck. Even at a distance, in the night, there was no mistaking Ferg.

Bull gripped his pistol, rage heating his blood. He had one bullet left—and if he could use it to kill one man in the world, that man would be Ferg Prescott.

His finger tightened on the trigger as Ferg rode up to the truck, reared the horse like the Lone Ranger, flashed Bull a triumphant smirk, and galloped away.

Bull lowered the pistol. Only the thought of going to prison for murder had kept him from firing the gun. Much as he hated the idea of retreat, there was nothing to do but drive away and take the boys back to the ranch. He would leave the water project until he could confront Ham and demand that Ferg be kept away from the property.

This weekend he would drive to Atlanta and do his best to win some desperately needed cash for the ranch. If Ferg was telling the truth about Susan, there'd be no need to fix up the house for her. But there were plenty of other places for the money to go.

Susan.

If she'd really gone back to Ferg, it was all over. He would never trust a woman again.

CHAPTER 14

"*B*UT WHY ON EARTH WOULD YOU WANT TO GET A job, dear?" Sitting in the shade of a blooming oleander, Susan's mother stirred an extra spoonful of sugar into her iced sweet tea. "You certainly don't need the money. Besides, you'll be in school. You won't have time to work—especially if you join a sorority. You *are* going through rush, aren't you?"

"I don't know. I haven't decided." At least living in a sorority house would get her out from under her parents' roof. But even thinking about it all—the social pressure, the parties, the snootiness, the silly songs and rituals—made Susan want to squirm. Maybe she was afraid that a sorority would turn her into her mother.

"I was a Chi Omega, you know," Vivian said. "They were lovely girls. I'm sure they'd be glad to have you. But you wouldn't have to move. You could live at home with us until next summer when you marry Ferguson."

Susan sighed, gazing across the blue-green expanse of the swimming pool to where her father, who was making a good recovery, was practicing his golf swing. Her parents had refused to hear her protests that she would rather go to prison than marry Ferg Prescott. She was young and didn't know her own mind, they'd insisted. But sooner or later she would come to her senses.

She knew better than to tell them about the rape. They would only shame her and redouble the pressure on her to marry and make things right. They wanted a secure life for their daughter. But mostly they wanted the Prescott Ranch in the family. For that, they'd be willing to overlook a few sins.

Last week, when she'd learned she wasn't pregnant, Susan had wept with relief. The worst part of her nightmare hadn't come to pass. But the helpless violation she'd experienced under Ferg's pumping, sweating body would be seared into her memory forever.

Through all this, she had never stopped wanting Bull. But if she was pregnant that would be the end for them. She couldn't even risk trying to contact him until she knew for sure.

Now that the worry was gone, the longing to see him, or at least hear his voice, was becoming more urgent with every day. She needed him to anchor her to the earth, to hold her until the pain of awful memories eased. She needed to know they were still there for each other.

She knew he was coming to Atlanta—all it had taken was a few phone calls to find out he was scheduled to ride. She had her own car, and she could always tell her parents she was going with friends.

She could get there, all right. But what then?

What if he'd given up on her, or simply lost interest?

What would she do if Bull turned his back on her and walked away?

Bull gazed past the chutes into what he could see of the huge arena. This was the big-time—the big crowds, the top cowboys, and the big money. He didn't have the talent to be here. He was too big, too slow, and too far out of shape. All he had going for him was grit and determination. But somehow, one miserable, bone-jarring ride at a time, he had made it.

By the skin of his teeth—and thanks to the bad luck of some younger riders—he'd qualified for the final round. But his two afternoon rides had been rough. The bulls here were champion buckers who could rack up spectacular points. But his body had taken a terrible pounding on both of them. He'd managed to hang on, though not with the style and control of the top riders who'd devoted all their time to the sport.

Going into the finals tonight, he had taped ribs, a strained back, and an old shoulder injury that was acting up. But he'd resisted the pain pills because he wanted to stay sharp. Two more rides remained if he could stay on. There'd be just one if he took a tumble. Either way, he'd be done for the season—and for good if he had any sense.

His next bull was ready. Geronimo, a burly black-and-white hulk, was banging the sides of the chute and tossing his massive blunted horns. Not a good sign. But for the few cowboys who'd managed to ride him, he'd racked up some impressive scores.

After securing his Stetson on his head, Bull strad-
dled the top rails of the chute and, with the help of
another rider, pulled his rope tight. Hearing his
name, and Geronimo's, on the loudspeaker, he took
a breath, dropped onto the broad back, and gripped
the rope handle with his gloved left hand. As Geronimo tried to smash his leg against the chute rails,
Bull gave the nod. The gate sprang open, and the
monster bull exploded into the arena.

Susan watched from the stands, her heart in her
throat. Because she'd arrived too late for the semifi-
nals, this would be the first time she'd seen Bull ride.

The black-and-white bull, a huge beast, bucked
and twisted, the heavy bell clanging below his chest.
Bull kept his grip on the rope, his right arm high
and clear. He was looking good. Then one powerful,
spinning jump tossed his body up and to the side.
Clinging to the rope, he hung on. But he was taking
terrible punishment. How long could eight seconds
last? Watching with clenched fists, Susan just wanted
the hellish ride to be over.

And then it was. Just before the eight-second
buzzer, Geronimo changed direction in midair.
Caught off balance, Bull lost his grip, flew off, and
landed rolling. As he struggled to his hands and
knees, the huge animal wheeled, hooked him with a
horn, and tossed him into the air. As the clowns
rushed in, Bull hit the dirt with a crunch and lay
facedown. A moan went up from the crowd.

While Geronimo was driven off to the pens, two
paramedics rushed in with a stretcher. Supporting
Bull's body, they eased him onto it and carried him
out of the arena. Susan realized she was sobbing.

What she'd seen that monster do could have killed any man, even Bull.

What if she'd lost him?

On her feet now, she shoved her way to the stairs and rushed down into the corridor under the stands. The fifteen minutes it took to find her way through a maze of people, animals, and equipment to the far side of the arena, praying all the way, seemed like an eternity.

When she finally spotted Bull through the crowd, he was sitting on a bale of hay, drinking from a bottle of Gatorade while a medic finished checking his vitals. He'd taken a terrible beating, and looked it. His shirtless body was bruised and battered, but he was alive. Right now, nothing else mattered.

"Susan!" He got to his feet. "What the hell—"

Her legs could barely hold her. She stumbled toward him and would have flung herself into his arms, but something in his eyes—something cold—stopped her like a wall. She hesitated.

"Are you all right?" she asked, sensing the awkwardness between them.

"I'm fine. Big bastard knocked the wind out of me, that's all." He scowled down at her. "What are you doing here, Susan?"

"I came to see you ride—to see *you!*"

"Did you?" His voice was flat with sarcasm. His gaze flickered to her bare finger. "What about Ferg? He told me you two were getting back together. And that wasn't all he told me."

"What did he—? Oh, Lord . . ." Susan went weak as the realization hit her. Ferg had told Bull his version of what had happened. And Bull had no reason to disbelieve it.

"Ferg lied!" she said. "It isn't true!"

Bull's expression didn't change. "So why haven't you called, or even written? What was I supposed to think?"

"We need to talk. Can we go somewhere?" Telling him the truth—everything—would be as hard as anything she'd ever done, but it was her only hope of moving past this painful time.

The medic had finished. Bull glanced around as he buttoned his shirt. "I'm done here. I'll take you to dinner if you'll settle for a burger and fries. I'm not dressed for anyplace fancy."

"That's fine, as long as it's someplace quiet. We can take my car."

Bull had told her he was all right, but he limped as they found an exit to the parking lot. Knowing Bull, he was hurting a lot more than he'd let on.

The sporty silver Mustang her parents had given her for her sixteenth birthday had been valet parked. The attendant took only a few minutes to bring it.

"I take it you know where we're going," she said. "Do you feel up to driving?"

"Sure. I've always wanted to try one of these little critters." Bull held the passenger door for Susan, then eased his body into the driver's side and slid the seat back as far as it would go. He was cool and polite, but as he drove, Susan sensed that he was holding back. He was far from ready to trust her again.

They drove to a quiet-looking roadhouse that served drinks and food. Bull had never been there, but he'd heard it was good. He parked the car, bit-

ing back pain as he climbed out. Inside, he ushered
Susan to a corner booth. The place was quiet, the
country music little more than a low, throbbing beat
in the background.

Excusing himself, he used the restroom to wash
off the worst of the dust and bull smell. The face he
saw in the mirror looked like a prizefighter's after
ten rounds in the ring. But the older bruises were
from the fight with Ferg—the fight over Susan.

He knew better than to pass judgment on her until
he'd heard her side of the story. But this woman had
left him with wounded pride and a broken heart.
Deeply as he ached to believe and forgive her, he
wasn't fool enough to let her hurt him again.

He returned to find her waiting with two cold
Bud Lights on the table. "I went ahead and ordered," she said. "I knew you wouldn't mind. Our
hamburgers and fries will be out in a few minutes."

"Thanks." He took a seat where he could face her.
The ice-cold beer glided down his dusty throat. She
sat looking at him, her eyes soft in the shadows. He
saw the glimmer of a tear.

"Oh, Bull," she whispered.

"Tell me," he said.

"I don't know where to begin."

"I'll help you." He still felt that angry edge. "Ferg
told me that you and he had a hot time in the stable.
Is that true?"

She shook her head. "Ferg . . . raped me, Bull. I
fought and cried and screamed, but he just went
ahead and . . ." Her voice broke.

Bull willed himself to ignore the rage welling inside him. Women had been known to lie about such
things. He couldn't allow himself to feel anything

until he knew she was telling the truth. But the need to believe and love her was winning the battle against doubt.

"Afterward he laughed and said maybe he'd gotten me pregnant. That was why I left, and why I didn't write or call you after that one time. I was afraid it might've happened. And I knew that if it had, we were finished. I couldn't contact you until I knew for sure."

"And you're all right now?"

She nodded, her lips pressed together hard.

"Lord, why didn't you tell me, Susan?"

"How could I? I didn't know what you'd think, or what you'd do. I still don't."

"What would you have done if you'd been pregnant? Married Ferg? Or maybe risked your life with some back-alley abortionist?"

She shook her head, tears glimmering in her eyes. "I don't know. None of the choices were good. I only knew that I couldn't make this your problem, too."

"What about now? Since you're not pregnant, what comes next?"

"I'm here."

The last of Bull's resistance crumbled as his eyes met hers. When he thought about how this precious, innocent woman had been hurt, part of him wanted to find Ferg and kill him with his bare hands. But the emotion that surged inside him now was pure protective love. She was his. Nothing on earth could change that. And nothing would keep him from claiming her.

He reached across the table and covered her hand with his. "I wish you'd told me, Susan," he said, meaning it. "Either way, I would have been there for you. I'm sorry I wasn't."

"I should have known that," she said.

"You know it now."

She glanced toward the kitchen. "You know, I don't feel hungry anymore. How about you?"

"I could pass on the burger. What have you got in mind?"

A faint but knowing smile teased her lips. "I have a room in a nice hotel," she said. "We can get there sooner if you let me drive."

Leaving cash on the table, Bull rose and followed her out to her car.

Susan's hand trembled as she thrust the room key into the lock. She'd driven to Atlanta, knowing that she wanted Bull to make love to her. Earlier, when he'd greeted her so coldly, she'd feared it wasn't going to happen. Now that it was almost a certainty, doubts and worries swirled in her mind.

What if Bull was put off by the thought that Ferg had been with her first? Worse, what if he didn't believe it had been rape at all?

Or what if the memory of Ferg, along with the shame and disgust she'd tried so hard to bury, burst to the surface and she froze or panicked?

Never mind, she wanted this. She wanted *him*. And she couldn't let her fears keep her from the man she loved.

Bull reached past her and opened the door. The room was dark except for a single lamp, glowing faintly, on the nightstand next to the king-sized bed. She had left the bed turned down.

Closing the door behind them, he turned and gathered her into his arms. He held her gently at first, kissing her with tenderness as if he knew, perhaps, that they'd both been wounded and needed to heal. Then the kisses deepened—tasting, nibbling, licking kisses that made Susan's pulse race. Her body responded with throbbing urges that shimmered upward from the place where she wanted him to be. She released a slow breath. She was going to be all right. But was he?

Pulling back a little, she gazed up at his battered face. He looked as if he'd run a gauntlet. But she would ask him about that later. Right now the only thing that mattered was giving herself to him.

"Make love to me, Bull," she murmured.

"Now?" He gave a low chuckle. "I smell like I've rolled in a corral. I could use a shower first."

Willing herself to be bold, she gripped his belt buckle and pulled him against her. "Now," she said.

With a raw laugh, he bent and kissed her again. This time his lips were rough and seeking. She felt the scrape of the stubble on his jaw and tasted the beer he'd drunk and the tobacco he'd gone back to using for the rodeo. The smells of the arena swam in her senses, strangely arousing. He was all man—her man.

He winced as she wrapped her arms around him. Her fingers felt his taped ribs through his shirt. "Oh—" She stepped back with a gasp. "Will you be all right to—?"

"We'll manage fine." He grinned. "But you'll need to do the riding."

He got out of his clothes. Lamplight sculpted a muscular body that was battered and scarred like a gladiator's. He lowered himself to the bed, easing onto his back and stretching out full length. Susan had looked away briefly to toss her clothes on a chair. When she turned toward the bed, she saw that he was fully erect and had managed to add protection. A shiver of anticipation passed through her. He was stunning, and she wanted him. But the next move would be up to her. What if she didn't know what to do?

"Just let me look at you," he said. "Do you have any idea how beautiful you are, Susan—and how much I've wanted you?"

Susan felt her skin warm as he filled his gaze with her. He was holding back, giving her time, she realized. And she knew why. He was letting her take control, giving her a chance to set the pace and back off if she became uncomfortable. He wanted this, their first time together, to be the furthest possible thing from the awful rape that was locked in her memory.

She loved him for that.

Leaning over the bed, she kissed him—letting her lips feather over his, then deepening the contact. As her tongue brushed along the sensitive inner surface of his lower lip, she felt his breath quicken. She could sense the strain as he willed himself to lie still.

She nibbled a trail down his throat, tasting the salt on his skin. Her heart was racing. She knew she could stop anytime and he would understand. But she didn't want to. All she wanted was Bull, loving her.

Reaching down, her hand closed around his big, hard shaft. He gave a low moan as she stroked him. She loved the baby softness of his skin there, but the sharp catch of his breath told her she was pushing him to his limit.

She could feel the pulsing of her own need, the slickness of moisture between her thighs. She'd expected to be fearful, or at least hesitant, but all she could think of was how much she wanted to be his.

Straddling his hips, she found the center of her slickness and lowered herself down the length of his jutting sex. As he filled her, it was as if she could feel his heat all the way upward through her body. Heaven.

Instinctively, she began to move. He responded with a groan. His hands came into play, clasping her hips as he drove into her, thrusting deeper and deeper. Shimmering bursts ignited inside her as she came, clenching around him in a climax that left her gasping.

"Don't stop," he urged, thrusting again. She matched her motion to his. This time she rode a rocket into the stars, reeling as his release mounted. He came with her, exploding with a groan, followed by a long outward breath and a low chuckle of satisfaction.

Susan sagged over him. Tears of relief and gratitude welled as she leaned forward and brushed a kiss across his smiling lips.

Ferg's rape had left her broken. Bull's loving had made her whole again.

As dawn crept through the curtains, Bull woke to find Susan curled against him, still asleep. He lay still, savoring her sweet warmth and the memory of last night—how they'd made love, showered together, made love again, and then lay talking and snuggling until they drifted into slumber.

Now their night was ending. They would wake up, get ready for the day, and go their separate ways. Susan would go home and prepare to start college. Bull would go back to the Rimrock and build it into a place where his lady would be proud to live. They would keep their relationship a secret for now. But they'd keep in touch and manage to see each other when they could. In a year, or however long it took them to be ready, they would marry and start their lives together.

It was a sensible plan, Bull told himself. Maybe too damned sensible. But whatever it took, he wanted to do right by his woman.

Thinking of the long day ahead, he leaned over and kissed the tip of her nose. "Wake up, sunshine," he said. "Time to get moving."

"Mmm?" She made a little muzzy sound. "Get moving where?"

"You back to Savannah to become a college girl. Me to pick up a few bucks' worth of rodeo money and head for Texas, to turn the Rimrock into a showplace for you."

"Not yet," she murmured, her arms sliding around his neck. "It's early. We've got a little time, haven't we?"

He kissed her and felt the warm pulse of early morning desire. Yes, they had a little time. Just enough.

It was nearly dawn of the next day when Bull drove the pickup into the ranch yard and pulled up to the house. After more than twenty hours behind the wheel, he was red-eyed, sore, and overdosed on caffeine and chocolate doughnuts. By now the interlude with Susan seemed like the memory of a dream. Bleak reality was the dilapidated ranch house, the drought, the livestock, the lack of money, and dealing with the Prescotts.

Jasper was on the porch drinking coffee, the dogs at his feet. He lowered his cup and came down the steps as Bull hauled himself out of the truck. "So how was Atlanta?"

"Not great. I'll tell you later." He knew better than to mention Susan. "Got any more of that coffee?"

"There's fresh coffee in the kitchen, and Rose is rustlin' up some ham and eggs. But you look like you could use a few hours of sleep."

Bull shrugged. "Forget sleep. You can catch me up on things over breakfast. Is Ham back home yet?"

"Not that I've heard. And Ferg hasn't come around, either. Maybe he figures he's already done enough damage."

Jasper didn't know the half of it, Bull thought. Sooner or later he would settle with Ferg—and he wouldn't go easy on the bastard. "What's the water tank looking like?" he asked, though he pretty much knew what to expect.

"Like a grave for the steers you shot. Even the pipe's tore up and broke. We took our stock in to water 'em at the creek like usual. Nobody gave us any trouble then. But there's nothin' left of that tank but a godawful mess. Damn Ferg Prescott—but never mind, come on in and eat. We got somethin' to show you. Somethin' Rose found."

Bull trailed Jasper into the kitchen. Rose was tending the electric stove. She gave Bull a quick, impersonal greeting, then went back to scrambling the eggs with a fork, adding a sprinkle of grated cheddar. She hadn't forgiven him, Bull surmised. But at least the girl hadn't run away.

"Sit down, I'll get you some coffee." Jasper filled a mug and set it at Bull's place. Bull took a sip. It was hot and strong enough to jar his senses fully awake.

"So what is it you've got to show me?" he asked.

"Hang on, I'll get it." Jasper strode down the hall

to the office and came back holding a dusty Muriel Cigars box, bound with a rubber band. "Rose found this under your dad's old bed when she was settin' a mousetrap. Here." He set the box on the table. "Take a look inside."

Bull peeled off the rubber band and lifted the lid. Inside was a clumsily folded, dirt-smudged sheet of business stock paper. Unfolding it, he stared. His pulse slammed. "Is this what I think it is?"

"If you think it's the deed to some property, I'd say we have the same idea. You know, your dad played a lot of poker. And he was pretty good at winnin'. That's how he got old Jupiter, our prize bull that you had to shoot because of some damn fool girl."

"Don't remind me," Bull said. "So what do you know about this piece of paper?"

"Not much. We only just found it a couple days ago. But seein' the name on it—Sam Perkins, who signed it over to your dad—got me thinkin' about something that happened a few years ago. I remember Williston came home from a game about three in the morning. The next day, Sam was out here, poundin' on the door, claimin' that Williston had got him drunk and cheated him out of the deed he'd put on the table. He wanted the deed back.

"Williston said he'd done no such thing, that he didn't have the deed, and that Sam had probably been too drunk to remember what had happened to it. Sam went stormin' off and we never heard anything else. He died just a few months after your dad did."

Bull shook his head. "So my dad cheated at poker and stole the deed! Lord, I didn't know the old scoundrel had it in him!"

"I'm guessing that's what happened," Jasper said. "Williston couldn't record the deed and claim the property because then Sam would know what he'd done. So he just hid it—maybe even forgot about it toward the end, when he was so sick."

Bull studied the deed. It looked authentic. And the property could be valuable. Why else would his father have cheated a friend to get it?

"All I see here is the legal description," he said. "It's nothing but letters and numbers. Do you have any idea where this property is?"

"Not a clue. You'll have to take it to the county recorder's office."

"I'll do that today, as soon as they open."

"First you'd better get some breakfast in your belly and some decent sleep, or you're liable to roll your truck in the bar ditch." Jasper slid a plate of bacon and eggs in front of Bull. "That deed's waited this long. It can wait a little longer."

At ten o'clock, shaved, showered, and barely rested, Bull was waiting when the recorder's office opened. The clerk on duty, a young man, was new and didn't seem to know him—all to the good.

"I want to register this deed to the Rimrock Ranch," he said. "But first, can you show me where the property is?"

"You don't know?" The young man stared at Bull from behind his horn-rimmed spectacles.

"This deed was with my late father's papers," Bull said. "It's all the information I have."

"Oh." The young man turned to the large map that was mounted on the wall. "Here's the parcel matching the legal description. It's here—west of the Rimrock Ranch, on the caprock above the escarpment. You're looking at about a hundred sixty acres. See?"

"You're sure?" Bull's pulse rocketed. The parcel wasn't huge, but caprock land was precious for one reason—the water-bearing rock under the flat plain. Sink a well and there'd be plenty of water for cattle, hay, or anything else.

"How would I get up there to see it?" he asked.

"There's a gravel road here." The clerk traced a line on the map. "It's a roundabout way, but it's the only way there is. I can mail you the deed when it's been recorded."

"Thanks, but I'll wait here for it," Bull said. "In case there's a question, I want evidence in hand that the land belongs to the Rimrock."

The clerk sighed. "Fine. Take a seat. It'll be about twenty minutes."

Bull waited in a folding metal chair, his thoughts racing. Now he could understand why Williston Tyler had cheated his friend to get the deed. If the land was everything he hoped for, it could mean the difference between success and failure for the Rimrock.

But what if all this was too good to be true?

If finding the deed was such a godsend, why did he have the feeling his troubles were just beginning?

CHAPTER 15

WITH THE RECORDED DEED IN HIS VEST, BULL FOL-
lowed the narrow, graveled road he'd seen on the
wall map and copied on a sheet of paper. It led him
up a broad canyon, to where it ascended the escarpment in a series of switchbacks with sharp hairpin
turns. He had no memory of such a road being
there when he was younger. It must have been built
during the years he was away from the ranch.

As he drove, his head swarmed with plans. If the
land was good for grazing—and he had high hopes
it would be—he could move the cattle up there until
fall, when much of the herd would be sold off. The
remaining animals could be brought down to winter
pasture close to the heart of the ranch.

For now, at least, stock and horses would need to
be trailered back and forth—a challenge on the narrow, winding road, but it could be done, especially with
the right kind of trailer. There was plenty of under-
ground water on the caprock, but if there were no

wells on the property, he'd need to get some drilled.
He could be looking at a lot of expense—at least as
much as he'd made on the rodeo circuit this summer. But this land could save the Rimrock. The
money he'd planned for the house, if needed here,
would have to be spent.

The road led up over the edge of the caprock and
joined with a paved two-lane highway. Bull glanced
at his map, made a left turn and headed south.
Here, for as far as the eye could see, the land was as
flat as a tabletop, the fields and farms green, irrigated with well water from the aquifer below.

According to the directions, the turnoff to the
property was seven miles down the road. Since the
parcel of land was bounded on the east by the edge
of the caprock, it shouldn't be hard to miss.

It wasn't hard at all. In fact, Bull knew the land the
minute he saw it. In a sea of cultivated green fields, it
was yellow, dry, and weedy. A length of rusty barbed
wire served as a gate. Clearly, the place hadn't been
worked since Sam Perkins had lost it to Williston in
that fateful poker game.

Bull got out of his truck to unfasten the wire from
the post that held it. Only then did he see—in the
distance—a log cabin with smoke rising from the
chimney. A small windmill turned on its wooden
tower.

Somebody was living on his property.

His .44 was in its holster, under the driver's seat.
He hoped to hell he wouldn't need it, but just in
case he took it out and laid it within easy reach. Cautiously now, he drove toward the cabin.

As he came closer, he could see a couple of old
cars, a small camping trailer, and somebody in the
yard chopping wood. A woman in a long skirt had

seen the truck. She pointed and must've called out because two more people, a man and a woman, came running outside. No weapons in sight, and nobody was trying to flee or hide. So far so good, but Bull knew enough to be wary.

He stopped the truck fifty feet from the cabin. The man who'd been chopping wood was coming out to meet him—lanky, and bearded, his long, stringy brown hair bound by a band across his forehead. He wore flowing green pants, a Mexican serape vest, and strings of beads around his neck. As he approached the truck he raised his right hand in a two-fingered peace sign.

Hippies, Bull concluded. Most of the ones he'd met seemed harmless enough, but Bull knew he couldn't be too careful. If things went bad, he'd be outnumbered here.

Slipping the gun into the back of his belt, he stepped down from the truck and waited for the bearded man to speak.

"Peace, brother. What can we do for you?"

"I'm the new owner of this property," Bull said. "I've got the paperwork, if you need proof. How long have you folks been living here?"

The man scratched his belly through the opening in his vest. "Going on three years. We thought the place was abandoned, so we fixed up the little shack that was here and moved in with our wives. My brother and I hire out to work in the towns around here—we're carpenters and general handymen." His speech, educated and articulate, belied his scruffy appearance. "We've never had trouble here. We don't want any now."

Looking past the man, Bull took in the cabin. The brothers had built an entire wing and a wide porch onto what must've been a small line shack. Most of the new structure was logs, carefully cut and laid. The windows were glass. The front door, which stood partway open, looked as if it had been salvaged from some expensive job. It was solid oak, with a stained glass insert. Below the porch, vegetables grew in well-tended rows. The dwelling looked solid and comfortable, even charming.

"Nice place," Bull observed.

"Thanks. We do a lot of scrounging. Most of the materials here were given to us or bought on the cheap as salvage. The name's Krishna, by the way. My brother's Steve." He held out his hand.

"Bull Tyler." Bull accepted the handshake and felt the light scrape of calluses on Krishna's palm. A good sign, although he'd bet his best horse that the fellow wasn't using his real name. Then again, neither was Bull.

At the cabin, he met the rest of the family—pale Steve who appeared as shy as his brother was confident, and their pretty young women, red-haired Venus and brunette Gypsy, who was visibly pregnant. They all smelled faintly of marijuana, but Bull decided that was none of his business.

"Now that you've seen how much work we've put in here, I'm hoping you'll let us stay and help take care of the place," he said. "Does that sound all right?"

"That depends." Bull gazed across the expanse of yellow grass, thinking how best to play this to his advantage. "For one thing, I plan to run cattle on this land with my men coming by to check on them. You'd lose the peace and quiet you have now."

Krishna nodded. "We could live with that. We'd even help keep an eye on the cattle for you. We could fence them out of the house and garden. You wouldn't have to do a thing."

Bull glanced at the windmill. "I see you've got a well."

"A small one, just for the house. We borrowed the tools and drilled it ourselves. There's a bigger well on the far side of the property, but it isn't working. It probably just needs parts. We could help you fix it and maybe set up an irrigation system. My brother's a good plumber."

A well already dug and someone to help fix it. Bull was encouraged so far, but he knew better than to show it. Silent, with his face fixed in a scowl, he waited. He was aware of Steve and the two women listening in the background, probably wondering how soon they'd have to pack up and clear out.

"If you're thinking about rent money, we don't have any to spare," Krishna said. "But we can work for you—we're good at carpentry and plumbing, even masonry. We can give you the names of people we've worked for. You can ask them about us. We could write up a contract that would be fair to both you and us . . ." His voice trailed off as he realized that Bull hadn't even twitched. "What do you think?" he asked, a quiver of uncertainty in his voice.

"I just might have a little work for you," Bull said, thinking of the house and what a stroke of luck this could prove to be. "What do you say you and I take a walk and talk about it?"

They spent the next hour walking the acreage, checking the soundness of the fences—mostly put up by neighbors—and inspecting the well, which looked reparable. All in all, the place needed a big investment in time and money to be fully productive. But he could start bringing in his stock as soon as the well was working.

Bull also learned a few things about Krishna, a former high school math teacher who'd grown disillusioned with what he called "the system." He'd joined up with his brother, Steve, who had some learning disabilities but was good with his hands. They'd searched out a place where they could live with their women in peace and quiet. Bull found himself liking the man, although he would hold back his trust until he knew him better.

They agreed that the brothers would each put in ten hours a week on Bull's house and property for the privilege of staying on the land. For any time over that, they'd be paid a fair wage. Bull would pay for all needed parts and materials, but Krishna would look for cheap salvaged goods to use where they could.

"We'll start with the well," Bull said. "But I'd like you to take a look at my house so we can talk about what needs to be done. I'll give you directions."

"No need," Krishna said. "I know exactly where you live. Come on. I'll show you something."

They circled back toward the cabin, following a route that took them along the rim of the caprock. Only as they paused and he looked past the edge did Bull realize that this parcel of land lay directly above his ranch. From where he stood, he could look down into the escarpment, including the petroglyph canyon where his father's body had been found. Beyond the escarpment and the foothills, shrunk to ant size by distance, was a bird's-eye view of his house and barn, along with the sheds and corrals. He could even make out Jasper's truck, parked next to the house.

"When you showed up, I recognized your vehicle," Krishna said. "As soon as I saw it I knew where you'd come from." He took a few more steps, then paused. "You're welcome to join us for lunch. We're vegetarians, so there's no meat, but there's fresh bread, and Venus makes a right tasty lentil soup."

"Thanks, but I've got a busy day ahead of me," Bull said. "I'll be back to start on the well pump tomorrow. Once we get it working, you can come take a look at the house."

"Sounds cool," Krishna said. "I've got a typewriter in the house. I'll draft two copies of our agreement for us to sign."

"Sounds like good business." Bull shook the man's hand and left.

His spirits rose and soared as he turned off the asphalt and drove down the winding graveled road. He'd grown used to hard times and disappointment. But lately it was as if a lucky star was shining over his head. He'd found the woman of his dreams. She loved him, and they were planning a life together. Now a vital piece of land that could provide water and summer pasture for the ranch had fallen out of nowhere into his hands. On that land, he'd found workers who could finish his house—hopefully for a fraction of what he'd feared it might cost.

Luck could be a fickle bitch. Bull knew that as well as any man. But on a day like this, with the sun bright in the sky and two golden eagles soaring above the caprock, how could he not dream about Susan, the fine ranch they would have and the family they would raise together—a dynasty of strong, proud Tyler men and women to carry their line into the future.

There were bound to be hard times ahead. But

nothing would kill that dream, Bull vowed. He would work for it, fight for it, cheat, lie, and even kill for it if he had to. Family and the land—nothing else was important. Nothing else could be allowed to matter—ever.

The day after Ferg's father got home from the cattlemen's meeting, he called Ferg into his office. Ferg never looked forward to these private father-and-son sessions. Once in a while, Ham might have something good to say. But more often than not, Ferg could expect the equivalent of a trip to the woodshed.

"Close the door, boy." Ham sat like a king on a throne in his massive leather chair, his vast walnut desk shielding him like a fortress. Ferg closed the door and took a seat facing his father. One day that big desk and chair would be his, he reminded himself. Until that day, he had little choice except to endure his father's bullying and toe the line like a good son.

"You look like hell." Ham frowned at Ferg's healing bruises. "What did you do, get into a fight?"

Ferg shrugged. "Does it matter?"

Ham let the comment pass. "So how did you handle being in charge while I was gone?" he asked.

"I handled it fine," Ferg said. "The best part was scaring the shit out of Bull Tyler. He was working on a plan to steal water out of the creek. Believe me, he won't try that again. Want me to tell you what I did?"

"I already know what you did. One of the men told me about it. He also told me that we lost four head of prime beef in that fool stampede you started. Do you have any idea how much money those steers were worth?"

"It was Bull who shot 'em. Go after him."

"He was within his rights. They were on his property and posing a danger to him and his men."

"What about the water he was getting ready to steal?"

"This isn't the eighteen hundreds. You can't just go charging onto another man's property and wreck what he's building. Bull Tyler could take us to court for this."

"You didn't say that when we pulled over his windmill."

"No, but maybe I should've. Bull and I had agreed not to fight over that water. You violated our agreement."

"You could've told me! Don't I have a right to know what's going on around here?"

"Maybe if you paid attention, I'd tell you more." Ham gave him a cold look. "No more shenanigans, hear? Maybe you ought to grow up and take a page out of Bull's book. While you're chasing women and pulling schoolboy tricks, he's running that hardscrabble ranch by himself."

"Damn you to hell!" Ferg was on his feet. "Why are you defending him? I'm your son! I was trying to protect our water! I thought you'd be proud of me!"

"I'll be proud of you when you start acting like a man." Ham shrugged, glancing up at the sound of a light rap on the door. "Yes? Come in."

The aging cook stood in the doorway. "Bull Tyler's here to see you, Boss. He's waitin' in the parlor."

Ham's frown deepened. "Send him in. And you—" He gave Ferg a dismissive glare. "Go outside and do something useful for a change."

* * *

"The boss says you can go on back." The aging cook, still wearing his stained apron, gave Bull the message and hobbled off toward the kitchen.

As Bull rose, Ferg came storming out of the hallway. Pausing, he cast Bull a look of pure hatred. Bull braced for a showdown, but Ferg wheeled abruptly, crossed the living room, and stalked out the front door. Bull resisted the urge to follow him outside and beat him until he whimpered for mercy. Not now, he told himself. His business was with Ham today. He would deal with Ferg later, at a time and place of his own choosing.

The door to Ham's office stood partway open. Bull rapped lightly, walked in without waiting for a reply, and closed the door behind him.

Ham didn't get up. "If you're here about the damage to your water tank, I've already talked with Ferg. He wasn't acting on my orders. That stampede was his idea, not mine."

"I figured as much." Bull remained standing. "That's why you aren't under arrest for murder. But placing blame won't pay for the damage to my property. I want compensation for the pipe and the liner, plus what I had to pay my workers to install them."

"What about my four steers, the ones you shot?"

"Ferg ran them onto my property. He's damned lucky they didn't kill anybody. Maybe you should ask him to pay me."

"Why should anybody pay you? You took a chance, putting in that pipe and tank. You knew you were courting trouble."

"I had a right to do that on my own property and to take my share of the water. I checked the law books to make sure." Actually, Bull had done no more than make an educated guess, based on what Jasper had told him, but he figured Ham wouldn't know any better.

"What if I say I won't pay you?"

"We talked about that. You know what I can do."

"You and that damned secret witness of yours. All for shooting a worthless old hermit who wouldn't sell me his land." Ham muttered an oath, opened a drawer, and took out his checkbook. "How much?"

"Five hundred should do it."

Ham filled out the check and tore it off but made no move to hand it over. "You know this is blackmail, don't you?" he said.

Bull gave him a slow, deliberate grin. "Not this time. It's just restitution."

"For all I know, you could be bluffing," Ham said, holding out the check. "Maybe that witness of yours doesn't even exist."

"Don't bet your life on that, Ham." Bull took the check, folded it, and slipped it into his shirt pocket. He'd be using the money to repair the windmill on the caprock property, but Ham didn't need to know that. "Just keep your boy under control and we'll get along fine."

He left Ham's office without saying good-bye. When he walked out the front door, he found Ferg leaning against the porch rail, his arms folded across his chest. The sight of him, and the thought of what he'd done to Susan, ignited a white-hot rush of fury. But Bull clenched his teeth and held himself in check. He'd resolved not to bring up Susan's name or say anything about their relationship. He mustn't even admit to knowing about the rape. For now, that would only make things more difficult for both of them.

"So what did you tell him?" Ferg demanded.

"Nothing he didn't already know."

"You didn't tell him about Cooper?"

The name stopped Bull in his tracks. "I haven't talked about Cooper in ten years," he said.

"Tell me the truth, damn you! Did you tell my father what happened to Cooper?" Ferg's voice shook, his question stirring a memory Bull had done his best to bury. His mind formed the words he'd sworn not to speak.

Bull fingered the small, ridged scar on his left thumb. "We took a blood oath never to tell," he said. "I take my oaths seriously."

"So you didn't tell him? That's a surprise. I always figured that sooner or later you'd spill that story, you son of a bitch."

"Damn it, Ferg, it didn't even cross my mind. I came to get payment for the damage your cattle stampede did to my property. Your father wrote me a check."

"He wrote you a check? Just like that? Man, he must think you hung the moon. He even told me I should take a page from your book. What did you do to make him say that, kiss his ass?"

"I'm leaving now, Ferg." Bull headed off the porch, keeping an iron grip on his temper. Pausing on the bottom step, he turned back. "But one last warning. Don't you ever come onto Rimrock land again. If you do, I'll make you sorry."

He'd started for his truck when Ferg called out to him. Bull glanced back over his shoulder.

Ferg's face wore a grin. "Just wanted you to know I was on the phone with Susan last night. That woman is so hot for me she can hardly stand it. Ever have phone sex? It's not as good as the real thing, but it ain't bad. Man, I could hear her comin' like a steam engine, right over the phone . . ."

"Good-bye, Ferg." Sick with disgust, Bull walked to his truck and opened the door. Knowing what he knew, Ferg's taunts came across as pathetic. Since they weren't true, the sensible thing would be to ignore them. Still . . .

Bull turned around, strode up the porch steps, and gave Ferg a hard left to the solar plexus and a solid right to the middle of his face. The crunch of his fist against Ferg's flesh felt wonderfully satisfying.

With Ferg fumbling to stanch the flow of blood from his nose, Bull drove away, a taut smile on his face. Ferg had deserved that and more. As for the rest of their exchange, he would never reveal what had happened that day in the escarpment, when a boyhood game of cowboys and outlaws had turned tragic. He hadn't committed the crime, but he'd witnessed it and helped cover it up. Legally, he was almost as guilty as Ferg. But if the idea that he might talk could serve to keep Ferg in line, he wasn't above using it as an implied threat.

Right now he had more positive things on his mind. For the present, he would leave the creek property as he'd found it and water the cattle from the bank. The money Ham had paid him would be better spent on the caprock, repairing the windmill and setting up a system to irrigate the grass. With that much done, he could start moving cattle to the caprock pasture and turn Krishna and Steve loose on remodeling the house for Susan.

He was going to need a trailer with a short wheelbase that could negotiate the hairpin turns going up. With luck he could find a used one. He would need to start checking the newspaper ads. The mental list of things to be done stretched before him with no end in sight. But Bull had never felt happier. He had his ranch; he had his woman; and on this bright, sunlit day, nothing seemed impossible.

Two and a half weeks after the confrontation over the cattle stampede, Ferg was once again called into his father's office.

"Sit down, boy," Ham said. "There's something we need to talk about."

Ferg sank back into the chair, wondering what the trouble was now. He'd done his best to keep his nose clean, but that was no guarantee of anything.

"This morning I got a call from Reverend Timmons," Ham said, and Ferg's heart sank. "Edith is pregnant again. She says you're the father. Congratulations. At least there's one thing you seem to manage well enough."

Ferg stifled a groan. "Isn't it a little too soon for that?"

"You're the one who ought to know." Ham wasn't smiling. "When she missed her period and started upchucking her breakfast, her mother got suspicious and took her to their doctor. It's early yet, but he said all the signs were there."

Ferg sighed. "So how much money does the good reverend want for this one?"

"Don't look for me to bail you out again," Ham said. "The last time you knocked that girl up, you were too young to get married. This time, Reverend Timmons is insisting that you make an honest woman of her. Marry her, bring her home, and claim young Garn as your son. For once, I have to say I agree with him."

"What?" Ferg stared at his father.

"You heard me," Ham said. "You're a man now. It's time you stopped fooling around, grew up, and took some responsibility for your actions. The reverend is expecting you to show up, on Sunday after the service, dressed in your best, for a good old-fashioned shotgun wedding. I told him you'd be there."

"And if I say no?"

"Then you'll be out of that pretty red car, out of the house, and out of my will. Understand?"

A bead of nervous sweat trickled down Ferg's cheek. "But . . . what about Susan?"

"She's gone, you fool. You had your chance with the girl. She was even willing to marry you, at least for a while. But then you had to go and show her what a horse's ass you could be, sneaking out to sleep with that waitress. I don't blame her for breaking up with you."

"It wasn't me that broke us up! It was Bull Tyler. He took her away from me!"

Ham's eyes narrowed. "Is that how you got those bruises on your face? From fighting with Bull?"

Ferg slumped in his chair. "I drove over to the Rimrock 'cause I'd seen that water-stealing operation he was rigging on the creek. We talked about that for a while—he pretty much told me to mind my own business. Then the talk got around to Susan. He made some claims about how he'd had her. That was when I went for him."

Ham's grizzled eyebrow slid upward. "I hope Bull got the worst of it."

"Pretty much," Ferg said. "I would've beat the bastard to a bloody pulp, but this crazy girl, about fourteen, came out on the porch with a pistol. The little wildcat shot in the air and said she'd aim lower next time if we didn't break it up. So I left. But I blacked Bull's eye real good. You know. You saw him."

"Never mind that." Ham leaned forward, his gaze focused and intense—like a snake watching a mouse. His hand reached across the desk and gripped Ferg's arm.

"Tell me," he said. "Tell me about the girl."

CHAPTER 16

*T*HE FOLLOWING SUNDAY, HAM AND FERG, DRESSED IN white shirts and Western-style suits with bolo ties, climbed into Ferg's freshly washed T-bird and headed for the Blessed Harmony Christian Church on the outskirts of Blanco Springs.

Ham had insisted on driving. Maybe he was afraid his son might floor the gas pedal and shoot off in some other direction. And he would've done just that, Ferg groused to himself as he gazed out the side window. Humping Edith in the backseat was one thing. Marrying her, when he'd hoped to do so much better, was something else.

Boiling with silent anger, Ferg cast sidelong glances at his father. Ham could've gotten him out of this mess if he'd wanted to. Offered enough money, the reverend would have settled for raising Edith's second child. But no—Ham wanted grandchildren to continue his damned dynasty. He wanted to settle his son on the ranch and end his wild nights once and for all. And he didn't give a shit about Ferg's happiness.

They parked in front of the unpretentious red brick church. The Sunday service had just ended. Families were trooping down the steps and out to the weedy dirt lot on the side, where they'd left their vehicles. A few people, however, paused to stare at the red convertible, then turned around and headed back into the church. If there was going to be a show, they didn't want to miss it.

Reverend Timmons, tall and storklike, his spectacles balanced on his outsized nose, stood in the doorway of the church where he'd been seeing his flock out. Spotting Ham and Ferg, he smiled, waved, and motioned them inside.

"This is a happy day," he said as they mounted the front steps. "The start of a new family is always something to celebrate."

Several members of his flock were within earshot as he said this. Ferg could only imagine what the good reverend was really thinking.

"We're here," Ham said. "Let's get this over with."

The organist had stayed on her bench. She began playing a hymn as Ferg and Ham entered and walked to the front of the small chapel.

Garn was sitting in a pew with his grandmother, a blond woman as nondescript as Edith. The other seven children in the family sat in the row behind them, arranged in stair steps from oldest to youngest.

Ferg had never paid much attention to Garn. Lord, he couldn't even remember how old the boy was. Dressed in a suit he'd outgrown, showing bony wrists and ankles, he looked like a younger, blonder version of the reverend. The child cast a nervous glance at Ferg, then looked down at his hands.

Ham took a seat alone on the front row. The people who'd invited themselves to watch the little drama sat in the back.

The reverend motioned for Ferg to stand at the foot of the podium. Then, as the "Wedding March" began, he strode back to the chapel entrance to escort his daughter down the aisle.

Ferg watched his bride walk toward him. Edith had made an effort to look pretty. Her dress was old-fashioned, as if it might have been her mother's, but she'd dabbed a little makeup on her pale face, and her veil was attached to her blond hair with a garland of fresh flowers. She looked like an innocent maiden, which she wasn't. Maybe that was all right. But if he had to be married, he could only wish that beautiful, sexy Susan was the woman coming down the aisle toward him.

Bull Tyler would laugh his head off when he heard about this.

The ceremony took just a few minutes, including a homily by the reverend. When it was done, Ferg gave Edith a self-conscious kiss and they left, trailed back up the aisle by Ham and by a scared-looking Garn.

At the curb, Ferg helped Edith into the backseat of the convertible and climbed in beside her. The reverend hurried out with two battered suitcases, one large and one smaller. Ham stowed them in the trunk and, with Garn in the front passenger seat, headed back to the ranch.

Ferg slipped an arm around his bride. At least he wouldn't have to pick her up on the corner for sex. But there was something about sneaking around that gave him a rush. He would miss that—and the time would come, he knew, when he'd go looking for it again.

No need for a honeymoon. By tomorrow, he'd be back in the saddle. Edith would be settling into the house and, he hoped, Ham would take over showing Garn around the ranch. For all Ferg cared, Ham could raise the kid.

Maybe in time he'd get used to the new arrangement. But now, as he glared at the back of his father's head, the only emotion Ferg felt was a burning hatred.

On Monday, Ham called Susan's parents to tell them about Ferg's wedding. The news sent Vivian to her room with a pounding migraine. It sent Cliff to his liquor cabinet for a bottle of Jack Daniel's.

Susan was on the patio, browsing the course catalog for the university's fall semester, when her father came outside with a half-emptied glass in his hand.

"I just talked to Ham," he said. "Ferg got a preacher's daughter pregnant. He's married."

For the space of a breath, Susan could scarcely believe what she'd heard. Then, as the news sank in, it was as if a pressing weight had lifted off her shoulders. *Free at last!*

"Well, what have you got to say?" Cliff demanded.

She hesitated, then shrugged. "Would congratulations be appropriate?"

Cliff emptied the glass, yanked out the chair on the opposite side of the table, and sat down. "Don't you understand what this means? That ranch could've doubled the value of our family holdings, not just for you but for your children and generations to come. Now it's gone, and it's your fault."

"My fault? Not Ferg's?" Susan laid the catalog on the table. "He'd already had one child with that girl. Now there's another one, and you say it's *my* fault?"

"If you hadn't broken up with Ferg, this wouldn't have happened."

"I told you why I broke up with Ferg. This isn't the eighteen hundreds. A woman doesn't have to put up with a man's sneaking off at night. And she doesn't have to let herself be auctioned off like a prize heifer, to whoever can put up the most cash."

Cliff's hand swept the table, knocking the catalog and the empty glass onto the tiles. The glass shattered on impact. Susan bent to pick up the shards.

"Leave that for the maid!" Cliff snapped. "I'm still talking to you! Ham told me something else. According to Ferg, it was Bull Tyler who caused your breakup."

Susan felt the awful weight settle in again. She'd taken pains to keep Bull's name out of the conflict with her parents. Now the game had changed, and not in a good way.

"That's not true," she said. "I broke up with Ferg because he was seeing a woman in town—I told you that, remember? Bull had nothing to do with it."

"I met Bull Tyler that night when he came to dinner. Proud, stubborn young fool without two nickels to rub together. When Ham and I offered to invest in his ranch as partners, he turned us down flat. You can't eat that kind of pride, girl. You can't wear it or drive it or live with it over your head. Marry that man and you'll be dirt poor all your life. Is that what you want?"

"What I want is to be responsible for my own choices. That's something I've put off too long." Susan rose and picked up the catalog that had fallen on the tiles. "Tomorrow I plan to start looking for a job. When I find one, I'll look for an apartment."

"And college? Don't expect any help from us if you walk out."

"I'll work to pay for it myself, or get a student loan."

"Go ahead," her father said. "Once you see how tough it is out there, living in some roach-infested walk-up and slinging burgers or scrubbing toilets, you'll be back. You'll see."

Susan walked into the house without answering. In spite of everything, she loved her parents. Once she was on her own, she might be able to have a better relationship with them. But as long as she was living under their roof, and spending their money, they would feel justified in controlling her life.

That night, on the pretext of an errand, she drove to a hotel with pay phones in the lobby and placed a call to Bull.

"My parents know about you," she told him.

"How much?" His voice, as always, calmed her.

"Certainly not everything, but enough to raise some flags. Ham told them that Ferg blames you for breaking my engagement."

"So you know Ferg's married."

"Yes. Thank heaven. I just feel sorry for that poor girl. How are things with the ranch?"

"Never better. I told you earlier about the new property on the caprock. The well is working now, and the grass is greening up. We're trailering cattle up there a few at a time, and the brothers have started on the house. It's going to take some time, but the place should be ship-shape for you by next summer. It's almost scary how well things are working out. I keep waiting for something to go wrong."

His words triggered an unexpected chill. "Don't say that. It scares me. I couldn't stand it if anything happened to you, Bull."

"Don't worry. Everything's going to be fine."

"How's Rose doing? I liked her."

He gave her a wry chuckle. "What can I say? She's restless and contrary, tired of being cooped up on the ranch, threatening to run away and take her chickens."

"In other words, she's a teenage girl. She sounds like me at that age. Don't worry, she'll outgrow it."

"I'm not so sure. I don't have much experience with girls—not even if I count you. I miss you, by the way."

"I love you," she said.

"And I love you, more than anything on this earth."

They ended the call. She drove her Mustang home through the sultry Savannah night, still vaguely troubled. She loved Bull with all the passion of her young heart. But if she expected their lives to be a romantic dream, she was a child, living in a fairy tale. She'd been spoiled and pampered all her life. But living on the Rimrock would be different from anything she had ever experienced. To be a wife and partner to Bull and a good mother to their children, she would need to be smart, tough, and utterly fearless. Right now she was none of those things.

If all went as hoped, she'd return to her love next summer and they would be married. Between now and then, Susan realized, she had a lot of growing up to do.

"How would you like to have open season on Bull Tyler?"

Ferg had barely been listening to the drone of his father's voice, but Ham's question snapped him to full attention. He sat up straight in the porch swing, where he'd been dozing.

"I thought you and Bull had some kind of agreement," he said.

"Agreement is the polite word for it." Ham pulled his chair close to where Ferg sat. His voice took on a conspiratorial tone. "Actually it's more like blackmail. Bull has access to a witness who saw me doing something illegal. He's been holding it over me ever since."

"Something illegal? Like what?" Ferg asked.

"Never mind. We're both better off if you don't know. But if Bull reported the crime, the testimony of that witness could send me to prison."

Ferg stared at his father. In the silence, a fly buzzed close and landed on his cheek. Ferg brushed it away. "This is about that girl, isn't it? The one at the Tyler place. Is she the witness?"

"She's got to be. Why else would Bull keep her around and so close to the ranch? She's his insurance policy. As long as he's got her, we can't touch him. But once she's out of the way . . ." Ham let the implication hang. Ferg could imagine the rest. He'd be free to punish Bull Tyler any way he wanted to.

"You're not planning to kill her, are you?" he asked.

"Hell, no. I'll just be sending her someplace where she can't hurt us anymore. A friend of mine's got connections with folks who deal in young girls— boys, too, but that doesn't concern us. I've already contacted him. His people are interested—even with that birthmark you told me about. Hell, we might make some money on her. But I'm going to need your help."

"Why me?" Ferg asked. "You've got your hired goons for that kind of thing."

Ham shook his head. "I can't trust those birds with something this big. They could demand a piece of the action, maybe blackmail me down the road, or run afoul of the law and spill everything they know for a plea deal. No, for this I need my own flesh and blood. I need family. That's you."

Ferg gazed past the porch and out over the rippling hayfields and the pastures, dotted with prime cattle. His eyes took in the barns and the stable, the paddock where blooded horses grazed. He thought about the money, the power . . .

All this could be his someday. But he sensed that his father was testing him—taking the measure of his strength and family loyalty. Pass the test and he'd be given the respect and responsibility that the heir to the ranch deserved. Fail and he'd continue to be treated like a child. He could even be forced out of his inheritance.

The choice was his. The decision could be the turning point of his whole life.

"Well, what do you say?" Ham made no effort to hide his impatience.

Ferg took a deep breath. "I'm in," he said. "What's the plan?"

Three nights later, they put the plan in motion. That afternoon, from a distance, Ferg had scouted the ranch with binoculars to make sure the girl was there. He'd seen her behind the house, feeding the chickens and gathering eggs. Everything looked calm, with no sign of trouble. There were two dogs with her, but they looked friendly enough. Even if they barked, it wouldn't matter.

Now, at two in the morning, Ham started the black pickup truck. Driving with the lights out, and Ferg in the passenger seat, he cut the engine and coasted to a stop just short of the Rimrock. The plan was in motion.

Ferg was to go to the pasture on the far side of the barn and create a distraction by firing his pistol at the cattle—not aiming to kill but to wound and scare them, creating a commotion. When Bull and the ranch hands went charging out to investigate, the girl would be left alone in the house. Ham, still powerful at his age, would go into the house armed with a pistol, get her into the pickup, subdue her with a chloroform-soaked rag, and drive off. Ferg would either cut around and join him on the road or walk home in the dark.

Ferg didn't think much of the plan. There were too many things that could go wrong. But he figured that by the time Bull and his men showed up at the pasture, he could make a clean getaway. Besides, there were worse things than having his father get caught and go to prison. With Ham out of the way, he would have free rein to run the ranch and go after Bull. All he had to do was stay out of sight and keep his nose clean.

When the truck stopped, Ferg climbed out, closed the door softly, and took off at a run for the pasture. Even at a distance, the sound, or perhaps the scent, had alerted the dogs. Ferg could hear them barking, but as the seconds passed, they didn't seem to be coming closer. The big mutts were probably penned or tied.

Never mind, Ferg told himself. However it went down, odds were that tonight's escapade would end in his favor.

Bull awakened to the sound of the dogs barking. It wasn't unusual for a passing coyote or skunk to set them off, but tonight their clamor was louder and more urgent, as if they sensed danger. Bull pulled on his jeans, cocked his pistol, and walked outside to the porch.

"What is it, you rascals?" he demanded. The dogs whimpered and pulled at their tethers, wanting to get loose and chase whatever was out there. Since their epic roll in the swamp mud, he'd kept them tied at night. They were bound by long ropes to a support under the front porch. They didn't like it, but it had to be done. Letting dogs run loose at night, especially in ranch country, was never a good idea.

By now the big mutts were getting used to the idea. They'd even taken to hiding their treasures— bones, sticks, and assorted dried animal parts— under the porch to amuse themselves when they were tied.

Bull's voice and presence seemed to calm the animals. He spent a few moments peering across the moonlit yard. Seeing nothing amiss, he was about to go back inside when Rose came out onto the porch, wrapped in Williston's old bathrobe.

"Is everything okay?" she asked. "They don't usually bark so loud."

"Everything seems fine," Bull said. "Go on back to bed, Rose."

The girl shook her head. "Something's going on. I can feel it in my bones."

"In your bones? Give me a break. I've never believed in that mumbo jumbo."

"No, it's real," Rose said. "Some women in my family have a gift. My grandma could sense things. Sometimes I can, too. And right now I feel like something's going to happen. Something bad."

Bull willed himself to ignore the unease her words roused in him. "Let's both go back to sleep," he said. "It'll be morning before you know it."

After they'd settled the dogs and Rose had returned to her room, Bull stood at his bedroom window staring out into the night. A warm, dry wind was blowing. The full moon cast the waving mesquite clumps into long, eerie shadows.

What if the girl was right? What if the dogs had scented danger and were trying to warn him?

Too restless to lie down, he dressed in the dark. The loaded .44 lay next to his pillow. The ten-gauge shotgun, loaded with two shells, stood behind the front door. Jasper had his own pistol, the old Colt .45 Peacemaker he'd carried for as long as Bull had known him. At least if danger threatened, they'd be well armed.

He'd picked up the pistol and was walking toward the rear of the house to check the back door when he heard a gunshot. Not close—it had come from the direction of the pasture beyond the barn. A second shot followed, then another. The dogs were barking again, and now, over the din, Bull could hear the frantic bellowing of cattle. He swore out loud.

Jasper burst out of his room, pulling on his jeans and boots. "Sounds like some bastard is shootin' our stock!" he muttered, barely awake. "We'd better get out there."

Rose had appeared in the hallway. "Stay put," Bull cautioned her. "Lock the doors. Keep down and keep the lights off."

Two more shots rang through the darkness as he rushed out the front door and off the porch with Jasper on his heels. On the far side of the yard, Patrick and Chester came stumbling out of the bunkhouse, still pulling on their clothes. The hellish shrieks of the cattle filled the night—but the gunfire had stopped.

Bull had rounded the back corner of the barn when the realization hit him. He halted as if he'd run into a wall.

"What is it?" Jasper stopped beside him, breathing hard.

"This is a damned diversion." Bull's voice rasped in his throat. "It's got to be. You and the boys see to the cattle. I'm going back. It's Rose they're after!"

Bull ran, his heart drumming in his ears. As he rounded the barn, the light of the full moon revealed Ham Prescott's black pickup truck, lights out, pulling into the yard and stopping about thirty yards short of the house. The driver's side door opened. Ham climbed to the ground, pistol drawn, and began walking swiftly toward the house.

"Ham, you crazy fool!" Bull's shout was drowned out by the bellowing cattle and the barking dogs, who were jumping and straining at their tethers. He kept running, but he was too late, and too far away, to stop what happened next.

The front door opened. Rose stepped out onto the shadowed porch carrying the ten-gauge shotgun. Before Ham could react, she steadied the heavy barrel on the back of a chair, aimed, and pulled the trigger.

The shotgun roared, blasting Ham backward as if he'd been kicked in the belly by a giant boot. He lay in the moonlit dust of the yard, legs twitching, one hand groping empty air.

Seconds after the shot was fired, Bull reached him. Ham lay in a pool of blood, eyes wild, teeth clenched against the pain. A straight shot would have killed him outright, but the blast of the heavy shotgun in Rose's small hands had struck a few inches to the right, ripping into his shoulder and side but missing his heart. All the same, the awful wound was bound to be fatal. Ham was losing too much blood to survive. But he was a tough man. Something told Bull he wouldn't die easy.

The dogs had retreated under the porch. Rose stood on the top step, pale as a ghost in the moonlight. The shotgun rested against her leg. "Is he dead?" she asked in a frozen voice.

"Not yet." Still numb with shock, Bull leaned over the dying man. "Rose—"

"He killed my grandpa, and I'm not sorry," she said. "If he doesn't die, I'll shoot him again."

"Run in the house and get some sheets and towels," Bull said. "Leave them on the steps and go back inside. I don't want you out here." When she hesitated, he snapped at her. "Go on! Move!"

She wheeled and darted into the house.

Bull stripped off his shirt and wadded it against the spot where the most blood seemed to be. It didn't help much, but instinct compelled him to do what he could. From the pasture he could still hear the cattle bawling. Jasper and the boys wouldn't be coming back anytime soon. He was on his own.

Ham's lips moved. "The little bitch . . . shot me . . ." he muttered.

"I can't say I blame her." Bull knew it was his last chance to ask the question that still tormented him. "My father. Tell me the truth, Ham. Who killed him?"

"Don't know . . . but you're barkin' up the wrong damn tree, Bull. It wasn't . . . us. Swear t' God . . ." He closed his eyes, grimacing in pain.

Rose had left the linens on the step and gone back inside. Bull fetched them and used a couple of folded towels to pillow Ham's head. With the rest, he made an effort, at least, to stanch the blood flow. He could've had Rose phone for an ambulance, but the hospital was an hour away in Lubbock—two hours round trip. Ham would never make it that far. And any call for help would also bring the police. What would they do when they found out Ham Prescott had been shot by a fourteen-year-old girl?

Sooner or later somebody would need to call the Prescott Ranch. Right now, all Bull could do was stay with Ham until somebody else showed up. After that, his first concern would be getting Rose out of harm's way.

Ferg had fired at random into the cattle herd, wounding a few animals and scaring the rest until they were bawling fit to raise the dead. When he'd heard the Tyler men coming, he'd vanished into the shadows and cut around through the scrub to the road that connected the two ranches. His original intent had been to wait there for his father. But why risk being caught in the truck with Ham and the girl? If he was smart, he'd go back to the ranch, crawl into bed with Edith, and play the innocent. If there was any trouble, his wife would vouch for his having been there the whole time.

He'd turned and started back when he heard the shotgun blast.

Ferg's first impulse was to keep going. But Ham hadn't carried a shotgun or taken one in the truck. Someone from the Rimrock would have fired the shot—most likely at Ham. If his father was hurt, in trouble, or even dead, it wouldn't do for him to bail out and leave. At least he needed to find out what was going on.

Keeping to the shadows, he circled back to where he could peer through the high brush. In the moonlight, he could see the black pickup parked at the edge of the yard. Closer to the house, Bull Tyler was bent over the sprawled figure of a man. On the man's feet, Ferg recognized the hand-tooled Mexican boots Ham had worn that night.

So the old man had gotten himself shot. Whether he was dead or only wounded, Ferg's actions now could make all the difference. After circling back, he came running down the road, out of breath.

"What the hell happened?" he demanded.

Bull rose to his feet. "I'm sorry, Ferg, your dad was doing the wrong thing in the wrong place, and he got shot."

"Is he alive?"

"Barely."

Ferg stared down at his father. Ham's eyes were closed, his breathing labored. Blood seeped from under the towels Bull had laid on his chest. "Lord, I don't know what got into him. He was acting crazy at the house. I didn't realize he'd headed over here until it was too late to stop him, so I just took off running. Who shot him?"

"Whoever it was, they were acting within their rights. Your father was walking up to the house with his gun drawn."

"What gun?" Ferg glanced around. "I don't see a gun."

"He must've dropped it. We'll find it later. Right now you need to get him home—or better yet, to a hospital if there's time. I can help you load him in the truck."

"The truck's got a reclining seat. I'll put it down." Ferg was calm and cooperative, the only way to be at a time like this. He could—and would—deal with Bull later.

When the seat was down, they eased Ham onto a bedsheet, picked it up from both ends, like a hammock, and hoisted him into the cab of the truck. The pain had to be excruciating. Ham groaned and swore as they moved him. But he was a tough old man and even he knew it had to be done.

"You'll want to call a doctor," Bull said. "At least he can give your father some morphine for the pain."

"I'll do that when I get him home." Ferg closed the passenger door and climbed into the driver's side. "This isn't over, Bull. Believe me, somebody's going to pay."

He switched on the headlights, started the truck, turned it around in a slow circle, and headed back along the road to the Prescott Ranch. Out of Bull's sight, Ferg pulled off the road and stopped the truck under a cottonwood tree. He had to have this conversation before it was too late.

He turned in the seat. The truck was in shadow, but a thin shaft of moonlight, shining through the

branches of the cottonwood, fell on his father's con-
torted face.

"Why the hell are we . . . stopping?" Ham's voice
was a breathy whisper, each word forced from a well
of pain.

"Maybe because we need to talk," Ferg said. "And
maybe because you always said you wanted to die
with your boots on."

Ham's eyes widened. "Hell . . . I'm not gonna die . . .
Get me to a doc . . . patch me up good as new."

"We'll see," Ferg said. "First tell me who shot you.
Was it Bull?"

Ham's head barely moved from side to side. "Not
Bull . . . The girl. That little bitch . . . Came out with
that gun, bigger'n she was . . ." His left hand moved
past the gears to clutch at Ferg's sleeve, the fingers
gripping like talons. "You get her, boy . . . Make her
pay."

"I will. And Bull, too. That bastard's going to wish
he'd never been born."

"That's my boy . . ." Ham's voice was getting weaker.
"Now start this damn truck and get me home."

Ferg shook his head. "You're not going to make it
home alive. Even if I wanted to, I couldn't save you
now. And that's fine by me. I've had enough of taking your shit, old man. Nothing I did was ever good
enough for you. But that's over. I'm the boss now.
You're done for, and the ranch is mine."

Ham stared at his son in sudden, awful compre-
hension. But Ferg wasn't finished with him.

"I've got a confession to send you off," he said. "It's
about Cooper. He never was much of a little brother,
being slow in the head and all. Well, he wasn't kidnapped by Mexicans, like we told you. He was hanged.

Me and Bull, we were playing cowboys. Cooper was the bad guy. I put a rope around his little neck and hanged him till he died. Then we took him and threw him down that rattlesnake hole on the Tyler property. He's still there. Think about that on your way to hell."

Ham's lips moved in a silent curse. Then the breath rattled in his throat and his eyelids closed for the last time.

CHAPTER 17

AS FERG'S TRUCK VANISHED DOWN THE DARK ROAD, Bull strode into the house. "Get your things together!" he ordered Rose. "Hurry! We've got to get you out of here!"

Rose obeyed him without question. But Bull could tell she was still grappling with reality. A simple movement of her finger had sent a deadly charge ripping into a man's body, most likely ending his life. It was a lot for a young girl to comprehend.

Jasper burst in through the kitchen door. "I heard the shotgun. What the hell happened?"

"Ham came after Rose and got himself blasted, probably to kingdom come," Bull said. "Ferg took him away. I've got to get Rose somewhere safe."

"*Rose* shot Ham?" Jasper looked stunned.

"Since you'll no doubt be asked, the less I tell you the better. I should be back tomorrow night or the next morning. If you don't know where I'm going, you won't have to lie."

"Fine." Jasper knew enough to keep his mouth shut.

"What about the cattle?"

"Luckily it was a small caliber weapon—I'm guessing a P32. Half a dozen wounded. A couple of steers will have to be put down. The rest can be patched up with tape and sulfa powder."

"Any idea who did the shooting?"

"Had to be one of the Prescott gang. Whoever it was, the son of a bitch was gone by the time we got there."

"Damn." Bull shook his head. "Well, do what you have to. If Krishna and Steve show up, give them a couple days off and send them home. I know I can count on you to look after the place while I'm gone."

"My chickens!" Rose burst into the kitchen, fully dressed, with her few belongings stuffed into a pillowcase. "I can't leave without my chickens!"

"We can't take your damned chickens!" Bull's nerves were frayed to the snapping point.

"I'll take care of your chickens, Rose." Jasper had found a cardboard box and was filling it with snacks and sodas from the kitchen. "Don't worry, I'll keep them happy."

"But when will I be coming back?" She looked stricken.

"Not till it's safe for you," Bull said. "That could be a long time."

"But—"

"You shot a powerful man, Rose. Whether he lives or dies, you'll be in a lot of trouble—and a lot of danger. Now come on. Let's go."

Jasper followed them out the front door to Bull's truck. The shotgun was lying on the porch where Rose had left it. Bull picked it up, wrapped it in a blanket, and laid it in under the camper cover, which was already on the truck bed. Rose's things and the box of snacks went in beside it.

Bull climbed into the truck next to Rose. Jasper stood by the open door to see them off. "Be safe," he said.

"You never saw us and you don't know where we went. I'll deal with things when I get back." Bull closed the door and started the truck. The engine roared as he headed up the lane toward the south-bound highway.

By the time Bull picked up Highway 277 out of San Angelo, the sun was a blazing ball in the cloudless sky. Rose had slept fitfully through the darker, cooler hours, curled on the seat in a blanket. Now she was awake and restless, gazing out the open side window. Loose tendrils of hair fluttered over her face.

She was probably hungry for a real breakfast. But Bull was hesitant to leave the truck outside a restaurant, where it could be spotted by some cruising lawman who might have been given the license number. Maybe in one of the smaller towns they could find a drive-thru. He could use some coffee himself.

"Are you ready to tell me where we're going?" Her tone was laced with annoyance. Bull couldn't entirely blame her. She'd been yanked out of her familiar world, even forced to leave her beloved chickens. She was sweaty and hungry and tired, and probably needed a bathroom. And, Bull suspected, she was just beginning to grasp the enormity of what she'd done.

"Did you hear me?" she demanded.

"I did. We're going to Mexico. I have some friends in a little town there—a nice family. I'm hoping they'll let you stay with them."

"Mexico! No way! I don't even speak Spanish!"

"You'll be fine. The father speaks good English. And you'll pick up the language in no time." He gave her a stern look. "You'll be safe there, Rose—from the law and also from Ferg Prescott."

"What if I don't like it? What if I decide to leave?"

"Then I can't stop you—or protect you."

She was silent for a long moment, staring out the window. "I really need to pee," she said.

"Fine. There's a truck stop just ahead. I'll fill the gas tank and get us something to eat. What would you like to drink?"

"Chocolate milk. A whole carton."

The truck stop had an inside restroom. Bull half expected the girl to do a disappearing act, but she emerged a few minutes later, her face washed and her hair smoothed. She accepted the chocolate milk and the half cheese sandwich Bull offered her, then climbed back into the truck.

"What if those people don't want me?" she asked as they drove back onto the highway.

Bull gave her a reassuring glance. Earlier he'd thought she was being a brat. Now he realized she was just scared. The poor kid had been through hell in the past few hours. And if she hadn't shot Ham, she could be going through a lot worse. Rose deserved more credit for courage than he'd given her.

"Don't worry," he said. "We'll deal with that if it happens."

Twilight was creeping over the Texas plain when they drove over the bridge at Del Rio and passed through the Mexican border station into Ciudad

Acuña. By the time they reached Rio Seco, the stars
were out. The little plaza was lit by strings of small
light bulbs, stretched between the trees. Couples and
families strolled the cobblestone pathways. Music was
blaring from the open cantina. Parked out front, in
all its polished glory, was Carlos's beloved old Buick.
The sight gladdened Bull's heart. Joaquin and Raul
must have made it safely home.

Bull parked behind the Buick. "Stay put while I
find my friends," he told Rose. "Don't worry, you'll
be fine here."

Ramón Ortega was seated at his usual table, playing cards with his friends. Catching sight of Bull, he
rose with a welcoming smile. "My friend! It's been
two years! What brings you to Rio Seco?"

Bull motioned him out of the cantina to where
they could talk. After an exchange of pleasantries,
Bull gave Ramón a brief account of Rose's situation.
"She shot an evil man, an important man," he concluded. "If she stays in the U.S., she could be arrested by the police or even killed by the man's son.
She's a good girl, a good worker, but she's been
through a bad time. Can you take her in and keep
her safe? I'll be glad to pay for her keep."

Ramón glanced toward the truck, where Rose was
looking nervously out the window. "But of course,"
he said. "I must ask my wife, but I know she'll say yes.
Carlos's sons are working on a sheep ranch near Za-
catecas. You taught them well, my friend. They are
sending good money home, but our little house is
lonely without them. And Maria would love a girl.
Wait here. I will go home and ask her to make sure."

He climbed into the Buick and turned down a
side street. His house was nearby, Bull recalled, but
maybe his lameness was worse—or maybe he just en-

joyed driving his late brother's beautiful car, even for short distances.

He was back in a few minutes. "Maria would love to take the girl," he said. "You can follow me to the house in your truck."

At the house, Bull opened the passenger door and helped Rose to the ground. Ramón's wife rushed out the front door and, speaking in rapid Spanish, enfolded the girl in a motherly *abrazo*. For an instant Rose looked almost terrified. Then, to Bull's surprise, her eyes flooded with tears.

"What is she saying?" she asked Ramón.

Ramón smiled. "Maria is saying that you are already her daughter."

Bull unloaded the truck, giving Ramón the shotgun for safekeeping. The box of snacks, rare in a place like Rio Seco, he presented to Maria. Rose took her things into the spare bedroom that was to be hers.

Maria insisted that Bull stay for supper before driving back. The meal of black beans, rice, and corn tortillas fresh off the *comal* was simple but delicious.

The Ortega house was built in the traditional Spanish style, with rooms around a central patio. They had just finished eating, and Rose was helping Maria clear the table, when something seemed to catch her attention. She froze, as if listening. Then, setting down the dish she was holding, she rushed out the screen door to the patio. Moments later she was back, her eyes alight.

"Chickens!" she exclaimed. "They've got chickens! And a goat!"

That was when Bull began to believe she would be all right here.

* * *

After recharging on black coffee, giving Ramón the eighty-four dollars left in his wallet, and cautioning Rose not to reveal her location by sending letters to him or to Jasper, Bull set out for home. He was bone weary, but the thought of what awaited him back at the ranch kept him too worried to nod off.

If Ham was dead—as he no doubt would be— Ferg would be on the warpath. True, there'd been no love lost between Ferg and his father. Rose had probably done Ferg a favor by killing the old man. But retaliation would give Ferg an excuse to hit the Rimrock with every dirty trick at his disposal.

Then there was the law. Ham had been conscious and talking when Ferg took him away. He would have told Ferg who'd shot him, and Ferg would no doubt involve Sheriff Mossberg.

It could be argued that Rose had fired in self-defense and run away out of fear. But Bull was the only witness to that, and he knew how the law could be twisted. With Rose nowhere to be found, he could try to clear her in absentia. But given the Prescotts' access to high-priced lawyers, that might be a losing battle.

He'd done the right thing, taking her to Mexico, Bull told himself. She would be secure and well cared for with the Ortegas, maybe even happy.

But the odds were, she would never be able to set a safe foot in the United States again.

The blinding rim of the sun rose over the eastern plains, shocking Bull to full alertness. He fumbled for the visor and pulled it down. For the past few hours, he'd been driving with his brain on autopilot, not really asleep but not really awake. Never a good idea, he told himself. But he'd needed to get home, and he was almost there.

He glanced at the gas gauge. The tank was low, but he'd run it almost empty before without a problem. He hadn't bought gas, or anything else on the way home, because he'd given all his cash to Ramón, and he didn't want to use his credit card on the chance that it could be traced. His belly was growling, his nerves screaming for a jolt of coffee. But never mind. He was in familiar country, and he knew that he'd be home in twenty minutes.

One hand raked his sweaty hair back from his face. He'd been dreaming about Susan, the taste of her sexy mouth, the way her lovely, naked body felt in his arms. He wanted her like a drowning man wants air. But she was better off in Savannah, where the evil that had drifted like a miasma over the ranch couldn't touch her.

She was bound to hear about Ham's death, and she'd probably be expected to come with her parents to the funeral. But even if she did, he couldn't involve her in this mess—he loved her, and cherished their future, too much for that. He could only hope she'd be understanding enough to keep her distance until everything was sorted out and the danger was over.

By the time he passed Blanco Springs and took the turnoff to the ranch, Bull's head was aching, along with every muscle and joint in his arena-battered body. The idea of a hot shower, warm food in his belly, and eight solid hours between the sheets struck him as pure heaven. Unless some new crisis had reared its ugly head, he planned to enjoy every minute of the rest he'd earned. He could wade into the ongoing problems with renewed energy when he woke up.

As he sighted the house, a curse escaped Bull's lips. Sheriff Mossberg's big tan Jeep was parked next to the porch. He and Mossberg had rubbed each other the wrong way ever since their first encounter, when the sheriff had refused to look into Carlos's murder. Today, one thing was sure. This was no friendly visit. With luck, the ex-military lawman was only here to look at the crime scene and ask a few questions. But when Bull drove closer and saw Ferg and a deputy standing next to Jasper, he sensed trouble.

Pulling up next to the sheriff's Jeep, he turned off the engine, opened the door, and dragged his aching body out of the driver's seat. "Sheriff?" It was both a greeting and a question. "What can I do for you?"

Mossberg wasn't smiling. "We've been waiting for you, Virgil," he said. "Turn around."

Heart slamming, Bull did as he was told. "What the hell—?"

Moving behind him, the deputy yanked his arms back and clamped a set of steel handcuffs around his wrists. The sheriff spoke. "Virgil Tyler, you're under arrest for the murder of Hamilton Prescott. Deputy, get him in the vehicle and read him his rights."

As the deputy shoved Bull toward the sheriff's Jeep, Bull glanced back over his shoulder. Ferg stood next to the sheriff. His face wore a triumphant grin.

Susan was at the table on the patio, searching the newspaper ads for job openings. So far she'd landed a couple of interviews, but most employers, she'd learned, wanted someone with experience or at least some marketable job skills, neither of which she had. Her father had been right. It was a tough world out there.

She'd circled several possibilities and was about to go into the house and make some calls when her father came outside. One look at his pallid face told her something was wrong.

Her first thought was, *Oh no, not more heart problems!* "Are you all right, Dad?" she asked anxiously.

"It's not me," he said. "It's something else. I just got a call from Ferg. Ham was murdered two nights ago. Bull Tyler's been arrested and charged with the crime."

Using every ounce of strength she possessed, Susan willed herself not to betray any emotion. On the outside, she was a statue. On the inside, she was spiraling into a bottomless black pit, with nothing to grasp and no one to hear her silent screams. This nightmare couldn't be real. But she had to make herself believe that it was.

Bull. She had to get to Bull. She had to be there for him.

"Tell me what happened." She forced out the words.

"According to Ferg, Ham got a call in the middle of the night from Bull. Somebody was shooting cattle on the Rimrock. Ham drove over to talk to Bull and tell him it wasn't his doing. While he was walking toward the house, Bull came out with a shotgun and killed him."

"How do they know it was Bull?" Susan asked. "Were there any witnesses?"

"No. The hands were all with the cattle. But it was Bull, all right. Ferg had seen Ham leave the house and was worried about him. He showed up before

Ham died and tried to get his father home, but Ham didn't make it."

"So nobody except Bull saw the shooting."

"No, but last thing before the end, Ham told Ferg that Bull had shot him. A dying man's words can be pretty powerful evidence—and there was a lot of bad blood between Bull and the Prescotts."

No denying that, Susan thought. "What about the girl—the foreman's niece? Wasn't she there?"

Cliff gave her a puzzled look. "What girl? I didn't hear anything about a girl."

"Never mind." Susan forced herself to breathe. The story, as Cliff had told it, was entirely believable. Except that she knew Bull, and she knew he would never destroy their lives by killing a man—even a hateful man like Ham—in cold blood. Something was missing.

"Did Uncle Ham have a gun?"

"Ferg says he didn't. And the sheriff's men didn't find one. Bull shot an unarmed man."

"What does Bull say?"

"As far as I know, he isn't talking."

Susan gazed down at the newspaper she'd spread on the table. A slow terror crept over her as she struggled to collect her thoughts. If it could be proven that he'd lured Ham to the Rimrock to kill him, Bull could spend his life in prison, or even be sentenced to death.

Something wasn't adding up. She had to help Bull, but to do that she had to know the truth—truth she could only get from Bull's own lips.

Or maybe from someone else—someone who had no reason to like her or even talk to her, especially now.

"I suppose we'll be going to the funeral," she said. "Did Ferg tell you when it's to be?"

"Three days from now." Cliff looked stricken. He and Ham had grown up together, Susan reminded herself. They were brothers in every way but blood. He was genuinely grieving.

"The coroner's agreed to release Ham's body to the mortuary before then. No mystery about what killed him. I've already booked our flights. Since we won't want to impose on Ferg's family, we'll be flying into Lubbock early that morning, renting a car, and returning home that night. I hope that's agreeable."

"It's fine." Susan wouldn't be making the return flight with her parents, but she could fight that battle when the time came. All she wanted was to stay in Texas and be there for Bull.

That night she drove to the hotel and shut herself into the phone booth with a handful of quarters. With a shaking hand, she lifted the receiver, inserted some coins, and placed a call to the Rimrock.

Jasper answered on the second ring.

"Jasper, this is Susan Rutledge. I know you might not want to talk to me—"

"You know right," he drawled. "If you hadn't let Bull steal you from Ferg, he might not be in this godawful mess."

"I want to help him," she said. "I can pay for a lawyer, a good one."

"You know Bull wouldn't stand for that. Anyway, he's got a decent lawyer, one the court gave him."

"Fine." Susan took a deep breath. "Jasper, maybe you can't say a lot. But please tell me one thing. Every instinct in my body tells me that Ferg is lying and Bull didn't do this. Am I right?"

"Yup."

"So you know what really happened."

"I didn't see it, but I know what Bull told me, and I believe him."

"So why don't you tell the sheriff the truth?"

"Because Bull ordered me not to. And because nobody would believe me—just like they wouldn't believe Bull."

"Can't you tell me more?"

"Not over the phone," Jasper said. Susan could only hope it was a veiled invitation.

"I'm coming," she said. "There's no way I can stay with the Prescotts. Will you let me stay at the Rimrock?"

"I will . . . for Bull."

By the time Susan ended the call, she knew what she had to do. At home she packed a bag, wrote a note to her parents, who were at a charity dinner, and left by the back door. Minutes later she was in her Mustang, headed for the interstate.

It was time to grow up.

Bull's court-appointed lawyer, Ned Purvis, had retired from active practice six years ago. But he still helped out when the court was shorthanded and needed a defense attorney. It kept him sharp, he liked to say. And there was nothing like a good murder trial to get the old juices flowing. Nearsighted and troubled by arthritis, he walked with a slight limp. In a movie, he might've been played by Walter Brennan.

Bull hadn't planned to tell him about Rose. But after Purvis assured him that lawyer–client privilege was inviolate and that he'd need the whole story to serve as his defense, Bull came clean, revealing everything.

"So a fourteen-year-old orphan girl shot Ham Prescott and you took her out of the country to protect her." Purvis shook his head. "I believe you. Nobody would make up such a crazy story. But it wouldn't hold up worth a damn in court. The prosecution would push the idea that the girl saw *you* kill Ham, and you got her out of the good old U.S. of A. to keep her from testifying—or maybe even killed her, too."

"I've thought of that." Bull sat on a straight-backed chair, wearing an ugly black-and-white-striped prisoner's jumpsuit. His wrists were handcuffed to the table in the interrogation room of the Blanco County jail. His arraignment, where he would enter a not guilty plea, was hours away. He had never felt more wretched in his life, but he couldn't give up his freedom and let Ferg destroy everything he'd fought for.

"I want to leave Rose out of this," Bull said. "If I get off on the basis of her guilt, it would make her a fugitive for the rest of her life. Besides, bringing her up would only complicate our case."

"So you're saying that you'd admit to killing Ham yourself, even if it wasn't true?"

"Rose shot Ham in self-defense. If I'd been in her place, I would've done exactly the same thing."

"Hold on an all-fired minute while I get this straight. You told me that Ham killed her grandfather—and that you used that information to control him. That's extortion and obstruction of justice. I can see why you wouldn't want it brought up in trial. But the basic question is this: Did Rose shoot Ham for revenge, or because he was a threat to her?"

"The revenge part doesn't make any difference.

Ham was walking toward the house with a pistol in his hand. I saw it myself. I knew he was capable of killing. So did Rose. Whoever shot him, it was self-defense, pure and simple."

Purvis's eyes narrowed behind his thick spectacles. "Are you trying to do my job, young man? Listen, Ferg's story is that you phoned Ham, lured him to your place, and shot him as he got out of his truck. That's first-degree murder."

"Ferg's lying. I never called anybody. You can check the phone company records."

"I'll do that." Purvis made a note on his yellow legal pad. "The other thing is the gun. The sheriff and his deputies searched every square inch of that yard. There was no sign of any gun, let alone one with Ham's blood and fingerprints on it."

The news caught Bull by surprise, touching the place where he felt fear. "I know Ham had a gun," he said. "It was a small one, in his right hand. I saw it with my own eyes."

"Could Ferg have taken it?"

"If he had, he would've kept it to himself. But I don't think he did. I helped him get Ham into the truck. His hands were in my sight the whole time." Bull shook his head. "Ham was shot mostly on the right side. The gun would've flown out of his hand when he was hit."

"Then why wasn't it found the next morning when the sheriff showed up?" Purvis stood up and shuffled his papers. "You'd better pray that gun turns up. With it, you've got good support for self-defense. Without it—you're up the creek, my friend."

CHAPTER 18

*T*HE SUN WAS HIGH AND HOT WHEN SUSAN DROVE her Mustang into the dusty Rimrock yard and pulled up to the house. Dozing in the shade of the porch, the two dogs roused and came bounding out to greet her.

"Whoa . . . Down, boys! Good doggies!" She shooed them away. She liked dogs, but these two furry bundles of mischief were into everything, and they loved collecting dirt and smells on their shaggy coats. If they were hers, she would take them to a groomer and have them washed and clipped. Maybe one day . . .

She began to shake. Only now, as she rooted her feet on Bull's beloved ranch, did it strike home that he was really gone, and he might not be coming back?

Exhausted after long hours of driving, her body craved rest. But the need to find out more about Bull was even more urgent.

"Hello?" Except for the dogs, the yard was empty.

The vanes of the windmill turned lazily in the breeze. Two magpies squawked and scolded from an overhead power line. The two pickup trucks, Bull's and Jasper's, were parked nearby. Where was everybody? Rose, at least, should be here.

"Hello?" she called again.

"Howdy, ma'am." The gangly young cowboy coming around the house startled her. "Jasper asked me to keep an eye out for you. He'll be along in a bit. Meanwhile, he says you can go inside and help yourself to a cold one."

"Thanks, I'll do that." Susan retrieved her purse from the front seat and her bag from the trunk. She opened the screen door and brought them inside, setting them in the living room. She'd been in the house only once before. Back then, Bull had apologized for its messiness. Now she could see that work was being done. In the kitchen, the flooring, plumbing fixtures, and refrigerator had been replaced, and some of the cabinets had been torn out. When she remembered that Bull had been fixing up the house for her, she almost broke down. But she mustn't cry. Not yet.

In the refrigerator there was nothing to drink except beer. But at least it was cold. She popped the tab on the can and walked back into the living room. The house was eerily quiet. Had something happened to Rose?

"So you came." Jasper walked in from the kitchen, his clothes dusty, his face dour. One hand held an open can of Dos Equis. "I was hoping you'd decide against it."

"I couldn't stay away," Susan said. "Thank you for letting me come. I hope I can help in some way."

Jasper sank into a battered armchair by the old

brick fireplace. "There's not much you can do here except wring your hands and fret. But you're welcome to stay."

Susan sank onto the arm of the sofa. "Have you seen Bull since the arrest?"

Jasper shook his head. "Only at the arraignment and bail hearing, and then I couldn't talk to him. The judge set bail at $300,000. Bull could've put up the ranch and made it, but he chose not to do that. He said there'd never been a lien on the Rimrock, and there wouldn't be one now. Proud cuss, maybe a little crazy in the head, but I understand."

"I need to see him, Jasper. How do I do that?"

"They've got him locked up pretty tight. His lawyer, Ned Purvis, is a good sort. Old geezer, but sharp. If you want to see Bull, your best chance would be to go through him."

"You've got his number?"

"It should be around here somewhere."

Susan glanced around, still puzzled. "Where's Rose? Is she all right?"

"She's fine. She's . . . gone." Something about that flicker of hesitation and the look in Jasper's eyes betrayed the truth. Stunned, Susan stared at him. She recalled the overheard conversation between Bull and Ham, and what Bull had said later about the girl being in danger. Suddenly it all made sense.

"Oh, my God." She breathed the words, scarcely daring to speak them aloud. "It was Rose who shot Ham, wasn't it? And Bull's protecting her. Where is she?"

"Bull hustled her out of the country after the shooting. I've got a pretty good idea where he left her, but I won't say more than that. The sheriff was waiting for him when he got back here. It was Ferg who called the law in and told Mossberg his version of what happened. Don't ask me if Ferg was lying, or if he really thought Bull killed his dad. I don't know the answer."

"But if Bull's innocent, why doesn't he just tell the truth?" Susan demanded.

Jasper rose. "No more questions. Anything else you want to know, you can ask his lawyer. Old Purvis knows more than I do, and he can explain it better." He turned toward the kitchen, then paused. "The phone number you want is on a piece of paper in the office. You can bunk in Rose's old room. It's the one that's empty. Clean sheets for the bed are in the closet. I'll be out by the pasture if you need anything."

He was gone without waiting for her to thank him.

Susan took a few minutes to put her suitcase on the bed and freshen up in the bathroom. She couldn't blame Jasper for being distant. She'd started out as Ferg's fiancée, then stirred up trouble when she fell in love with Bull.

If she'd left well enough alone, would Bull be in jail now? But even if she could answer that question, it was too late to change anything. Now was now. The man she loved was in trouble, and she would do anything in her power to save him.

In the office she found the phone number and called Ned Purvis. The lawyer answered the phone himself. His voice was that of an old man with a note of warmth that put her at ease.

"Bull didn't tell me he had a fiancée," he said after she'd introduced herself.

"We're keeping that under wraps for now," Susan said. "But it's urgent that I talk with you. I need to understand what's happened and maybe give you some insight into the Prescott family. Most of all, I'm hoping you can get me into the jail to see Bull."

There was a pause. "No promises, but I'll see what I can do. I've got some free time this afternoon. How soon can you get here?"

"I can leave now," she said.

He gave her directions to his home, which was on a country road east of Blanco Springs. Fatigue forgotten, she raced out to her car. Thirty minutes later she pulled up in front of a charming, old Victorian house with roses in the front yard and gingerbread trim along the roof that shaded the broad front porch. A small, neat-looking man in shirtsleeves rose from a wicker chair.

"Miss Rutledge." He nodded, as if tipping an imaginary hat. "Please have a seat. It's cooler out here than inside."

"Thank you for seeing me, Mr. Purvis. You have a lovely home." Susan sat in the white wicker chair he'd indicated. A pitcher of iced lemonade and two glasses sat on a matching wicker coffee table.

"Thanks. Since my wife passed away two years ago I don't have much to do except take care of the place—unless a case like this one happens along. Here." He poured a glass of lemonade and handed it to her, then picked up a yellow pad and a pen from the table. "Now, let's talk."

Susan told him as much as she knew. "What I don't understand is why Bull doesn't just tell the truth," she said.

Purvis nodded. "All I can tell you, because of lawyer–client privilege, is that we discussed that option and it wasn't the best one—mostly because the jury wasn't likely to believe him. I did check out Ferg

Prescott's claim that Bull called Ham at the house that night. Bull was telling the truth. There was no phone call. Of course, Ferg could wiggle out of that one by claiming he'd heard something else and jumped to the wrong conclusion."

"He could also be lying about what Uncle Ham told him."

"Or Ham could've been lying. See what a complicated mess this is?"

"My father and Ham were stepbrothers," Susan said. "I was even engaged to Ferg for a while. I broke it off because he was cheating on me, but he always blamed Bull for coming between us. Ferg would say or do anything to destroy Bull and get his hands on the Rimrock. You can't believe a word he says."

"Maybe not, but a jury might. That's the problem. Sympathy will be on the side of a man who's lost his father."

"Ferg despised his father—and the feeling was mutual."

"I understand." Purvis jotted down some notes. "We'll be going before the grand jury next week. As things stand, our best chance of an acquittal—one that would clear Rose as well, by implication—would be to put all this aside and plead not guilty by reason of self-defense. Ham was on Tyler property, and Bull insists that he had a pistol in his hand when he was shot. I believe Bull. But there's just one problem—no sign of the gun."

Susan felt a chill. "Could Ferg have picked it up?"

"Maybe. Bull says he never saw Ferg take the gun. But the deputies searched the yard. So did Jasper Platt. Nothing. Find that gun, with Ham's prints or his blood on it, and Bull stands a chance of going free. Otherwise . . ." Purvis shook his head. "Otherwise it's a crapshoot, and the dice are loaded in Ferg's favor."

"I'll do anything I can to help," Susan said. "The funeral's the day after tomorrow. I'll be going with my parents. I might get a chance to talk with Ferg. Maybe he'll let something slip. But right now I need to see Bull—and to let him see me."

"I already called the jail," Purvis said. "You can go in with me tomorrow morning. Nine o'clock. We can meet in the parking lot. All right?"

"Yes!" Susan blinked back tears. "Thank you so much! I'll be fighting this with every ounce of strength in my body."

"So will I. And this fight's a long way from over." Purvis smiled as he rose to see her off. But Susan noticed that the smile failed to reach his eyes.

"Visitor to see you, Tyler." The guard that stopped by Bull's cell was holding a set of handcuffs. Rising, Bull submitted to having his wrists cuffed before being led down the hall to the interrogation room, which doubled as a space for private consultations between inmates and their lawyers.

Lord, how he hated this!

His visitor would be Ned Purvis, who'd promised to come by for an update. As far as Bull knew, the old man was doing a decent job. But why did the process have to take so long? The thought of this ordeal dragging on for weeks, months, even years, while he rotted away in a cell, made him sick to his stomach.

Even so, he kept his head high and his gaze defiant as he prepared to walk into the room. Nobody—

not the sheriff, not the guards, not his lawyer, or the court—was going to see him crack.

The door opened. Bull stepped inside ahead of the guard—and almost lost control as Susan broke away from Purvis and ran to him. Before anyone could stop her, she flung her arms around him, holding him painfully tight. With his wrists cuffed in front, he could only stand still and feel her trembling against him.

"Back off, miss," the guard said. "I can't leave until he's cuffed to the table."

Reluctantly, she backed away. Bull could see that she was struggling not to weep. She knew he would want her to be strong. He loved her for that.

She was dressed simply in jeans and a denim shirt, her golden hair falling in waves around her face. She looked so beautiful that it almost broke his heart.

Accustomed to the routine, he let the guard lead him to the far side of the table and run the chain between his cuffed wrists. He could tell by the look in her eyes that his own appearance dismayed her. With his rumpled, ill-fitting jumpsuit, unshaven beard stubble, disheveled hair, and bloodshot eyes, he looked every inch the prisoner that he was. And seeing him chained, he knew, had to nearly destroy her.

He waited until the guard had left, locking the door behind him, before he spoke.

"What are you doing here, Susan?"

She took the single chair across from him. "I came to be here for you—to help in any way that I can."

"This mess is none of your damned business," he said. "And there's no way you can help. Go home to Georgia. Get back to your life. That's the best thing you can do for me."

Her silver eyes seemed to darken. She rose to her feet, quivering. "Bull Tyler, you're the proudest, most stubborn, most maddening person I've ever known. It would serve you right if I walked out of your miserable life for good! But I'm not going to. I'm going to stay here and fight for you, all the way! I'll find that missing gun, or harass Ferg until he breaks, or do whatever I have to. I'm not giving up on you—ever! Understand?"

As Bull sat stunned, a patter of applause came from the corner of the room. Bull had almost forgotten that his lawyer was still here. "Bravo," said Ned Purvis. "Bull, you've got a tigress on your team! Stop being so damned noble. Let her give it a shot."

"Listen to him, Bull," Susan said. "If I give up and go home, it will be my decision, not yours. But I've no intention of leaving. I'm staying in this fight until we win."

Bull gazed at her across the table, his throat too tight to speak. He had never loved her more. But if he could force her home, away from the miasma of shame and danger that hung over him, he would do it without hesitation.

There was a rap on the door, the signal that time was up. The door slid open. Susan and Purvis were escorted out of the room. Bull slumped in his chair as the door closed behind them. He couldn't fault Susan for coming, but seeing her only served to remind him of all he had to lose.

Waiting for the guard to come back, Bull muttered a string of the vilest curses he could dredge from the black depths of his soul. He knew better than to feel sorry for himself. He hadn't fired the gun that blasted Ham Prescott to kingdom come, but every other step in this tragedy had been his own doing. He had set a trap of blackmail, secrets, and deception, then walked into it himself.

Anybody who knew the whole story would say that he deserved to be here. But that didn't mean he had to accept his fate. He wanted out of this hellhole! He wanted his life back! He wanted Susan.

But his old life was gone. He'd taken too many shortcuts, opened too many of the wrong doors. Susan deserved better than the man he'd become— and the man he would be if he ever walked out of here on his own. He knew she'd stand by him. Susan was loyal to a fault. But she deserved so much bet-ter—an upright man who'd treat her like the queen she was, a man who'd never ask her to give up any-thing she loved for his sake.

With every tick of the clock in this place, his hope for life as a free man, with his own land and his own family, grew fainter. In time, he knew, it would be no more than dust in the wind.

After the jail visit, Susan drove back to the Rim-rock and spent the next hour searching for the gun. Common sense told her she wouldn't find it, and she didn't. But at least she knew that she'd looked. The dogs trailed her around the yard, tails wagging, tongues lolling in the heat. Susan did her best to ig-nore the filthy mutts, but they seemed to have cho-sen her as their favorite person. Only after she'd gone inside did they plop down in the shade of the porch and go to sleep.

She'd asked Jasper their names. "Shep and Pal," he'd told her. "Don't ask me which one is which."

She was doing her best to be useful around the house, buying food in town, cooking, cleaning, and running loads of laundry through the aging washer and dryer. The two hired boys usually warmed their own food and ate in the bunkhouse, but Susan had invited them to supper last night to ease the awkward silence between her and Jasper. She knew he didn't like her much, but she tried not to take it personally. Jasper had been like an older brother to Bull in Bull's youth. He was still fiercely protective of his young boss.

The next morning, after breakfast and chores, Susan dressed for her uncle's 11 a.m. funeral, to be followed by an informal luncheon at the house. She dreaded the thought of going. Her parents would be furious with her. And she would be seeing Ferg for the first time since the rape.

His wife and son would be there, too, she reminded herself. That might make things easier. She had nothing but pity for the young woman he'd married and the son who'd gone unacknowledged for years. But her real purpose in being there was the hope of getting Ferg alone and learning more about the night of his father's death. The prospect of facing him chilled her. But she would do it for Bull.

Dressed in a simple black knit sheath and black pumps, she was tucking a clean handkerchief into her purse when Jasper rapped on the bedroom door. "I found somethin'," he said. "Take a look."

She opened the door. He was holding a twisted red bandanna with something inside. When he opened it, Susan saw half a dozen brass shell casings from a small caliber weapon. "Found these outside the pasture fence," he said. "The varmint that shot the cattle didn't have enough time—or maybe enough sense—to pick them up. I used my knife to put 'em in here. Figured they might have prints on 'em. They might not count for much, but who knows?" He gave her a hopeful look.

"Yes, they could be helpful," Susan agreed. "Would you like me to drop them off at the sheriff's office?"

"Not there. I don't trust those birds. Take 'em to Ned Purvis. He'll know what to do."

"I'll take them by on the way home after the funeral." She accepted the bandanna and put it in her purse.

"Thanks," he said. "We both want to help Bull any way we can." His wise eyes met hers. In that moment, Susan realized that Jasper had begun to trust her. They were becoming a team.

Ham Prescott's funeral was to be held at the Blessed Harmony Christian Church. Ham had never been a churchgoer, but since the pastor was Ferg's father-in-law, it was a natural choice.

As she drove into the weedy parking lot, Susan was surprised at the small number of cars. She'd made it a point not to arrive early. Still, the lot was less than a third full. Ham had made more enemies than friends in his fifty-odd years of life, or so it seemed.

The organ was playing as she walked in the back door. Her gaze swept over the pews, seeking her parents. They were already upset with her. If she didn't sit with them, they would be even angrier.

In the third row, she spotted Vivian's lacy, black funeral hat. Next to her was an empty seat. Susan

slunk down the aisle and slipped into place. Her
mother's narrow-eyed look and her father's scowl
spoke volumes. But at least, since the service was
starting, they couldn't lecture her.

The casket was closed. The only speaker appeared
to be the reverend. As he droned on and on, eulo-
gizing a man he'd barely known, Susan's gaze wandered to the front row, where Ferg sat with his new
family. His wife was pretty in a conservative sort of way,
her plain black dress accentuating her pale skin. Her
shapeless black hat was pinned to her wheaten hair,
which she'd twisted into a bun. She sat with her arm
around her son, who bore more of a resemblance to
his preacher grandfather than to the man who'd
sired him.

Susan avoided looking at Ferg. Even the back of
his head—glossy chestnut hair curling low on his
neck—awakened memories of terror, rage, and disgust.

After the service, cars and pickups followed the
hearse in a solemn parade through town and out to
the Prescott family cemetery on the ranch. After
Ham was laid to rest beside his late wife, friends and
family drove back to the house to eat barbecue,
drink, and unwind. So far, Susan had avoided the
clash with her parents. But sure as night followed
sundown, it was coming, and she knew it wouldn't
be pretty. She needed to talk to Ferg, too—something she dreaded even more.

Anxiety had robbed her of her appetite. She nibbled at the beef, bread, and salad on her plate,
barely tasting the food. Giving up, she abandoned
her plate on a side table, picked a cold Tab from a
tub of iced drinks, and wandered out onto the
porch. With a sigh, she opened the can and leaned

against the porch rail. How easy it would be to just go out to her Mustang, get in, and drive off. But that would be taking the coward's way out. She needed to resolve things with her parents once and for all. And she owed it to Bull to ferret out whatever she could learn from Ferg.

"There you are, young lady!" Her mother's voice shattered Susan's temporary peace. "You've got some explaining to do!"

"I explained in my note," Susan said. "I came back to Texas to be here for Bull. He's innocent, and I'm doing my best to prove it."

"Innocent? That's nonsense!" Susan's father had followed his wife outside. Looking tired, he sank into a chair. "Ham named Bull as his killer before he died. There's no question of his guilt."

"It isn't true," Susan said. "But that's all I can tell you."

"Well, never mind, dear." Her mother laid a controlling hand on her arm. "Once we get you home again, you'll look back and realize this was all a silly mistake. You'll forget about it, and so will we."

"But I'm not going home, Mother. I'm staying here."

Vivian gasped, looking faint. "You can't stay here! What about college?"

"College can wait. I've moved to the Rimrock, to be there for Bull."

"Enough of this foolishness!" Her father rose. "We've got your plane ticket home. You're coming with us tonight."

Susan lifted her chin, eyes meeting her father's stern gaze. "No. I'm sorry, Dad, but I'm not leaving."

"If it's your damned car you're worried about, forget it. We'll buy you another one."

"It's not the car. I'm staying for Bull. I love him."

"But darling, you're our only child!" Vivian's grip tightened on Susan's arm. "How can you do this to us—especially given your father's health?"

Susan took a deep breath. "I love you both. I always will. But I won't be responsible for your happiness. And I won't let you manipulate me with guilt. I've made my choice. I've chosen Bull."

Her mother's hand dropped from her arm. Her father's eyes had gone cold. "This is your last chance, Susan," he said. "Either you forget Bull Tyler and come home now, or you'll no longer be welcome in our home. You won't receive another cent from us, and if you marry that murderer who killed my brother, you'll be written out of our will. It will be as if we never had a daughter."

Stunned but resolute, Susan shook her head. "I'm sorry, but my mind's made up. I'm not going home with you."

"We'll mail you your things," her father said.

Vivian had begun to weep, tears streaking mascara down her cheeks. "I can't go back inside looking like this, Cliff," she said. "Let's just go." She might have hugged her daughter one last time, but her husband drew her away and led her down the steps toward their rental car.

Susan stood on the porch, her throat tight, her hands gripping the rail as she watched them drive away. Would her parents forgive her later, especially if she had children? But that couldn't be allowed to matter. She'd made her choice. So had they.

She didn't feel like staying, but she couldn't pass up the chance to talk with Ferg. After what he'd done to her, the thought of facing him sent a shudder through her body. But she was doing this for

Bull, she reminded herself. That made all the difference.

She was turning to go back inside when Ferg came out onto the porch. He was alone, one hand holding a glass with two fingers of liquor in it. The smirk on his face made her want to turn and flee down the steps, but she willed herself to be strong.

"Hello, beautiful. I've been wantin' to get you alone." Sounding more than a little drunk, he held up the glass. "Peach brandy. Want some? I can get more. Along with my other inherited duties, I'm now master of the key to the sacred liquor cabinet."

"No thanks. I've got something." She picked up the Tab she'd set on the coffee table. The can had already lost its chill. "I'm sorry about your father," she said.

"Me too, I guess." He raised the glass. "Cheers, old man. Rot in hell." He raised the glass, downed the rest of the brandy, and set the glass on the table. "So take a look at the big boss of the Prescott Ranch!"

"I suppose it's too soon to congratulate you," Susan said.

"Oh, never too soon." His eyes roamed her body, lingering on her slim waist and flat belly. "You're lookin' good, girl. I take it I didn't get you preggers."

"No." Susan forced a tight smile. "But from what I hear, you had better luck with somebody else."

"Yeah. Got me a ready-made family. Edith's okay. But I always hoped it would be you."

"Well, it's too late for that now."

His mouth widened in a leering grin. "Maybe not. Will you be around long? Maybe we can get together."

"Sorry, my parents booked a flight out tonight."

Susan sipped her lukewarm Tab, masking her disgust. If Ferg assumed she'd flown in with her parents, then he wouldn't likely know about her involvement with Bull. All to the good if she could put his mistaken assumptions to use.

"I hear it was Bull Tyler who shot your father. Is that true?" she asked.

"That's what my old man said with his last breath, when he passed away in my arms. A man's dyin' word is as good as you can get. And now I've got Bull Tyler by the balls. If the bastard gets the electric chair, believe you me, I'll be front and center to watch."

How can you hate him so much? Susan wanted to ask. But that wasn't why she was here.

"My father wants Bull punished as badly as you do," she said. "But according to him, Bull's insisting that Ham had a gun when he was shot. Do you know anything about that?"

"A gun?" Ferg shook his head. "Why the hell would he be packin' a gun on a nice, friendly visit—especially when Bull had called and asked him to come over?"

"So if there was no gun, why would Bull shoot Ham in the first place, knowing he'd be caught and arrested?"

"Who knows? Maybe it was just because they didn't like each other." Ferg leaned close to Susan's ear, his hand sliding around the small of her back. "How about a quickie in the stable?" he whispered. "Nobody'll miss us that long. C'mon, I got a powerful yen . . ."

She twisted away, fighting the panic that would have sent her flying at him, scratching and clawing. "That's over and done with, Ferg. You've got a wife and family now. So behave yourself before I punch you in the eye!"

He reached for her again. This time she was rescued at the last moment by one of Ham's old friends, opening the front door. "C'mon, Ferg!" the man said. "We're drinkin' toasts to your pa. You'll want to break out the good whiskey."

Susan was left quivering on the porch. Suffering Ferg's drunken abuse had been bad enough. But worse was knowing she'd gone through it for nothing. Ferg hadn't told her anything she didn't already know. It was time to leave.

She'd turned to go down the steps when she noticed the empty glass on the table. The glass would have Ferg's prints on it. If they matched the prints on the brass casings, that could place Ferg at the pasture, shooting cattle, before his father's death. It was a long shot but well worth a try.

Using the clean handkerchief from her purse, she wrapped the glass, tucked it out of sight, and hurried to her car.

She'd already planned to drop off the casings at Ned Purvis's place. Now she had more evidence. Maybe she could even talk Purvis into getting her name on the jail's visitor list so she could see Bull more often.

Purvis was watering his rosebushes when she pulled up to his house. Inviting Susan to follow him, he took the glass and the casings to his office and slipped them carefully into the evidence bags he had on hand.

"The fellow who runs the lab owes me a few favors," he said. "If I push him, we could have the results back tomorrow. No promises, mind you, but if we get a match, it would suggest that Ferg and Ham were on the Rimrock for no good reason. That would take first-degree murder off the table for Bull. But a jury could still go for second degree or manslaughter, so don't get your hopes up."

"Speaking of hopes," Susan said, "I was really hoping you could get me in to see Bull again, maybe even get me on the visitors' list so I could see him every day, on my own. Can you do that?"

Purvis took his time, arranging a stack of papers on his desk. When he looked up at her again, Susan knew something was wrong.

He cleared his throat. "I spoke with Bull this morning. He gave me a message to pass on. You're not to come to the jail again. If you do, he'll refuse to see you. And you're not to stay on the Rimrock. You're to go back to Georgia, move on with your life, and forget you ever met him. It's over—for good."

CHAPTER 19

*T*HAT NIGHT ON THE PORCH STEPS, SUSAN TOLD JASPER about Bull's decision.

A long time seemed to pass before he replied: "Bull's a proud man. I'd call him a fool, but I understand where he's coming from. He wanted to give you a perfect life. Now, as he sees it, that's not possible. For him, there's no such thing as half measures."

Susan gazed up at the waning moon. "I can be proud, too, Jasper. Too proud to grovel on my knees to a man who doesn't want me. I'd planned to spend the rest of my life here on the Rimrock. Even if Bull went to prison, I told myself I'd be here for him. Now he's told me we're finished, and I don't know what to do next. My parents have disowned me. I need a job, a place to live . . ." She struggled to hold back the tears. She'd be damned if she was going to cry about this—at least not in front of Jasper.

"You don't have to leave right away," Jasper said.

"Stick around a while—at least until the grand jury rules next week and we know whether there'll be a trial. Bull's a stubborn son of a gun, but he's crazy in love with you. If he gets off, things are bound to look different from the other side of the bars."

"I wish I had your confidence." Susan picked up a pebble from the step and tossed it into the yard. The dogs, tethered for the night, pricked their ears, then settled back into their spot next to the porch.

"Believe me, I know what it's like to love a woman the way Bull loves you, and then lose her. You never get over it. If Bull lets you go, he'll regret it for the rest of his life. But right now he's not thinking of that."

Susan knew about Jasper's fiancée. She suspected he would never love again, being the man that he was. But she couldn't believe Bull loved her the same way. He'd had other women in the past. It wouldn't take him long to find someone else.

"I'll stay," she said. "But only until I can make other arrangements. Bull said it himself—it's over."

Jasper stood. "I'll be damned," he muttered. "You're just as mule-headed as he is. I'm goin' to bed."

The screen door closed behind him. Susan waited until his footsteps faded and she heard the click of his bedroom door. Only then did she bury her face in her hands and give way to wracking sobs.

She woke the next morning to a quiet house. The time on the bedside clock was 7:10. Jasper would have long since risen, made coffee, and gone out to start the morning chores.

After pulling on jeans and a shirt, she pattered barefoot into the kitchen. The coffee Jasper had left her was cold. She made a fresh pot, poured herself a mug, added creamer, and wandered out onto the porch.

Perching on the steps, she sipped her coffee and watched the last pale tint fade from the sunrise. She'd hoped her outlook would be brighter this morning, but after a night of too many worries and too little sleep, the days ahead of her loomed like a mountain of heartbreaking decisions. She'd been handed a new kind of life to build—a life without the man she loved. And she didn't know where to begin.

As the sun rose, shadows melted in the yard. A meadowlark trilled from the pasture beyond the barn. The two dogs, let loose at first light by Jasper, frolicked in the sunshine. One dog thrust his head into the space under the porch and came out with something that looked like a dried rabbit skin. Playing, he raced in circles, tossing his prize in the air and catching it.

The other dog seemed more interested in Susan. With a low whimper, he came up the steps and sat down close beside her. Her first impulse was to move away, but the dog seemed to sense her troubled mood. It was almost as if he wanted to comfort her.

Gingerly, she scratched one shaggy ear. "Hello, boy," she murmured. "Are you Shep or Pal? I guess as long as you want to keep me company, that doesn't matter."

The dog closed his eyes and sighed as she scratched downward past his collar and worked her way toward his chin. His tail thumped against the step. "So you like that, do you?" Susan teased. "I bet you don't get enough petting around here. If you two would clean up your act . . ."

Her words trailed off as her fingers touched something small and hard stuck to the fur at the corner of his jaw. She bent closer to look.

Ugh! Her hand jerked away. It looked very much like a drop of dried blood, tangled in the long hair. Where could it have come from?

From anywhere, she reasoned. When they weren't tied to the porch at night, those dogs roamed all over the ranch. The blood could have come from the pasture, or from some small animal, like a prairie dog, killed and eaten.

Susan tried to dismiss what she'd found. But her thoughts were racing. The dogs would have been tied to the porch when Ham Prescott was blasted with that shotgun. They had witnessed the shooting. Could the blood on the dog's fur be Ham's? Even the thought made her shudder.

The dog in the yard, tired from tossing his rabbit skin, had brought it back to the shade of the porch, where he lay in the warm dust, worrying the thing with his teeth.

Susan remembered the missing gun—the gun that, if found and proven to be Ham's, could set Bull free. Would a dog pick up a metal gun, even a small pistol, and carry it off to hide? It didn't seem likely.

Unless the gun had blood on it.

The rabbit skin had come from under the porch— a natural place for storing treasures like sticks, bones, and whatever else might catch a dog's fancy. Susan's heart began to pound. Scarcely daring to hope, she rose, then walked down the steps and around to the side of the porch, where she crouched to peer into the low space beneath.

It was dark under the porch, the smell mildly repulsive. Fingers of light, falling between the boards above, outlined a clutter of odds and ends. No way was she going to reach under there and feel around with her bare hand. Pushing to her feet, she hurried into the house to put on her shoes and get a flashlight.

The light helped some. By shining it at different angles, she could make out several bones, a wellchewed sock, a shed snakeskin, and an old leather strap. A desiccated bird lay within easy reach. So far, no gun.

She could always get a rake and pull everything out into the open, but even then the gun might not be there. Maybe Ferg had taken it after all—in which case it would never see daylight again and perhaps neither would Bull.

She was weighing her choices when suddenly she saw it. Half buried in the dirt was the dark metal grip of what appeared to be a small pistol. Pulse racing, she reached for it, then checked herself. The location of the gun was important, as were any prints that might be on the weapon. As vital evidence, it would have to be properly handled.

She was eager to give Jasper the news. But first she needed to go into the house and phone Ned Purvis.

The lawyer picked up on the first ring. "Don't touch a thing," he said. "I'll be right there."

When Purvis's vintage station wagon screeched to a stop in the yard, Jasper and Susan were waiting for him. They'd shut the dogs in the barn to keep them from getting in the way.

Purvis had come well prepared. First he used a Polaroid camera to take a picture of the house front with the porch. Then he had Susan hold the light while he photographed the gun in place. "I don't want the prosecution to have any doubt where we found this," he said.

"Why do I get the feeling you've done this before?" Susan asked.

"Didn't I tell you?" Purvis gave her a grin. "Back in the day, I used to be a big-city cop. After a few years my wife and I got tired of the stress, so I earned my law degree and we moved to the country. No regrets. But I do enjoy dusting off my old skills now and then."

He used tongs to reach under the porch, lift the gun out of the dirt, and drop it in an evidence bag, after which he took another photo. He studied the pistol, which was caked with dirt and what looked like more dried blood. "A Beretta three-eighty," he said. "That sounds about right. Looks like it's taken a beating—even got tire prints on it. My guess would be that it fell out of Ham Prescott's hand when the blast hit him. When Ferg turned the truck around to leave, or maybe when Bull drove off with the girl, it got run over and pushed into the dirt, where one of the dogs dug it up the next morning."

Susan's heart sank as she saw the small gun. "It's a mess," she said. "How can you find any prints on it now?"

"Not to worry," Purvis said. "If Ham loaded the gun, there should be prints on the magazine and the ammo inside. And the blood traces can be matched to type, at least. Just to be sure, I'll snip off that bit of blood you found on the dog. Then everything can be logged into evidence."

They walked to the barn to collect the sample and let the dogs out. By now Jasper had gone back to work.

"So, have you made any plans?" Purvis asked her.

Susan shook her head. "I'm still at square one. Jasper says I'm welcome to stay, but if Bull doesn't want me here, I need to be gone."

"You know that Bull's been under a lot of strain."

"Of course I do. But that doesn't mean I can ignore it when he says he doesn't want me."

"You need to understand something," Purvis said. "When a good man, especially a man as proud as Bull, has his back to the wall, his first concern is protecting the people he loves. That's what Bull is doing. He's protecting you from shame and hurt and disappointment—from danger, too. He knows that if he's in prison and Ferg decides to go after you, there'll be nothing he can do."

"But won't finding Ham's gun be enough to clear him?"

"Let's hope so, but the legal system can take unexpected twists and turns. Even if Bull goes free, he'll always be known as the man who killed Ham Prescott. There will always be people who'll believe he's a murderer. If you're married to him, you and your children will be tarred with the same brush. He wants to spare you that."

Susan sighed. That was Bull, all right. Proud and protective to a fault. The worst of it was, she loved him for it.

"Bull's the only man I've ever wanted to be with," she said. "How can I convince him that he's wrong?"

"I don't know that you can. Bull has to convince himself of that."

They went into the barn, and Susan held the dog while Purvis snipped off the dried blood and bagged it. Letting both dogs out, they walked back into the sunshine.

"I have a suggestion for you," he said. "With my daughters gone, the whole second floor of my house is empty. You're welcome to stay there. In return for a little light housekeeping and office work, you'd have your own room with your own bath. And you'd be close by for Bull, when he comes to his senses."

"You said *when*. Do you think he ever will?"

"He'd be crazy if he didn't. My wife and I had a wonderful marriage. I could wish nothing better than the same for you two. So what do you say? Do you want to come on board?"

"That sounds perfect. Thank you so much."

Susan clasped the lawyer's arthritic hand. For now, at least, Purvis's offer was like the answer to a prayer. But with Bull's future and her own hanging in the balance, it was too soon for relief.

"One thing," she said. "Whatever happens with Bull, promise you won't tell him where to find me. As far as he's concerned, I'm just gone. That's all he needs to know."

"And Jasper?"

"I'll tell him, of course. Same promise."

Purvis gave her a nod. "Understood."

On the following Thursday, the grand jury convened in an upstairs room of the Blanco County courthouse to determine whether Virgil Tyler should be indicted and bound over for trial.

The hearing lasted less than forty minutes. In light of the strong evidence—Ham Prescott's pistol, Ferg's fingerprints on the brass casings, and proof that there'd been no phone call to the Prescott house on the night of the shooting—the prosecutor requested that the charges be set aside.

Bull walked out of the courthouse a free man.

He followed Ned Purvis to the lawyer's old brown station wagon and climbed into the passenger seat. The sense of unreality lingered, like the dregs of some otherworldly dream. He'd never gotten used to the idea of being in jail. Now that he was free, his most powerful emotion was not so much relief as a smoldering rage.

"Let's go," he told Purvis.

"Go where?" The lawyer waited, maybe wondering whether Bull would bring up Susan. But Susan was only a bittersweet memory now. He knew that she'd found Ham's missing gun. He owed her for that. But he'd ordered her to leave, and she'd taken him at his word. The fact that she wasn't here waiting for him was enough to let Bull know that she'd already gone.

"You can drop me off at the Rimrock," he said. "When I get my legs straight under me I plan to buy you a good steak dinner and a bottle of the best whiskey in Texas."

"You know where to find me," Purvis said. "Meanwhile, no need to worry about payback. I've already billed the county for my services."

Bull had called Jasper from the courthouse to give him the good news. The cowboy was waiting on the porch when he climbed out of Purvis's wagon.

"So what now?" Jasper asked as Purvis drove away.

"Right now I'm going to take a shower and wash off the jail stink," Bull said. "After that, I've got a score to settle."

Jasper gave him a worried look but said nothing. It was as if he sensed that his boss was in a dangerous frame of mind and needed to be left alone.

Twenty minutes later, showered, shaved, and

dressed in clean work clothes, Bull walked out to
his truck, climbed into the cab, and drove off toward
the Prescott Ranch.

Ferg poured himself a brandy and walked into the
parlor. It was midafternoon, about three. Edith had
gone to Lubbock with her mother to shop for ma-
ternity clothes. Old Joe, the cook, was napping on
the back porch. Garn was sitting in the corner with
his nose in some kind of book.

Looking at his son, Ferg mouthed a curse. If he
didn't know better, he might've suspected that
somebody else had knocked up Edith and fathered
the kid. Garn had no interest in ranching. He dis-
liked cattle, hated chores, and was an indifferent
rider. All he wanted to do was read and wander
around by himself. But never mind. A fertile woman
like Edith would give him more sons, stalwart boys,
born to rope and ride, and strong enough to carry
on the Prescott legacy.

The sound of a vehicle caused him to glance out
the front window. His pulse lurched as he recognized Bull's pickup.

Ferg had gotten a call from the prosecutor's office after the grand jury decision, so he should've
been prepared for a visit from Bull. But he hadn't
expected it to happen so soon. He wasn't ready.

From below the porch came the slam of a metal
door as Bull got out of the truck. "Garn," Ferg said.
The boy looked up from his book. "Mr. Tyler is coming to see me. I want you to answer the door and
send him back to my office."

Garn shrugged, laid down the book, and rose out
of the chair. As the doorbell rang, Ferg hurried back

down the hall, opened the office door, and slipped into the throne-like leather chair that had been his father's. He could hear Bull's voice in the parlor as he opened the desk drawer on his right, checked the .38 revolver that Ham had kept right in front, and made sure it was loaded. He wasn't sure what Bull had in mind, but if it involved violence, shooting an armed assailant in his own home would be justified under the law.

He slid the drawer partway shut, leaving enough space for his hand, as Bull appeared in the doorway.

"Ferg." Bull wasn't packing a weapon. He didn't need one. The ramrod stance, the slitted gaze, the firmly set jaw, the lightning hands poised to strike at the slightest provocation, all whispered *danger*. Ferg shrank into the chair. He glanced at the gun in the drawer, sensing that it wouldn't do him any good. Bull was like a panther, sleek and taut, reining back his fury by sheer force of will.

"What do you want, Bull?" Ferg asked.

"What I want is to kill you." Bull's voice was low and icily calm. "But I came here to give you a warning. Stay away from the Rimrock. Stay away from me, and from anybody I care about. I have evidence to place you on my property, shooting my cattle, the night your father died. Keep your distance and I won't press charges. There are other things I could do as well—but we're both adults, and you've got a family now. We're getting too old for fistfights and silly pranks. Don't you agree?"

"What about Susan?" Ferg asked the question, knowing it would sting.

Bull flinched, the only sign that he could still be vulnerable. When he spoke again, a trace of emotion had crept into his voice. "Susan's gone for now.

But wherever she is, if I hear that you've so much as breathed on her, so help me, I *will* kill you, damn the consequences. Don't doubt it if you value your life. Do we understand each other?"

"I'd say so. You leave me alone, and I'll leave you alone. It sounds like a sensible bargain." Ferg rose. Neither man extended a hand.

"Fine. As long as it's settled, I'll be going. Don't bother to show me out." Bull turned and, at an unhurried pace, walked back down the hall and left by the front door.

Ferg slumped in his father's chair. To his surprise, he was sweating like a horse.

Bull picked up two extra-large pizzas and a six-pack of Mexican beer in town. After returning to the ranch, he took half the booty out to the boys in the bunkhouse. He shared the rest with Jasper while they watched a rerun of the past weekend's regional rodeo finals.

When the broadcast was over, they wandered outside and sat on the porch steps. In the late-night sky, the crescent moon was a silver scimitar amid the stars. The windmill creaked softly, turned by a breeze that smelled of sage and cattle. Bull filled his lungs, savoring the scents and sounds of home.

Lord, he loved this place, this ranch. He'd never wanted to come back here but the land was part of him, and always had been. His father had been right, the land was everything.

"When do you figure it'll be safe to bring Rose back?" Jasper asked. "I miss that spunky little gal."

"Not for a while yet," Bull said. "She's in a good

place, with good people. And if she were to come back now, she could still be in danger from Ferg. I know he said he'd leave us alone, but I don't trust the bastard."

"I see." Jasper's terse comment spoke volumes. Bull knew he was thinking of the land that was rightfully Rose's. But that issue could wait until she was older. He'd do right by her then.

Jasper rolled a cigarette from the pouch in his pocket and lit it with a miniature dime-store lighter. He smoked in silence a few moments before he spoke again.

"So when are you goin' to come to your senses and call Susan?" Jasper asked.

The sound of her name triggered a stab of longing. Bull struggled to ignore it. "I don't know if she'd even have me," he said. "I was pretty brutal."

And he had been. He'd thought he was doing the right thing, telling her to go away. But he was just beginning to realize how hurtful he'd been.

And how much he still wanted her . . .

"She'd have you, all right. The gal was a real trooper while you were locked up. Helped around the place and everything. Hell, you wouldn't even be here if she hadn't figured out where Ham's pistol had gone to."

"I know that," Bull said. "This isn't about Susan. She's everything I could ever want. But how can I give her any kind of future? I just got out of jail. I can barely support this place, let alone a quality woman like her. And the house—"

"For once in your life, shut up, Bull!" Jasper snapped. "What makes you think everything has to be exactly the way you want it? Hell, life isn't perfect.

You have to learn to be happy and make the most of what you've got, even when there are things you can't change."

"You mean like the way my father died—and me not being able to put it to rest?"

"Hey, we were talkin' about you and Susan," Jasper said. "Where did that come from?"

Bull turned to face his most trusted friend. He'd long suspected that Jasper was keeping secrets about his father's death. If his suspicions were right, it was time to demand the truth.

"You know I've never felt like I knew the whole story," he said. "Locked in that cell, I got pretty black. Not just about Susan but about my whole damned life. I must've spent hours thinking about my dad, how hard he was on me and what he went through to save this place for me. If he slipped or jumped off that cliff, I'll deal with that. But if somebody killed him, I need to see justice done. I need to make it right."

Jasper didn't reply.

"For a long time I thought it might've been the Prescotts," Bull continued. "But Ham swore that it wasn't. So I got to thinking of those people up on the caprock—Krishna and Steve and the rest. They were living up there when my dad died. Maybe they did it. Maybe he saw something they didn't want him to see."

Jasper laid a hand on his arm. "Let it go, Bull. Forget it. Marry that beautiful woman and move on with your life. That's what Williston would have wanted you to do."

"But—"

"No." Jasper tossed his burning cigarette butt into the yard. "That's enough, damn it. It wasn't the

Prescotts that killed him. And it wasn't those fool hippies up top."

"How do you know that, Jasper?" Something closed like an icy fist around Bull's heart.

Jasper looked Bull straight in the eye. "I know because it was me. I pushed Williston off that cliff."

Bull stared at him, mute with shock.

"Don't say a word," Jasper said. "Just listen to the whole story. I've told you how sick Williston was, how much pain he was in. Toward the end, even being drunk didn't help. He wanted to live to see you again, but he was in agony. He couldn't stand it any longer. He told me he wanted to end it and asked me to be there with him.

"We took a bottle and walked up the back of the ledge. I had a little to drink. Williston had most of it. We'd agreed on a story to cover what was supposed to happen, to make it look like an accident in case anybody wondered.

"When the time came, he told me, 'Jasper, I want to do this on my own, but you might have to help me. I'm going to stand on the edge and count down from ten. If I haven't jumped by the count of one, promise you'll give me a good push.' So I promised him, and that's how it happened."

Tears were flowing down Jasper's cheeks. "I never had more respect for a man than I did for your father. Helping him die, and hiding the truth afterward, was the last kindness I could do him. But I'll live with that memory every day for the rest of my life. And now you'll have to live with it, too."

Bull's eyes were moist. An aching lump had risen in his throat. "Why didn't you tell me?" he whispered.

"Because your dad didn't want you to know. He swore me to it before he died. I turned his horse loose and spent the next day pretendin' to search, knowing the whole time where he was and how I'd find him. And I never told anybody till now. It was all for you, Bull. That was the promise I made—the promise I just broke. Wherever he is, I hope to hell Williston will forgive me."

Jasper gazed up at the stars, as if wondering whether his old boss was listening. "I broke a whole passel of laws doing what I did. I'm hoping you won't turn me in."

"I'd never do that," Bull said. "What you did, you did out of friendship."

"If your dad was here, he'd tell you to go get that woman, make babies with her, and be happy. Since he's not here, I'm tellin' you for him. Life is too short—nobody knows that better than I do. I put off marryin' my Sally because Williston needed me, and after that because I thought *you* needed me. You know the rest."

After some silence, Jasper stood, stretching his long, skinny frame. "I've said enough. Time to turn in. You think on what I've told you. If, by morning, you've decided to take my advice, I'll break one more promise."

"What promise is that?" Bull asked.

"I'll tell you where to find Susan."

Bull's pulse skipped. "She's still here?"

Jasper nodded. "I wouldn't keep her waitin' too long if I was you, Bull. You put that girl through hell. You don't want her changin' her mind."

"More coffee?" Susan poised the carafe over the beautiful china cup, one of a set that had belonged to Ned Purvis's late wife.

Purvis, who was reading the morning newspaper, shook his head. "Thanks, but I've had enough. You're spoiling me, young lady. Any more of those muffins you made and I'll have to let my belt out a couple of notches."

Susan smiled at the comment. She'd had very little baking practice, but in one of the cabinet drawers she'd discovered a well-used copy of the red-and-white *Better Homes and Gardens* cookbook. She'd tried several recipes. The failures had gone into the trash. But the muffins, made with blueberries she'd found in the freezer, were spectacular.

Cooking would never be high on her list of accomplishments but, at least for now, it helped divert her thoughts from Bull.

Yesterday Purvis had passed on the news that Bull was a free man. Susan had been giddy with relief. But as the afternoon dragged into an evening that slowly darkened into night, she'd forced herself to face reality. He'd meant it when he'd told her to leave. She wasn't going to see him again. It was time to start planning the rest of her life.

A life without Bull. Without the sight of his face, the sound of his voice, and the strength of his arms around her. This morning it felt like a prison sentence.

As Purvis finished the paper, she carried the breakfast dishes to the sink. "As soon as I clean up here, I'll file that stack of briefs you left on your desk," she said.

"No hurry. Take some time for yourself." Purvis rose from the table. "If you need me, I'll be out front trimming my roses. Best to get it done before the heat sets in."

Alone in the house, she loaded the dishwasher, wiped the countertops, and dusted the table. She was folding the newspaper when, on impulse, she decided to check the want ads. Maybe jobs were easier to find in Texas than in Savannah.

She'd pulled out a chair and was about to sit down when Purvis, who hadn't been outside long, opened the front door. "Susan," he said, "you have a visitor."

He moved discreetly out of the way, back onto the porch.

Bull stepped into the doorway.

Susan's heart dropped. She forgot to breathe as he walked toward her and stopped a few feet away. He looked careworn, as if he'd spent nights without sleep. She checked the urge to run to him. First she needed to hear what he had to say.

Silence hung between them as they looked into each other's faces. A small eternity seemed to pass before he spoke.

"Forgive me, Susan. I've let pride make a fool of me."

She forced herself to remain rooted to the floor with one hand on the back of the chair. "You've been a proud fool, all right," she said. "But as long as you've learned your lesson, I'll forgive you—on one condition."

In his eyes she saw fear, hope, and love. "Go on," he said.

"I'll forgive you only if you promise to spend the rest of your life making up for what you did to me."

"Come here and try me, lady."

She flung herself into his open arms. He held her tight. She could feel her tears wetting his face.

"I'm sorry," he said. "I wanted everything perfect for you—the house, the ranch, even me. When I knew I couldn't give you that—"

"Hush, my love." She silenced his lips with her own. "I don't care about perfect. I only care about building a life with you—together."

He chuckled, deep in his throat. "I think you just proposed to me," he said. "The answer is yes."

A week later they were married in Ned Purvis's rose garden. Susan wore a simple, white summer dress. Purvis walked her across the lawn to where Bull stood, with Jasper beside him as best man. The two young cowhands, Patrick and Chester, served as witnesses. A justice of the peace performed the ceremony.

One other event made the day memorable. As they began their vows, a breeze sprang up. Dark clouds swept in above the tall cottonwoods. Thunder rumbled across the sky.

They had just exchanged rings and kissed when the clouds burst open, releasing a torrent of rain, like a blessing on their marriage.

Purvis and the justice raced for the cover of the porch. Susan, Bull, and the rest of them splashed and danced, laughing like children in the sweet, life-giving downpour.

EPILOGUE

August 1975, three years later

BULL STOOD ON THE PORCH BEFORE SUPPER, WATCH-
ing the last blaze of sunset fade above the shadowed
cliffs of the escarpment. The air was fresh and cool
after the midday cloudburst. The smell of raw, damp
earth was heaven to his senses.

A rare satisfaction stole over him as he contem-
plated the fact that, in every direction he looked,
most of what he saw was his own land.

Over the past couple of years, he'd picked up
pieces of neighboring property wherever he could.
The swampland to the south was his now, with a
good spot to drill a shallow well if the need arose.
And he'd jumped at the chance to expand the
caprock parcel when the owner had retired. Now he
had enough land and water up there to run a thou-

sand head of beef and still have enough acreage for growing hay.

The heart of the ranch had seen improvements as well. Months of living in the house while Krishna and Steve remodeled it had been a bother, but the end result had been worth it. The house was now a handsome edifice of timbers and river stone, with a cathedral ceiling and a high rock fireplace in what Krishna called the great room, as well as hardwood floors, a formal dining room, and even a small apartment added on the back for Jasper.

At Susan's insistence, he had also graveled an area around the house to keep the dust and mud from tracking inside. Susan had also insisted that the dogs be professionally clipped and groomed. Without their shaggy fur, they were as sleek and trim as show dogs, but as mischievous as ever.

As if the thought could bring them, the two mutts came up the steps and crowded around his legs, begging to be petted. Bull scratched each eager head. He liked them all right, but in their doggy hearts, they really belonged to his wife.

He heard the screen door open and close as Susan came out onto the porch with their two-month-old son in her arms. "Look who's awake," she said.

"Give him to me." Bull took the tiny boy in his arms. It had taken some time for Susan to get pregnant, but they'd done the job right. Young Will—named Williston, after Bull's father—was stamped in his father's image with dark hair, deep blue eyes, and a stubborn nature that was already showing. Healthy and alert, he was just beginning to notice things around him.

"I took him in for a checkup today," Susan said. "Everything's fine. But a woman in the doctor's office mentioned that poor Edith Prescott has miscarried again. That's the second time. I feel so sorry for her, especially when I look at our perfect little son and think what a blessing he is."

"Well, at least they've got Garn to carry on the family name." Not that Garn was much for a father to brag about. Bull supposed that he should feel sorry for Ferg. But after the things Ferg had done, he couldn't muster much compassion for the man.

Bull cradled the baby partway upright, turning his face toward the yard beyond the porch. "Take a look around, son," he said. "Someday, you'll be the big boss of this ranch. All this, and more, will be yours."

"*And more?*" Susan looked up at him, frowning. "Good heavens, Bull, isn't this enough?"

"Never," Bull said. "I'm going to keep building this place till the day I die. It's not just a family ranch we're creating here. It's a dynasty."

All true, Bull mused. But right now, on a soft summer evening with the sun gone down, supper on the stove, his woman by his side, and his firstborn son in his arms, it almost seemed like enough.

*T*HE MEXICAN VILLAGE SLUMBERED UNDER A PALLID
crescent moon. Around the deserted plaza, the cantina was closed for the night, its tables and chairs
shut away behind corrugated metal doors. A bat fluttered from the tower of the old adobe church and
melted into darkness. A skinny dog foraged for leav-
ings in the empty marketplace.

The night was almost peaceful. But the stillness was
heavy with tension—especially in one small house on
a dusty side street. Nothing in Río Seco was the way it
had been before the Cabrera cartel took over the
town. And for Rose Landro, after tonight, nothing
would be the same again.

The click of a boot heel on the tiled patio startled
Rose to full alertness. Lying fully dressed in the dark,
she checked the impulse to sit up, fling aside the

covers and bolt out of bed. She was a small woman. Face to face, she'd be no match for the burly intruder who was stalking her. Her only chance of survival lay in surprise.

The loaded Smith and Wesson .44 lay under her pillow. As the footsteps clicked across the patio of the small adobe house, she closed her hand around the grip, cocked the hammer, and slid to the floor. Her free hand bunched the pillows into a semblance of her sleeping body and covered it with the blanket.

She knew who was coming for her. Lucho Cabrera, younger brother of the local cartel boss, was built like a short pile of bricks. He wore high-heeled cowboy boots to make him appear taller. The sound of those boots, clicking across the kitchen, chilled Rose's blood. Gripping the heavy pistol, she belly-crawled across the floor and pressed upward to stand against the wall, in the dark shadows behind the door. Her breath came in shallow gasps. Her pulse hammered in her ears.

The cartel killed anyone who stood against them. They had already murdered Ramón and María Ortega, who'd taken Rose into their home eleven years ago. Rose would have fled for her life before now, but she could not leave without avenging the couple who'd cared for her like their own daughter.

Honor. The Ortegas had lived by that code. Now it was Rose's turn to carry on the tradition.

The footsteps were coming closer. Would Lucho stand in the doorway and fire at the lump in her bed, or did the sadistic pig plan on raping her first, as he'd done two months earlier, when he'd caught her walking home alone after dark?

At the memory of his filthy, sweating body, her

finger tightened on the trigger. If ever a man deserved killing, it was Lucho Cabrera. Only his older brother, Refugio, was worse.

The bedroom door creaked open. Rose held her breath as Lucho stepped into the room, his pistol drawn. Moonlight, falling through the high, barred window, cast black shadows across his fleshy face. As he neared the bed, he holstered the gun. One hand fumbled with his belt buckle. *Good.* This was almost too easy. She could shoot him now, in the back. But something in her wanted more. She wanted him to see her. When the bullet tore into his body, she wanted him to know who had fired it.

She forgot to breathe. Every muscle was a coiled spring as she waited for the right moment.

"*Brujita fea . . .*" he muttered. The name, given to Rose because of the birthmark on her face, meant ugly little witch. Over the years she'd learned to bear it with a measure of pride. Superstitious people tended to fear her, especially men. But that wouldn't stop Lucho. He might even be planning to take a trophy back to his brother, as proof of his bravery.

Still muttering, he loosened his trousers and jerked back the blanket. That was when he realized he'd been tricked. He spun around, cursing as Rose stepped out of the shadows, the .44 gripped between her two hands.

"*Muera, pendejo.* Die, you bastard," she said, aiming the heavy revolver at his chest.

Lucho had no time to draw his weapon, but in the instant her finger tightened on the trigger, he lunged for her. The pistol roared, but Lucho's move had thrown off her aim. The bullet struck his right shoulder, barely slowing the brute's charge.

Slammed by the recoil, Rose staggered backward. Her feet tangled in the rug on the floor and she went down on one arm.

She managed to keep a one-handed grip on the gun, but now he was standing over her, blood streaming down his sleeve. He reached for his holster, but her shot had disabled his shooting arm. The flicker of distraction it took for him to draw with his left hand gave her the only chance she had left.

She cocked the .44 and fired.

lifted his hand and raised his battered leather hat in farewell before turning into the forest. He felt the remembrance of the woman's arms tighten around his waist and her warm breath against his neck. He smiled again. He was home. He was happy.

THE END

A SELECTED LIST OF FINE NOVELS
AVAILABLE FROM CORGI BOOKS

14058 9	MIST OVER THE MERSEY	*Lyn Andrews*	£5.99
14974 8	COOKLEY GREEN	*Margaret Chappell*	£6.99
14581 5	KATE HANNIGAN'S GIRL	*Catherine Cookson*	£5.99
14451 7	KINGDOM'S DREAM	*Iris Gower*	£5.99
14452 5	PARADISE PARK	*Iris Gower*	£5.99
14895 4	NOT ALL TARTS ARE APPLE	*Pip Granger*	£5.99
14896 2	THE WIDOW GINGER	*Pip Granger*	£5.99
14537 8	APPLE BLOSSOM TIME	*Kathryn Haig*	£5.99
14771 0	SATURDAY'S CHILD	*Ruth Hamilton*	£5.99
14906 3	MATTHEW & SON	*Ruth Hamilton*	£5.99
14820 2	THE TAVERNERS' PLACE	*Caroline Harvey*	£5.99
14220 4	CAPEL BELLS	*Joan Hessayon*	£4.99
14603 X	THE SHADOW CHILD	*Judith Lennox*	£5.99
15045 2	THOSE IN PERIL	*Margaret Mayhew*	£5.99
14872 5	THE SHADOW CATCHER	*Michelle Paver*	£5.99
14905 5	MULBERRY LANE	*Elvi Rhodes*	£5.99
15051 7	A BLESSING IN DISGUISE	*Elvi Rhodes*	£5.99
14903 9	TIME OF ARRIVAL	*Susan Sallis*	£5.99
15050 9	FIVE FARTHINGS	*Susan Sallis*	£6.99
15052 5	SPREADING WINGS	*Mary Jane Staples*	£5.99
15138 6	FAMILY FORTUNES	*Mary Jane Staples*	£5.99
14911 X	SUNSET IN ST TROPEZ	*Danielle Steel*	£5.99
14118 6	THE HUNGRY TIDE	*Valerie Wood*	£5.99
14263 8	ANNIE	*Valerie Wood*	£5.99
14476 2	CHILDREN OF THE TIDE	*Valerie Wood*	£5.99
14640 4	THE ROMANY GIRL	*Valerie Wood*	£5.99
14740 0	EMILY	*Valerie Wood*	£5.99
14845 8	GOING HOME	*Valerie Wood*	£5.99
14846 6	ROSA'S ISLAND	*Valerie Wood*	£5.99
15031 2	THE DOORSTEP GIRLS	*Valerie Wood*	£5.99